Within the Veil

Within the Veil

Brandy Vallance

Cover Design: PixelWorks Studios
Photo Illustration: PixelWorks Studios
Cover Image: Period Images
Interior Design: Polgarus Studio

ISBN 978-0-9974997-1-1

First Edition
14 13 12 11 10 / 10 9 8 7 6 5 4 3 2 1

Praise for *Within the Veil*

Lushly descriptive and emotionally evocative with touches of humor and spunk to drive the romance along, *Within the Veil* is not only lovely to read but entertaining, as well. Add this one to your TBR—it should not be missed! Highly recommended!
~*USA Today*

Passionate and riveting (with an absolutely gorgeous cover) Brandy Vallance's sophomore novel is impossible to put down until every last glimpse of Alasdair and Feya has been fully savored. The romantic tension steals your breath, yes, but the timely themes of racism and discrimination, synesthesia and abstinence, elevate this story to one of beautiful depth and make it exceedingly relevant for today's readers.
~RT Book Reviews, Top Pick

Vallance combines unique characters, historical facts, and powerful writing to transport readers to 19th-century Scotland. Spunky characters must battle their for their faith and overcome systemic barriers, including poverty and discrimination. While the ending is expected, the journey is wonderful, and Vallance uses an engrossing narrative to speak about delicate social issues in this impressive tale.
~Publisher's Weekly

One of the most passionately and powerfully written tales I've had the pleasure of reading, *Within the Veil* is an irresistible blend of Victorian Britain and Gypsy history with a refreshingly unique hero and unforgettable heroine. Written with the same panache that won her the Operation First Novel Contest, this second novel is sure to win many reading hearts. I only hope Feya and Alasdair's story has a sequel!
~Laura Frantz, author of *A Moonbow Night*

Lush and poignant, *Within the Veil* is a treasure in the historical fiction field. From the first page, Brandy Vallance's determined characters jumped into my heart and made me root for them equally–even as they fought each other and surprised me on every page. Vallance feeds all the senses and emotions while leading us through a fascinating story of Gypsies in Scotland–and the

horrible racism that knows no age. Fans of Liz Curtis Higgs' Scottish novels will love *Within the Veil,* and readers of all historical romance will lose themselves in this gripping, page-turning read.
~Sally Bradley, author of *Kept*

Brandy's novel *Within the Veil* is a complex, unique and interesting period read that has a sense of wild romanticism that's hard to ignore. It's an atmospheric and arching romance that is sure to please any reader who enjoys fiction.
~The Silver Petticoat Review

Within the Veil is the second outing from Brandy Vallance. Her first book, *The Covered Deep,* was surprisingly brilliant for a first novel, and this follow up is no less. Feya is a fabulously well-rounded character with depth, vitality, and anything but a caricature personality. As she travels through this perilous journey, she learns much more about herself than most characters do over the course of an entire series . . . Vallance has given light to a world that is relatively unknown in the Christian fiction realm. Not many write books about Gypsies, and I guarantee none of them do it with the grace or style Vallance brings to the table.
~Radiant Lit

I cried as I turned the last page of *Within the Veil.* This incredibly tender story is absolutely stunning – from cover to cover and every ink-stained, heartfelt, adventurous page in between. *Within the Veil's* raw, organic beauty will move you in the depths of your soul. It is an absolute must read.
~Baker Kella

I knew this book would leave me in pieces. Vallance has a particular magic when it comes to characters and imagery. She sits her characters down in your mind's parlor and proceeds to lay them bare and bind your emotions so thoroughly as to make them into lifelong friends . . . This is a story of prejudice and revenge on a grand scale, but also an intimate, thread-by-thread weaving together of two characters from very different backgrounds who never would have guessed they needed each other. Be warned, if you pick up this book there's no going back, no choice but to fall in love, and no chance of remaining unchanged.
~Evangeline Denmark, author of *Curio*

For those who see: May your gifts always lead you back
to the One who gave them.

And for those who ache: Don't we all?

"Which *hope* we have as an anchor of the soul, both sure and steadfast, and which entereth into that within the veil."

Hebrews 6:19

Prologue

London, England
Palace of Westminster
August 1885

"Order! Order, I say!"

Shouts echoed in the dark-paneled chamber of the House of Commons. Every member stood, waving papers and thrusting insults. The press peered over the balconies, frantically scribbling every insinuation, backhanded compliment, and outrageous lie. Not that they could tell the difference.

Ranald Aldourie pushed through the crowd and stepped to the parliamentary lectern. Control. He must appear controlled. The muscle at his jaw betrayed him.

Minister Coreley continued. "This is a bill to provide for the registration and regulation of traveling vans used as abodes. Surely the House can acknowledge that Gypsies ought to be subjected to certain sanitary regulations."

"Hear, hear!" From the right, fists pounded on the backs of the benches.

Ranald's stomach clenched. He placed his hand upon the insignia of the crown—the lion and the unicorn, gilded on the red leather of the despatch box. The law . . . Decency would prevail. Surely they would see.

Minister Coreley inflated himself, pushing out his chest like the buffoon that he was. His voice was the punctuated *thwack* of a hammer. "These roadside Arabs shamelessly flit about in our midst. Their children cannot function properly in our society and are brought up completely without restraint or information. They must be educated in the proper ways." He thrust his hand into the air as if holding the Sword of Justice. "If that were not reason enough, this bill would also prevent their *particular* infections from being carried from one end of Great Britain to the other."

Ranald clasped his hands together to keep from strangling the man. "I am sorry to disagree, but this bill would do nothing but harass the Romani people. Parts of this bill speak of caravans being searched at leisure, even upon the *suspicion* of any moral infringement. I would ask my fellow members whether they would give up their freedoms and have their houses searched upon any man's whim. Have we sunk so low that we must enact race laws once again?"

From the right, voices erupted once more.

"They are black spots upon our horizon!"

"Reducing our own riffraff to their level."

A voice called from the back. "They do not consider lying and cheating to be sinful."

"They dabble in sorcery!"

A member from the left yelled. "What are their religious views, if any?"

"Order!" Mr. Speaker scowled, red faced.

On the right, a member stood on a chair. "There are reports of them poisoning the cattle and then bringing the cure—for a hefty price."

"Order!" Mr. Speaker pivoted, shouting at both sides of the chamber. "There will be order!"

A member from the back shouted. "Bound up in their nature is an insatiable love of plundering and gold!"

"Do you dare defy the order?" Mr. Speaker's voice rose, a boom over the chaos. His white hair shook as he jutted out his finger. "Minister Coreley will continue, and the rest of the gentlemen in this House will conduct themselves as their status requires or kindly leave the chamber!" His frown carved a deep line in his face as he firmly sat.

Minister Coreley stared at Ranald, drawing out the moment. "Gypsy life may find favor in the East, but in the West this system cannot thrive. A real Englishman hates the man who will not work and scorns the man who would tell him a lie. Perhaps my honorable friend has been too long in Scotland and has been jaded by the wild antics of the locals."

Ranald felt heat creeping below his starched white collar. And something else that was very familiar: rage. "You would have us believe that we have the resources to search every caravan? Perhaps my most *honorable* friend is merely trying to insert a precursor into his true aims: reenacting the Egyptians Act of 1554." Murmurs flew through the room. "Have we not moved beyond the wrongful sentiments of such a time when being part of an ethnic community was punishable by death? Perhaps we should add, as Queen Mary did, that merely fraternizing with Gypsies should bring about the gallows."

The whispers in the back surged. He drew out his words for effect. "Perhaps we need only to look to the Diet of Augsburg, where it was declared law that whoever killed a Gypsy was not guilty of murder!"

The room erupted once again.

Mr. Speaker shot to his feet. "Order!"

Minister Coreley shuffled the papers before him. "Perhaps my most honorable friend makes these outlandish points because there is something deeper driving his motivations. Indeed, let me see . . . If the House will direct their attention, I give to you Minister Aldourie's certificate of marriage."

Panic washed over Ranald, gripping him by the neck. The man wouldn't dare. If he did, his reputation was ruined—legally, socially, and every which way around.

Minister Coreley thrust the paper into the air. "You will notice, of course, that this page is blank. That is because no legal record exists. My most esteemed members, Minister Aldourie was never legally married to his wife. No British ceremony ever took place, sanctified by any British church." He narrowed his eyes. "And now, most shocking of all, I reveal to you that the woman he took into his household was a common Gypsy. Some say he participated in some sort of outdoor Gypsy shenanigans—jumping a broom or a bride kidnapping."

Outrage swirled through the room. Papers flew in the air, skittering across desks and the ceremonial mace. Ranald kept his gaze low, away from the scrutiny of the journalists.

Hot laughter hit him like a slap from all sides. He pushed past the men crowding him and quit the room. The heavy oak door shut firmly behind him, but that did nothing to muffle their cruelty. Questions—he could still hear the incensed questions.

How could someone of his status fall so low?

Why not just have a tumble and be done?

Their hearts are filth. Their language is low and violent, an insult to the ears . . . How could he actually bind himself to someone like her?

Someone like her. How dare they presume to know what she was like? Ranald reached for the wall, forcing himself to focus. So many souls relied upon him now. And the money was almost gone. If these lawmakers had their way, there would be no end of destruction. Death had followed the Romani people all across Europe. It was a cloak they wore from the moment of their birthing.

Ranald's mind slid back to the day when Elspeth's life had been snuffed out. Now he thought of the smells of that morning: the clove in his shaving lotion, the beeswax of the furniture polish used by the maids. And then the noises—the resounding, urgent knock upon the front door and the distant sound of gunshots . . .

His hands trembled so badly that he hid them in his pockets.

No. The bill would not be taken to the House of Lords and then sent for royal assent. He would stop this monstrosity before it ever reached the third reading. Every tiresome dinner party and false smile had led him to this. Finally, he knew the chink in the monster's façade—the one who was responsible for Elspeth's death and the pressure to pass the bill. One key player was all he needed: the favored son in Scotland. After he had him, the monster would crumble. By the time the division bells sounded and the bill was called to vote, the Romani people would be safe.

He owed his wife's restless soul that.

Making his way through the hallways and out onto the walkway bordering the Thames, his eyes searched the passersby. There—the dark-skinned man dressed as the perfect Englishman, staring into the river with an expression as murky as the water.

Ranald went to the rail and pretended to study a boat. "Do it."

Two words.

A slight nod, barely discernable, was the man's reply.

Ranald stepped away and headed back into the lofty halls of Parliament. The members flooded out from the Commons, taking a recess. They jeered and scoffed like the spoiled children that they were. Ranald smiled as if their words did not still cut him. As if he could not feel anymore, which wasn't far from the truth. Only one thing would work now: brutality. The members had decided, not him.

The blood that would be shed was on their lily-white hands.

Chapter One

Edinburgh, Scotland
August 1885

The glowing orange veins on the coal faded. The strong wave of the fire, the heat in the crumbling fireplace, had all but died. The light flickered, reaching for the torn hem of her dress, trembling over the scuffmarks on her shoes. Shadows scraped over the walls, pulling at the ripped wallpaper like thieves.

One last cinder split, sending up sparks that lingered before they fled.

Light and dark.

A contradiction. Just like the fear that she felt.

And the thing she thought, but shouldn't.

The smoke rolled upward, long grey fingers grasping for the mantel. "Da, I could get the two shillings if ye wait." Panic rose like the smoke, twisting, curling, playing with her fears like a toy. "I just need a little more time—"

"Window tax won't wait, girl. Landlord's already keening down my neck like a bleedin' banshee." He shoved another brick into the window frame. The wet mortar ruptured and fell to the floor.

The cold Edinburgh wind blew through the gaping hole. Feya breathed deep, wanting to savor the smell of something fresh, hoping to catch a whiff of the wind that came from beyond this part of city, somewhere where dreams weren't sold for a farthing.

"Selfish, brutish, heart-lackin' man." She said the words because she was used to them, not because they could make a difference. Nothing made a difference in the slums. You worked. You ate if you were lucky. You died. "Wastrel of a government, squeezing us all like sporran oats . . ." The curse died on her lips, paralyzed from too much use.

The wind brought tears to her eyes—the bite of it, the cold. How long since she'd really cried? She breathed in again, enjoying the pain in her lungs because she could feel it.

"I should have taken us to Glasgow. There's better work there." Da's voice was full of the past and the things he'd already said a hundred times. He stacked another brick, and then another— blocking out the belching chimneys of the tenement, the silver-brown waters of the Port of Leith, and the ships they'd never sail on.

Feya wanted to reach for the bricks and tear them away. Instead, she stood there like a fool, squeezing Ma's Scottish cross necklace in her hand. Ma would have thought of something by now. Ma always made a way.

"Waste of a man I am, Feya, and no mistake. The same thing would have happened in Glasgow." Da smiled, despite his words. "They all told it to yer ma, but she wouldn't listen. Not even when she had to sell her granny's brooch to marry me, pauper that I was." He put his hand on the side of his head. "And then when we moved here, I sold the books she was so fond of readin' to ye." He stumbled back and sobbed.

The sound cut her deep, rending and tearing like a broken saw. "Ma knew what she was doin'. She loved ye." Feya tested the words, hoping he wouldn't say anything more on the subject. "We're only going through hard times, that's all." Times so hard they had to block up the window because they couldn't pay the tax. They weren't even allowed light any more. She reached for Da's arm. "Everyone here's fallen on the times hard."

"Not everyone. Are ye blind, girl?" He pulled away, his long black hair blowing like a madman's in the wind. "We've been cursed fer a long time because of me." His dark eyes, wide and hazed, went to the empty whisky bottles scattered upon the floor. "The old tinkers were right. The first time I looked upon yer ma's bonny red hair, the curse came." He stepped toward Feya and lifted a lock of her long hair. "And ye with hair just like hers. But me darkness shows up in yer eyes. And here . . . look close." He skimmed his calloused finger along the skin of her arm. "Me kind whisper here in yer coloring." He lowered his voice. "Ye'd be better off without me. Say it."

Feya saw in his face everything that frightened her, everything she didn't want to be. "I won't, Da."

"I can get it over with tonight." He laughed, a sound full of emptiness and the weight of misfortune.

"Stop it." She wanted to shake him. "I told ye not to talk like that anymore."

Da clutched her arm, pulling her so close she could smell the whisky. "A knife's a friend to a man in a tight spot. I could wander down the wrong alley and have someone do it fer me." He dug his finger into her side. "Right here."

Feya winced and tried to pull away. "Don't say those things."

Da tightened his grip. His eyelids drooped to slits and he seemed to forget what he was saying. "Ye'll do fine in this world because ye always do what's right, don't ye?" He stumbled and reached for more mortar. "Me own, strong girl."

Anger flared in her cheeks, but anger she was used to. Her anger was the only thing keeping them alive.

Her baby brother cried in the corner, a little bundle of rags. Feya lifted Hamish and held him close, feeling the breath that should be tinged with milk but wasn't. The red curls of his hair were sprinkled with black residue from the coal smoke that choked the entire city. Specks of it lay on his tiny face, as though a fairy had dusted him. But this fairy did not bring sweet dreams to bairns in the night. It choked their lungs till they couldn't breathe and sent them to lie in the cold, hard ground. "Hamish, me love." She kissed his cheek and cooed at him, bringing him close, as if that would help.

As Da worked, more of the coal smoke collected around the ceiling. They were being plunged into the pit, light disappearing, no hope of escape.

There wasn't even enough money for a chimney sweep.

Da laid another brick, and the view of the wharf was gone.

"Listen to me," she said to herself as much to Da. "I'll get more work." The tightness in her chest increased. She coughed. "Things are goin' to be fine."

"Fine," Da sang as he held up the trowel. "Me Feya's goin' make it all fine." He pushed his hand through the last bit of open air above the bricks as if to taunt her. His accent grew thick and stumbled back through the years to the time before he'd married Ma. To the time when he'd spent all his evenings around an open fire, singing the old tales of the Gypsies. "'Clean and bright, me girl always does what's right . . .'" His words slurred into the old language—the cant—a mixture of Gaelic and Romani. The sound of it always made Feya think the devil was coming, and soon.

A thump came from the other room, and then a crash. She whirled around.

"Brenna! Gillis! I'll have yer guts fer garters!" The laundry line lay on the floor, the work she'd done all morning a pile of soot-covered wrinkles. "Ye naughty bairns! How will I send ye to school if I canna collect me washin' money?"

Da laughed low. "What use is school to the likes of them? Their blood's tainted." He scraped the trowel against the bricks and went back to singing, in and out of the cant. "'Me daughter does the work of three women and her blood's tainted . . .'"

Brenna wrapped her arms around Feya's legs. "I didnae mean to ruin the washin'. Was only tryin' to get Gillis his horsey." Fear made its way into Brenna's green eyes. The look had nothing to do with being afraid of being punished; it was deeper, feral, as if the girl understood more than was possible. "Why's Da singin' again, Feya?" She gripped Feya's skirt. "I don't like it when he does that."

Feya sighed and felt the weight of it in her bones. "*Ach*, lassie . . ." There wasn't an answer she could give.

A tear made a pale pathway down the dirt on Brenna's cheek.

Feya still hadn't managed to get the bairns into the bath. Hadn't yet given them supper. She'd failed them. She took her sister's chin and tilted it up. "Ye hold up your head like a thistle, do ye hear me? We are of Scotland, and we will be strong."

Gillis sat in the middle of the laundry, his shamble of a toy horse broken. His tears fell into his hands where he held the pieces, the expression on his face far too grim for a boy not yet seven years old.

"Oh, my wee little man, don't cry." Feya wiped his face with her apron and kissed his cheek. She picked up the gnarled toy she'd taken from the rubbish bin near Prince's Street over a year ago. Only one strand of yarn remained on the tail. The yellow paint that had once made the saddle shine was completely gone.

Feya ran her fingers over the broken pieces. She remembered walking past the shops when Ma was still alive. Dreaming of when they'd move back to the country. Looking at the wedding dresses. But that was before. A time when dreams were possible.

No one would take her now.

She gathered the children together, along with baby Hamish in her arms. "Here, now, don't despair. There's always hope." Even as she said the words, she didn't feel them. She only felt the burn marks on her hands from the rubber mill and the ache behind her eyes from sewing by candlelight. She forced the words out again. "'Hope springs eternal.' That's what Ma would say."

Da appeared in the room, his frame silhouetted by the wastrel of a fire. He tried to tie his hair back with a ribbon, but he only managed to gather half. Past him, the last crooked brick sat tucked into the window frame. "She was sayin' that even when the Death Angel came and ripped her away." Da's eyes focused on a place that only he could see, a place where his demons had come to call.

Feya thought of those last moments—the way Ma had turned pale after the bloodletting, how her spirit had left in degrees. She closed her eyes and shut off the memory, hardening herself.

The smoke clogged the air, thick and ugly like sin, wafting through the room.

Da walked past her, saying nothing. The door didn't make a sound as he opened it, but Feya felt the shift in the air in the room— a shift that said he wouldn't be back until the morning, or a few days.

Noise carried through the thin tenement walls: Da's heavy footsteps in the hall, angry words with the men he met on the stairs, the thump of someone being shoved. Behind her, the mortar still dripped on the floor. With each sound, the wall around her heart grew harder. She had to kill the feelings, keep them down.

Feya went to the washbasin and started the work. Scrubbing. Tidying the room. Mucking up the mortar. Peeling the last potatoes and making the soup. The work she was used to. The work she could do.

When she'd finished, she tucked the bairns into her bed and lay down beside them. She'd stay until their eyes closed. Until the noises didn't frighten them anymore. The work from the day wore against her bones, the aches begging her to sleep.

Gillis wove his fingers through her hair, combing and pulling. "My stomach hurts."

"Be quiet, Gillis." Brenna lashed him with her eyes. "Sayin' it doesn't make the food appear."

"Here, now." Feya sat and took a sheet from the floor. She spread it over the rickety headboard. "We'll make a Romani tent and sleep underneath. Remember the stories I told ye?" She tied the end of the sheet to the footboard and lay back down. The candle flickered through the thin, flower-print fabric. "Skim yer fingers along it, like so." Feya traced the outlines of what used to be pink petals. "When I was yer age—"

"I don't like those stories." Brenna stared at the wall, her face as dark as the wallpaper stains. "And I don't want to play that."

Noises came from the other side of the wall—moans like someone dying. A thump. Gillis jerked and whimpered. He reached for Feya's hand.

Before she could respond, Hamish shuddered and let go of his tattered blanket. His head lolled to the side and the fight seeped out of his face as though some malevolent spirit drew it, stroking his cheeks, lulling him to give in.

"Hamish!" Feya pushed away the sheet and gathered him close.

"Fey-Fey . . ." Hamish's head drooped.

Feya brought him to her, her heart pounding. "What's the matter, little man?"

Brenna reached to touch him, then widened her eyes accusingly. "Why's he so hot?"

"I don't know." Feya swallowed, wishing the answer would come to her. He hadn't been hot just a minute ago, and he'd eaten the little bit of soup she gave him.

Brenna reached for him again, as if Feya's hold wasn't strong enough.

"I have him." Feya pulled him closer and rocked on the bed. "He's not ill." The words rang false. "He's just tired."

His eyes, Gypsy dark like hers, were far too dim.

The memory of Ma's death night pressed back in. Same hopeless room. Same bed. Her last words echoed in the dark. *"Don't put yourself in divers places, Feya. Stay at home where it's safe. The good Lord will protect you as long as you don't go provokin' things."*

"He didn't protect ye."

"What are ye sayin', Feya?" Brenna's voice dove into the pain and the fear.

Ma's lips had trembled as the next words came. *"God watches over us all. Always has the best things in mind."*

Feya tightened her hold around Hamish. Did God mean for them not to have fresh air? Did He mean for them to never again have any light? To starve?

The smoke still swirled in the room. The moments were measured by her siblings breathing. The last ember in the fireplace died.

Feya squeezed Ma's Scottish cross in the darkness. She'd always worn it. And what good had it ever done?

"Don't put yourself in divers places, Feya." Places where a girl ought not to be. A woman has her place. *"Don't go provokin' things."*

"Or what?" Feya ran her thumb over the place on the cross where years had rubbed it thin.

Ye shalt not tempt the Lord thy God . . .

The wind howled down the chimney like a ghoul, spilling the remnants of the coal onto the floor.

Brenna tugged on Feya's sleeve, tears pouring from her eyes. "He needs a doctor."

Feya nodded, her body like ice. She could never afford a doctor. She rubbed Hamish's back as if that could help.

"Take him fer a moment, Brenna." She went to the loose floorboard and lifted it.

Gone.

The coins were gone. Just as she knew they would be. Da had found her last hiding place.

Feya sat on the floor, put her arms around herself, and squeezed. The bairns . . . They cried. They looked at her and they cried.

The thought she'd been thinking earlier . . . That thought she shouldn't think . . . It took root, twisted deep in her heart until it bled cold stone. The woman she'd met in the market—Maggie— she'd said she could help. She'd said . . .

Da's blue Romani scarf lay upon the floor, forgotten. He wore it around his neck to remember the days in the camps. She'd use it to remember too—that what she did now was because of him. She reached for it and stuffed it into her pocket.

"Bairns, get up. Come with me."

"Where are we going?" Gillis slid off the bed and stumbled. He rubbed his eyes.

"Yer going to have a visit with Annie fer a while." She reached for Hamish and moved toward the door. "Hold onto me, Brenna. Gillis, hold yer sister's hand."

She led them into the hall, around the rubbish and the people sleeping on the floor. Shouts came from behind doors—words the bairns shouldn't have to hear. A woman sobbed from somewhere down the hall.

"I'm afraid." Brenna looked up at her in the dim light.

"We only have to be strong, lassie. And do what has to be done."

Feya forced her eyes away from her little sister and knocked on the last door. Wood scraped against wood as the inner bar lifted.

"Please." Gillis moved closer and pulled on her skirt. "I don't want to go. I'll work harder at the mill tomorrow."

Feya swallowed against the hotness of the hall burning her eyes.

"I won't be naughty again." Tears wove into Brenna's soft voice. "I'll do all the mendin' tonight." She sniffled. "Ye can sleep."

The door creaked open. The shadows on Annie's face told what sort of a day she'd had. The purple bruise rimming her eye told more. "I told you I couldn't watch them anymore, Feya. They'd be better off sleeping in their own beds."

"No." Feya reached for Annie's arm. "I'll not leave them alone. Please. I need this . . ." Her words came too quickly. "I need to go somewhere—to do something fer the bairns."

Annie looked her over and sighed. She opened the door wider. "Only till the morning, mind you. You don't want them here when Albert comes straggling back."

She shifted her gaze to Hamish. "What's wrong with that one?"

"He has a fever. I . . . I'll bring back medicine. And pay ye extra this time."

"I'm still waiting on the money for the last time." Annie crossed her arms. "This is your last chance. If I don't see any money—"

"Ye'll see it." Feya took a slow breath. "And ye'd better treat them well." She looked the woman directly in her eyes.

Annie shrugged and went back inside, leaving the door open.

"Please." Gillis pushed his face against her leg.

Feya's breath came hard. She crouched and held them close. "Listen to me, bairns." She kissed their foreheads and the tops of their heads. "Just a few hours, and then I'll be back."

"I don't want—"

"Hush, now." Feya placed her hand on Gillis's wet cheek. "Ye hold on to each other and try to sleep." She handed Hamish to Brenna. "I promise I'll be back before the morning."

The rain that fell on the Royal Mile was weak, like a man's promises—weak like a father's promises to take care. Feya pulled her threadbare wrap tighter, put her head down, and walked. One foot in front of the other. A man passing her on the street stopped and stared, as if he knew what she was about to give.

Deacon Brodie's Tavern gleamed in the rain, its green paint a coat that hid deeper things—horrible things, things that had to be. A wooden sign swung above the door, creaking on rusty chains. She didn't have to look up to know what images it bore; for the past two weeks she'd seen them in her dreams. On one side a locksmith held a key. On the other side stood a masked man—the same man. Locksmith by day, thief by night.

Sounds traveled from the windows above—laughter, the clink of silverware.

It was only work. And work she could do. She pushed open the door. Sweet warmth hit her in the face. Light from the lamps made her squint.

"Oy, girl. What are ye doin' in here? This be the door for the patrons."

Feya raised her chin and moved through the crowd. She only had to get to the stairs.

"She knows where's she's going," another voice said. "And from the looks of that one, I'm following."

Hot laughter hit against her back and pushed her on. Upstairs, the room burst with noise and bodies—men everywhere, basking in the glow of the gaslight, shoving in cottage pie and cherry crumble, steaming chicken, and thick sausage. The smells ripped through her stomach until it clenched. The man closest to her scooped up a spoonful of neeps and tatties—those creamy, crispy, dripping-with-butter potatoes that were her absolute favorite in the world.

"And didn't I know you'd come after all." Maggie's voice cut through her thoughts. The woman sauntered across the room, her smile wide.

"What do I do, Maggie? How—"

"It's all right, pet. Everything's going to be all right." Maggie laced her arm through Feya's and led her to the back. "What changed your mind?"

"Money, Maggie. It brings us all down in the end."

Maggie led her into a small room, sparsely furnished—a dresser, a bed. She took a brush out of her pocket. "We can't have you looking like this for your first night. The rain's made you look more red sheep dog than woman."

The bristles caught in tangles. Sharp pain lanced her scalp. "I'm just here fer work. Ye don't have to pretend like we're friends."

In the mirror, a slow smile crossed Maggie's mouth. "Oh, we're going to be friends, you and I. And I'm going to teach you everything you need to know."

Chapter Two

As Maggie talked, Feya felt something like shock, but she couldn't really tell. Shock was like hunger—after becoming accustomed to it day after day, it didn't have a name anymore. It was only a numbness, something consistent.

Some things just were.

"A nod's as good as a wink to a blind horse." Maggie leaned in and took Feya by the shoulders. "You get my meanin'?"

"Aye." Feya drew her eyebrows together. She had no earthly idea what the woman meant.

The gaslights flickered. On the wall, the shadows of Maggie's curls looked like maggots. "You pick a man who won't hurt you. It's not always good to go for the bonniest ones. Especially in this part of town."

Feya stood and crossed her arms. "But this is the good part of town. Ye said there'd be more money here, better prospects."

"There's more money for sure." Maggie withdrew a faded yellow ribbon from her pocket and tied it around Feya's neck. "But men are men, no matter what part of town you're in. I'd be my granny's mother if I didn't tell you the truth. The handsome ones aren't always the gentlest, and the strongest ones aren't always kind."

A wave of pure fear rushed over Feya. Her gaze went to the bed—the simple blanket, the thin pillow. Images built in her mind, nightmarish and cruel. She squeezed her eyes shut. "So, choose a man who's poorly?"

Maggie gave her a sad smile. "Sometimes, lass."

The flame of the gaslight hissed and rose, licked at the dark like a living thing.

"You're going to be just fine." Maggie wrapped her arms around herself and slid her hands slowly down her shoulders. "After awhile you won't even think about it anymore. It just becomes who you are."

Just somethin' ye do. The thought didn't feel authentic, like a tin cup used for tea. Feya breathed deep to stop the shaking—the tremor that was always there.

Maggie curled her fingers around the cracked door. "The night wanes on. We'd best take advantage while we can."

"Yer right. No use wastin' time." Feya stepped into the hall, feeling like someone else was doing the walking. The light below the main door pulsed—a fleeting heartbeat, yellow and orange, flickering as someone on the other side passed.

Glasses clinked. Voices rose and fell. Greedy voices, full of want and obsession. Feya fisted her left hand into a ball, felt the place where there would never be a ring. There was no room for weakness. Not now. Not ever.

She stepped in front of Maggie and pushed open the door. The heat from the fireplace whooshed against her. Thick wooden beams stretched across the ceiling like a giant's ribs. The windows in the back of the room showed the dark Royal Mile—lights beyond the glass flickering here and there like ghosts waltzing in the dark. And there, to the right, the shadow of St. Giles Church, all sharp spires and menacing towers—a place for royalty. She felt it staring at her, judging.

Maggie took a rag and a pitcher off the bar. "Just go fill their glasses. The rest comes naturally."

A few other women stood around the room, mingling, some taking food to the men, others just talking. Feya forced a smile. She needed to look appealing.

Men flicked their gazes at her, then looked back down into their glasses. Some were too lost in conversation to look up at all. Still, the smell of the food pulled at her, every scrape of a fork torture. And the happiness . . . That was worst of all—the smiles and light conversations amongst friends.

A man stood next to the fireplace, his elbow casually propped upon the mantel. Firelight shone over his suit, washing around the contours of his shoulders in orange and yellow light, spilling onto the silver pinstripes of his grey waistcoat. He was handsome, but his eyes were shallow and restless. His smile was cruel and his blond hair too perfectly combed.

Feya shivered. He must be English.

God forbid.

She scanned the room again. Maybe that one, with his head bent low over the candle. Feya walked closer and grabbed a rag, wiping tables just because.

The voice of the man at the table faded in and out. His eyes shifted. "We're the New Resurrection Men . . . steal the bodies . . . the graves . . . sell 'em to whoever's buying . . . twelve pounds a stiff."

Feya inched closer, pushing in chairs and trying to look busy. Surely she'd heard him wrong.

The shadow of the candle danced off his companion's thin cheeks. "Thought all that was over years ago when Burke and Hare were executed. And what about the Anatomy Act of '32? What need does the medical university have now?"

The shifty-eyed man smiled. "Let's just say there's been a decline in bodies donated to science. Executions are down . . . People are getting all religious." His gaze lifted to the ceiling as if he were trying to pass off innocence. "You'd be surprised how exhilarating a moonlit stroll over to Greyfriars can be." He tipped his glass and drained it. "Especially with a wooden shovel. Less noise."

Feya's eyes widened. He was an anticlockwise devil, this one. She squeezed the handle of the pitcher. She should hit him over the head and save the world from his trouble.

"You're lying." The sallow man's voice was thick with shock.

"We're not burking 'em, mind you, so there's no problems."

"You're not murdering them, you mean? To save yourself the trouble of digging?" The thin man slammed money down on the table and stood. "That does make all the difference, doesn't it?" He peeled his greatcoat from the chair and shoved it on. "I hope you enjoy being detained at Her Majesty's pleasure."

The shifty-eyed man watched him go. He smiled, looking satisfied, then caught Feya's gaze and locked eyes with her.

There was no way she'd consort with the likes of him.

His smile spread like a sickly disease. He leaned back in his chair as if she were a curiosity on a stage. He followed her every move— the fisting of her hands, the way her skirt shifted around her ankles when she moved.

"You're new here." Another man's voice sounded behind her. His tone was deep and dusty, like something locked away too long.

Feya narrowed her eyes at the body snatcher before she turned. He winked.

The man who'd spoken sat alone at his table. His features were perfect—a thick shock of brown hair, eyebrows that slanted gently, and a mouth that gave the impression of smiling even though he wasn't. His skin was smooth and his beard closely trimmed. His clothing was flawless—starched and very good quality.

"Yes . . ." Feya stumbled over the word. "This is me first time here."

"Is it indeed?" The effect of his smile was strange, like finding something lost, but hated. "Would you like to sit with me?" He gestured to the chair opposite.

Feya turned to look for Maggie but couldn't catch her attention. The man Maggie was talking to laughed uncontrollably. Probably drunk. Feya sat, her heart pounding.

"And before tonight?" He raked his gaze over her face, lingering around her neckline. "Where did you work before tonight?"

Why would he want to know that? The candle flame grew urgent, reaching high then swaying toward her. The rim collapsed and bled beeswax down the side, pooling onto the dark wood.

The man leaned forward and placed his arm on the table. There was need in his eyes.

Understanding came like a sunrise. Slowly she watched it unfold in his expression, the thing he most desired for her to say: he wanted to know if she'd ever been with a man, if he would be the first.

The room swelled with heat. The conversations slacked and then rose again.

"Well?"

"Nowhere." Feya whispered the word like a criminal's sentence. She dropped her gaze and let the judgment fall. The years fled away, and she remembered a moment when she'd been a child, sitting in Glen Affric with Ma, weaving each other's hair as well as their dreams.

"Promise me that you'll wait for the man who'll love you. A man who'll fight for you till he bleeds his last drop of blood. A man like your da."

Feya twisted her resolve and killed the memory. Da was the reason she was here—the reason for all of it, and all her days to come.

"Is that right, then? You've not worked anywhere else." The man said the words slowly, as if he was unwrapping his thoughts. "Well, then, seems fate is a beautiful woman with bonny red hair." He touched the tips of her fingertips. "Tell me your name."

Feya jerked back her hand. He caught it. His fingers were cold from the empty ale glass.

What should she say? She couldn't tell him the truth. "Brenna." Voicing her sister's name gave her a little strength. She pictured Hamish and Gillis and gained some more.

The man turned her hand over, keeping his eyes locked with hers. He placed hot, heavy coins into her palm. Just pieces of metal, but so much more.

A movement to the left caught Feya's attention. Maggie reached across the table and knocked the coins from Feya's hand. They plinked upon the table and spun. "Beggin' your pardon. I hope you'll excuse us."

"I will not." The man's voice was iron. He gripped Feya's wrist.

"Maggie." Feya drew her eyebrows together. "Please." The men at the adjacent table stared, their hot glares tangible on her skin.

Maggie tugged Feya's hand away and pulled Feya out of her chair. Ignoring the man's protest, she led Feya to a corner. "Saints preserve me . . . I didn't know that one was here."

"Who?"

"That. One." She inclined her head toward the man, who had leaned back in his chair. "His heart's as black as the Earl of Hell's waistcoat. What'd I tell you? When I said not the bonny ones, I meant *that* one."

Feya widened her eyes. Although she didn't know Maggie well, the woman's distress was infectious. "Why?"

"Just pick another one." She brought her face close. "Maggie's always right." With a final nod, she turned and filtered back into the crowd.

Feya looked back at the man, who sat watching her. He suddenly pulled his gaze away and focused on the body snatcher.

Was he one of them?

The body snatcher rose, put on his greatcoat, and exited. The man she'd just sat with waited. One second. Two. Then he rose and followed.

Devils, the lot of them. Feya smoothed her skirt. Her gaze went to the window and the shadow of St. Giles Church. She supposed if she believed God was watching out for her, she might thank him now. But that's what weak people did. People who lived in fancy houses and had the means for another day.

Feya looked back at the other men scattered about the room. Too old. Too young. Too handsome. She gripped the wainscoting on the wall and closed her eyes. "All right, ye stupid girl, turn around and the first one ye see, go with him."

She slid her hand from the wall and opened her eyes.

A thin man across the room bent over his table. He scribbled like mad upon a paper.

Feya forced herself to walk. Past the stares and past the sneers.

The man muttered to himself as he wrote. Dark hair curled just below his ears. His eyes were large—almost too big for his face. His nose was fine and long, giving the impression of a privileged birth.

Feya took a breath, forcing out the feeling that she should run. He would do. It didn't matter. After him, it would be easier.

He wore a plain suit with a velvet coat draped over his shoulders. His mustache moved as he talked to himself—strange phrases, things that made no sense at all.

Just so long as he had money. That was all that mattered now.

The window behind him was cracked open, the rain a silvery slash against the dark. The fresh smell of it promised a new beginning. Feya let her eyes linger on the falling droplets. Just one last moment for herself. Ma had always told her and the bairns stories about how it used to be when it rained.

Melancholy forced its way in, only a momentary lapse, but one that cost her dearly.

The sound of scribbling grew louder.

Fool. What was she doing? Staring at the rain like the Blue Men of the Minch—those water spirits the Gypsies spoke of. She forced her gaze back to the man. "It's a poor evenin'."

The man stopped his pen. He looked up, his eyes distant. "Aye." He went back to writing.

Feya looked to Maggie across the room. Her curls bounced as she nodded in approval.

Feya slowly lowered herself into the chair beside the man. She stared at him, willing him to do whatever it was men did during these occurrences.

The man's lips moved, then his voice grew louder. "'Embarrassed in discourse; backward in sentiment; lean, long, dusty . . . dreary and yet somehow lovable.' Perfect!" His mustache lifted when he smiled. He scooted his chair in and scribbled some more.

Feya leaned toward him. "I said it's a poor evenin'."

The man raised an eyebrow. "Would you be wanting something then?"

"Are ye not understandin' me?"

"I understand you just fine." He looked out the window and shrugged. "It's always poor weather here in Old Reekie." A coughing fit made him fumble for his handkerchief. He doubled over.

"Are ye all right?" Feya hit him on the back. "Do ye have the grippe? Perhaps catarrh of the larynx?" She grimaced. Just her luck. He probably had cholera. "Have ye been drinkin' cold water and eatin' unripe fruit?"

"I . . . no." Sweat shone on his forehead. He looked back down at his page, but it didn't look as though he was reading the words.

She'd chosen a sick one.

Feya placed her face in her hands. She didn't feel so well either. Her throat felt too tight and her face burned with heat. How long had she been there? In just a few hours the bairns would be wanting breakfast.

"Is something wrong?"

"No. I'm sorry fer botherin' ye." Feya stood, tiredness hitting her like the grave.

"Wait. Something troubles you. It's in your eyes."

"What are ye, a doctor? I think ye need one yerself."

A sad smile crossed his face. "I've had plenty of doctors, none of them worth much good." He gestured at the opposite chair. "Sit. I am fond of stories. I'd like to hear yours."

"I didn't come here to tell me story." Feya frowned, but she sat anyway. "I came here to make a new one."

"Then we're more alike than you might think." The man raised his hand and yelled over the buzz of the crowd. "Liam, tea for the young lady. And more coffee for me."

"Yer buyin' me a cup of tea?" What kind of strange sod was he? Feya watched the man at the bar pour hot water into a pot. The tendrils of steam danced in the air, twirling like fairies. The noises in the room were too loud, the temperature too hot. Dizziness pulled at the edges of her mind.

A smile transformed her companion's face. He leaned in close and whispered.

My tea is nearly ready and the sun has left the sky;
It's time to take the window to see Leerie going by;
For every night at teatime and before you take your seat,
With lantern and with ladder he comes posting up the street.

The rhythm of his voice calmed her a little. She could see the pictures in her mind. The sound of the words strung together seemed to be woven from silver and dripping with gold. "That was beautiful. What was it?"

His expression appeared lighter, the tension from the cough gone. "Penny whistles. The dreams of a child."

"Dreams." Feya wanted to laugh, but couldn't. She didn't have any dreams anymore. She dropped her gaze to his papers.

A maid servant living alone in a house not far from the river had gone upstairs to bed about eleven . . . the lane, which the maid's window overlooked, was brilliantly lit by the full moon. It seems she was romantically given, for she sat down upon her box, which stood immediately under the window, and fell into a dream of musing.

The words were like beautiful prodding forks, forcing her to pay attention. "What is that?"

"I'm not entirely sure, yet. I'm fiddling about with an old play of mine." He tapped the paper. "Shadows of ideas are toying with me. Things I can't quite reach." His smile was full of mystery. "I do know that this will be a sinister story, very different. Potions and hidden identity."

Feya smiled and realized she hadn't forced it. "Yer a writer."

"Aye."

"What's yer name?"

He tapped his pen on the table. "What's yours?"

"You first."

"Robert."

"Robert what?"

He shuffled the papers in front of him until he came to the first one. His name was scrawled there, half eloquent, half dashed off: *Robert Louis Stevenson.*

"Yer . . ." Feya swallowed. She'd tried to sell herself to Robert Louis Stevenson!

"I take it you've read my writing?"

"I beg yer pardon." She rose from the chair, stiff with humiliation.

"Here now, your tea." Mr. Stevenson gave her a look that forced her to sit.

"I feel . . ." No answer came. Perhaps he didn't know.

He folded his hands like a teacher. "I saw earlier that you came in with Maggie."

"Maggie? How do ye know—"

"Everyone knows Mad Maggie."

"Mad Maggie?"

"Oh, aye. Been that way for quite a while." He leaned in and gave her a look full of conspiracy. "Fancies herself a lady of the night."

Feya wished she could die. Sink through the floor and disappear like the mournful wind. An old rhyme came to her mind: *If wishes were fishes then beggars would eat.*

"Poor thing comes in night after night. Always gets thrown out before she's been here an hour."

As if hearing his words, the man at the bar went to Maggie and took her by the arm. "We're respectable folk in here, Maggie."

Mr. Stevenson opened his pocket watch. "Right on time."

Feya picked up her teacup and guzzled.

"But you'll have to forgive me for telling you such a story, a nice young woman like yourself." He narrowed his eyes.

Her teacup clinked against the saucer. "Above the board. That's me fer sure. Only doin' what's right."

Mr. Stevenson smiled to himself and stirred his coffee. "That's good, because there was a police officer in here earlier trying to catch those who aren't above the board. You were sitting with him, actually, before you came over here. I happened to look up just then."

"Me name's Feya." The words tumbled out like a confession.

"Feya." He repeated it slowly. "Now that would make a good name for a heroine." He scribbled her name on the side of his paper. "Maybe I can get you into a chapter."

"Please." Feya held up her hand. "I think I'd like to forget this night ever existed."

"Feya." A faraway look came to his eyes. "Reminiscent of the fae. Yes, you do seem somewhat fairy. A little lost, perhaps." He gave her a kind look. "But being lost is often the beginnings of a grand adventure."

Feya took another gulp of tea. "I can't say adventure is a priority at this moment."

"Pity. You have the look for it, you know. Something about your eyes."

Of course he'd notice her Romani eyes from Da. Everyone noticed. She lowered her lashes so he couldn't see.

He must have sensed her unease because he changed the subject. "I used to come here as a young man." He looked around the room as if remembering. "In fact, Deacon Brodie may be inspiration for this current story." He laid his hand upon the stack of papers. "I can't get Brodie out my mind—the locksmith by day and thief by night." He touched his finger to his temple. "How does one transform into the exact opposite personality?"

"Ye tell me," Feya said. "Yesterday I went to work in the rubber mill. Now I'm here, with ye. Ten minutes ago I would have . . ." She couldn't finish the sentence. Her shame was too strong.

"Ah, but you didn't," he said, leaving no doubt that he knew what her purpose had been. "There's something for thought." His eyes bored into hers. "It's not in you."

She should have been pleased at his observation, but she wasn't. If it wasn't in her, the bairns would starve. "Circumstances intervened."

He raised his gaze to the ceiling, as if the words he was about to say were hanging there. "Odd that you chose this place and not another. Odd that Maggie took you under her broken wing."

"Not odd, just unfortunate."

He stopped his coffee cup mid-air. "You seem to be fond of stories. Shall I tell you one?"

Feya took a breath. With every flash of the fire and patter of rain against the window, time seeped away from her like sand.

"A long time ago, on a rainy night just like this, a young man sat at this very table holding a yellow ribbon in his hand. The man was wealthy, from one of the oldest families in Scotland. For our purposes, we shall call him James. He was very handsome, and well favored, but he had a secret."

Feya allowed herself to relax. What could one indulgence hurt when she'd most likely be dead in a week? How she used to love stories, reading every one of her mother's books. "I prefer me heroes to have secrets, especially when they originate abroad. I am particularly fond of India."

"Are you?" He looked pleased and scooted forward in his chair. "I've been tossing a story around on that very subject. I only have bits and pieces, but I've got a wonderful title." He spread his hands in the air. "'The Master of Ballantrae: A Masterful Tale of Revenge Set in Scotland, America, and India.' What do you think?"

She nodded, her imagination roaming. The feeling was strange— this part of herself that had lain dormant for so long. "Sounds fascinating. I'd love to read it."

She took another sip of tea. What was the last book she'd read? It had been . . . Disbelief made her mouth go slack. "I was very fond of *The Suicide Club*."

"Were you?" He leaned in as though they were two gossiping friends.

Feya returned the gesture and even placed her hand upon his arm. "Yes. Prince Florizel and Colonel Geraldine . . . The young man with the cream tarts." She closed her eyes as if in rapture. "What an amazing opening."

"My dear, you do know good literature."

She snickered. Where had that come from? She hadn't laughed in how long?

"Ah, but we're getting off the subject." He once again pulled his coat closer. "The story . . ."

She reached behind her and closed the window, thinking he might be cold. "Go on." She put her elbows on the table and fisted her hands under her chin.

"I must warn you, Feya, a really good story has a way of altering the hearer. Are you quite prepared?"

She wanted to laugh again, but thought better of it. After all, how could a story alter anything about her, or change what was already written in stone?

Chapter Three

The light had changed in Mr. Stevenson's eyes. His expression darkened, as if a specter inhabited his body. "A young woman worked here, around that same time James frequented this place. A common beginning, you might say. But ah, Feya, how a moment can change a life for all eternity."

Feya scooted closer to the table, the very air around them changing.

"The girl had a curse upon her. An ancient curse that many before her had borne. There was no escaping it; from the time she was old enough to play she saw it in the eyes of the men who came to her house." Mr. Stevenson's expression pinched. He paused.

"What was the curse?" Feya asked, expecting some hideous thing.

He drew his gaze over her face. "Beauty."

Feya crossed her arms. Beauty, if she had it, was the only thing a woman could use. But she did not. Her hands were too rough from working, and her hair was always too wild. And then there were her Gypsy eyes, dark as the curse Da said flowed through her veins.

"The woman was used by many. But she was strong. When she came here, she hoped for a new start and a path to her destiny."

Feya sneered. "I wonder, Mr. Stevenson, if the lateness of the hour hasn't clouded yer judgment. I am not yer pupil."

"No, you are not. But I believe we were meant to meet." He tapped his fingers like the steady tick of a clock. "If one believes all the Scottish foolishness about predestination."

"Foolishness indeed." Ma's Scottish cross lay heavy at the base of her throat. She had no idea why she'd brought it. "So, back to the story. The woman came here?"

"Yes." He said the word slowly and still seemed to be considering something. "She drew the attention of James."

"Did they fall in love?" A log fell in the fireplace, followed by a great cough of cinders and smoke from beneath the mantel.

Mr. Stevenson lowered his gaze to the table and acted like he dreaded his coming words. "There was a child—a little girl. James didn't marry the woman." He held his hand to his chest and stifled another cough. "Those sort never do."

She waited for him to continue, but he didn't. Instead, he only watched her and coughed. Then watched her again. And then it all made sense.

He was using this as a moral story. Knowing what she'd almost done, he wanted to warn her of the dangers of her choices, as if she were a child.

"Let me try to guess the rest." Heat flooded her body, familiar anger at being judged. "The baby starved. The mother was never the same." Loneliness wove around her, worse than when she'd walked into the tavern. Yes, this was worse. This was almost having someone understand you and then having that ripped away. "A very familiar tale fer Edinburgh, don't ye think? Somehow I expected more from the greatest storyteller of our age."

Mr. Stevenson started to speak, clutched his chest again, then took another drink. "Don't you want to know the woman's name?"

"Why not?"

"Maggie."

Feya stilled. Her eyes shifted to the doorway where Mad Maggie had been taken away.

"The very same." His voice was sad. "And the yellow ribbon you wear was the child's."

Feya's hands went to her throat. She untied the ribbon and threw it upon the table. "Why did ye tell me this?" Despair washed over her. For just a moment she'd forgotten her pain. But then he'd given it back to her with a vengeance. Time still ticked away. And the bairns waited for her to provide.

Mr. Stevenson looked sorry. "Writers often fiddle with stories and give readers what they want: a happy ending. But life is often different, as I expect you know." He looked older somehow, and his face concealed more than he was saying. "One thing is not often learned in Scotland, and that is the way to be happy."

Feya stopped the protest that wanted to come. Hadn't she come to the tavern trying to find a bit of that happiness? Trying to get money, to provide?

"All human beings are commingled out of good and evil, Feya. You can't go tilting the scale by provoking things. It's not long before you forget the person you used to be. Then you're in so deep you can't go back." He pulled his frock coat tighter around his shoulders. "I am a great sinner. I should know."

"Don't go provoking things." Ma's words. The coldness crept in again, and the squeezing around her heart. The smoke from the fireplace swirled around the ceiling. It reached for her with tendrils of grey. Feya shut her eyes. Smoke always did bring a wetness to her eyes that she despised.

"I told you this story because—" Mr. Stevenson coughed again, the sound mixing with the others from the room—laughter, glasses clinking, life moving on.

As her life never would.

Feya stood and was hit by a wave of dizziness. Without a word—for what good would it do to even say good-bye—she made her way through the chairs, littered across the floor like black rib bones. And the men—they still gawked, looking down their noses whenever she caught their gaze.

"Feya." Mr. Stevenson's voice behind her was urgent. "Wait. I may be able to—"

Nothing he could say would make a difference. She set her gaze upon the exit. No use in lingering any longer. What did it matter if she still didn't have any coins in her palm? There were always ways. Before the sun broke the darkness she'd have something to feed the bairns.

Robert Louis Stevenson clutched his handkerchief tighter. Another spasm of coughing came, but there was little he could do. Time. There was never enough time. He reached for Feya in hopes she would stop. She stood by the stairs, gave him one last look, then slipped behind the doorframe like a dream before waking, remnants of what could have been.

He wiped the sprinkles of blood from his mouth. Just a few more minutes—that's all he would have needed. He could have turned the course of events. Maybe even eventually proved his father wrong that everything was set in stone.

His writing was good. They could have afforded another maid. Fanny wouldn't have liked it at first, but she would have eventually softened. Possibly. Maybe. One never knew for sure with his wife.

Feya. Such a name. He'd liked her. He'd wanted to help. He'd felt like he was supposed to help. Like their meeting had been higher than themselves. And those feelings came so sporadically of late.

He shouldn't have tested her temper by telling her that story. But the last woman he'd tried to help had ended up flying into a rage and robbing him blind before she'd been at the house for a day—something Fanny never let him forget.

It was like he'd told Feya: all human beings were commingled out of good and evil. The trick was to see what side they most heavily leaned to.

Tiredness came upon him like the Edinburgh fog—thick and deceiving. He leaned back against the wall and gazed at the half-written pages before him. Good and evil. The two sides of all people.

The excitement of the story that had gripped him before Feya came had been like a drug, coursing through his body, making him feel alive. But that was gone now. Only the ache in his lungs remained, the haze of pain that robbed and battered.

He rested his head against the cold windowpane behind him. Outside walked a desperate red-haired girl who'd no doubt destroy herself. Take any road she had to . . . to do what? Earn enough money for a day? Two days? And then what?

He could have helped ease her life.

But he hadn't.

Edinburgh. Tiresome, tiresome Edinburgh. Time to go back to Bournemouth. And then after that . . .

The South Pacific Islands were looking better all the time.

The rain ran like vipers down the ancient buildings. Not quite a downpour and not quite a drizzle, mostly it just maddened the senses. The cold bit and clawed and threatened to take her down, but what did it matter? What did any of it matter at all?

There was only what she had to do. And what the bairns needed.

Feya blended with the shadows, up against the buildings—a soggy scrap of nothing and cold, hard stone. When the closes—the alleys between the buildings—came, she slipped into the darkness like a thought that had never been. Stories came from these places—the plague, doctors with masks like demon birds, murder and darkness.

She made way up the Royal Mile, the cobblestones slick and black like blood. On the left she passed the house of John Knox, the old reformer. Even in the dark she could see the gold inscription above the door: *Love God Above All.*

It was rubbish, true and firm.

The only thing that was, was the hunger.

That she could understand.

A little further, and she was at the pub—the one that she and Ma had eaten at so long ago. Ghosts of her own making floated behind the glass—a mother and a daughter, both full of life and possibility. Feya laid her hand on the thin window; the rainwater running over her skin like a glove.

The haddock they'd eaten that day had been crisp and mild. The peas had tasted as though they'd come from a garden outside of the city—a place where the plants could breathe and the sun glowed on the leaves like gold.

Inside there was bread so fresh it was better than cake. A person could eat that bread alone and be satisfied. The crust, powdered with flour, had made her mouth water when she bit down. The inside of it, soft and light, had melted like a child's dream—slowly, mixing with the butter in such a perfect way that she had hesitated to swallow.

That bread had not been like the paper-thin bread in the tenements, made of the leavings of better men.

Feya tried to stop her hand from shaking against the glass. Cold filtered deep into her bones and her soul. Her breath rattled.

She would do it quickly. She could carry enough food back to feed them for a week at least. If the people around were sleeping deeply, only the rain would hear the glass shatter. No one would watch, except for Edinburg Castle on the hill.

Feya knelt and picked up a rock. She could barely feel it in her hand.

There was a chance the owner was sleeping upstairs. If so, she might be dead within a few moments. Stabbed or shot. Her blood left to drain upon the ground like the rain.

But maybe . . . Maybe no one was at home. It was possible. Not every store owner slept above stairs. Or so the thieves who lived in the tenements said.

Feya lifted her hand and shielded her face with the other.

A devil wind ripped up the Mile. It howled and grabbed at her skirt. Rain pricked against her face. She reached to keep from falling . . . and almost did. Another shiver coursed through her body until her back felt like it might snap.

A poster in the corner of the window drew her eyes.

Mary, Queen of Scots' bedroom is one of the suite of apartments in the north wing of the Palace . . . Her Majesty is delighted to offer viewing to the public, as well as certain historical artifacts of note . . . A very fine jewelry box discovered by the 8th Lord Belhaven in a secret drawer at Holyrood palace contains a lock of Mary, Queen of Scots' hair. Lord Belhaven gifted this find to Her Majesty, Queen Victoria. The small box, lined with water-creamed silk, is now on exhibition within the historic apartments.

The wind reached into Feya's boots and pushed against her drenched socks. "'Historical artifacts of note . . . small box . . .'" She dropped the rock. With one such item, their entire lives would be solved. Da had once told her of a man who dealt with such pieces. If she could get it to him, they'd be fed for much longer than a week. Months, even. Perhaps years. She could take the bairns to the country and disappear. Say she was widowed. Buy a little cottage by the sea.

The thought made her breath catch and her teeth chatter.

At the end of the Royal Mile stood the Holyrood Palace gates. They lingered there in the dark below the shadows of the moon. There wouldn't be many guards since the queen wasn't in residence this time of year.

Maybe, just maybe . . .

Alasdair Cairncross stood at his post and counted the hours. Sometimes he counted them by the way the moonlight slanted—the blues and blacks seeping over the lawn like a cloak. Sometimes he counted by how the sun's rays hit the top of the great hill—Arthur's Seat—above the palace.

The white came first, just a bit, like a teasing of a veil. And then the darkness pushed back, changing the white to dark blue. Then the colors muddied, like men's lives, merging into nothing that was definable. But after that, the great bowl of the sky showed itself and the orange came, like a trembling heartbeat, battering against the cold and the dark. But it never succeeded. Not even when the sun brought its fire over the hill and slowly parted the misery that was Edinburgh.

The chill was always in the air. Like an ancient spell cast over the land, impossible to break. But at that point, when the orange and fog blended—then he only had five more hours to go on his watch.

On Tuesdays he walked through the garden. That, at least, was a change. But it was always the same path. Watching for murderers, miscreants, or even the wrong kind of admirer of the queen. A year and a half ago a Spaniard had managed to slip through the gate and hide by Queen Mary's sundial. That had brought some action. Sadly, only five minutes' worth.

A year ago, by the stone forecourt fountain, that Russian fellow had come bent on assassinating Queen Victoria. Alasdair stretched his foot in his boot. The knife scar on his leg still pained him when it rained. But at least that had been *something*. At least that had made him feel alive.

He stepped out of the guard box, walked the two hundred and fifty-seven steps to the abbey, and stood still again. He knew every one of the graves behind him by name. He knew their sizes to the exact dimension. He'd taken the dates off the graves and added them together for no particular reason at all.

But that wasn't entirely true, was it? There was a reason. His brain ailment dictated it like an overbearing master. He saw things. Strange things. And, since he was thinking about it, he might as well indulge and look.

Madeleine Valois. The numbers and letters on the gravestone converged into colors. Always colors. So many that he was certainly on the verge of an apoplexy—scarlet reds, variegated greens, flaming oranges, and violet blues. The shades floated above the engraved letters like vapors from another world. The *M* was not unpleasant— a soft yellow. However, the *DE* combination put him in an extremely foul mood. The dark-brown hue it produced gave him the feeling of being displaced. And that feeling was already too familiar.

Every corner of the ruined nave was his own tomb. Hardly any sound day after day—only the crunch of rocks beneath his boots and the echo of a life that could have been lived.

Alasdair lifted his gaze to the place where the windows used to be. On particularly starry nights he framed the orbs there, setting them between the stone frames. He didn't know why. It was just something he'd always done. Like fading into the shadows, as he did now. He was used to that. He had been trained well; his father had made sure. Like he'd made sure of everything else in his life.

There were benefits to having such a methodical father. He had been taught self-discipline. He was trusted by the nobility and smiled at on occasion by the queen. What more could he possibly want?

Memories jangled like bells. Attending countless religious meetings. Immature delusions from before the Horse Guards—a passage booked across the sea and then cancelled. It was all the height of embarrassment, simply put. One of the many narrow escapes of his life.

The moonlight slanted. Orange slid into the fog like powder falling from the sky. Alasdair took a deep breath and clenched his jaw, shaking loose the memories. He applied the proper pressure and opened his pocket watch. Exactly as he thought. Only two more hours to go.

He followed the arch of the ruined window with his gaze, then stepped three paces to the right, framing the first star of Orion in the middle pane. That was an excellent place to start.

Chapter Four

The palace gates looked easy enough to climb, as far as easiness went. That word never had been something familiar. *Easiness* was when the frost she found on her blanket in the morning didn't make her bones ache. *Easiness* was the mold on the meat that hadn't eaten clear through.

Feya shoved her hand into her pocket and withdrew Da's Romani scarf. She tied it around her head, the way she used to in the camps. It felt familiar—soft against her forehead, gathered at the nape of her neck, trailing down her back and moving in the cold, Scottish wind.

The tipped cup of the moon was suddenly covered by clouds, like a woman caught without her clothes on.

Darkness was on her side.

A shiver crept down her back. The rain had slacked, but the mist remained, pushing its way between the buildings like a floating demon—an ancient thing, unstoppable. Her gaze followed the mist's fingers and the way it touched the windows in the Tudor houses down the close. Those people didn't have cares like her. Living so close to the palace, they'd always been given more. And there they slept, heads on plush feather pillows, while she stood in weather that wasn't fit for a dog.

She ran her fingers through the long fringe of the scarf. Tonight the Romani blood that beat in her veins would serve her well. The earliest games Da had taught her were how to be unseen and unheard. How to blend in with the night until those standing around saw only a shifting of the wind or a well-concealed shadow.

This part of her was easy.

She closed her eyes and let herself remember—the wailing of the women around the camp, the men with their sharp knives, Romani words coming from her mouth before Scots English—the things deep within her that she always tried to push away. She let the whispers from the past come—songs from around the Gypsy fire.

"O shoshoy kaste si feri yek khiv sigo athadjol . . ." "The rabbit which has only one hole soon is caught . . ." And when her mother wasn't looking, her grandmother, the old Gypsy woman, would bend her head low. *"May mishto phabol o kasht o chordano . . ." "Stolen wood burns better for being stolen, Feya . . ."* She could almost feel the old woman's paper skin and bony hands.

She pushed away from her hiding place against the wall and walked when the rain dripped from the eaves, masking her steps. Dizziness churned around her—up and down and then over again. Her stomach clenched. She fell against the gate.

"Bleedin' . . ." She couldn't finish the words. Another spasm ripped through her belly. The cold of the iron gate seeped into the bones of her hand. She gripped the metal tighter, then swayed. The dark pavement bowed like a nightmare.

It felt like the grippe. Or maybe Mr. Stevenson had passed along his blessing and given her whatever death ailment he had, which she couldn't afford.

Especially now.

A cry rose within her, but she pushed it down. She'd been a fool to be out in the rain for so long. First there'd been the walk to the tavern, and then the bread shop, and then the walk all the way down the Mile.

She gazed up at the half-hidden moon again. If He who was supposed to be watching really existed, she wouldn't be feeling this way.

"More proof."

She clenched her teeth and climbed. She couldn't go back, not without anything to feed the bairns. No matter if she retched on the ground or fainted she had to try.

The hem of her skirt caught on the gate spire. Up in the air, with the ground swaying, a shaking started in her hands and moved to her shoulders. She tightened her grip and tipped her weight to the other side. Bit by bit, she lowered herself down. When her feet met the gravel on the other side, the wind hushed like a well-fed babe.

Her fingers unwrapped like rusty hinges from around the bars. Another chill came, but then she felt warm—too warm. The gate blurred.

The huge monster of a house loomed behind her; she could feel it—all rounded towers and perfect symmetry. She breathed in, the air thicker now with the fog that rolled through. It was too risky to go sauntering across the gravel. She'd follow the gate and try the servant's entrance.

Her feet felt too heavy. Sweat mixed with rain dripped down her forehead. The palace walls were closer now. They swayed.

The side door looked ancient—iron studs in well-worn wood. Something from dark fairy tales from long ago.

Feya stumbled. Splinters of ice shoved into her lungs. She coughed, covered it up, and almost choked.

The door handle wouldn't turn. Locked.

Feya shoved her back against the wall. The cold, frosty sky beat down, a smothering blanket over the land. The pounding in her head amplified.

"There has to be another way in." Her whisper came out as smoke. She nodded, more to convince herself that she hadn't failed.

She followed the wall, grabbing at the stones to stay upright. The sun was coming, surely. More light crept into the fog. The devil's breath was at her neck, making the hair stand up. Heat surged around her shoulders, pressing. She was tired—tired like the snow falling on a wounded man and rocking him into a wakeless sleep. If she could just sit for a moment . . . If the walls could just stop swaying.

The gravel changed into pebbles. She stumbled along the path, cringing when her feet dragged the ground.

A tall, skeletal ruin rose up into the blanket of the sky. An abbey—she remembered now—a place where kings had been crowned and tombs desecrated. Feya wiped the sweat out of her eyes.

Mist swirled around the hem of her skirt—dancing circles and long fingers reaching as though playing the harp. And the notes . . . She could hear them, repeating over and over again. High like the tinkle of rain on glass. But the notes hurt; thinking about them brought a sharpness behind her eyes. She blinked and felt ice on her eyelashes.

Maybe she should go back. Only a few hours' sleep . . .

The wind came down from the great hill—Arthur's Seat—and whipped around the stones. It was a slap in her face, a wall of pain raking into her lungs. She threw her body into a crevice in the wall and reached for something to hold onto. Her right hand found air— a gap in the wall, an old entrance.

Surely the perfect way in.

She slipped into the gaping black between the stones and stood still for a moment, afraid to move, afraid to breathe. The ruined walls of the abbey moved in and out like the ribs of a skeleton breathing. The wind blew again, through the queen's garden, rustling the leaves of the bushes and the trees.

Her gaze followed the abbey wall—brick after brick and then nothing. More mist where the stars should be. The colors were wrong somehow, the blacks and blues muddled.

She leaned against three columns twisted together like rope. Beside her, archway followed archway until disappearing into the covering of night. Moonlight slid through the mist in patches, over the headstones like a candle flame, glowing and shrinking and then back again. The portico behind her was as black as the hour of death.

The wind came again. And then a shifting in the dark. She felt it more than heard it. Like the way one feels something in a room and then turns around to see no one there.

She stood still and listened, her heart near exploding.

It must have been the wind again. Wind could do strange things, especially in Scotland. There were stories of grown men dying from fright out in the Highlands just because of the noises of the wind. That had to be it. Only the dead walked here. Only bones and memories. Things that would never rise again.

Stone after stone scraped against her palm as she walked. The heat was back again, and the dizziness stole her thoughts away. And her lungs . . . Why were they so tight?

A door. A cold handle that felt like brass. Inside, the air was warm. She could fall into that feeling, the comfort. Even with her clothes wet and clinging, this warmth was something—a sigh before dying, a gasp before a scream.

She stumbled against the wall and pulled her hand back when it made a wet print.

The bairns.

Food.

That was all.

She had to stay steady.

Water fell from her skirt. She knelt to wring it out, but her fingers wouldn't do what she wanted. They were too stiff, too useless.

No matter. One step and then another. Down the hall.

A heavy door creaked when she opened it. She cringed. They would catch her now, and it would be all over. Except for the pain when they hung her. But she supposed that would only hurt for a little while. Not like this . . . not like this swaying and clenching and ripping.

She didn't know how many moments passed, but no one came. No voice shot from the dark to change her fate forever.

Just ahead rose a grand stone staircase. Above it a plaster ceiling. Around and around the staircase turned like a never-ending apple peel. She passed window after window and saw the court outside where she'd come from. Plaster angels stared down, disapproving. They held the emblems of Scotland—the crown, scepter, and sword. Noble things. Not like her.

At the top of the stairs she wandered. Room blended with room. Strange shapes loomed in the dark. Furniture covered with sheets, she knew, but the shapes were monstrous and seemed to breathe.

In the next room, the coverings on the wall were thick, only letting bits of light creep in—spears of blue-white moonlight on a lush red carpet. The reds and golds throughout the space throbbed in the dark, shamelessly.

The thought that she was wandering around the queen's throne room registered somewhere in her mind. She could almost feel the woman's presence, hear the rustling of her fine skirt. All the more reason to hurry.

Down a hallway, the air was different. An old door with a massive iron hinge beckoned from the top of the stairs. The door creaked when she opened it.

Inside, tapestries lined the walls. There was a closeness about the room, as though one might speak something and the tapestries would hide the words forever.

An intricate pattern of wood lined the ceiling—beams that crissed and crossed. A lush red canopy framed the bed. "Her bedroom . . ." Feya held back a cough. "Mary, Queen of Scots."

Paintings lined the walls in the next room—faces from other eras, long gone. Glass cases were set about the room at different intervals.

Surely the jewelry box was here.

A few more moments and she'd be done.

The jewelry box sat in a case in front of a window. Long, velvet curtains brushed the glass on either side. Feya laid her hand on the lid.

"There ye are. So little . . ."

She lifted the lid and plunged her hand inside. Slowly, her fingers wrapped around the box, more than three hundred years old.

"Don't move."

Feya turned, and the glass lid slammed shut. She saw a shadow of a man, and then a force shoved her to the ground. A hand gripped the back of her head, pressing her face into the carpet. Her hands were clasped behind her back, held by grip so strong she thought her arms would break.

"I said don't move." The voice was thick with the sickening tones of the English.

She kicked.

The man brought his knee down on her.

Feya screamed. The floorboards faded. Black hovered at the edges of her sight.

"I would ask what you're doing here, but the answer seems clear."

She felt like she was breathing under water. "Sir . . ." Wooziness played at the edges of her mind, and other things—things like grassy green fields in the middle of summer, a mother's hand against a daughter's back, and laughter. So far away, these things. Darkness— darker than what filled the room—blurred those images and called in a sing-songy voice. She should go there . . . It was safe . . . Feya felt her shoulders relax.

Someone lifted her body. Her feet barely touched the ground.

The sharp sound of keys rattled, making her cringe. Because it brought her out of the dark. It tried to force and pry, that noise. And then there was the other noise: a man's voice.

The voice was taking her somewhere. She felt her legs moving. And somehow she recognized the room she was walking through: the bedroom of the executed queen.

But then a door opened where a door shouldn't have been. Before her lay a passage she didn't recognize.

"Mad as the day is long, are you?"

She didn't know who said that. But it wasn't right. She wasn't mad. She was just Feya. The strong one. The one who was going to rescue the bairns.

Feya felt herself slipping again, going into the dark place. But that was all right. She could disappear.

Something hard held her body still. There was one color that she could still see: blue. Blue eyes like the water at Loch Leven when the clouds shifted just right and let the sun shine through. A man's eyes, the rest of his face obscured by the dark.

"Brenna." Panic reached in and tugged. She was in the palace. And she'd been caught. "Gillis! Hamish!"

She tried to hold on. It felt like trying to catch silk on the bottom of the sea.

The man was there again, and he held her, his hands crushing her wrists. But that didn't matter any more. Only the darkness mattered.

She called to it. In Romany and Scottish slurs that women weren't supposed to say.

Darkness smiled hard, and then he wrapped his arms around her and took away her pain.

Chapter Five

Alasdair flung open the door to the barracks and hurried down the hall. Water dripped from his greatcoat, his hair was disheveled, and his shirt was completely soaked—the consequences of carrying the thief to a part of the palace where he could secure her. Finally, some action. Finally, he felt worth the wage he was paid.

He needed to change. He couldn't appear in front of Father in this state.

The cold he so desperately hated clung to his skin and strained his muscles until he shook. It had been far too many hours since his room had held a decent fire. He struck a match, lifted the globe of the oil lamp, and set the wick aflame. The yellow light pushed against the cramped walls and cast shadows upon his simple metal bed.

He hated sleeping here. The room was far too small. And small places forced the nightmares in. His memory slid to that night that haunted him: September three years ago—the Moonlight Charge at Kassassin, the mudbrick dwelling after his capture, the rattle of chains. He could still feel the thirst that the desert had brought, still feel the sting of African sand. And, if he listened to his memories instead of the cruel Scottish wind, he heard the slurs of the pointy-shoed Asiatics who stepped as softly as cats. What came after would always haunt him, he supposed.

He closed his eyes and regulated his breathing. Sometimes it helped. He thought of his rescue; that helped too. He remembered the day of his return to the greatest country in the world—blessed, civilized England. That brought a smile. It had taken some time before he could rest on a proper bed again, and even now sleep was a fickle mistress. But at least outwardly he was able to pass off the appearance that everything was fine.

Alasdair shook out his greatcoat and hung it on the mahogany rack. Peeling off his clothes, he opened the dresser. He pushed the medals aside as he rummaged, but he could feel their presence as if they were alive—Royal Horse Guard medals, the Egyptian Campaign medal, and the Victoria Cross, given to him personally by the queen. The lion engraved on the front had always seemed too proud. So he kept it at the back of the drawer. And he supposed it would stay there, tucked beside the old tattered shirt with the thistle embroidery he also didn't like to remember.

He shoved on an undershirt and went to the wardrobe to get freshly pressed livery. In a few moments he was dressed, his hair was combed back into place, and he was out the door.

He made his way through the hallways and back into the palace. He still didn't understand why Father chose this remote part of the west wing in which to sleep. However, this thought was as redundant as the Scottish rain. Every time he descended the stairs and passed the long row of gaslights, it knocked on the recesses of his mind. Perhaps it was the way his boots echoed on the naked, cold pavement. Maybe it was the way the ancient house groaned above his head.

Such things did have some influence and suggestion. At least that's what the countless novelists of Edinburgh were always toying with—atmosphere and foreshadowing. In his view, it was utter and complete tommyrot. Evidence of a mind too often left to wander.

But that's exactly what his mind had been doing for weeks. Alasdair rubbed his eyes. He needed a holiday. A little time where he could just *be*. Somewhere where he didn't have to think about everyone else's motives. Where he wouldn't have to check every parcel, every shipment that came onto the grounds. Somewhere he wouldn't have to stare at the same walls.

Maybe a nice, modern cottage in Cornwall. He could take up sailing again. Cornwall was a place where a man could hang his troubles on the cliffs and forget things with the blowing of the warm, fair wind. Where the sun shone and gave the water the illusion of glass. That sea—endless blue possibility. Fathomless depths undiscovered. God's rolling clock of time.

Such thoughts. What the devil was happening to him? Obviously, his brain was going flaccid. He ought to read *The Dictionary of National Biography* again. That should do the trick. Fifty-five thousand entries did lend a certain point of convergence for the mind.

No matter how many times he read the *A* section, the excerpt on Sir Robert Abercromby was especially entertaining. And the bit about Andrew Amos was probably the best two pages of the entire volume. After all, the man had written all the laws of England down for posterity. What nobler cause could there be than that?

Alasdair stretched as he walked, spreading his arms. The wood above him groaned again, but it was only the moving of the Scotland centuries. Too much wind, that was all, and a palace in some desperate need of renovation. The only thing that was, was logic and strategy. Like the twists and turns of the subterranean parts of the palace, the numbers of stairs it took to get from one place to another—life was like that. Planning was essential. Step upon step. Foundation upon foundation. One had to meticulously build a life. That alone brought success. Not emotion.

Never that.

He turned down the last corridor and allowed himself the liberty of slouching. After so many years of preparing—Oxford College, the training at Windsor, and worst of all the hellish Anglo-Egyptian war—he was finally going to get what he had worked so hard for: a permanent appointment in the queen's household as the most senior personal guard. Not just guarding the palace or standing on ceremony, but being her eyes and ears when she was at leisure.

The most important job in the world.

The best part was that the queen didn't lodge in Holyrood many months out of the year. The less Scotland he had to deal with, the better. London was preferable, Buckingham Palace ideal. Windsor Castle was pleasant, and then there was Osbourne House on the Isle of Wight, the place where the queen spent the majority of her time. Osbourne House would be a rare treat after Scotland. Best of all, the Isle of Wight was warm and secluded from the world.

The island . . . Alasdair took a deep breath. Just thinking the word brought comfort. A private beach. Long paths in the woods where one could walk for hours. Exactly what he needed.

Nothing would stop him from reaching that island and protecting the queen. Especially not the Gypsy upstairs he'd just caught in the midst of stealing. She was a minor detail. That was all. One that would be signed, sealed, and dispatched within the hour.

Alasdair opened his pocket watch. Half past five. He pushed away the thoughts of his past and the oddities about his father. If there was one thing Alasdair knew for sure, it was that his father was not to be questioned. Experience had taught him that. And a long road that stretched from the dark woods of northern Scotland down to London and then back again.

He knocked.

"Enter."

His father's door, which had squeaked last time, was now perfectly oiled.

"I trust this is important." Father sat at this desk with three evenly spaced candles in front of him. He flipped through a stack of papers, making quick marks with his pen. The black hair that so perfectly mirrored Alasdair's was slicked close to his head. Despite the early hour and the fact that his official duties didn't begin for quite some time, Father wore his ceremonial clothes—white shirt starched to perfection and his dark, embroidered robe with the fur-lined collar.

"There's been an intruder."

Father looked up, his grey eyes hardening. "You won't disappoint me and say this person escaped."

Alasdair raised his chin a notch. "Of course not. But as we don't have a dungeon, I locked her in the kitchen storage room."

"'Her'?" Father sat back in his chair. "How interesting."

Alasdair leaned against the wall. "Indeed."

Father cleared his throat. Alastair stood back at attention.

"What was she seeking?"

"The box containing Mary, Queen of Scots' hair."

Father laid his pen down. "With the Darnley Jewel four feet away?"

"I thought the same thing." The feeling Alasdair always got when something was off resurrected. "It's odd."

Father tapped his finger on the stacks of papers. "You said you locked her in the storage room. She's alive, then?"

"Of course." Alasdair furrowed his brow. "She's a woman."

"She's a thief. That is all." Father lowered his gaze to the candle flame nearest his hand. The light of it danced in his eyes. "Had you disposed of her quickly, as you did that Russian fellow, we wouldn't have to answer the question of what to do with her. But now . . ." He gazed back up, and his grey eyes were thick with disapproval.

"Now, Alasdair, I have Sir Walter and your fiancée coming today. I definitely can't have a thief lingering about."

"What do you suggest?"

"A long rope," he said without emotion. "Or a dagger. It's all the same in the end, you know."

"She's a woman," Alasdair repeated.

"Yes." Father circled a paragraph on his paper. "I heard that part."

"She deserves a trial. The proper courses must be consulted."

"Believe that, do you?" Father looked bored. "And tell me, Alasdair, since your knowledge of the law is obviously superior to my thirty years of dealing in it: what will they do with this woman in the end?"

Alasdair knew the answer. They'd hang her. Especially since she'd been trying to steal from the queen. One did not simply steal from the monarch who ruled an empire where the sun never set. And women criminals in Edinburgh most always got a heavier sentence because the crimes they committed were against their feminine nature.

Father opened a drawer to retrieve the house ledger. "Do you think the months she will spend in prison, waiting for this trial, will benefit her? Reform her in some way?"

"No." It was an old argument between them: the evils of the lower class. But even after hours of debate on his nights off, Alasdair still wasn't entirely convinced. "Father, I think the woman might be mad. She was obviously deranged. Indeed, the things she said—"

"You do know they're all mad, don't you? Your time in the academy surely taught you that."

"You're speaking of criminals in general, I suppose. Those who haven't had the benefits of a proper education."

"In general?" Father's chair scraped the floor. He stood and walked around his desk. "Perhaps I've been remiss in posting you on the night watches. Too much time alone can have one of two effects:

hardening a man . . . or making him soft. But then again, perhaps it is your other ailment that clouds your judgment?" The last syllable lingered in the room like a serpent speaking in the dark to a child.

Alasdair stiffened his shoulders. He made sure to keep his gaze locked with his father's. He hoped his pupils weren't dilating. "Have I not proven myself to you?"

"Not quite." Father said the words casually, as though talking of the temperature of soup.

The pull to look at the colors above Father's head was the strongest call, like a light to a lost man. They floated there, rippling and pulsing.

Father rested his hand on Alasdair's shoulder. "Rome wasn't built in a day, my boy. And neither will Scotland be." He went to the desk and rolled the papers there into a neat scroll. "Progress, that's the thing." He tapped Alasdair on the cheek with the edge of the roll.

Alasdair forced himself to remain still. The words he wanted to say stayed down. He was good at that. Father had made sure.

Father raised an eyebrow. "Do your job."

Alasdair nodded a fraction of an inch, then he quietly closed the door behind him.

Images flashed in the corner of Feya's mind—a pane of glass, bread she couldn't reach, a man with the bluest eyes she'd ever seen. And anger—so much of that. But then, just as suddenly, the pictures blurred, as though a giant's hand wiped them from her dreams. A woman's voice sounded as if it came from under water.

"Ach, lass. What a situation."

Feya felt the cuffs about her wrists first, burning like circles of flame. "What—"

Something wet slid across her face. A rag. She sputtered and opened her eyes.

"I assume this is the young master's work." The woman wore a white cap. A servant. Her cheeks were rosy and full. Storage bags lined the floor. An overburdened shelf held gleaming jars. A side of beef hung from the ceiling,

Feya's heart lurched and sped. The light from the lantern was too bright. A monstrous bolt of pain plunged behind her eyes.

"How did you come to find yourself here?"

The woman's voice was kind, but the noise made Feya want to retch. "I don't know." Sweat dripped down her cheek.

The woman mumbled something, then dipped her rag into a bowl of water. Feya cringed at the sound of the dripping water, and pain exploded in her wrist. "Why am I chained to the water boiler?" The sound of the heater's sharp ticking shot through her head like a spike. "Who are ye? What have ye done to me?"

The woman plunged the rag into the bowl again. "I'm the cook in this great house. Perhaps the better question is 'Who are you and why are you chained up in my pantry?'"

Footsteps sounded outside of the door. The older woman looked up, apprehension etched on her features. Her gaze slid back to Feya.

The door opened. A man stepped through.

He was tall, with hair as black as death. His face was smooth and his features chiseled. His eyes . . . Familiar, somehow. His uniform was bright red and the buttons shone gold. A guard, perhaps, a military man of some sort. His collar was high and stiff, just as formal and emotionless as the man's face.

He was looking at something above her. He snapped his gaze back down. "You're still here, I see."

Feya knew that voice. The tones were deep and flat, disgustingly proper and very English. "You." It all came rushing back like an ill-fated wind bent on destruction. She sat forward, rattling the chains.

He surveyed her with his cold gaze as if he looked upon a piece of rotten meat.

She narrowed her eyes and fought the desire to spit on the English dog's shoes. Instead she made her voice as sweet as possible. "Shall I turn so ye can further yer inspection?"

"I'm sure it's the same as the front—bedraggled and fit for the—"

"And a good morning to you, Mr. Cairncross." The cook hefted her large body to stand. She wiped her hands on her apron. "I suppose you have an explanation as to why this poor lamb is chained in my pantry, soppin' wet."

The man scowled. The look was actually an improvement. "This *poor lamb* tried to steal something very dear to our queen."

"No." The cook drew out the word like hot candy. "Not this one, surely."

"Oh, I can assure you: *this* one." He took a step toward her. His cape flared in the small space. Feya scooted backward, feeling the heat of the radiator dangerously close.

He stepped closer.

Feya's back met the radiator. Searing, scalding heat blazed against her skin. A wild scream tore from her throat.

The cook lunged, bumping the shelf. Jars fell and shattered upon the floor. The tinkling of glass and slosh of the contents filled the air. Feya smelled Bloody Ploughman apples and Scotch Bridget. The room spun as the tin ceiling faded to black.

"Be still!" The man knelt beside her, gripped her shoulder, and held her away from the heater.

Black warred with the bright lamp in the room. Her head fell against his hand. *Let the darkness take me. Take me away from this pain.*

"Be still," he said again, as if it mattered. She stared into his eyes, saw dark circles around fathomless blue. A chill ran over her, starting deep and radiating to the tips of her hands and feet. Those eyes—she felt that she was drowning. And the iron grip of his hand held her under the water, pushing her down.

This man would be her undoing. She knew this better than she knew the hills beyond Kilbride and the mists of Cannich. Better than the way heather felt in the palm of her hand. The Gypsies spoke of moments like these. But she'd never believed them. It came quickly, this feeling—sudden and urgent. Fate had come to call.

Feya tried to shut her eyes, but couldn't. She was powerless. The rain slapped against the windowpane as the moments passed.

The man's eyelids flickered. His grip lessoned. "Mrs. Fergus, I would be very much obliged if you saw to your duties in the kitchen."

The cook shifted her weight from one side to the other, her voluminous black skirt swaying. "But—"

"Now, please." His voice held the same calm as before, as if he were taking tea in a grand house. But something lingered below the syllables this time; it was in the way he ended the words—a lilt that sounded oddly familiar.

The cook furrowed her brow. "What do you mean to do with her?"

His gaze never wavered. "That is for me to decide. You should not concern yourself with matters of the law."

"She's sick." The woman's protest came out weakly, like an afterthought to a sleepy prayer. "The way she takes in a breath—can't you hear that wheeze?"

The man stood and looked down at the cook. "Some esteemed guests are arriving for luncheon. Isn't there a pudding to be mixed or an oyster soup to be tested?"

"Aye." The woman drew her eyebrows together. "That there is."

"Then you should see to it." The man put his hand on the cook's back and guided her toward the door.

"Wait!" Feya coughed and almost choked.

The woman looked back, but then the swinging door blocked Feya's view. In the other room, the man and the cook exchanged words, none of which Feya could discern.

There had to be a weapon in the room. "Carrots, onions, bags of flower . . ."

A shard of broken glass lay upon the floor. Perhaps if she reached.

The swoosh of the door brought cold air upon her neck. Gooseflesh rose on her skin. She dropped her eyes to the man's perfectly shined shoes. "Sir, please. I know I've done wrong. I was only tryin' to get somethin' I could sell, fer food." The words made her feel dirty; they dug down deep and rooted in the corner of her soul.

She couldn't bear to look at the upstanding lawman. The shame drove her gaze out the window. The light was just beginning to break, and even that looked dirty, like a smudge of curdled cream against black.

Hamish would be crying for his breakfast, and Gillis would be running his cold fingers through the tail of his broken horsey. And Brenna . . . Brenna would be scared. Feya risked looking at his face. "I won't do it again."

"I know you won't." His words were final, like a benediction beside a grave. His dark-blue eyes were expressionless as he gazed at her. He could have been the devil in disguise—all black hair and heart cold as stone. He reached under his cloak to something at his side.

"What are ye planning?" Feya's heart pulsed, her blood surging through her body as the man slowly knelt, his hand still under his cloak. A muscle worked at his jaw.

Feya squeezed the rag behind her back. The little piece of glass was a hard, hot thing.

Quickly he pulled a ring of keys from his belt and plunged one into the lock. At the *click* of the lock she lunged, aiming for his face.

The man's hand shot up, blocking. The glass met his palm and sliced.

Blood splattered his sleeve.

He grabbed her like a vice and drove her to the floor. The fruit juice seeped into Feya's skirt and slathered against her leg. She kicked, flailed her arms, and tried to jab again.

He clamped his hand over her wrist and squeezed. Unable to help herself, she unclenched her fingers. The rag and the glass fell.

The man pinned her hard, his weight crushing. Shock rang on his face, and then rage. "You will regret that." His voice was low and guttural, the earlier control in his tones gone. "When I get up, you are going to walk." He brought his lips close to her ear. "And if you don't, I will put my hands around that little Gypsy neck of yours and break it." He increased the weight of his body, his shoulder digging into her arm. "Do I make myself clear?"

"Yes." The word strangled as it fell from her lips. A tear fell from her eye, made a hot path on her cheek, and then died upon the floor.

Chapter Six

Cairncross was the perfect name for the devil.

Feya could feel the man behind her—his anger at what she'd done . . . hate for people like her . . . people from the wrong side. Emotions seeped off of him like heat from a funeral pyre. Wave after wave rolled and stroked her back as she walked in front of him. She could almost hear the words he thought.

Rubbish.

A waste of human flesh.

Nothing.

That's what he thought of her. He'd tied her hands behind her back and held the end of the rope like a leash for a dog.

When she'd sliced him with the glass a switch had turned inside him—cool, calm, strength to absolute rage. Fire shone in his icy depths of blue. His pale English cheeks flushed with complete loathing.

The thought made the corner of Feya's lips turn up. If she was going to die—or worse—at the English devil's hands, she'd make him suffer. He'd rue the day he ever crossed with a Scotch half Gypsy.

"To the left." His voice was sharp like a surgeon's knife.

Early morning mist stroked the ankle-high ruins on the ground.

They were laid out in squares, like a giant child had played with blocks and then carelessly forgotten them. A gravel path led into a tall, wild garden, which would have been pretty in another circumstance.

Her feet dragged like brass. There was a moment when she didn't know if she walked at all.

The wind picked up, snatched flower petals, and threw them down. They would shrivel in a few hours and die in the rain puddles. Much like life. No one cared for things that were cast away.

Color shifted in the puddle—the black blur of Cairncross's greatcoat. He stepped behind her, closer, as if trying to intimidate her with his nearness. "Sightseeing, are you?" His voice was low. "Enjoying your tour of the garden?"

Feya stood still, her breath coming too fast. The fever, as well as his words, raked at her. The tone of his voice played on her skin, prickling the hair at the back of her neck. She turned and glared at him.

Cold indifference shone in his eyes. He smiled, like a monarch ready to declare death. "Were you hoping to divine your future in the water puddle?"

Feya smiled back at him, just to taunt his arrogance.

His expression grew hard. "Move."

"Or what? Will ye kill me? Are ye that sort of a man?"

His hand clutched the back of her neck before she could think. She felt the wet blood where she'd cut him. "I am not the sort to be trifled with, Gypsy. Or didn't I make myself clear?"

Feya winced as the pressure on her neck increased. "If me hands weren't bound, I'd scratch out yer eyes."

"I've no doubt." He pushed her forward. "Walk."

The walls of the garden were like the shoulders of ancient guardians, cold and impenetrable. Cold like the world.

A stone building came into view, towers on either side. A perfect place to dispose of someone.

She glanced at Cairncross. Two high brush marks of red flamed in his cheeks. He focused intently on the building, and a shiver passed through her. Perhaps she should say that she hadn't intended to kill him. "I only meant to—"

"Escape?" He raised his eyebrow.

The sickness, whatever it was, made her body sway. She coughed, deep and rumbling. "What do ye mean to do with me?"

The wind blew through his orderly hair, barely disturbing the strands. "That is my affair." He raked his gaze over her as if looking at an infectious animal. "I can assure you, I mean to be done with you as soon as possible." His lips twisted into a frown. "Now . . ." He swung his hand out toward the stable. "If you please."

Feya lifted her chin just to spite him. She stepped into the building. Horses stood in every stall.

Cairncross walked past her, led her to a stall post, and tied the rope around the end. A precaution, she supposed, so she wouldn't get away. Not that the animalistic way he'd bound her hands wasn't already precaution enough.

She narrowed her eyes, hoping he thought she had the look of a tinker bent on invoking a curse. He'd called her a Gypsy. Let him think that she was. Let him think that she was mad. And a heartless thief. What difference did it make? He'd already made up his mind.

His hands were quick, taking down a saddle from the wall. He went to the stall beside her, where there waited a magnificent black horse. Cairncross's every movement was calculated—the way he checked the bridle, even the way he removed an almost invisible smudge from his boot. Despite the poor weather, he brushed the horse.

The creature was beautiful, not like the draft horses in Leith—

dirty, damaged, and begging for a scrap of kindness. This horse was something out of a story, not unlike those of Mr. Stevenson's she'd read long ago. The animal's nose was slender and fine, its mane black silk. The horse watched her with intelligence. It whinnied and raised its head in her direction.

Cairncross gave her a sideways glance and then went back to brushing. The horse whinnied again.

"I know." He said the word quickly, like he was hushing a child who'd said too much. He ran the brush over the length of the horse's back, white bristle over black, over and over again.

Feya leaned against the pole. She focused on his hands—the gentle way he moved the brush over the beast's back and hip. She hadn't expected him to be gentle. She'd expected him to be a brute like the way he'd held her in the queen's gallery and pinned her body to the floor. Instead, he lightly touched the horse's neck and then followed its leg down, squeezing behind the painted number on the hoof. The horse lifted its leg, and he checked for rocks. That, too, was done with disgusting precision.

Reeking rot, but the English were a troublesome race. Feya felt like spitting. Right on his shiny boots.

The horse was fond of him. It nuzzled his shoulder, the perfect display of master and pet.

Here, the horses slept better than most people in Edinburgh. Certainly better than people in the tenements. She looked at her torn skirt and her muddy shoes. The tile below her shone. Not even a single strand of hay sullied the aisle. The walls were dark, polished wood and the windows were lined with heavy velvet. Above, a wooden rotunda. Light streamed through the high windows like arrows from angels' bows.

Disgusting. Revolting. The excess of the rich.

Feya wanted to make it dirty somewhere, anywhere—to make it

look like a place for horses. The contrast was too much. The sickness was like a thick blanket, draped around her, pulling her down. She craved sleep. To forget. Not to feel. Not to worry. Her eyelids were heavy. She let them fall.

The warmth of the stable. The cleanliness. The soft noises of the horses breathing. The sweet smell of hay . . . She felt her body sway. Her head dipped. If she could only rest, just for a little while.

"Let's go."

Her wrists jerked up. Feya snapped open her eyes and inhaled sharply.

Cairncross tied the rope to the pommel of the saddle. The leather groaned as he placed his boot in the stirrup and mounted.

"Go? As in ye draggin' me behind ye like a slave?"

"No one rides my horse except for me."

The *clop* of the horse's hooves was too loud on the cobblestone. The rope tightened. Her hands jerked up and she walked.

Across Holyrood Palace grounds.

Past the gate she'd so foolishly climbed over last night.

And onto the cobblestone of the Royal Mile.

Men, dressed in fine tailored suits and holding walking sticks, stopped to stare. Some laughed. Some pointed. Some winked. Men were men, Mad Maggie had said.

She was right.

Their calls sounded in Feya's ears and made her feel dirtier. Deep down in that place she kept only for herself. The place that said she might be pretty and good some day.

The sunshine broke through the clouds, as if even it came out to see.

Women shielded their children. Children that looked like dolls full of frill and fat, holding candies and new toys—sweet things that Brenna, Hamish, and Gillis would never know.

Feya dropped her eyes to the back of the horse and the nonchalant swinging of its long, black tail. The women were right to shield their lovies from the gutter slum—the Gypsy witch from the other side.

Cairncross turned down a side street. Smells came to her—potatoes rotting for too long, the contents of chamber pots upon the street.

That, at least, was familiar.

The road sloped up toward Calton Hill. He was taking her to the jail—that dark, devil-infested place where people never got out.

"Please." Feya pulled against the rope. "Not there."

Clop. The horse moved on. *Clop-clop* on the slick pavement. Cairncross's black greatcoat snapped in the wind.

"Turn around." Anger raked against her skin. She pulled against the ropes until her wrists bled. "Face me!"

The towering gates of the prison loomed close, a behemoth in stone.

"I need to explain." The words caught in her throat. If he put her in there, the bairns would die. Feya looked back at the city—the countless windows, the endless smokestacks, and the spires of St. Giles. "Please, sir. Isn't there another punishment?"

Clop. Clop. Still he didn't turn. Not even a glance.

The shadows of the gates fell heavy against her, the sorrow of the place mingling with her own. "Let me talk to ye."

Cairncross dismounted and finally glanced at her, his face frozen as hard as his heart.

The heavy prison door creaked as it opened. A guard came out. "Alasdair, I haven't seen you in ages. How is it, old top?"

Feya squeezed the rope. Cairncross's parents weren't even good enough to give their son a proper English name. They'd gone and stolen a Scottish one: Alasdair. But since the English had stolen everything else in Scotland, why not take the names too?

Cairncross shook the man's hand. "The queen reigns and all is well."

Feya scowled at him. He would say that.

"Still keeping the peace at Holyrood?"

"Of course."

"You posh beggar. How I'd love to change jobs with you. What do you say?" He leaned in close to Alasdair. "You come in here with this rot, and I'll go watch after Her Majesty's petticoats for a while."

Cairncross's face flushed. His voice flattened. "Who is your superior?"

"My—" The man's face pinched. "Alasdair. I was only joking."

"One does not make light about the sovereign."

"Of course not." The soldier stood straighter. "How can I be of assistance?" His gaze went to Feya. "Bringing this one in, are you?"

"Yes." Cairncross flicked a glance at her. "Is the warden about? I'd like to get this one processed as soon as possible. She's been blasted inconvenient."

Looking her up and down, the soldier grimaced. "Understandable. Where'd she come from? The Highlands?"

Both men laughed. Like it was actually funny.

The soldier took the reins of the horse. Cairncross led her inside. The room was plain, with a sickly kind of white on the walls. An older man sat at a desk overflowing with papers. The sound of barred gates slamming came from behind a door.

Cairncross stood as stoic as a lead soldier.

The man at the desk looked up. "Ah, Alasdair. How are you, my boy?"

"I am well, sir."

"And your father? I regret that I could not attend his dinner party Thursday last." The man spread his hands out over the papers. "As you can see, I have been quite busy."

Cairncross dipped his head in acknowledgment.

A woman's scream came from behind a door. The warden didn't flinch. "So, what do we have here?"

Cairncross flicked his gaze at Feya. "A thief."

The warden opened a large black book. "What sort?" The words came out like he'd said them too many times.

"She broke into the palace last night."

"She *what*?" The man jerked his head up.

Cairncross took a breath, but his gaze never faltered. "Broke into the palace."

"Who was on guard?"

Pink flushed Cairncross's neck. "I was."

The warden gave Feya a second look. "Were you asleep, man? It wouldn't take much more than summer wind to blow this one away."

Cairncross stood straighter, if that was possible. "I thought it wise to allow her entrance into the palace to see what her purposes were."

The shelf of the warden's forehead lifted. "You thought her capable of conspiracy?"

"These are dangerous times. One never knows."

Another scream sounded behind the door. It ended in a sob.

"Hmmm. I think not much enters her mind except where her next meal comes from. Or which chap she can take advantage of." The man sighed. "What's become of the world? More and more women acting against their gentle natures these days."

Cairncross looked her over again, his black hair fading into the shadows. His face was a pale smear against the dark. "Indeed."

The fever rolled over Feya's body. The edges of the room blurred.

"Does your father know you *allowed* her entrance into the palace?"

Cairncross hesitated. "No."

"I will have to tell him, of course."

Red seeped upwards on Cairncross's neck. "As you see fit, sir."

The warden consulted his book again. "The timing isn't the best, that's for sure." He turned a page. "We admitted seven prisoners this morning, and that takes us to fifty over limit." He shut the book and slammed his fist upon the desk. "Grinstead! Where the devil is the other ledger?"

A man with legs like sausages flung open the door and almost tripped. His wire-rimmed glasses slid down his bulbous nose and landed at an angle. "Yes, sir. What is it you asked for? The ledger? Will you be wanting the ledger for offenses, the ledger for prisons, or the ledger for punishments?"

"Of course I want the prison ledger, you idiot."

"Yes . . . the prison ledger." The clerk turned and knocked over a stack of books. Loose papers fluttered to the floor. "It's just—"As he stumbled, the man's fat jiggled like Christmas pudding.

The warden rolled his eyes at Cairncross. "How hard should it be to find a ledger?" He bent down, dug through the books, and tossed them aside. "Here it is. Grinstead, I beg of you, go and do something useful. Kill yourself or tell the doctor there's a new prisoner to be inspected. Your choice."

"Yes sir. Quite the—"

"Now." The warden stood and rubbed his hand over his haggard face.

Feya widened her eyes. Escape was impossible. The soldier had locked the door behind them. Cairncross stood beside her, still holding the rope. Her gaze landed on the open ledger.

Stealing a book—9 months
Smoking on the omnibus—2 days
Assaulting one of the Masonic procession—2 shillings, dismissed
Riding Furiously through the streets—3 weeks

> *Dirty clothes in public—6 days*
> *Beating carpets not within permitted hours—17 days*
> *Keeping irregular houses full of thieves, prostitutes, and disorderly persons—60 days*
> *Stealing one rasher of bacon—5 years*
> *Stealing 130 oysters valued at 8 shillings—5 years*
> *Ann McQuillan, aged 11 years, theft by housebreaking—4 years' sentence*
> *Eliza Dalton, aged 76 years, theft of two bed sheets—5 years' imprisonment*

Feya tried to breathe, but couldn't. The room pressed in, too small, too hot.

She was done for. She'd never see the bairns again.

The warden turned to Cairncross. "You can see what a mess we're in since the duke of Richmond became secretary for Scotland. Things before were just fine, but no, they had to overturn the entire prison system."

The room spun again. Feya's stomach clenched.

Cairncross's gaze passed over her like the sentence that was coming.

The side door opened. The hefty clerk blocked the doorway. "I brought him, just like you said." A wide amphibian smile split his face. He stepped to the side.

Shock gripped Feya's body. The body snatcher from the tavern wore a long, white surgeon's coat. "Is this her?"

The warden ran his finger along a line in the ledger. "Seems a redundant question, don't you think?"

"Very good." The surgeon wiped his nose on the back of his sleeve.

Feya took a step back. She looked from the doctor to Cairncross to the warden. She was completely surrounded by English devils.

"What's she done, eh?" The surgeon came closer.

"Not your business." The warden turned a page.

The surgeon's breath smelled like greasy pork. He reached for her with his boney hand. Feya's whole body shook. "Don't touch me."

The surgeon wheezed out a laugh. "Now, now. Be a good girl. I'm just going to have a little look and then you can get what's coming to you."

"I'll bite yer hand off."

Cairncross bit his lip as if to keep from smiling.

The warden looked up from the ledger. "A feisty one." He chuckled. "Did she give you any trouble, Alasdair?"

Cairncross went back to staring at the wall. "Some."

"I'm warnin' ye." Feya lowered her chin and stared the body snatcher directly in his soulless eyes. "Ye touch me with that hand and ye'll come back with a stub."

The surgeon raised an eyebrow. His gaze swept over her face. His eyes widened.

Good. He recognized her.

"I . . . Gentlemen . . ." His tongue twitched in his mouth. "You might have to hold this one down."

The warden rolled his eyes.

Cairncross looked bored. He took a step toward her. "Allow me." He clamped his hand upon her shoulder. That blue gaze said things that chilled her to the core—no tolerance, no leniency. If she made the slightest protest, he would make her pay.

Feya was afraid to breathe. Her lungs ached. Her back would soon snap from holding still.

The body snatcher smiled. And then he winked. Just like he had in Deacon Brodie's.

A wave of nausea hit her when he touched her face. His hand slid along her cheek and then rested on her forehead. "She has a fever. Quite high." He reached for her throat. "Pulse is abnormally elevated." He opened his bag and withdrew a medical instrument, which he laid against her breastbone. "Breathe."

Feya turned her head to the side and obeyed.

"Open your mouth."

"Me mouth?"

"That's what I said." He squinted at her mouth and then wiped his nose on his sleeve again. "Just as I suspected. This one's infectious. Far too sick." He stepped back quickly. "I recommend she be kept elsewhere." He gave the warden a poignant look. "I can assure you, it is of the utmost importance."

"Excuse me?" Cairncross clipped the words.

The warden closed the ledger. "I concur. We're far too overcrowded, as I said. Five thousand eight hundred forty-six prisoners at present. Quite past capacity."

Something like panic registered on Cairncross's features. "Surely you could take one more."

The warden threw the book into the pile. "Impossible. And not my problem."

"Surely you're not suggesting . . ." Cairncross ran his hand across his jaw.

"You apprehended this criminal. She's your responsibility. Since your father is the bailie of Holyrood, he should have decided what to do with her. Oh, I forgot. *Bailie* is sort of a ceremonial title, isn't it? Like the twelfth duke of Hamilton is actually the keeper. The only thing that man keeps is the queen's money and lavish apartments."

Cairncross's cheeks went white.

"The crime happened on Holyrood grounds, yet you bring her to me."

"Sir, I cannot be shackled with this right now. The timing is most inconvenient."

The warden placed his finger upon his desk and ran it through the dust. "Tell it to the wind, Alasdair. We all have our problems."

As if on cue, the screaming started again.

The warden sat and withdrew a piece of paper. He lifted a pen and held it over the page. "You have two choices, and only because I like you. There are a few honest men left in Scotland, and I think you might be one."

Cairncross closed his eyes, as if he knew what was coming. "Sir . . ."

"Perth or Stirling?"

"Might I beg you to recon—"

"No. Choose."

"Stirling." He said the word like a disease.

"Excellent." The warden scrawled the word on the page and then stamped it. The thud echoed in the room. "Young lady, I'm going to need you to tell me your name."

"Why?" Feya whispered the word.

"Because this man is now your keeper. And he's going to deliver you to Stirling Prison."

Chapter Seven

Cairncross locked her in an abandoned guard shack on Holyrood Palace grounds. Without so much as a word, he slammed the door behind her, blocking out the light just like Da had done the day before with the window in the tenement.

The heavy lock fell into the chamber, sending a final echo into the room.

Feya stared at the crack beneath the door and followed the movement of his shadow until it flicked away. She supposed she should be thankful she wasn't in Calton Jail. But instead, she only felt rage at Cairncross. If he hadn't been there . . . She swallowed hard and wadded her tattered skirt in her hand. Of course he'd been there. How had she actually believed that she might break into a palace undetected?

She pulled a dull brown thread that hung, and then another. Threads spilled upon the ground like shorn hair—strand after strand. What use was it trying to preserve any dignity? She'd already patched this skirt so many times.

Here she was, just a walk away from the bairns, and she couldn't reach them. She closed her eyes and saw their faces and the tears that would shimmer there. What would Annie do with them since she hadn't returned? Cast them into the streets? And that husband of hers . . . Feya wrapped her arms around herself and squeezed till it hurt, as if the pain could make the images go away.

"I'll be right back," she'd said as she left them with Annie. And then she'd promised to make Brenna oatmeal just the way she liked it—with brown sugar that they sold down by the wharf and northern walnuts that the ships brought in. But the morning had come and gone, stolen by the Englishmen with blue eyes as unreadable as the pagan glyphs in the north.

When she'd left the tenement yesterday to go to Deacon Brodie's, she'd promised herself she'd mend Hamish's blanket when she returned. After making breakfast, she was going to use the money to buy him pants that didn't squeeze. He always had tiny red rings on his ankles by the morning. How long had she been tracing those lines with her finger, hating herself?

Hamish would never remember her.

If he survived at all.

Brenna's fate would be worse. And Gillis . . .

Feya stood, clutched an old, broken chair, and threw it against the wall. Wood splintered and rained upon the floor. There was no chance of escape—no windows, no weakness in any of the stone walls.

She collapsed on the iron bed. Dust surged and then fell in the shard of light, making her cough. "Ach, this ache in me lungs . . ." Sweat broke out on her forehead.

Just give up. There isn't any use. The words were old and familiar.

The light from under the door stretched, touching her fingertips. She turned her hand into the glow, illuminating the lines upon her palm. "What use is light if it doesn't warm ye?" She made a fist. "What use is light if ye can't see a way out?"

The stones in the wall were muddled—dark and light grey, an

indecisive swirl. Images came to her mind: leaving the caravans and coming into the city . . . the hope on Da's face that day . . . Ma taking her to the good part of town to look at the fancy people and have her first taste of shortbread.

Another image. And she hated it. It was Cairncross standing in the palace kitchen. The sculptured lines of his face faded in and out of her vision like something beneath the water just out of reach. His eyes burned into her like stolen sapphires. And still there was the feeling that something about him was important. Something about him she needed to know.

She wasn't romantic; that was certain. Life was too hard for that kind of weakness. But in the quiet moments throughout the years she'd allowed her mind to stray to what kind of eyes her husband might have. Only that. The answer had always been the same.

Blue. Always blue.

Just like Ma's father, her grandfather, the Scotsman. The only man she'd ever known to be kind. But after his death, the money had stopped coming and Da started doing what he was best at: destroying everything that was precious by tipping up the bottom of a glass.

And this man—this Cairncross, the devil Englishman—had black hair just like Da.

Another chill threatened to take her down. The ceiling bowed. Sweat dripped down her neck. "This fever . . . Making me see things."

If there was a God, He was taunting her. Probably created the devil Englishman just for this moment, gave him blue eyes that a woman could get lost in, even when they were looking on you hard.

Feya laughed bitterly. He was the perfect English soldier. Slinking in the dark behind her like a fiend. If not for the sickness, she would have gotten away. Even though he had legs that had seen more than a few days in training. Even though his shoulders were strong like the Highlanders and broad.

The years wrapped themselves around Feya as the sun set. Nothing good could be said in the way the light began to fade. It was like all promises—they started out strong and then left you alone in the dark without a friend. Only cold walls remarked on the sun's passing. Only the ache in her bones told her she was alive.

"You did what?" Father's lips turned into a snarl.

"I took her to the jail. I thought it best." Alasdair looked into his father's burdened eyes.

"And now, instead of being here to meet your fiancée—who, I might add, has traveled all the way from London—you have to take a thief to Stirling."

"Yes." He put no inflection in the word. He'd long ago learned there was no place for emotion.

"Yes?" Father stepped forward and took hold of Alasdair's jacket. "Is that all you can say?"

Alasdair was used to this. This was familiar. So much so that the sands of the Egyptian desert had been a relief. "That is all I can say."

Father turned away and his words fell into curses. "Of course you had to take her on the day the warden likes to pretend to work."

The irony was strange, Alasdair did have to admit. It was rare for the warden to be at the prison, and had the under warden been there, he would most likely not be having this conversation. Alasdair wanted to curse and rave and join Father in the misfortune of it all. But outbursts weren't allowed. He wiped his hand over his forehead instead.

"You'll have to go, of course."

Alasdair snapped his gaze back. "Excuse me?"

"It's unavoidable. I cannot afford to anger him."

"Father, you are the bailie. You can get one of the new guards to take the woman to Stirling. If she survives, that is. The surgeon said she's quite ill, and to tell you the truth, I'm still not entirely convinced she isn't mad."

He squeezed the wound on his hand that ached like his first flogging. What he'd really like to do was wrap his hands around the little she-cat's neck and be done with it, as his father had suggested. But this wasn't war. And she was a woman. Nothing Father could say would make him that ruthless. "We hardly need to follow precedent in this instance. The queen is away."

Father crossed the room, a wild look in his eyes. "Oh, we're going to follow precedent. After all . . ." He came so close that Alasdair could smell the cheroot on his breath. "Isn't precedent what you've always been so fond of? That's the reason you took the woman to the jail in the first place."

"Father, you do realize it's eighteen eighty-five? Not sixteen eighty-five."

"We cannot afford any scrutiny. The Moveable Dwellings Bill will pass. I have almost turned the vote."

He didn't have to elaborate. It was an old conversation, one that seemed to thrum through his father's blood—redefining Scotland, ridding her of the parasites that infested the land. Namely the Gypsies.

Alasdair rubbed his temple and closed his eyes. For that reason, he hadn't mentioned the scarf tied in the thief's hair or the darkness of her eyes. Two lectures were enough for one day. "I'm sorry, Father. I know you didn't need this right now. Not when you're so close."

Father stepped forward and pointed. "You will not ruin this for me. Nor will anybody."

"I understand." Alasdair's voice came out lower than he'd intended. He did understand. All the sacrifices his father had made followed him like phantoms. He could never repay them all, but doing his duty was a good place to start.

Father stepped back and smiled. "It's all right. We all make mistakes." He looked at the ceiling medallion like he saw more there than plaster and gold. "Stirling is around sixty kilometers. You can be there and back in four, maybe five, days. I cannot spare you today; there is the Soldier's Parade to think of." He handed the warden's orders back to Alasdair. "This thief is in a secure place?"

"The old guard shack."

"Well done."

Alasdair bowed and headed for the door.

"I am told that Miss Wanesley and her father are fond of history. Perhaps a tour of Edinburgh Castle is in order. After that, maybe Rosslyn Chapel. I will tell them you've been detained on matters of the utmost importance."

Alasdair's hand stilled on the door. "Would you, Father?

"You are my son."

Alasdair raised his chin. "I will not fail you."

The shadow of a smile crossed Father's face. "With Miss Wanesley to come back to, and your wedding approaching, I know you will make haste to dispatch with this little interruption."

Alasdair thought of Amberlyn's blonde hair and how he longed to run his fingers through it. And her skin . . . A man could get lost in that softness. But he'd waited. Even when they'd been alone and he'd had opportunity.

Always playing by the rules, down to the letter.

But soon Father would have his dream and Alasdair would be free.

The sweetness in Amberlyn's eyes called him as he walked into the hall. And her smile—there was no guile there, just a heart that would give to him. And he would give back.

Sunlight streamed through the windows of the gallery. Red dots moved in and out of the yellow light, floating like embers. A servant opened a door. Green spiked in the air beside the man. Alasdair rubbed his eyes.

Soon he would tell Amberlyn everything. He only hoped she wouldn't laugh. Or run. Or do any of the things people were prone to do when he told the truth.

Quick, sharp bursts of pain needled Feya's temple. How long was Cairncross going to leave her locked up?

The sound of keys rattling stilled her thoughts. The door cracked, just enough to let the day's dying light creep in. A woman slid through the opening. She shoved the key into the lock again before Feya knew what was happening.

The woman's face was plain and her features sharp. Her brown hair was neatly arranged to either side of her face and split down the middle. "Allow me to establish one thing, missy." Her words were quick, like a nervous rabbit. "There are two guards outside, and should I scream, things will not go well for you." She took off her bonnet like she was making a social call. "Do we understand one another?"

Feya sat up. "Who are ye?"

"That hardly matters as we shan't be acquainted long." She smiled sweetly despite her words. "But, as I am not in the business of rudeness—even with a thief—you may call me Mrs. Thurston." She opened the basket she'd brought. "And you are Miss Feya Broon."

"How did ye know?" Feya pushed her damp hair out of her eyes.

Mrs. Thurston lifted a lid on a metal pot. The smell of lamb mixed with carrots wafted through the room. "I know a lot of things. Being housekeeper in a palace does have its advantages."

"Please." Feya swayed. She closed her eyes under the weight of the delicious smells. "Might I have some? I haven't eaten in so long. I need . . ."

Mrs. Thurston dipped it out and placed a bowl in her hand. "Of course." There was compassion in her eyes.

The lamb was perfectly tender and the gravy salty. The onions were better than any she'd ever had.

"Not too fast. You'll regret it if you do."

Feya looked up at her, numb. She savored the stew, holding it in her mouth until it melted. But the bairns had no such food. She swallowed, and it went down like poison.

"Eat more, child. I didn't mean for you to stop."

Feya scooped up another bite and slid the food into her mouth. Her lips trembled. *Because I have to. I'll do it for them.* She swallowed. And then ate again. And again, until there was no more.

Mrs. Thurston took the bowl and filled it. "The whole pot's for you, so eat your fill." A dark look crossed her thin features. "You'll need your strength."

Feya knew what she implied: the devil Englishman. Soon he would drag her all the way to Stirling.

Mrs. Thurston reached into her pocket. "I brought you this." She withdrew a small brown bottle. "I heard you could use a little medicinal fortification."

"I am ill."

"So I see. You've quite a fever in your cheeks." The woman inclined her head to the side. "Almost the same dark red of your hair." She pulled the cork from the bottle. It squeaked against the glass. "Here you go, then. Drink it all."

The medicine tasted vile—like sourwood and whiskey. It burnt her throat like it was peeling her flesh away.

"There, now." Mrs. Thurston clasped her hands together. "It

won't heal you completely, but my remedy has never failed. You'll be able to sleep, and in the morning you should feel somewhat akin to your old self."

Feya squeezed the bottle. "Why are ye helping me?" Her words slurred. Warmness crept into her veins.

"I'm only doing what I've been asked to do. The young master told me a bit of your plight and what you'd done."

"The young master?" She couldn't mean Cairncross. That devil didn't have a sympathetic ounce.

"The man who caught you. Young Master Alasdair." Mrs. Thurston pursed her lips together and looked as though she considered saying nothing more. After a moment, she continued. "It's a name we gave him because he always has a book in his hand when he's off duty."

The information made Feya's eyelids close. The warmth was taking her down. She stretched her legs and couldn't feel them anymore.

"He thought perhaps you hadn't eaten in a while. He suggested I bring you something hearty."

Surely the woman was lying. The devil Englishman couldn't have been so thoughtful.

"He'll be taking you to Stirling in the morning."

Feya nodded against the thin pillow. She supposed he couldn't take a dead woman. That must be his motivation. He had to do his job. And get the reward at the end for doing so. It was cut and dry, neatly packaged in a little bow.

Laughter escaped her mouth. Once it started, Feya couldn't stop.

Mrs. Thurston narrowed her eyes but then bent at the fireplace. She hummed, keeping her gaze on Feya. Before long, she'd started a fire.

"I was freezing." Laughter wove in and out of the words, but then

Feya felt lost. Tears knocked but she didn't answer. The only thing she had left was her strength not to cry.

Mrs. Thurston handed Feya a piece of bread. She turned and headed for the door.

"Wait!" Feya reached for her and almost fell off the bed.

"Yes?" Mrs. Thurston raised an eyebrow. "Do you have something to say to me, child?"

Feya fought to keep her eyelids open. Only a few more minutes, that's all she needed. "I need to tell ye something." The sound of deep humming filled her ears. Words were heavy things, sitting in her mouth like rocks. "I can't go. They're waitin' fer . . . me . . ."

Chapter Eight

"Get up."

A hand fell upon her shoulder, shaking her.

Feya pulled the blanket closer. There was a jerk against the cloth and then a sudden draft. She pried open her eyes.

Cairncross frowned down at her. "It's time to go."

Every strand of his dark black hair was in place, the blue of his eyes a startling contrast. Feya drew in her breath like she'd been struck. The way he looked at her shook her, made her weak. It was like standing on the edge of a cliff and staring into the vast valley below. One false blow of the wind, and she'd fall to her death.

She couldn't show him the fear that she felt—nothing that wouldn't work to her advantage. "All right." She stretched her legs, which still felt weighted and warm. Mrs. Thurston's medicine was the best kindness she'd received in an age.

"Two minutes. And then you'd better be outside." The wooden boards of the floor creaked as he walked.

Feya kept her eyes on his perfectly shined shoes until he left. She sighed, sitting a moment. The day ahead of her seeped into her bones like a death cloak.

He beat on the door. It shook against the hinges. "Thirty seconds."

Feya stood, walked to the door, and jerked it open. He stared back at her, less than a foot away. "Took an extra moment to tidy up?" A hard look seeped into his eyes. "What a shame there was no improvement."

Feya raised her chin. "What a shame I prefer prison over time spent in yer company."

He smiled like that was exactly what he wanted from her. Then he clucked with his tongue like one would scold a child.

She would make him pay for that.

He grabbed her arm and led her out to where two horses were tied—the same fine black he'd ridden yesterday and a plain, sable brown. At least he didn't expect her to walk all the way to Stirling.

"Get on the horse, unless you want me to throw you."

Feya jerked her arm away and hefted herself into the saddle. Immediately, he tied her hands again. A rope was also tied between the two horses. More security, she supposed, assurance that she would not flee.

Feya hid a smile. It would take a lot more than ropes to keep a Gypsy.

Cairncross mounted his horse. "You don't want to be here, nor do I." He looped the reins around his hands. "If you insist on acting like an animal, as you did yesterday morning, I will treat you like an animal." His gaze flicked to his bandaged hand. "I will break your ankles or your feet or whatever appendage happens to be nearest me. Do you understand?" He drew his gaze back up to her eyes and held it there.

It took everything within her not to look away. He had such coldness within him, such resolve. He towered over her, almost twice her size. She knew that he could easily break her—her body at least. Her will, and her love for the bairns, was another matter.

She would escape. No matter what. There was always a way.

One woman against one man. How hard could it be?

"I understand." Feya let the words drip with sweetness and then faced forward. The wind came down from the hill that overlooked the palace, bringing with it the smell of something fresh. Something she'd not smelled in a while. There was hope in a wind such as that. It held notes from the rain last night, but it was lighter, better, like it had risen above. A wind like that made a person strong—warm and fragranced with the smell of wild Scotland.

Cairncross spurred his horse on. As her horse did not have a bridle, she could only hold on to the pommel. At least there was a saddle.

It was the little things. She had to focus on that. Little victories led to big ones, Ma used to say.

Like mixing the rubber at the mill or cleaning their hovel at the tenement. The work she could do.

She would study this man—the devil Englishman Cairncross— and she would find his weakness. Then she'd be back with the bairns.

As he led her back into the square, people stopped to look upon him with respect. She was the dog, the scourge they were thankful he was cleansing. As the *clip-clop* of the horses' hooves rang on the cobblestones, the hundreds of years of Romani cleansings sang in her blood. Forced slave labor. Abduction of children. Brandings. Head shavings. Severed ears. Special taxes, mandatory hangings, and unpunished government-sanctioned killings. All across Europe they had been hunted, cast out, and despised. Why should it be any different now? What did it matter that yesterday she'd been one of these proud Scots, working in their mill? She still had Da's scarf tied around her head, hiding her red hair, and they saw only the dark eyes. They saw only the filthy clothes. They saw only the cursed Gypsy.

The cramped streets and ancient houses gave way to grass, and the city dwindled off like a bad dream. The horses whinnied and jerked their heads high, as if they wanted to play. But Cairncross killed that, too, reining his mount in, bringing the beast under absolute control.

Although she'd dreamed of the countryside's beauty, seeing it was like a breath coming out of water. The mist on her face was soft and light, like fingers urging her awake. The grog of the medicine began to fade. Feya let her shoulders fall into the relaxing rhythms of the horse, and she just looked, scanning the countryside that had been denied her for so long.

The hills were clothed in yellow velvet—flax. And there—linseed. The purple stalks bent with the wind and the sun hit them just right, like a thread running over a quilt, only touching the tips and weaving in here and there. The fields would smell like nuts if they were closer, and fresh, good earth.

The green of the hills was the depth of summer. Feya breathed in, feeling a pang in her chest—like a bell ringing from long ago. It was a rare gift, that green. Sometimes, when the winter in the city was at its worse and she'd been stuck in the corner of their tenement, she'd thought on that color. But, oh, her memory had dulled it. She'd matched it to the flat colors of the tenements, meshed it with dirt, sorrow, and pain.

A fence ran through a pasture and there, in the distance, were sheep. Fat and ready for shaving, she could plainly see that. She wanted—no, longed—to weave her fingers deep into the wool and feel a living breathing animal underneath. Not the rotting meat she saw day after day in the markets of Edinburgh.

To the left there was barley on the hill, and from the looks of it, it was due for a threshing. Feya smiled, surprised to feel that the gesture was genuine. There'd been just such a wheat threshing when she'd been little, before Da had got his big ideas of coming to the city. Ma's apron had been full of the chaff and her face had been bright with exertion. The horses had worked by threes, wading through the barley like it was waves.

"Is something amusing?" It was the first time Cairncross had spoken to her in the past hour.

Feya considered cutting him with her words. She decided to tell the truth. "I was rememberin'. I used to live in the country."

"You should have stayed."

She ignored the bite in his tone. "Yer right."

He narrowed his eyes. "Excuse me?"

"It wasn't me decision." She didn't want to tell him the rest. But if she didn't, he wouldn't talk. And then there'd be no hope of finding his weakness. "Da wasn't content to stay in the country. Me mother was from a well-to-do family in Edinburgh. But she left all that to marry me father, a Gypsy."

He made a pompous sound that only an Englishman could produce—indifference, hardness, and superiority wrapped up in just one sound.

"Even though me mother said she was happy, Da never believed it. He only saw what he couldn't give her. And the fine place where she'd come from. Her father forgave her for running away and helped us with some money when I come along, but that was worse, ye ken. Wounded Da's pride." Feya curled her fingers around the edge of the saddle. "It destroyed him when Ma had to sell her harp." She bent over her hands, captured the edge of her scarf, and pulled it from her head. Her long hair whipped around her.

Feya glanced toward the Englishman. He was watching her.

Good. Very good.

An excellent place to start.

Alasdair let his gaze linger on a pile of rubble down the way—a broken fence, no doubt. Some Scottish farmer's neglected business. And it had probably lain that way for weeks.

Good Lord, but these ruffians needed guidance. Not two hours from the city and already there was evidence of blatant disrespect for the crown. What sort of testimony was this to Her Majesty? Broken fences led to broken lives. One act of carelessness spilled over into another. That's what Father always said.

Alasdair switched the reins to his left hand and stretched the fingers of his right. His leather glove protested, creaking with the movement.

He could feel the Gypsy watching him. She was like fire—strong, raging fire—beside him, hate rolling off of her in waves. She tried to mask it with smiles, but he wasn't so easily duped. She would try to use emotion. And if that didn't work, she would try pity. It was all so tiresome. And always the same.

He would tame her. As he had all the criminals that had passed through the frames of his existence. It wouldn't take much. She was a woman, after all.

Alasdair sighed. He could choose not to talk to her. That was an option, and a good one. It was better not to become entangled. And besides, his head roared from the pain medication he'd taken last night for his hand.

She was beneath him. A thief. Staying indifferent was key.

That was one of the first things the Horse Guards had taught him. Especially when the length of his sword was buried in another man. When foreign blood was pooled upon the ground and they begged for mercy.

No entanglement.

Just do the job.

It was a reasonable request. It had kept him safe in two wars, and all the years before. He understood rules, and the reason for them.

What he didn't understand was the way the Gypsy looked at the countryside. How there were almost tears in her eyes. And that wasn't contrived. Perhaps neither was her story about her family. Yesterday she'd tried to cut him to the bone. Today she spoke of regrets—and harps, of all things.

He hated complications.

And now all he could think about was Scottish harps and how the woman who'd sold it must have had the same wild hair that this ragamuffin beside him possessed. And that got him thinking of the whole impropriety of a woman of good birth marrying a Gypsy. Which was even more complicated.

Worse than that was the feeling that something wasn't right. Alasdair shifted in the saddle and stared at the Gypsy. When she didn't think he was watching her, there was something quite strange about her unguarded expressions, something that made him want to know more. Besides that were the colors around her in the air, lacing her head like a bright, rainbow crown.

All the time alone he'd spent on night watch really was starting to fray his mind. Either that, or his brain ailment was progressing. He dropped his gaze to the nearest pile of sheep excrement and willed the kilometers to fall away.

The sun hung in the sky too heavy to last. Behind the thin orange clouds, stretched out like rope, it faltered, setting the pine needles on fire, making them almost too bright to look at.

Feya closed her eyes and stretched her neck, trying to alleviate the ache. The horse beneath her still swayed, back and forth, careful against the rocks and bearing down to climb the valleys.

Just like Cairncross. Careful about everything.

There'd not been much conversation since she'd told him a little about her family. If anything, he'd locked himself down like a monarch's treasure box. No crack in the perfect palace guard façade.

He was good, this one. And although she didn't like to admit that she knew such things, he'd not bent when she'd tried the tactics Da had taught her: give a secret to get a secret, over-exaggerate your own weakness to gain a strike . . . Nothing.

She'd tried slumping in the saddle to play to his chivalrous side. Nothing. He'd only kept his face forward as the horses walked.

She'd tried staring at him to annoy him. Nothing. He'd not even turned his sickening, princelike head. Or bothered to lower the angle of his nose—stuck so high up in the air.

She'd made comments here and there—the beauty of a white-washed farmhouse as they'd passed it, the sad disrepair of a fence, the way the sunlight turned clumps of grass in the valley gold and purple.

Nothing. He gave nothing.

Just like a man. Brainless and an instrument of trouble.

One thing kept her from the bairns. And he sat just a short space away.

Alasdair Cairncross.

She'd have to kill him. It had come to that.

He had to fall asleep sometime.

The sun slipped closer to the hill, and almost immediately a chill crept in. The colors in the sky dulled and then faded.

The night was coming. And hopefully her freedom.

Feya rubbed her arms and narrowed her eyes at the Englishman. His guard jacket was thicker than any cloak she'd ever owned. He didn't even have a chill in his cheeks. Not the slightest tinge of pink.

Suddenly he pulled back on the reins. "We stop here for tonight."

Feya scanned the clearing and the trees beyond. She nodded. If someone were going to murder somebody, perhaps this would be a suitable place. Not a house for forever.

Another chill came through her. Her shoulders shook on their own accord.

"Get down." Cairncross stood beside her horse. She hadn't even noticed him approach.

Feya gave him a smile full of venom. "That's a little difficult with me hands tied to the saddle."

"It is not your place to question, but to do." He untied her, grabbed her waist, and pulled her to the ground, depositing her like a bag full of rubbish.

"Ye might have given me a warnin'." Feya blew her hair out of her eyes and tried to cover her ankles. The last thing she wanted was for the Englishman to be getting any ideas on how to pass the long hours of the night.

He reached down, grabbed the rope, and forced her to stand. Pain sliced through her shoulder. "Didn't yer mother ever teach ye how to treat a woman?"

His body grew still. "You will not say anything to that effect again." Pale orange from the sunset brushed his face, making his eyes look otherworldly.

Bleeding banshee. What the devil had she said to give him such a look? Da had just such a look every time the drink was about to take him down.

The sun slid behind the hills and the light with it. Feya could feel the heat from his body and all his coats of importance. More than that, she felt his anger. Whatever he'd been thinking about the last couple of kilometers hadn't been pleasant.

"I'm . . . sorry." Feya pulled her gaze away from his eyes and watched the rise and fall of the fancy buttons on his jacket. "I dinnae mean nothin' by it. But ye dinnae have to try to rip me arms off. Or throw me on the ground. I am a woman, not some brutish man yer used to confrontin' in battle." Her full Scots speech came out, and she was sorry she'd let it slip.

"You are correct." He said the words slowly. "Even though you're a thief, and beneath me, my actions were uncalled for."

The fact that he didn't ask for forgiveness was not lost upon her. Neither was the fact that he made sure she knew repeatedly where she stood in relation to his loftiness. However, it was an admission—something she never expected to come from his lips.

"Well." She was glad for this softening. Even though it was as disgusting as maggots on a pile of rot. "As ye said earlier, we both find ourselves in strange circumstances. And there's nothin' pleasant about it."

"Right." She didn't think it possible, but he inflected the word to make it sound ever more English. "I need to make a fire."

"That would be good."

Neither of them moved, both locked eye to eye, as if the first one who broke contact would be the loser.

His grip on the rope was not so hard as before. And his steps were a little more relaxed. Where method and perfection had been before, now he just seemed tired.

Tiredness was good. She could use that. Feya decided to go easy on him. After all, she would be killing him anyway.

The wind blew, flipping out the black hair that had been neatly combed down before. He led her just beyond the forest line. Immediately, the light dropped again, like a blanket had doused it. The smell of earth and woods was strong. Night noises came—an owl, a cricket. Just beyond them somewhere was a stream.

Cairncross bent and gathered wood. His gaze never left her. There was wariness in his eyes.

"There's better wood over there." Feya inclined her head to the left. "I could help if ye untied me."

"I'm not that stupid, Gypsy."

"Suit yerself." She pretended to study the way the leaves shivered above them. "But the longer ye take, the colder it will become."

"Like to state the obvious, do you?"

"Excuse me, me lord." Feya bowed her head to him like he was royalty. "I had no intention of offendin' yer noble sensibilities."

He drew his mouth into a thin line. "My sensibilities are noble. If you made a little more effort about yours, perhaps you wouldn't be in this situation."

"Ye don't know anythin' about me or me kind." Anger swirled like the dark, and the mist coming in over the ferns. "Maybe if yer kind paid a little more attention to what was goin' on a few streets over from yer posh palace and yer precious Mile, ye wouldn't be findin' yerself in this situation—shackled to a *worthless* thief."

His knuckles turned white on the hilt of his sword. "Madame, you would be wise not to assume what I know."

"Why is that?" Feya took a step closer. "What would I find if I looked beyond yer surface? Ambition? That's more than clear." She twisted her mouth. "It seeps from yer pores, don't ye know?"

Shadows crossed his face. "I don't see the problem with that."

"There's only a problem if yer English, because that kind of ambition robs and rapes and takes away everythin' that's precious. Especially if ye happen to not speak in the same way."

He took a step closer, narrowing the space between them. "The problem with Scots is that their minds are perpetually stuck in the time of King Edward the First. Don't you people realize it's the nineteenth century?"

"Ah, but we on the worthless side have long memories. And yer more than daft if ye think the crimes ended with Edward."

He mumbled something and turned, pulling her along, walking

past the forest line and back to where the horses were tied. He threw down the wood. "I think I've encountered more modern thought at the backside of a camel in Egypt. Sit. Down."

Feya lowered herself as if she were a princess alighting upon a pillow. She glared at him.

He retuned the look, went to the saddlebag, and withdrew more rope. "As I wouldn't want to disappoint your outstanding opinion of the English, you will, of course, understand." He gave her a mock look of concern and held the rope a loft. "Your ankles, if you please."

Blatherskite of filth. She hadn't counted on that. Killing him with her hands bound was going to be a hard enough feat. "Is there really a need fer such precautions? If I didn't know better, I'd think ye were afraid of me killin' ye in the night." She laughed, making her voice trill like she'd heard a fine lady do once on the Mile.

"I may be English, Gypsy, but I wasn't born yesterday." He tied her feet together, looping the rope in and out, knotting it three times.

Feya studied his handiwork. Fancy. Precise. Completely thought out and executed, curse him. "Ye must think I'm very dangerous."

"No, not much." He stacked the fire and had it quickly blazing. "If I thought you dangerous, I would have drugged you for the journey, which I can assure you, is still possible."

"Oh, I don't doubt it." She widened her eyes for effect. "Your kind is capable of a lot."

He rolled his eyes to the night sky, boredom etched in his features.

The English were always so good at that—looking bored.

He reached into the saddlebag and withdrew something. Feya scooted to the left so she could see. Although she'd eaten all the soup last night, she was starving again. There'd been nothing for breakfast and he'd only given her a piece of bread for lunch. "Will ye be sharing that, then?"

He hid whatever it was in his hands. "I'm sorry, are you hungry?"

"You know I am."

"I'll give you some—" He adopted a look of pure innocence and walked to her. "—if you say please."

Suddenly, the wind coming over the hills seemed more mournful, and Feya felt even more alone. She dropped her gaze to the fire and watched the way it licked the wood. Her back ached like mad where she'd burnt herself in the palace kitchen. Her shoulders ached like claws sunk deep. Her wrists stung from the rope.

She was tired. And just like the way the fire was licking the night, greedy and vain, this man was going to try to break her. She should have seen it coming, after all. Wasn't she trying to do the same?

Tears were forcing their way. Real tears. And she hated herself for them. Crying was the worst weakness. She thought of the bairns to make it stop.

Cairncross mumbled something.

Dried meat landed in her lap. Followed by a blanket tossed at her side.

Chapter Nine

He never should have had her portrait painted.

Ranald Aldourie sat in the worn leather chair in his bedchamber and tried not to look. The firelight played on the frame, painting it with a golden, otherworldly glow. He'd only have to raise his eyes and he would see her—Elspeth, his Gypsy wife, the ghost that haunted his heart. He squeezed the chair arms until the brass tacks bit into the old leather and threatened to bend.

He should have covered the painting long ago. Perhaps that would have stopped the whispers in the corridors by the servants that he was indeed going mad. But covering the painting—covering her—was unthinkable. It kept her memory strong, and the doubt from crashing in.

"One doesn't talk to the dead." He spoke the words although he knew he would break them. He slid his hand into the contours of the chair that had been worn by her body years ago. She used to sit here and reflect upon the hours, much like he did now.

Everything that he was, he had carefully crafted. From the obscure courtrooms of Scotland all the way into Parliament. But not even privilege could get him what he desired most in the world right now.

He wanted to feel Elspeth's skin against his. He wanted to feel her long, dark hair slide between his fingers. And her laughter—sometimes he could still hear it in the halls of the castle. He'd turn a corner and his mind would taunt him, bringing the tones from his memory like a dangling, unreachable prize.

Ranald tipped back the thin glass that he held and drained it. A cold Scottish breeze pushed in from the loch, inching through the window he'd pushed open earlier. The wind was sweet, like the first breath of youth. It brought the scent of the silt from the banks of Loch Ness, an easy walk from the castle door. The fading sunlight fell upon the water, as well as sprinkling rain. This was this time of the prevening—when the afternoon opened its hands and gave way to the eve. It was a moment when the veil lay thin. A time when heaven touched the earth with the tip of its toe and stirred the water.

Such thoughts . . . Ranald reached for the decanter and poured another glass. If God cared at all, Elspeth would have lived. She wouldn't have been at the camp that day. And Edan Cairncross never would have ventured north, raining down hate and destruction like the eleventh plague.

Ranald placed the cold glass against his forehead and closed his eyes. What had the man received for his ambitious campaign against the Gypsies? A promotion. The guardianship of one of the queen's palaces. The wicked prospered. Wasn't that always the way?

Ranald drained his glass again. All the years of his naiveté passed before him like the mist wafting by the window. He hated that person—that hopeful person he had been, believing that order and right would prevail. The lines of law and government were blurred. They always had been. But now, finally, he would be powerless no longer. He would make his own law—be his own law—playing the game the white wigs played and crushing them all with one fell stroke.

A knock sounded on the heavy bedchamber door. Bersh came in, the smell of the forest thick on his clothes. "Everything is going as planned." The wind had blown the ages into the old man's face, and the grief of the ones he tried to save still lingered in the lines around his eyes.

"Excellent." Ranald took a deep breath and let his head fall back to the cushioning of the leather chair. He rested his gaze on the bottom of the portrait frame.

"Once we have him, the father will crumble. All his work to turn the vote will come to nothing. All those dinner parties wasted. All that money, as if he'd thrown it into the River Forth."

"Most assuredly." Ranald ran his fingers along the cut glass of the decanter. Hours. It was only a matter of waiting a few more hours. He would have his revenge and the Gypsies would be safe. Two beautiful birds with one palace guard stone.

"Remember the raised pie she used to make for the children? How they'd come in from the camp and sit in that fancy kitchen of yours?"

"How could I forget?" Ranald attempted a smile but knew he failed as miserably as Bersh at such things. She had been a beautiful mix, his Elspeth, carrying the wild spirit of the Gypsies even while on some days she played at being lady of this house.

Bersh scowled and rubbed his shoulder. The English bullet wound would always bother him, especially on days like this. "If you can't pull this off, bury me on my feet. I've spent too many years on my knees." He turned and walked toward the heavy bedchamber door.

Ranald swirled the amber liquid in his glass, higher and higher, to the brink of the lip. It was a game he played with himself, this delay. Somehow, drawing out the moments dulled the pain. If the drink took effect quickly enough, he could look at the painting with absolutely no feeling at all.

But not yet . . . He turned his head and let his gaze go far, across the loch to the place where the birch trees bent low—where the peregrines nested and their feathers fell. The Gypsy caravans were there. As they would always be. Safe.

The wind picked up and made the trees dance. Ripples moved across the water, over the smooth, tan rocks of the shore. Blood always cried out. The Scottish ground knew. It remembered.

The last light slipped. The orange glow of the fire surged, as if preparing for what would come. Ranald walked to the painting and lifted his hand to the frame. The metal knob was there, carefully concealed. He pressed it and then lifted his eyes to Elspeth—his lovely ghost. A shock surged through him. Her voice . . . He could hear it so clearly, telling him what to do.

The deep protest of hinges came from behind the wall.

The false bookshelf opened up, revealing the torches in the secret stairwell that had already been lit in preparation.

Yes. This was the way.

Yes.

Feya lay next to the fire, its heat lulling her. On the other side the Englishman sat, searching the darkness of the woods like he knew someone was there. The tree branches above him stretched and contracted, black fingers against the hazy aura of a lovesick moon.

Hold on. Feya clutched the edge of the blanket as if it were Hamish's. *Brenna, Gillis, just a little longer.*

She stared at the Englishman's lips, once again twisted into a frown. They would have been fine, full lips on a Scotsman. Lips to make a woman beg and obey.

Feya drew her eyebrows together and cursed herself. That was no way to be thinking, especially considering what she had to do. She took a breath and pictured him lying dead upon the ground. She'd leave him in the field, just over there. Before anyone found him, his blood would freeze solid to match the state of his heart.

Cairncross turned to her, fire shadows on his face and his coal black hair blowing in the wind. "You're a loud thinker, Gypsy." He narrowed his eyes, as if he knew the dark things sliding through her mind.

Feya sat up. It was now or never. "I need to take care of somethin'."

"I imagine there's a lot you've left neglected."

His condescending tone gave her strength. "I need to go to the woods."

He inclined his head, as if considering. "Make it quick. And stay at the edge of the tree line."

"All right. Feya kept her face expressionless. It was possible that belladonna grew in these woods. Poisoning him would be the easiest way. "You'll have to untie me ankles."

She didn't look him in the eyes as his fingers worked. His presence so close to her was warmer than the fire.

The ropes fell. She stood and walked quickly, his gaze burning her back. The mournful wind followed, kicking up leaves and small branches, tearing across the ground like a scythe.

Please don't let it be too late in the year. Belladonna was common. Otherwise known as deadly nightshade. Ma had warned her of it on their way to Edinburgh.

"It looks like common berries, lassie, but don't be fooled. Your da's people told me about it. It'll take you down faster than you can sing 'The Ghosts of Culloden.' The first thing that goes is the eyes. The light will hurt, real bad. The mouth will feel as dry as tinder. Speech will slur worse than a drunkard. The roots and the leaves are the most poisonous. Witches used it in their dark rituals. Some said it gave them the ability to fly."

Feya glanced back. Cairncross stood by the fire with his arms crossed. He wouldn't be looking away.

Her feet snapped branches and sunk into plush, green moss. She pretended to be looking for a proper place, passing through ferns and over fallen trees.

The Englishman called to her. A warning. The wind brought his voice like the slap of a hand.

"Please," she said. She didn't know who she said it to, but it came from somewhere deep.

There—a mulberry bush. Broken twigs. Wet leaves.

Feya's breath came fast. She circled her hands around her neck and imagined the hangman's noose. There were stories of hangings going wrong. Especially when the hangman was drunk or wanted to make a spectacle.

What would the moment before dying feel like? A relief? Or terror hard and pure?

To the left, wide green leaves trembled in the wind. Her heart caught. The leaves were tinged with brown, most curled in on themselves. And there, just below, wilted purple flowers that looked like bells. And berries—shriveled black berries.

Feya dropped, ripped a clump away, then stuck her hand into the cold ground and dug. The root wasn't far down, sitting like a pale treasure of old.

The Englishman strode across the field. Feya shoved the root and leaves into her blouse. She stood. He must not suspect anything.

"What were you doing?"

"Nothin'."

"You were doing something." He accented the *g*'s, another way to highlight their differences.

"Do ye expect me to give an account of what a woman does in these instances?"

He stepped closer. "What, Gypsy, were you doing besides *that?*"

"Just like I said. Nothin'." Feya raised her chin and hoped it passed for a look of truth.

He arched his eyebrow. "Shall I search you to find out?"

"Yer welcome to do so, but ye'll find nothin' but dirt and a body that's far too thin." Feya locked eyes with him—Gypsy dark to dark, English blue.

A moment passed. The Englishman's expression shifted to pity. Relief swayed her body.

It was only a matter of time.

The leaves against her skin itched like stinging nettles. If the Englishman would just look away, she could adjust her bodice and maybe find some measure of relief. But the gaze of Alasdair Cairncross was like the plague. Once it latched onto you, it stayed until the bitter end.

As the horses stepped off the kilometers, the forest grew dense and thick. Although the sun shone bright on the ruts in the mud, Feya only had to look to the left between the trees and it was as dark as the alleys in Edinburgh she purposely avoided. It gave her the feeling of being lost in time, as if things had gone on in this place that only the leaves could tell. Maybe, as the Gypsies said, some nightmares did roam.

The branches twisted and groaned without the aid of the wind. But how was that possible? She must still have remnants of the fever. Indeed, sleeping on the ground last night had made her wake up dizzy, and her lungs still felt far too tight.

Branches snapped deep in the forest. Underbrush shook. Feya brought her bound hands up and crossed herself out of habit, the effects of going to the kirk with Ma.

"Afraid, are you?" Cairncross smiled like the notion gave him pleasure. "Are you familiar with the name for these woods?"

"No." The word trembled and Feya hated herself for the weakness. She felt like a child again, hiding under a blanket as the old Romani women told her the tales.

"This is the forest of Torphichen, very ancient. The Knights Hospitaller did many strange things here, at the invitation of King David the First in the twelfth century. Before that, the Celts buried their dead in these hills." He breathed in, as if he smelled something sweet. "And Cairnpapple Hill . . . Well, it isn't far." He looked at her from the corners of his eyes and his lips tightened. "All manner of atrocities."

"What does it matter what happened ages ago?" Feya spat the words at him.

He acted as though he hadn't heard. "Some say the name means 'cairn of the eye.'" He took on a look of innocence, if that was possible. "What do you reckon that means?"

"I've no idea." Feya sat straighter in the saddle. "How do ye know so much about this area anyway? Were ye up here murderin' and subduin' the Scots?"

"Something like that." He looked at an overgrown path. "The people here are backward. I'd wager even more backward than you."

"And how would ye know what they're really like? Have ye ever taken the time to talk with someone who's not English?"

"Yes." He said the word slowly and then smiled like the devil. "It's time I wish I could've retrieved, so much did I waste on the attempt."

Feya's mouth dropped open, but only a void of words was there. "It is ye who are to be pitied, judgin' a people simply from the way they talk or the country they were born in." Her accent was back, full force, and she didn't care. There was no use keeping up pretenses. "I am sorry fer ye."

Cairncross set his jaw hard and looked straight forward. "And you give all Englishmen a fair chance when you meet them, do you? You don't assume certain things?" He scanned the fading orange in the sky. "Just because I have black hair instead of red, just because I talk differently . . . You think you know everything about me."

"I've met yer kind many times." She knew she was almost repeating his words from earlier. She didn't care. "Ye'd drive us all into the sea with no regrets so ye could have more. Why is yer blessed England never enough? Yer English queen sits upon our throne like she's earned it."

He turned in the saddle. "You don't know her. Don't pretend like you do."

"She makes time fer ye, does she? Let me guess? Yer one of her lap dogs."

He reined in his horse too quickly. It danced across the road, mirroring the emotion of its master. "Father was right. Killing you would have been easier."

"Oh, I see." Feya pursed her lips. "An Englishman who has never met me spoke of dispensing with a Scottish life as easily as if he were raising taxes."

He rubbed his temple and closed his eyes. "I find this conversation tiresome, and I have a headache. Perhaps you could contemplate the beauty of nature instead of talking. If that is possible."

"Oh, aye. A lot is possible with me."

A *clang* came from his horse. Cairncross snapped his eyes open and leaned over his saddle.

"He's thrown a shoe," Feya said.

"Obviously." He dismounted.

"He can't walk like that. He'll do himself damage."

The anger on his face turned to sarcasm. "Oh, do you reckon?" He spoke softly to the horse and ran his hand down its leg, giving it the command to lift its hoof. The horseshoe hung at an odd angle, and part of the hoof was splintered.

"Queen's guard, indeed." Feya sniffed. "Who'd ye get to shoe the creature? A street vendor?"

His voice was deathly low. "I'll have you know that I take very good care of my horse. This animal has been with me through two wars, the African sand, and your vexatious Scottish rain. And, most important of all, he has more common sense than you will ever have."

Feya drew her eyebrows together in mock repentance. "Beggin' yer pardon m'lord."

He mumbled something and then scanned the landscape. There was only forest and hills that stretched on as long as an English court hearing.

"How far to the next town?"

"Too far." He glanced back down at his horse's hoof. "Stirling is about thirty—" He cut off the words, obviously so she wouldn't know.

They were that close. A chill passed over her back. "Ye mentioned the people of Torphichen." She peered into the darkness of the woods. "Perhaps there's a blacksmith?"

He sighed. "Yes . . . there's a blacksmith."

Feya stared into the woods and the strange fear wrapped itself around her again. The deep green of the trees looked almost black, and the thick moss on the ground seemed like you could fall through it to another world. The weeds swayed with the wind, bending over long neglected ruts in the road. Leaves turned over like pages in a book. Cairncross followed the movement with his eyes. But just like Da when he was drinking, what this man saw was not what his mind was on.

The sun hid behind a cloud, casting the road into shadows.

Cairncross worked the muscles in his jaw and then stared down the road that led to Torphichen.

Chapter Ten

Eriness lay all around them, in the ground beneath and the stroking lightness of the wind. *Come closer,* it seemed to say.

The *clop-drag* of the horse's shoe didn't help ease Feya's fear. Especially since there didn't seem to be any other sound. Not even when the wind blew.

"We're almost there." Cairncross inclined his head to the bend. "The town, if it can be called such, is just ahead. Don't say anything, do you understand?"

"Why is that? Don't want the people to know yer transporting me? Of course the ropes around me wrists wouldn't be givin' that away."

"Woman, just do as you're told. I am in no mood for negotiation."

She mock bowed to him. "As yer highness wishes."

"Stop being a fool." He gave her a sour look, but it didn't last long. His eyes were drawn to the opening in the trees and the hint of stone just beyond.

The forest thinned and opened up like they'd stumbled upon a well-kept secret. The village was small, with an old stone kirk across the yard. The dwellings were rustic things—practical. Smoke rolled out the chimneys at a leisurely pace, dissipating into the soft pink sky. The dwellings reminded Feya of her days in the crofter's cottages when Da had worked the land by day and then fished as the sun set.

Sheep dotted the hillside like puffs of clotted cream. It was simple here. And simple was something Feya hadn't had for so long.

The Englishman's gaze was still far away. He was paler than usual. *Must be bad memories come to call. He surely must have plenty of those.* Good. She would need him to be distracted for what she had to do.

Sourness settled in her stomach. She would look at him as little as possible. That would make it easier. The world would be better for the lack of him, wouldn't it?

One man. How much difference could the death of one man make?

She had to stop these thoughts. It must be the hunger getting to her, and the cold.

The tools of the blacksmith shop swung in the wind and clanged together like chimes. The coals were hot on the fire, but no flames shot up. Feya smelled the wood chips on the floor—fresh and clean.

Cairncross tied the horses and stepped inside. "Hello?"

A pop of the fire was the only answer.

An iron door handle sat on the table. It was a black dragon, its tail twisting into the handle. This place was Scotland through and through. Even simple people loved beautiful things. Feya wanted Cairncross to look at it, to see the contrast of the rough wooden table and the beautiful iron. "Fine craftsmanship here."

He paced and didn't answer.

She broke her agreement with herself and looked at his face. His scowl looked to be born on the vestibule of hell.

"The blacksmith is obviously not at work." He turned over a rock with the toe of his boot. "Surprising."

"Ye could ask at the tavern." Feya inclined her head toward the building at the end of the row. Laughter and the bright glow of a fire beckoned from the windows. "Everyone's probably there."

"Don't you think I've already deduced that fact?"

"Pardon me, m'lord. Far be it from me to tell a man what he already knows."

"Get off the horse."

"Why?"

"Because I asked you nicely." He strode over to her. "Unless you'd like me to knock you off."

"I didn't think it possible, but yer manners have exceeded yer charm." She gave him her sweetest smile just to provoke him.

His face darkened like a storm seeped into his eyes and overtook his soul. If she'd had any doubts about killing him, they were gone. Hate mingled with pain radiated from him like the heat from the blacksmith's fire.

The pain surprised her. It was easy to notice living in the tenements. Everyone wore it like a heavy cloak. It just was.

But not people like him. Pain lurked about the corners of his eyes even though he tried to hide it. Just a moment, and then it was gone.

"All right." She leaned over the horse's neck and then dismounted.

"Come here, woman."

Everything within her rebelled. What she really wanted to do was to be done with him. She could run to the tavern and say he'd kidnapped her. Maybe the townsfolk would believe her. Maybe.

The corner of his lips turned up. "You can try running if you like. I could do with some sport."

Feya widened her eyes.

"Trust me, you're not that hard to figure out. We are in a game of chess, you and I. And I can assure you, I've played this game to the end many times before."

Feya walked to him.

"Closer."

She took a step.

"Closer." His whisper went over her, like a pet on a dog. "I know you can do it." Cairncross tilted his head. "Just one more step." He smiled, exactly as she had done earlier. It must have been the smile he used on court ladies as they passed.

"Yer a devil."

"You're not the first woman to call me that."

"I'm not surprised." Only a few more steps and she'd be standing nose to nose with him. She turned her head and pretended to admire the vines on the blacksmith's roof.

"I'm still waiting. I said come here."

"Ye want me close, do ye?" She took another step. "How's this?"

"Just right." He lifted the end of the rope that bound her hands and tied it to the blacksmith's post. "I will return momentarily. In the meantime, don't do anything foolish."

"I'll be the perfect Scottish lady."

"Pity. I'll have to be even more on guard." He stepped past her, then stopped and turned, his eyes just as dark as before. He rested his hand on his sword. "If I'm not mistaken, that shack—" He pointed to a small building opposite the tavern. "—holds certain persons who might know something about this little rot of a town. You will, of course, notice the strategic position of the window in the corner. I will be watching." He strode across the gravel, his boots crunching on the stones.

"'I will be watching.'" Feya mimicked the smooth tones of his voice and looked at the back of him until he disappeared from view. Her heart picked up its pace. His horse was only a few feet away. And, more important, his water flask was tied to the saddle on her side.

His horse lifted its head and stared at her, as if he knew what she was thinking.

She dropped her gaze. It was the only way. Of course it was. She had to think of the bairns. "Don't look at me like that, ye beast. Ye don't know what I've been through."

The horse snorted, then lowered his head to eat grass.

Cairncross had left some slack in the rope. Feya reached into her blouse and pulled out the root. She rubbed it against the post and caught the small shavings. Some spilled upon the ground.

Feya looked back. No movement from the window.

She tossed the root into the woods and stepped closer to the horse. The creature's eyes turned toward her, great brown depths of questions.

"Forgive me." She unscrewed the water flask and dumped the powder in. The root floated on the top, but then rolled and sank like a dead man in a river.

It was done.

Feya stepped back to the post and gripped it. The wood there was worn, like other hands had touched it—maybe children that had played there for a hundred years.

The leaves above shivered. Water drops rained down like tears.

The Englishman's footsteps approached behind her. His presence was large, radiating life and threat. She turned and kept her eyes down. His shiny black boots were covered in mud.

He withdrew his dagger. It scraped in the sheath.

"What are ye doin'?" Feya clutched the post.

He lifted the knife, expressionless. The blade sliced and the rope fell.

Feya stepped back and rubbed her wrists. She was free.

His hand shot out and grabbed her arm again. Cold metal replaced the rope.

"Ye've handcuffed me!"

He latched the other handcuff around his wrist. "Your ability to state the obvious is astounding."

"Why handcuff me now?"

"You're still my prisoner, or did you forget in the space of ten minutes?"

"What—"

"I don't trust the people here. And I don't trust you. This way, you can be done with any ideas you have of escape, and they will know exactly what your status is."

"Ye had these handcuffs all the time, and yet ye tied me to the saddle like an animal? Ye led me around like a donkey!"

"It suited my purposes."

"'It suited—'"

"Yes. Now be quiet, if that is possible. We're only going to be here a short time. Understand?" He didn't wait for her answer but pulled her toward the tavern. The building was whitewashed and very old. It was two stories, and the roof looked to be something from the days when dragons were said to roam the land.

"What's the red cross?"

He sighed. "Ah, three seconds of silence. A personal record of yours?"

She raised her chin and didn't answer.

"The cross is the Knights Hospitallers'. As I told you earlier, they have history here. William Wallace does as well. He held his last parliament here prior to the Battle of Falkirk in 1298." The Englishman scowled at the slanted inn roof. "In this place he prepared the only surviving document that names him as the Guardian of Scotland." He gave her a sideways glance. "One of your heroes, I am sure."

"He was here?"

"Indeed. You're looking at the hotbed of Scottish conspiracy." He eyed her like she was part of it.

"Are we goin' in? Or do ye just want to stare at me like I'm guilty of everythin'?" Her own words condemned her. She was guilty. In a short time he would be dead.

Laughter came from inside. Surely they would go in now.

But Cairncross just stood there beneath the red cross.

"What's the matter?" Maybe he had seen what she'd done to his water bottle. "Afraid the ghosts of the Knights Hospitallers will curse ye fer comin' this way?" She shifted her gaze across the road to the kirk. Strange marking stones were placed in the yard.

"Something like that." He pulled her toward the door and had to bend to keep from hitting the frame.

Loud voices made Feya cringe. Too many bodies packed into the small room. After being out in the wild for two days, the shock of it was sudden and sure.

Heads turned. Conversation died.

Cairncross's face blanched whiter than when the wind had stolen his blood away. His dark-blue eyes were locked on a place that Feya couldn't see.

Glass shattered across the room.

The crowd parted.

An older woman with hair as red as Feya's stood with dishes broken at her feet. "Alasdair." She reached out, her hand trembling. "My son."

It had been a possibility. He'd known that. And, of all the luck, Haven just had to throw a shoe near Torphichen. The one place he'd never wanted to return to.

His childhood home.

But when he'd done some private inquiry after the war, the man had said that Morna was dead. She certainly deserved to be.

Now he stared at the dark-blue eyes that so closely mirrored his own, and he wanted to kill the woman himself.

"Alasdair . . ." The accent was still as thick as he remembered, just as backwater as the thief's beside him. "How I've prayed I'd get to see ye again."

He swallowed and smoothed out his expression. "It wouldn't have been that hard. You knew exactly where I was."

"I tried to find ye, son." Tears brimmed in her eyes. "I didn't know where he'd taken ye exactly."

"Is that so?" There was too much emotion in his voice. He hated himself for it. No doubt the thief would see it as a weakness and try to use it somehow.

"Aye." The woman who had borne him into the world lowered her eyes. A tear fell. "I headed toward London. But I didn't make it far. Ye know what we earn in Torphichen. A journey of that magnitude would have cost—"

"Ah." He'd imagined the lies she would tell him if they ever chanced to meet. Hearing them was worse. "Spent all the money he gave you in a week, did you?"

She drew her eyebrows together. "What—"

"I see. You spent it in a day. Hope it was worth it." He pushed past her and addressed the crowd. "I need a blacksmith. Who here can be of assistance?"

The questions from the thief beside him were tangible in the air, radiating from her worse than the heat of the fire. As if on cue, she whirled around and stepped in front of him. "This woman is yer mother?"

"You're a quick one, aren't you?" He gave her the smile that irritated her the most. The small space of the room pressed in on him, all the colors—swirls of blackish purple dipping from the ceiling like ghosts, hideous green floating up from the people like hell vapors. Sweat broke out on his forehead. Air. He needed air.

The thief's eyes widened. "But . . . she's Scottish."

"Do you reckon?" Alasdair tried to control his breathing. Doom latched on like a parasite. Always this way in crowded places . . .

The smoke of the fire merged with dull yellow, like the hiss of steam from a soup pot. Ugly orange crisscrossed in the air until he thought his head would burst.

Rage seeped onto the thief's face, just like he knew it would. "All this time . . ."

"Aye, lassie." He looked her straight in the eyes and brought his old accent back. "I was born here in this little village, to that woman over there. I'm half Scottish, believe it or not." He shifted back to the English accent he'd worked hard to cultivate. "However, my very *English* father rescued me from this filth." He flicked his gaze toward Morna, who still stood in the same place. "That woman sold me."

Feya's mouth fell open. "But yer father and yer mother . . ."

"Englishmen have many weaknesses, as you have been so kind to remind me during this journey. Morna was my father's weakness when he was tired and drunk." He clucked his tongue. "Oh, don't look like that. I'd reckon you were conceived in much the same manner as me."

For once, the thief was speechless.

"Shocked you, have I?" It brought a satisfaction that almost took the edge off the splitting in his head. Almost.

Morna was at his side. "Alasdair, will ye come upstairs so we can talk?"

"The time for talking ended about twenty years ago, wouldn't you say?"

"Don't say that." She looked down at her dirty apron. "Please."

"Someone wantin' a blacksmith?" A short, whiskery man pushed through the crowd.

"I do. My horse has thrown a shoe."

The man nodded, then raised an eyebrow at Morna. "What's the matter, love? Ye look like ye've got yerself into a wee bit of a row."

"This is me son, Angus. The one I told ye about."

"Is it?" He took a long drag from his pipe. "I told ye today was a peculiar day, didn't I? When the wind came over the cairn and whistled past the kirk."

"That ye did."

Alasdair rubbed his hand over his face. Of course they'd digress into superstition. The conversation even included talk of the weather. He was Fortune's favorite for sure.

The man turned his scrutiny onto him. "Ye picked a poor day to have yer horse throw a shoe. That's also a fact."

"Is that so? Let me guess. Earlier you saw two knives crossed upon a table. Or perhaps you saw a pig on your way to a wedding?"

The man frowned like Alasdair was mad. "No. Blacksmith's just taken ill. Got the costiveness and camp fever somethin' terrible. Seein' his arse with his eyes, that one."

Alasdair lifted his hand. "The details aren't necessary. Surely someone else in this respectable village can shoe a horse." He gritted his teeth. "It's not a very difficult task."

The man yelled over the crowd. "Bobby, anyone else 'sides Collin do horse shoein'?"

A man by the fire rose and spilled his drink down the front of his shirt. "There was one, but he died thirty years ago." He guffawed like the village idiot, which he probably was, and spilled the remainder of his tankard upon the floor.

"No, you oaf. Anyone do it now?"

"Oh, there was Finnigan, but remember that girl from Stirling came over and turned his heart to porridge."

The crowd laughed, and the man stood on the bench and started telling the tale. Which was just as dull as Alasdair knew it would be.

Torphichen. Only in Torphichen.

"Are ye hungry?" It was Morna. "I made a deer stew. It's very fine . . . fer these parts."

He was hungry, curse it all. And the thief beside him looked like she was about to blow away. If he got her to Stirling before she died, it would be a miracle.

Alasdair nodded, knowing with everything within him that he'd regret it in the end.

Chapter Eleven

Being handcuffed to the Englishman was the definite worst part of Feya's day. Similar to the time the landlord had tried to kiss her in the hallway of the tenement and then left her with bruises on her face when she'd refused. Or akin to burning her hand last year in the mill while

curing the rubber. She still couldn't feel her thumb, and the pale half-moon scar would no doubt be with her forever.

Elbow to elbow with Cairncross, his body shoved against her on the rough wood bench, she shivered, even though the fireplace was only two tables away. The orange glow reflected on the handcuffs, washing over the metal in waves. Feya made a fist to keep from touching his hand. The metal bit into her flesh, rubbing against the place already raw from the rope.

Cairncross sat across from the mother he hadn't seen in however many years, studying the grain patterns of the table as if they were the most interesting sights in Victoria's kingdom.

Men were all the same. Puffed up, cruel, always ignoring the obvious, and eternally looking down upon women, even if only in their thoughts.

Morna set two bowls of stew on the table. "It has parsnips in it from the glen where we used to sit. Remember?"

Cairncross picked up the spoon and shoveled in food, saying nothing. Feya wanted to kick him. If it hadn't been for the cuffs she would have tried. She turned to Morna. "Thank ye fer the stew. It's much appreciated."

"Yer welcome." Morna smiled, and there was kindness on her face.

Her blue eyes truly were beautiful, just like the eyes of the man beside her. Feya hated to admit that. Every time the thought came she felt like her own traitor.

Great tiredness washed over her. The smoke of the fire was cotton in the air—great big tufts shoving down her throat. Sharp laughter from the table behind them beat against her back like a hand.

Feya coughed, but it didn't make a difference to the pain in her lungs.

The road today had been too long. The room faded in and out—time swelling and contracting.

She scooped up a piece of lamb and chewed. It was better than the stew at Holyrood, although that had been grand. This was the taste of the fields and the open air, of a full day of work and satisfaction at the end. A bite of onion had the flavor of being kissed by sun and deep, dark earth. The country taste of Scotland.

"Ye got yerself into some trouble." Morna's voice roused her. "If Alasdair's anything like he used to be, he's given ye a run with his stubbornness, no doubt."

Cairncross stiffened his back. Feya turned her laugh into a cough and almost choked.

Morna smiled. "Some things never change."

Cairncross stood, lifting Feya's arm as he did. "We need to leave."

The bench teetered at Feya's knees. She grabbed the spoon with her left hand before it fell onto the floor.

"Yer not done with your stew." Morna's eyes pleaded.

Cairncross scowled. "There's the horse to see about."

Morna looked over at the men who were still telling stories about the last blacksmith. "The horse will keep fer ten minutes more." She gave him a look that would have stilled Auld Clootie. "Now finish yer stew."

He opened his mouth to speak, then closed it again. He sat down.

Feya leaned over her bowl to take another bite. Cairncross pushed the bench back again as if he would stand. Feya's spoon clattered on the table.

He shoveled in more stew, at a maddening pace.

"How'd ye find yerself in this quandary, lass?" Morna rested her elbow on the table, as if she had all the time in world.

"Well . . ." Feya drew her eyebrows together.

"She broke into the palace and tried to steal Mary Queen of Scots' jewelry box."

"Holyrood Palace?"

Feya sat up straighter. "Aye."

A look of awe crossed Morna's face. She shifted her gaze to Cairncross. "How long have ye been guardin' at Holyrood?"

"Three years." There was no emotion in his eyes. "Before that I almost died in the shadow of a pyramid. Not that you would have cared."

"That's not true." Morna looked like she wanted to reach for him. She flattened her hands on the tabletop instead.

"How have you been filling your days, then?" His tone said he didn't really want the answer.

"Seven years ago I married."

"Did you now?" He lifted his cup. "Glorious, happy day. And who is my step papa, then?"

"He died."

"Pity." Cairncross swallowed hard and set his cup on the table with a thud. "What was it? Syphilis?"

Feya's face flushed. "She's yer mother!"

"Don't I know it." He clenched his jaw and locked eyes with Morna—blue to blue, both unwavering.

A movement caught Feya's gaze. A large dog with wavy black fur padded across the room. A little boy walked alongside, his fingers intertwined in the dog's fur. The boy's red hair was slicked back and parted in the middle, making his ears look bigger. He wore a small, checkered suit—complete with a tan button-up waistcoat. The black leggings under his checkered short pants were tight against his legs, giving him the appearance of a baby bird. The boy had his eyes locked on Cairncross.

"Want to see me dog?" He patted the beast, and it wagged its tail like a scythe, knocking against the chairs. "Her name's Nessie after the monstie. She likes to eat turnips."

Morna leaned over, emphasizing her words with her expression. "Rowan, dear, why don't ye go and see if there's any pie left in the larder."

"No, thanks." Rowan climbed onto the bench and then Cairncross's lap.

"I beg your pardon, little man." Cairncross stiffened.

"Yer buttons are nice." Rowan's little fingertip skimmed them and then the fabric of Cairncross's sleeve.

"Yes, well." Cairncross scooted the bench back again, moving Feya with it.

"What does it mean?" Rowan pointed again to the button.

Cairncross cleared his throat. "It's . . . ah . . . the crown's for England . . . And the letters are the Royal Cypher."

"What's a cypher?"

"It's a monogram of the reigning sovereign. V.R.—*Victoria Regina.*"

"Why?"

Cairncross took a breath and then exhaled. "It just is."

Feya could see his foot tapping under the table.

"All right, silly." Rowan lifted his head and looked into Cairncross's eyes.

They were the same eyes.

Feya turned to Morna. The woman looked as pale as milkweed juice. She shoved her hair behind her ears and looked down.

Cairncross stared at his mother. And from the way he was looking, he knew he was holding his little brother on his lap.

"Da died," Rowan said suddenly.

Cairncross turned his gaze back to the little boy. "I'm sorry."

Rowan twisted his expression. "Wasn't yer fault."

"No." Cairncross whispered the word. For the first time since Feya had known him, the Englishman looked sad.

"I miss him somethin' horrible." Rowan leaned against Cairncross's chest and wrapped his hand around his lapel. He worried the fabric, moving his thumb back and forth like a baby with a blanket.

Feya thought of the bairns and pain stirred deep. She ached to hold the boy. Her hands itched with it. She wanted to get on eye level with him and ask him childish things, something to make him feel better—his favorite toy, games he played with his dog. She'd tell him a story of some sort, something where the hero always won in the end.

Cairncross's gaze shifted from the boy to the ceiling and then back again.

"Rowan." Morna stood. "Nessie hasn't had her supper yet. Why don't we go and find the bone we saved earlier?"

"All right." He reached for his mother and rested his cheek against her shoulder. As Morna walked away, he waved.

Feya waved back with her uncuffed hand.

Cairncross brought his fist to his lips and breathed hard. His foot still tapped under the table, jogging his leg and shaking the bench. He didn't appreciate Feya looking at him, that was certain. He drew his lips into a thin line when he caught her eye. "Enjoying yourself?"

Feya mirrored his expression. "Not at all."

Morna walked back and sat. "He's a wild thing, that little man." Feya could tell she held back for Cairncross's sake. Her words were an apology, but not for Rowan. There were unspoken things in the lilt of the words. She seemed to consider saying more, but then turned to Feya. "Ye didn't get to tell me yer side of the story. How is it ye find yerself at Torphichen with me son?"

Feya ignored the man beside her and the feelings that radiated from him. He was a storm, this one. A brooding, unmerciful cloud ready to spill out wrath and judgment. Well, he could shut up and hold his tongue for a moment longer.

She leaned forward, over the table, to let him know she'd be saying her part. She liked Morna, regardless of what the devil thought. The words came easily. She told the woman of Hamish, Gillis, and Brenna. She mentioned Da, his drinking, and the window tax. She even talked about the Gypsy blood that flowed through her veins.

Once she got that out, it was like a fire infused her bones and loosened her tongue. It had been ages since she'd had a sympathetic ear or another woman to share her story with. Two years. Since Ma had died. The realization made her shake as the words poured out. The women at the rubber mill were brutal as alley cats, and they didn't care about whom they sunk their claws into as long as they got to do it.

Morna didn't look away once through the telling. Before it was over all the stew was gone and the candle had burnt down to a puddle.

Cairncross sat as still as a gravestone through every word, never looking at Feya.

Morna crossed her arms. "Alasdair, surely ye can see Feya is in a hard predicament."

He lifted his chin as if waking from a dream. "Aren't we all?"

Morna sighed. "Ye've both been on the road too long and it's gettin' colder. Why don't ye stay here tonight?" She leaned into Cairncross's line of sight. "The rooms are nicer than they used to be when ye were here."

"There's no time." He rubbed his hand over his face. "I can't believe I've left the horses. What time is it?"

Morna ignored his question. "Angus took yer horses to the stable. I heard him talkin' when I took Rowan to the kitchen. There's a man who's a farrier, but he's up past the cairn visitin' his sick mother. He'll be back in the mornin'."

"And why didn't someone just say that in the first place?"

"Ye know how it is here."

Cairncross laughed, a hollow sound. "All too well." He moved to stand. "We'll sleep in the barn."

"Give her to me." Morna put her hand on his arm. "She looks like she could use some takin' care of."

He snorted. "Absolutely not."

"If yer takin' her to Stirling, those buggers will put her away fer the next fifteen years at least. Yer not a cruel man, Alasdair, despite what you've tried to portray to her."

He jerked his arm away. "You've no right to say what kind of man I am. And I'm quite sure, Morna, that the past years you've not thought of me more than as a reference to your own sin." The Scottish accent wove through his words. Red flared on his neck around the collar of his uniform. "I know how to do my job. And I always do it well. I fully intend to deliver this prisoner and see that she gets what she deserves."

Morna stood and walked around the table. "Is that right?"

He stood, dragging Feya up, and faced Morna. "That's—"

Morna grabbed the keys hanging from his belt.

Cairncross stepped back, seemingly burned by her touch. At the same time Morna reached for his wrist and plunged the key into the handcuff.

He gripped Morna's arm. "Don't even think about it."

She locked eyes with him. The lock clicked. The handcuff fell from his wrist.

Shock registered on his face. He clenched the back of Feya's neck.

"That hurts!" Feya stumbled back, tipping over the bench, and kicked him in the shin. He jumped back and narrowed his eyes as if he was going to kill her. And would take pleasure in doing it.

Paralysis seized her body. She should run, she knew that. But the dizziness . . . it came again like pounding rain upon her head—rivulets and waves washing over her. And the noise from the room—like grinding rocks upon her soul. As if every word, every phrase was a stoning—accusations more and more. Tremors ripped through her hands, and then her arms. Falling. Sinking. Disappearing . . .

Morna grabbed her shoulder.

Cairncross's cold, blue stare held her still. It terrified her, that look. He'd never appeared that ruthless before. She swayed, her spirit wanting to flee, but her body staying rooted to the floor.

"Give her to me, son."

"Are you mad, woman?"

"Sometimes." Morna locked the handcuff around her own wrist.

Cairncross's face bled red. He took a measured breath, looked down, and then smiled. "I will go against my better judgment and let this thief stay upstairs tonight. But, Morna, if you try to help her escape, know this: I will take you to Stirling prison along with her. Where you both belong."

The keys rattled as he snatched them out of her hand. He strode away and pulled open the door. The cold night air whooshed into the tavern and stirred the fire. The flames leapt higher, like raised arms making an offering.

Cairncross slipped out, and when he was gone, it was as if he had never been. The conversation went on. The fire still crackled.

Just like that, Feya was free.

Chapter Twelve

Morna guided the bedroom door back to the doorframe with the utmost care, as if she didn't want to make a sound. Which was strange, considering the tavern was downstairs, and the men and women there were as loud as pirates, eating and drinking as if this night would be their last.

Feya didn't move, a voyeur to something strange. Deep emotion passed over the woman's face—the crinkle of the skin about her eyes, the corner of her lips turning down. She swallowed like something was wrong with her throat.

The door met the frame, but Morna didn't release the handle.

"Are ye all right?" Feya put her hand on the woman's shoulder. The bone there was sharp, her arm too thin.

"Aye, lass." Morna looked up, her blue eyes brimming with things unspoken. "'Twas only that I was hopin' fer more the first time I saw him. I suppose some things just can't be." She held out her free hand toward the bed. "Would ye like to sit?"

"Aye. That would be good. And thank ye fer what ye did just now."

"Yer welcome." The words came like the scent of something costly—a fragrance deep and rare. The moment lingered and Feya breathed in it. Morna had given and not asked for anything in return.

It was odd and frightful, all the same.

Surely she wanted something, didn't she?

Feya tried not to look at her. She didn't know what to say. Was conversation called for?

They both just sat there, on the mattress that was far too thin. Feya wanted to ask Morna so many questions. And yet, that was not her way. People who pried were little better than the highwaymen who hid along the roads. She wouldn't take what another didn't offer.

Silence shrank and expanded like the kneading of dough. Morna pressed her lips together. Feya looked away, as the woman appeared on the verge of weeping. An *A* was carved in the floorboard beside them. The sight of it was a hot, sharp jolt. The past had an awfully loud whisper. Even if it wasn't yours.

Morna opened the bedside dresser. The green paint was chipped. Faded eternity knots decorated the drawers. She rummaged, casting aside papers, an old tattered book, and a long goose feather with a broken nib. "I think I have just the thing to get us out of these handcuffs."

"Get us out?"

"Unless ye prefer to stay in."

"Of course not, but—"

"I told ye earlier that ye had a look of trust about ye. Unless I'm mistaken, ye'll not jeopardize me relationship with me son by runnin' away."

"I . . . no." Feya didn't know why she agreed. She owed Cairncross no loyalty, especially since he was taking her to her doom. And this woman . . . Even though she was kind, she'd only just met her.

"I was thinkin' ye might like to wash." Morna smiled through loose strands of red hair. "If I were in yer situation, I know I'd covet such a thing."

"Please." The word dropped like summer sweetness. Washing would ease her muscles and make her feel half human at least.

Morna nodded, shoved her hand deeper into the drawer, and blew the hair from her face. "Here it is." She withdrew a long silver hairpin. "I did many things in me youth, such as yerself. Some more respectable than others." Her smile was full of mischief as she plunged the pin into the handcuff lock, wiggled it back and forth, and then made a satisfied sound. The lock clicked.

"Still got the magic!" She unhinged both cuffs and threw them onto the bed.

"Ye did it." Feya rubbed her wrist. "And so easily, I might add."

Morna tossed the pin back into the drawer. "Yer not the only girl who found herself at the mercy of an Englishman." She went to the fireplace, removed a teapot, and poured the water into a bowl on a washstand. "Ye can wash here." There was an old screen. She pulled it across to hide the bowl from view.

Feya crossed the room. "I can't remember how long it's . . ." She couldn't finish the words. The days were a mess of rubbish all jumbled together. She shoved her clothes from her body. And it felt good to be rid of them. They'd been in the dirt in the tenements, the dirt of what she'd almost done at Deacon Brodie's, and then the disaster in the palace kitchen.

She plunged a rag into the warm water and scrubbed her face. It felt like a sigh just before sleeping, that soft rag. She laid it against her eyes and let the warmth seep deep. Rivers ran down her face, her neck, her body. She shivered in the drafty room. But she didn't care.

She was alive.

Next, she ran her fingers through her hair. The tangles wouldn't break free, so she ripped them, clump after clump, digging her nails into her scalp and then pulling. The ruined hair skimmed against her pale, naked legs like the touch of a spider. The red became brighter as more of it nestled around her toes. She saw everything she hated in the ravaged strands. Da. Poverty. Hunger. Want.

And the Englishman. Especially him.

He had done this to her.

Feya ripped more until she could comb her fingers through without a hitch. Even then, she still pulled, wanting to free herself somehow. As if removing her hair might cleanse her deep inside.

She plunged her head into the water—deeper and deeper—until her scalp and the tips of her ears tingled. She soaped her hair until the foam was heavy.

When she lifted her head, the firelight caught the threads of water dripping down from the strands. Colors ran along the drops, just flashes, and then they were gone. In the bowl, leaves and sand floated in dingy brown.

"Allow me." Morna reached around the screen and took the bowl away. She flipped open the window and pitched the dirty water. The sound of it falling upon the ground was amplified by the cold.

The wind whipped into the room. Feya crossed her arms against it. "I don't know why yer so kind to me . . . With me being yer son's . . ."

"Oh, aye. Yer his captive." Morna shut the window, poured fresh, hot water into the bowl, and replaced it. "Alasdair always did have more degrees than a thermometer."

"He's a multifaceted personality, yer sayin'?" Feya rinsed her hair and wrung out the water. She didn't want to know about how he used to be. She didn't want to know anything about him at all.

"One time he saddled a cow and rode it all the way to Bathgate. He wasn't much older than Rowan. While he was there he took the money he'd been savin' fer a year and bought me special string fer embroidering. Then, as the sun was settin' over the cairn, he came back riding that same cow, a smile on his face like he'd conquered all of Scotland."

Laughter floated up from downstairs, and it seemed out of place. A sound from a different time. Feya plunged the rag into the water again and brought it to her neck and shoulders.

"I put thistles on a shirt fer him. He was angry when he saw it, because he'd wanted me to embroider my dress." The hinge over the fireplace moaned as Morna pushed the kettle deeper into the heat. "Alasdair was as givin' as the day was long. Despite what ye saw downstairs, I imagine that hasn't changed. He was a complicated boy, but one who could love as deep I've never seen." Her voice broke off, but then she found it again. "Rowan's different . . . They all have their gifts, ye ken? Having Rowan was a mercy from God. He makes me smile when I don't feel like goin' on."

The subject felt too sacred to speak of. Feya stared at the sloshing water in the bowl. The thick wooden beams above were reflected there, as well as soot from years of fires. Years of happenings in this room.

"Alasdair was stolen from me."

Feya's hand stilled on her chest. Snakes of water ran down her waist from the rag. "But, downstairs—"

"When he was eight years old."

Feya peeked around the screen. Morna stared at the wall like a phantom floated there. "The man who planted him in my belly took him in the middle of the night."

"Cairncross . . ." Feya swallowed. "He said that ye sold him."

"I imagine that's what his father told him. He left me with child then came waltzin' back on that night eight years later like he belonged . . . Gone and married some mouse of an Englishwoman who had money, but she couldn't have his child."

"Did ye . . . love him?" She didn't know why she asked and heat flooded her cheeks as soon as she did. It was a stupid question, considering what the man had done. It brought back her conversation with Robert Louis Stevenson about Maggie. Lies and loving. Taking and giving. It always left a woman with the burden in the end.

"Aye." Morna was looking into another time; her gaze was thick with it. "I met him in Perth when I was about yer age. Innocent as a lamb back then, I was. And when Edan smiled at me fer the first time, I felt like I died."

It was a strange name, and knowing the name of Cairncross's father made her feel hot and cold at the same time. The pieces of his life were coming too fast. And she'd never asked to know. It would complicate things.

"I spent a summer with him. There was a boat . . . Every day he'd row me down the river to a cove covered with heather. I was naive. We'd lie together and listen to the sound of the water . . . He made me a mother there. And I thought he was makin' me his own."

Somehow the story embarrassed Feya worse than when she'd been in Deacon Brodie's. Worse than when she'd almost given her body to a man. There was longing in Morna's voice. And that, above all things, Feya did not understand. Nothing came from a man lying with a woman. Nothing but pain.

"Alasdair looks a great deal like Edan. When he came through the door tonight, I thought fer a moment that it was him. But, he has me eyes. And when I saw them, it was like a knife ripped my body, deeper than the day he was born." She placed her hand on her stomach as if she could still feel the pain.

"Did Edan know about . . ." She almost said Alasdair, but she'd never do that. Names were an intimate thing—magical, the old Gypsies said. "The baby."

"That's why he left. On that day a part of me died. But somethin' else came too. I grew up."

Feya took the towel that Morna offered and moved to stand in front of the fire. "Havin' a baby makes ye grow up, does it? I can say I don't want one, then. I've already done enough growin' up because of Da drinking our lives away."

Morna drew her red eyebrows together and looked into the fire. "Pain has a way of bringin' responsibility. Some growin' up is good, but some comes too fast and too raw." She took a heavy breath. "The good Lord makes it all even out in the end."

Feya widened her eyes as heat flashed in her body. "Yer happy with the way God sorted yer life out, are ye? Ye think having yer son stolen from ye was part of His plan?"

"People always think that, don't they? When something bad happens, they think it's the doin' of the Lord—some punishment. Or that it must be His will. But this is a fallen world. Not everythin' that happens is His doin'. The choices of men and angels matter, Feya. There's always more goin' on than we can see."

Feya's mouth gaped. Who was this woman? And which side of crazy had she gotten off on? "What are ye talkin' about? Spooks and whispers in the dark?"

Morna looked older than what she must have been. She locked eyes with Feya as if searching her soul. She lowered her voice. "Somethin' like that. Just remember: fer those who love Him, God works everythin' into good. Sometimes that just takes time."

The room suddenly changed. It seemed as if the walls were listening. As if some presence were there, focusing on the conversation. Feya turned and looked, hugging the towel tighter. Nothing was there. No one. Now her mind was playing tricks on her for sure.

Morna went to the wardrobe and pushed aside clothes. "When

Edan came back, he wanted to pass me boy off as theirs, because he looked so English. He'd seen him in passin' on a northern campaign to subdue some Gypsies."

Feya swallowed. The Gypsy cleansing in the north was one of the reasons Da had decided to move to Edinburgh.

"He came here. We were arguin', and when I wasn't lookin' he put drugs in me drink." The lines around her eyes deepened. "Those herbs carried me down so low I almost died. Many times after I wished I had. He took Alasdair while he was sleepin'. I didnae even get to say good-bye."

Feya brought her hand to her cheek. What must he have felt when he woke? She closed her eyes and pushed the thought away. She couldn't think about him like that. Anything but that. She pictured the belladonna in his water. "Why didn't ye tell him the truth?"

"Truth like that needs a little time to buffer it into belief. And trust."

She was right. He wouldn't believe a word she said; Feya had seen it in his eyes. He hated the Scottish with a vengeance, even though the same blood ran through his veins. It was the blood of the mountains and the Highlands, the lochs, and the stories of old. But he denied it all. Because he lived with being denied by his own mother.

His entire life was a lie.

Feya went to the bed again and sat. Her head swam. There were too many words. Too many thoughts to sort.

Of all the Englishmen in the world, why Alasdair Cairncross?

"Right now he's angry." Morna nodded like she was trying to convince herself. "If he's anything like my poor departed husband, a little time alone in the barn will do him a world of good."

Feya snapped her head up. "How can ye be so calm?"

"Do ye think me calm? I've only learned to hide my emotions,

Feya. It's somethin' that might benefit ye."

Feya jerked like she'd been slapped. "I'm sorry. It's yer business. He's yer son. I just happen to be here." She glanced out the window. The sun was setting. Day two without the bairns. If she believed in God, she'd pray that He'd keep them safe. But that was like spit in the wind. The only thing she had was the moments and the fight within her. There was no room for weakness. Nothing this woman said was going to change that.

"I might have a dress that will fit ye."

"Why are ye helpin' me?" It didn't make sense. And what was worse, Feya knew that the only thing she'd have to do to escape was overpower this woman and run. She could use the teakettle and sock her over the head. But that would leave a nasty burn, and she didn't deserve that.

"I've been in tight spots more than once throughout me life, Feya. I often wished fer help and none came." She pulled out a pretty skirt—dark green plaid. There was also a white blouse with puffy sleeves and a bodice that tapered down in a *V*. "I'm only offerin' ye what I would have wanted."

"I can't take it from ye. It looks expensive." Feya gazed out the window again. Had Cairncross drunk from the water flask yet? She swallowed, feeling the poisoned water going down her own throat. Panic played on her body like a harp.

He deserved it.

He was the only thing standing in her way.

The bairns would die without her. Didn't that make it right?

Morna ran her hand over the skirt. "This will suit ye. It's just somethin' of mine from a long time ago."

"It looks dear. I'll not take it." Feya went to the window. The roof of the stable was fading into the blackness of the sky.

"You can't wear those clothes again. They're not fit fer the gutter."

The gutter. Yes. That's where she'd come from. That's where she belonged. Because she'd killed this woman's son for sure.

Feya pulled the towel together until it hurt her shoulders. Rowan was still downstairs. She'd killed Rowan's brother. Before they'd even gotten to speak to one another with the knowledge of it.

Feya breathed in, and the air felt like fire. "I don't deserve to live. I should have died in the rain that night at the palace."

Morna crossed the rug and took Feya in her arms. "Shhh. Don't say that."

"It's true!" Feya pushed away and reached for her filthy clothes.

"No." Morna snatched the clothes from Feya's grasp and pitched them into the fire. "Ye are worth more. Ye deserve better."

The fire hissed and spat and billowed smoke.

Morna pointed to the fire and the clothes burning there. "That is not who ye are." She stood straighter and the tone in her voice was like a warrior's. "Ye listen to me, girl. Ye are not what ye keep tellin' yerself. No matter what ye've done, ye still have a chance." Her face scrunched as if she was drawing painful memories to the front. "We all make mistakes, and don't I know that. But there's One who can forgive them all."

"What are ye sayin'?"

"I wonder if yer not running away from the One who made ye— the One True Living God."

"I don't know what yer talkin' about." Anger flared again, worse than the way the flames were consuming the old, ugly dress. "There were only two people who lay down, and I was the result of it." Feya put her hand in her hair and couldn't think. If she could get to Cairncross, maybe he hadn't drunk the water yet. "Give me the clothes."

Morna nodded and handed her the blouse.

Feya jerked it on. "I have to talk to yer son."

"Do ye now?"

Feya reached for the skirt.

Morna jerked it back. "Maybe ye ought to give him some time. He didn't seem so keen on talkin' to ye earlier."

"Obviously. He hates me."

"I wouldn't go that far. He's only doin' his job."

"Give me the clothes. Or I'm going stark-ravin' naked. Yer choice."

"All right. At least put these shoes on and brush yer hair. Let's put the cuffs back on and go together."

Feya shoved on the shoes and grabbed the brush. She ripped it through her hair, not caring that strands were snagging and breaking from not being dry.

"One more thing, then we'll go down." Morna led her to the vanity stand and pushed her down to sit. "Let me braid yer hair."

"There's no time." Feya knocked her hand away. She wanted to tell her the truth. It would have been the right thing to do. "I don't have time."

Morna anchored her hands to Feya's shoulders. "It won't take long. I promise."

Feya opened her mouth to say something. Anything. She saw her reflection in the mirror, and it looked strange—like the girl she'd been so long ago. And Morna behind her with her red hair might have looked like her own ma.

The older woman's hands stroked Feya's head—soothing—over and over again.

The old numbness came then, the same one that wrapped its arms around her when Da was drinking. She could feel it banking the fire within her, and she hated it. Wave after wave told her that there was nothing she could do anyway. Just shut her mouth. Survive. Stay secret and stay low. That which had always been would ever be. She'd never make a difference.

Wasn't this what she wanted?

Her only way out.

The death of one man against three children.

Feya closed her eyes and fell into the sound of the Scottish wind blowing against the window pane. The fingers running through her hair weren't Morna's. The mirror was right—they were Ma's.

Love. Feya felt love.

Finally, she was safe.

Chapter Thirteen

Alasdair set down his water flask and wrapped his fingers around the low stable door. The brittle planks would splinter if he asserted enough pressure. Just from the movement of this thumb, shards of wood rained upon the dirt floor.

Blatant neglect. Just as he remembered.

The years fled away, and he saw himself sitting by the ramshackle trough—clothes not fit for a dog's bed, hair unkempt. There, just to the right of the hole in the roof—that had been his favorite place to dream.

And when it rained, the water came in like a thin white rope. He'd reach out and catch the falling stream in the middle of his palm. He held his hand out now, under the jagged hole, almost seeing the white-blue drops bounce above his palm.

Haven nickered as if he understood the grief of remembering.

Alasdair closed his fist and brought it to his side. The hole in the roof was also the place where he'd first framed the stars. That was before he'd discovered their proper names in the astronomy books Father had given him that first Christmas.

Two days ago, at Holyrood Abbey, he'd framed the stars in the ruined windows. His face burned with the memory. The childish habit should have died.

Still, he squinted and peered through the hole—beyond the jagged thatch, through the crooked trees. "Andromeda." The irony made him sigh. "Constellation of the chained woman." A rush of heat surged up his back. Remorse clawed at him—for what he had said to Morna, although she deserved it. For how he'd beleaguered the thief.

The wind outside cut the corners of the stable, moaning and whispering—syllables from another time. The tree limbs above the thatch scratched on the molded hay. Moonlight flashed through the branches and into the hole, spilling down like a searching beam.

The light touched the tip of Alasdair's boot. He stepped back.
Life.

Alasdair's skin prickled. The word was an echo, something he felt more than heard. His breath caught in his throat and he stumbled. Dust from his boot flew up into the moonlight beam.

The wind blew again, ripping around the stable like a chariot from another world.

A presence was to the right—heavy and extravagant like the sun. Alasdair couldn't move. Didn't know if he was breathing.

Waiting.

Watching.

That's what the presence was doing.

Sweat broke out on his forehead. He ached with the desire to turn—to see. He tilted his head to the right, just barely.

Black and blue exploded in the corner of his vision—bursts and then lines that trembled and fainted upon the floor. His heartbeat throbbed in his neck. Shaking started deep. Worse than when he'd been in Egypt.

The air swung toward him and gasped. Alasdair turned and widened his eyes.

No one was there.

The colors had come from a shutter, blown by the wind, bouncing against the outside wall. His cursed brain ailment, that was all.

He sucked in his breath. The blue and black kept coming, wave after wave, in perfect timing with the will of the wind.

Haven made a sound like a laugh, his head bent low in his trough.

Alasdair wiped his hands over his face. Exhaustion had finally taken its toll. Now he was imagining specters. And the word that he had heard . . . He shook his head. The tumor, or whatever it was, was surely progressing.

The blue lines that came from the sound of the shutter were brighter now, collapsing into the air like waves.

Since they'd left Edinburgh, the colors were harder to ignore. Death, that cruel mistress, would come soon. That's what all the doctors said. What had just happened confirmed it.

He steeled himself, placing a well-practiced wall around his heart. He had to get the thief to Stirling tomorrow and then get himself back to the city.

He would have to tell Amberlyn that he was dying. If she chose to marry him anyway, he could offer her the protection that his position afforded. Father would have the influence of Sir Walter 's vote where it was needed. Loose ends would be tied. Everything, apart from him, would go on.

Alasdair laid his hand against Haven's back. He breathed again, smelling the wet birch and mold that was so familiar.

Beyond the stable window and across the grass, two shadows stretched in the upper window of the inn. Morna's room. It used to be his too. The shadows swayed against the bedroom wall as the fire flickered. One shadow stood over the other, lifting strands of hair with long, grotesquely thin fingers.

He was staring. And he hated himself for it. Regardless, he stepped closer to the stable window so he could see them better. A log in the fire must have shifted. The shadows angled upon the ceiling like something had frightened them. Just as quickly, they came back down and settled against the wall.

Had Alasdair not known her, he might have called the thief's profile somewhat pleasant. Her shadow cheek and chin did have a certain . . . slant. But it was no doubt only the fire that cast it so. Defiance and stubbornness—that's what graced her. In the daylight those traits hung about her neck like a chain.

Alasdair worked the muscles at his jaw. He admired the thief's inner strength. She'd given him quite a run.

He considered the other shadow—the hands that looked gentle, the way her head tilted just so as if listening. Or perhaps talking, saying whatever it was women said in instances like those.

Alasdair walked back to Haven and thread his fingers into the black mane shimmering with moonlight. The fact that the woman who had borne him was still alive meant nothing. She'd never wanted him. "All lies." His breath formed smoke in front of him.

The horse snorted and leaned into Alasdair's body, as he'd always done when he sensed something awry. The beast had an uncanny sense about Alasdair's moods. Even in the wasteland of Alexandria and the sands of Kassassin.

Alasdair's hand stilled on the pale, jagged line on Haven's flank. The long scar from the Bengal lancer he'd met in battle would never disappear.

His own wounds itched with the memory—the scars on his stomach where they'd tried to cut him open on his last day of torture, before the 4th Dragoon Guards burst in. The place in his throat where they'd ripped the rag out after it had been there too long.

Alasdair swallowed and looked at his water flask in the corner.

The thirst was always with him. No matter how much water he drank, he still felt the need for more. His throat ached with the longing and woke him often. It came from the severe dehydration in the desert, the doctors said. Once a man experienced that kind of want, his body never forgot.

Footsteps shuffled somewhere outside. A scruffy young man opened the back door of the inn, dumped a bucket of rubbish into a cart, and pushed it toward the woods. Muddy green waves floated in the air by the wheels.

Tiresome, that. Why couldn't the color be bright blue like the sea?

Alasdair rubbed his hand over his eyes and sighed.

Of course the memory of another cart would come now. And he'd seen the same muddy green back then, when he'd woken from the sleeping tonic Father had mercifully given him to get him away from Torphichen.

The stars were stretched out above him. His body swayed with the movement of the wheels. Father's black hair blended in with the night.

"Who are ye?" The words came from his mouth like ice.

"I'm your father, Alasdair."

Alasdair had stared at him. When he'd been at the market in Stirling, this man had watched him from the shadows. "Ma!"

"Here, now, my boy. You're going to come and live with me."

Panic, such as he'd never experienced, had gripped him and shook his body to the core. "I want Ma."

Alasdair closed his eyes against the shame that coursed through him now. He'd clawed at the edge of the cart that night and tried to escape. Father had held him down.

"That feeling will fade." Father's grip had tightened. "I'm going to take you to London."

"I don't want to go!" His dirty face left streaks on Father's snowy white sleeves.

"That doesn't matter. You're going to live a life of privilege, Alasdair. And learn what it is to bear the name of Cairncross."

Alasdair's eyes had shifted away from Father's and upward to the cold, fathomless moon.

"'You'll never want again.'" Alasdair repeated Father's last words from the night of his rescue.

Haven bit the edge of Alasdair's sleeve, tugging him out of his thoughts. The horse lifted his head and whinnied, pulling Alasdair's arm into the air and holding it there. It was an old game. But this time it didn't make him smile.

Alasdair searched the saddlebag and found an apple. The horse reached with his velvet lips, careful not to bite Alasdair's hand. Apple juice foamed at his mouth and dripped into the hay. The horse would be content now.

If only Alasdair's life was so simple.

Little things had never pleased him. There'd always been the next mountain to climb. The next war to win.

When did it end?

He used to like it in this stable. He'd dreamed here—ridiculous things. Sadly, most of that time had been spent contriving ways to make Morna smile. And then there were the things that all boys dreamed of: having a life full of adventure and conquest, a battle to fight.

Alasdair ran his hand though his hair. Mostly, the definition of adventure and conquest was murdering and blood. Other men's causes across the sea. It never seemed as glorious when the end of your bayonet was stuck through another man's heart. Especially when his eyes glazed over and you could see his soul fading away.

The tree limbs scraped against the roof again. Dried mud fell into the hole and clumped upon the ground. Hay from the thatch skittered down the moonlight shaft in spirals.

A storm was coming. And wasn't that just the Scotland way? When he needed fair weather, it snowed. When a gentle wind would suffice, a man had to gather his coat around him to keep from being stripped and ravaged like a slave.

The falling thatch drew his gaze again. The sound of it was like rats running. The color was yellow—a bright yellow that stood out against the dark, following the straw in twisted lines like ribbons.

And only he could see it.

Only him.

He swallowed, dryness creeping down his throat.

Feya grabbed Morna's wrist. "I can't do this."

"What, lass? What can't ye do?"

Feya stood. She looked at the handcuffs on the bed then headed for the door.

"Wait."

Feya flung the door open.

"Don't be stupid, girl! Me son . . ." Morna stood behind her on the landing.

Men and women were still eating and drinking without a care in the world. Little Rowan played with his dog in the corner.

Feya searched the crowd for Cairncross's black hair. She looked for a flash of bright gold buttons. Nothing. An ache surged in her chest. He hadn't come back in.

She ran down the stairs and almost tripped, the skirt too long.

A group of men lingered at the bottom of the stairs, drunk out of their senses. Their beefy arms were slung around each other. They sang an undecipherable tune.

"Excuse me!" Feya pushed a man's back, but he didn't move.

"Ease up, my love." A red-faced man slid his expression into a toothless smile. "How's 'bout ye come home with me tonight."

"I need to get through!"

The smoke in the room forced Feya to cough. The noises swirled like insects over rotting meat. She lifted her gaze to the ceiling and couldn't breathe. "I need . . ."

She heard a bark and looked down.

Rowan's dog pulled one of the man's coattails.

"What's the mutt doin'?"

"Shut up, Sam, he ain't doin' no harm."

"He's trying to eat me, he is."

"I told ye to shut yer mouth. And move away so the lassie can get by."

The crowd swayed and broke. The man who'd smiled at her punched two men at once. They fell into the corner.

A roar came from the crowd, and a cup whizzed past Feya's head and smashed against the wall. She pushed through the bodies. Someone picked up a chair.

Feya threw open the tavern door and sucked in a deep breath.

No one walked in the square. Only the wind moved.

She ran to the grass in the center of the buildings and turned in a circle. Nothing looked like a stable.

A cold breeze blew against her face and chilled her damp scalp. It stirred up the scent of the bog myrtle soap in her hair. Fog crept over the hill, inching closer, like a death angel, floating into Torphichen.

"Don't come." Feya felt weak and light, like the next blow of the wind would take her down. She ran past the kirk. Malevolent faces smiled from the gravestones—demons etched in stone. The words were illegible, their meaning long forgotten.

A horse whinnied to the right. Feya followed the sound.

"He's dead," she whispered. Surely she'd find him lying on the ground.

She stepped inside the stable and squinted in the dark.

He stood at the end of the paddock, his hand against the rail, his back turned.

Feya reached out her hand and froze. Cairncross was alive.

He was going to kill her.

The moonlight cast a glow about his body. His hair was wild in the wind.

Feya took a step back.

The wind whipped around her skirt, its hem fluttering like the beat of wings. She winced and stepped back again, setting her foot upon the hay.

Cairncross shifted his head and seemed to be listening.

Don't turn around.

His black hair blew in the wind, a stark contrast to his pale cheek.

Stay there.

He lifted his arm, the water flask in his hand.

Feya's throat clenched. If he'd already drunk, there was nothing she could do. She could still get away. Run. Forget.

Cairncross lifted the water flask.

"No!" She ran toward him and reached. Her hand hit the flask. It dropped, spraying water up the side of her face. She slammed into his body.

His hands closed around her arms. She grabbed the lapels of his uniform to keep from falling.

Their bodies swayed.

He righted her, and she stared at the gold buttons on his jacket, afraid to move.

Her breath, coming out as smoke, mingled with his.

"I would think, Gypsy, that you should be running the other way." His voice raked over her like the wind. Chills came in waves.

Her gaze went to the water flask on the ground. She could lie. She probably should. She felt the moment like the edge of a knife. If she told the truth, there'd be no way she would escape. He'd believe all the things he'd ever said about her—because they would be true.

The wool of his coat under her fingertips burned. His chest beneath her hands rose and fell.

Feya dared to lift her eyes, degree by degree. Condemnation whispered again on the wind. When she found her voice, it was hoarse. "Did ye drink any of the water?"

His grip on her arms tightened. "Why?" The word fell like a blade into a beast. Steel bled into the blue of his eyes.

"I . . ." The wind stole the word away. "I . . . poisoned it." Heat surged into her body, mixing with the chills. Her heart flipped over and trembled.

"Did you?" Cairncross showed no emotion. He didn't blink.

Feya nodded slowly.

An owl called somewhere nearby.

"How did you manage that?" His voice was too gentle. Too false.

She shouldn't tell him. Every word she said only dug her deeper into the grave. The wind stung her eyes. "Belladonna from the woods, before we left this morning."

"Clever Gypsy." He let go of her arms, turned away, then stared at the moon. The moments were counted off by the wind. "Pity you weren't five minutes earlier."

Feya spread her fingers in the open air. She was too late.

"Why tell me?" His voice was low.

"Because I didn't mean to do it." The words came out as an accusation. "I thought it was the only way to get back to me brothers and sister." She looked out the window and up at the bedroom that must be Morna's. "I'm everything ye said." Feya nodded, accepting the fact. She was a thief. And now a murderer. A Gypsy gutter rat.

Cairncross turned his head to the left. His cheek gleamed white in the moonlight. The beginnings of a beard bristled along his jaw. Oddly, the hair had red through it, given from his mother. The realization twisted inside her. "And now I've killed ye when ye've only just seen yer mother again, and little Rowan." Feya stumbled and collapsed in the hay.

The horses made contented sounds as they chewed.

Contentment was something she would never know. She'd stolen a life away.

He walked to her and stood at her feet, his boots still an impossible shine. "How long do you think I have?"

"An hour, maybe." She put her arms around herself. "I'm sorry. I wish I knew some way to help ye."

His black eyelashes fell as he watched her. "And would you?"

"Of course I would. I didn't want to kill ye, not really. It was a moment of desperation." She flung out her hand. "Ye kept me tied to that horse. Said nothing but how I was from the gutter. I can't help it that I have a temper." She scooped stalks of dry hay into her hands and squeezed.

Cairncross bent down so he was close to her. "Why did you really break into the palace?"

His nearness, still, was like a blast of heat. Feya scooted back in the hay until her back met the wall. Somehow, she'd felt safer when she'd been bound by his ropes. "Were ye not listenin'? Their names are Hamish, Gillis, and Brenna. I'm the only person they have. If ye take me to Stirling, they'll die."

"You could have chosen something easier. You couldn't possibly have believed that you could break into the palace and not be caught."

"I made the last potatoes we had, and I didn't eat any. The bairns needed them. There was nothing else. Da always finds where I hide the money. He usually drinks it away the same night." She thought about not telling him the worst of it. She'd left the information out when she'd told Morna at the table. But, he'd be dead soon, so it didn't matter. "I went to Deacon Brodie's tavern to try to sell meself." She closed her eyes. "But I couldn't do it, because I'm too weak."

"Is that so?" His voice was quiet.

"After that I tried to steal some bread so the bairns would have breakfast." She ran her hands over her damp hair. "But I couldn't do that either. And then I saw the advertisement for Queen Mary's box and I thought—I don't know what I thought. It seems stupid now."

"How old are you?"

Feya lowered her hands. "What a strange question when yer bound fer the grave."

"Humor me."

She drew her eyebrows together. "Three and twenty."

The wind blew, casting shadows and moonlight across his face. "You could have married by now. That would have solved everything."

Feya's mouth fell open. "And have some man beat me? Or do worse than Da?"

"Marriage would have been an option." He gave her a sideways glance. "All men aren't devils."

"Bah." She sat straighter. "So speaks a man who bound me and wouldn't even allow me basic necessities."

"That was, perhaps, overkill." He nodded. "I apologize."

She leaned forward so she could see his eyes. "Apologize? Tryin' to get things off yer chest before ye die?"

"Confession is good for the soul, they say."

His blue eyes unnerved her. The mint on his breath was worse. "Do ye want to go to talk to yer mother now? Rowan?"

He didn't answer, but only stared at her—her clothing, her hair, her eyes.

"Can I do anything fer ye, to make ye more comfortable?"

"Yes." His expression fell, and it tore through her heart. He really would have made some woman a nice husband if it wasn't for all his arrogant ways. And the fact that he was half English. "Come with me." He stood and walked out of the stable.

Feya crossed the meadow with him, walking a few steps behind. How many more steps until he keeled over? His gait seemed straight, but at the top of the hill he stopped. He took a shaky breath. "Let's go to the church."

"All right." He probably wanted to pray. A good idea, under the circumstances. "Should we find a priest?"

"No." Cairncross swallowed and seemed concerned with the way the wind moved the grass on the hill. "I saw him in the inn and I knew him as a boy. He'd do about as much good as spit in the wind."

"Oh." Feya wadded the sides of her skirt in her hands. "But I can't help ye. God and me aren't exactly on speakin' terms."

"Aren't you?" He made a *tsk*ing sound. "That's unfortunate." He crossed his arms like he was cold. The poison must be working on his extremities.

Feya frowned and crossed her arms, too, mimicking his gesture.

"We'll do the best we can." He drew his lips into a thin line and looked up at the moon. He shook his head, as if in pain. "Come on."

They walked around the graveyard wall and then entered. Feya studied Cairncross's profile. Would they bury him here?

He walked to the kirk door and opened it. The black interior gaped like a mouth. Feya peeked around his shoulder to the shadows of archways. "Where would ye like to pray? The sanctuary?"

"No. If you don't mind, I'd like to go where I spent some fond moments as a child."

Feya nodded. That seemed reasonable. And as she was the one who'd killed him, it was only right that she follow him there.

He walked into a room with ropes hanging from the ceiling. Bells must be above. Beyond, the stairs twisted and turned. Almost to the top, the stairs split off to the right. "Just here." His eyes looked hollow. There were shadows underneath.

She'd cut down a great man—a warrior. It was a crying shame.

He lifted a heavy beam that served as a lock for the door. "I'm sorry for the way I treated you." He closed his eyes and caught himself against the wall.

His words pierced her like a knife. She'd always been too impulsive and as crazy as the old tinkers. Da had always said so, and every one else in between.

And now, here, didn't she see the effects of all her faults?

"Would you allow me to show you something before I die?" He gestured to the inside of the room. "Just a few moments, and then you can go."

Inside was a table and chair, a rug of some sort. It looked to be a place where a monk might be alone with his thoughts and offer up prayers to the brass heaven above.

Feya stepped inside.

Something slid onto the floor and landed at her feet.

Cairncross's jacket.

The door slammed. The beam scraped the wood on the other side as it lowered into place.

Feya ran to the door and hit it with her palm. "What are ye doin'?"

No sound came from the other side.

Chapter Fourteen

There was a reason the Romans had thought of *paterfamilias*—the right of the man to have absolute rule over his wife and daughters.

Women like Feya Broon forced men to such notions.

Alasdair hurried down the church stairs, grabbed the lantern and lit it, then shoved open the church doors. The cold wind hit him full force, making him gasp. He flipped his collar high around his neck, put his head down, and walked.

He could name every departed soul in the old church cemetery: William Arthur, Jennet Hutton Arthur, Marion Allan Walker. The letters were faded now, but oh, how he knew them. He knew the etchings by what they said and by the colors that the letter combinations made in his mind.

The dates were like old cloaks—1775, 1815, and on and on. He knew them backward, forward, added, subtracted, and multiplied. Just like the gravestones in Holyrood Abbey.

Alasdair wiped his hand across his face and passed the carved men on the most cryptic gravestone. The toothy face at the top still smiled like a demon emerging from the stone. He used to sit in front of the tombstone for hours as a child, partly because he was terrified, partly because he thought it had a secret to tell.

But Torphichen didn't hold any secrets. Beyond these woods there was only freedom. Not the shadows and horrors he'd imagined as a child. No bogeymen hid behind the trees.

Alasdair didn't bother with the gate; he jumped over the low stone wall, crossed the sad excuse for a road, and headed for the woods.

The old shortcut was still there, howbeit grown over. The moonlight bled pale white over the fallen trees and undergrowth, washing away the color of the world. Once again, the wind brought turmoil to his senses, painting strips of color through the air.

Alasdair forced his eyes back to the path before him. It was an old habit—not looking at the veils in the wind. Father had taught him that. If people didn't see him look at things they couldn't see, they wouldn't ask questions. They wouldn't smile like they understood or call the warden of the insane asylum.

He knew how his eyes appeared when he focused on the moving colors. No matter the light in the room, his pupils expanded, as if opening to another world.

The wind gusted, and red taunted him out of the corner of his right eye. He shouldn't raise his gaze. He knew that. He'd only get caught in the dance and lose precious time.

Thin blue strings beckoned like fingers, sliding out of his periphery and onto the path. Alasdair narrowed his eyes and shoved his hands into his pockets. But then—*then*—yellow flashed, drawing his gaze up by force. As if something took hold of his chin and pulled his head to the side.

His back stiffened in shock. There—spinning color wrapped around countless trees, spiraling down. And there—puffs of green, as far as he could see. A symphony of wind and swiping brushstrokes of red, orange, and purple, as if the hand of God was real and tangible, creating every second as he walked.

Alasdair's heart caught in his throat. He'd forgotten what it was like to really see. To really look. To let his guard fall. It was beautiful. Utterly and completely beautiful.

The colors spun everywhere, completely surrounding him—to every height, and then to the depth of all he could see. The field was illuminated. He lifted his hand into the wind and a red veil of light slid over his fingers. A smile formed at the corner of his lips, and that was a very odd feeling. Hadn't he enjoyed this once? Getting lost in the colors? Hadn't it made him feel like he was in a holy place? Hadn't he felt close to God? He used to pray like this—with his eyes and his heart wide open . . .

He made a fist and pulled his hand to his side. Why were these thoughts more present of late? Disgust raked through his body and lodged in the pit of his stomach. Thoughts like those had turned him into a religious zealot. Pity that he'd just been the victim of sensationalism—shocking stories from across the sea.

Thankfully, that life was gone. He'd made his choice by joining the Guard, and now only duty remained. But sometimes—only when he was extremely bored, mind—occasionally he still felt a pang when he thought of those men laboring on the islands, fighting for the people lost in darkness. Sometimes he thought of John Paton and his fascinating account of the angels . . .

Alasdair groaned in frustration and clenched his jaw. He had to kill these thoughts. For however long his moments remaining were, he'd spend them in an exemplary fashion—bringing honor to the queen and honor to the father who'd thought enough of him to rescue him from the backwoods of Scotland and a life of meaningless obscurity.

He forced his eyes away from the colored veils in the fields and looked down at the path in front of his feet. One step and then another, that was all. But still he saw the colors in his periphery. *Look at us,* they seemed to whisper. *Dance with us. Linger here.* A pang shot through his heart—something akin to longing. But that feeling he was used to. He only had to push it down.

Two more seconds and he would have already been a dead man. He let the thought sink in. "Had the thief not knocked away the water . . ." He shivered and thought of how cold she must be in the tower, even with his jacket. But thoughts like that . . . Alasdair hardened his face and pulled his collar higher. Tomorrow night at this time, he'd be free of the thief. She'd be in Stirling, and his job would be done.

Tonight was more proof that Father knew what he was talking about. Never in his life had another person given him so much trouble. And what kind of name was Feya anyway? Sounded like the fae—fairy. Could he never escape the superstitious rot of Scotland?

He'd survived being tortured in Egypt only to be brought low by a Gypsy and some belladonna. What had Morna been thinking, giving her clothes? She didn't even look like a thief anymore. On top of that insult, her hair had been washed and braided. And now . . . Well, now . . . she didn't quite look like the gutter scum he'd been dragging through Scotland for the past two days. It wasn't that she was pretty—no, she could never be beautiful as Amberlyn was beautiful. She only looked different. And he didn't appreciate the transformation. Transformations were complicated. Like the Scottish kelpies of old, luring men into the water to drown them.

There would have been no problem marching her into Stirling this morning, but now the constable would want the entire story. If Fe—the thief—did that annoying thing with her voice that masked her accent, there would be even more problems.

But he had the warrant. The law would hold.

Order would prevail. Just like the dome of night above him, the constellations never changed. Law was law. Black and white.

The path ahead curved. Alasdair stepped out into a small field hidden by a square of poplars. He'd purposely let Morna take the thief as a test. And as the thief came running into the stable without handcuffs, his hypothesis had been answered.

The woman who had borne him was no better than the thief.

Father had told him stories throughout the years—of what Morna had been capable of. Naively, he'd never believed them. After this plague of an excursion was over, he'd never doubt again.

In the field, the wind blew across the long, untended grass and made it sway. Moonlight hit the tips of the weeds, making them resemble the white crests of waves. Just like so much in Torphichen, twenty years had passed, and the field hadn't changed.

The old ache came back, for this was where it had been born. Sailing. Exploration. The sea.

Alasdair gritted his teeth. "I don't need the sea. Salt water is inconvenient. Makes everything smell like fish." He reached for the moonlit grass and ripped it as he walked.

Maybe by this time next year he'd have a child. If he lived that long. Alasdair tried to imagine a baby with Amberlyn's blonde hair and clear blue eyes. Rowan's face inserted itself instead. No doubt Morna would cast the lad away at the first opportunity. Alasdair knew the kind of scum that roamed these hills. If some passing tinker took a liking to him, he'd no doubt be stolen away.

But it wasn't his problem.

Just like the thief wouldn't be after tomorrow.

What did her history matter—all that rot about a Gypsy father and a dead mother and three bairns? She'd probably lied about it all. Her sort always did.

As soon as the thought came, he knew it wasn't authentic. The way she'd bent over the table as she'd told Morna . . . He'd be stupid not to recognize there'd been truth in her dark-brown eyes.

Alasdair searched the waves of shadow grass. Once he'd imagined murders and thieves hiding amongst the stalks. In the northwest corner was Cairnpapple Hill. On the road he'd tried to scare the thief with stories of it. She had no way of suspecting that the tales used to terrify him as well.

He stepped between the large stones hidden in the grass. The shadow of the ancient cairn rose up out of the darkness. A cold arc of wind bent low and rushed against his side, ruffling his collar and his hair. The ancient stairs were still there—cracked and overgrown with moss. So, the villagers still wouldn't tend them. Superstitious idiots. Still believing the cairn was a gateway between two worlds.

The wind dropped. The grass bowed and then stilled.

A branch snapped in the woods behind him. Alasdair turned. Nothing but forest shadows. Only animals wandered in these woods.

Alasdair bent and lifted the cracked edge of the step out of the ground.

The toy boat. Just where he'd left it. Twenty years of rain had seeped in and rotted the wood. He brushed away the dirt and laid the object in his palm.

If Father had never come, he'd still be here, barely educated enough to calculate the weight of grain. He'd probably have married one of the farmer's daughters, and he would know nothing of the world.

He climbed to the top of the cairn. The remnants of lives long ago rested below him in the ground. Bodies long turned to dust. Primitive people. Much like the people of Torphichen. Not a lot had changed in a few thousand years. They ate. They drank. They fought. They spewed out offspring as ignorant as they, and then they died.

His life would be different. What little of it he might have left to live.

Alasdair ran his thumb around the stone in the middle of the cairn. He'd always been afraid of what waited on the other side. But not now. Some deep places had ways of calling even when you were thousands of kilometers away across the sea.

The wind tugged at his shirt and a cry came over the trees—shrill, like an animal dying. The hair stood up on the back of his neck, but he didn't look back. The earth under his fingers was cold.

Alasdair lifted the stone. The air around him fled into the hole, hissing and moaning. He flipped over the stone and threw it onto the ground, gripped the handle of the lantern and plunged it into the hole.

Old mortar and earth. The curving of the mound. That's what was inside. Ghosts in the dark that were never there.

Alasdair waited. Nothing came to claim him. Nothing at all. He looked up, past the field and into the thin place of the forest. The lights of Torphichen winked through the shivering trees.

The real demons were there. But the time for that was done as well.

He threw in the old toy boat, replaced the stone, and sealed it, brushing back the dirt around the edges so no one would know where he'd been.

This would be his last night in Torphichen. And his last night with the burden of Feya Broon. He'd lied to her to get her into the tower. There she'd stay until the morning came.

He walked down the cairn stairs for the very last time. He didn't have to look back. Childhood memories should stay buried, like the bones.

There was only one more thing to do before he got some sleep— he'd talk to the woman who called herself his mother.

He had questions. And Morna was going to answer them all.

Morna's door stood cracked open, as if she expected him.

She sat by the fire, embroidering. From what he could see, she meant to form thistles out of the green thread. That, too, never changed. He envisioned the thistle shirt back in his drawer at the palace. He'd throw it in the rubbish when he returned.

He knocked. He didn't know why. Why should he keep pretenses with this woman? Why, when she didn't even have the decency to say good-bye?

"Come in, Alasdair."

He pushed open the door the rest of the way. "You didn't look up. How did you know it was me?"

Morna pulled the needle through the fabric. "A mother feels her child without lookin'." She glanced at Rowan sleeping on a pallet in the corner. "Each one is special and feels a different way—like a soft, fine shirt and the way it fits around ye."

"I see." Alasdair rolled his eyes and ran his finger along the fireplace mantel. Surprisingly, it was clean. Spotless, in fact. "I only came to ask you why you took the thief's handcuffs off." He leaned on the long, rugged wood. "She's locked in the church, by the way. Your plans to help her escape have failed."

Morna dipped her needle back into the cotton, the green thread a stark contrast to the white. "I didn't try to help Feya escape. I only wanted to help her get back some of the dignity that was taken from her."

Alasdair looked down on Morna's red hair that he used to curl his fingers in as he slept. "That's an awful lot of compassion for a stranger. Especially when you didn't give me a fraction of that twenty years ago."

The needle stopped mid-air. "I've thought fer many years how to answer ye if ye ever asked me that question."

"I didn't ask you a question."

"Yes ye did, son. It's been in yer eyes since ye walked through the door of the inn."

He considered denying it. "The truth would be nice, although I doubt I'd believe you."

Morna placed her embroidery on the side table. Alasdair tried not to look at the left-hand corner where he'd carved an *A* as a child. He failed. There it was—only now a frame of vines was painted around it, and words in gold.

One True Living God
Be my eyes where I cannot be
Wrap your love 'round my stolen child
Set the captive free
O, Life, answer me

"He's answered, praised be His name." Morna raked her eyes over Alasdair's face like she could see into his soul. "And I reckon He has a lot more to say."

Words lingered on the tip of Alasdair's tongue, but he couldn't find them. The prayer bothered him. And the letters that formed it on the wall—they had no other color beyond the gold paint. No unearthly glow like usual. Unlike every other letter he'd ever seen— books, street signs, gravestones. Never in one instance had letters just been plain.

The fire crackled, and he noticed the smell—alder wood, from down by the stream.

Images washed over him like the firelight—Morna singing hymns when she'd put him to bed as a child. Stories—the miracles of Jesus,

Daniel in the lion's den, Queen Esther. How could he have forgotten? It had taken place in this very room.

Alasdair searched the small space, half expecting to see some earlier version of himself. His eyes fell on Rowan and the easy rise and fall of his chest.

That couldn't be where his faith had begun. Surely it was at Holy Trinity Church in London. And all those days spent with his aunt, Alice.

Morna had her hand under the mattress, searching for something. "Do ye remember a man who used to live in our village? A metal worker?" She stood and walked to him. "He was here, in this room, when you were born. He brought the midwife."

Alasdair twisted his mouth and tried to look bored. He'd perfected the expression over the years. "A circus show, was it? How many other men did you have here when I drew my first breath?" Guilt speared him instantly.

Morna ignored his comment and unwrapped one corner of the cloth. "There was lightnin' that night, even though there was no rain. The noise of it ripped through the valley like God on His chariot, bringin' in the end of the world."

Alasdair raised an eyebrow. Leave it to the Scots to be dramatic.

She unwrapped another corner and revealed a gold chain. "There was a presence in this room, just as real as you standin' here." Morna slid her gaze over his shoulder. "There, in the corner by the window." Her voice softened, as if someone was there now, eavesdropping. "Power was radiatin' off him something fierce. It was like he was curious, some kind of watcher. I knew in that moment that ye were destined fer great things."

The experience in the stable earlier resonated like a bell. Chills ran up his neck, despite the closeness of the fire. He turned to the empty corner.

"I haven't put anythin' in that corner since. It just didn't seem right." Morna seemed lost in her own thoughts. "Ye almost died during yer birth, and I almost died with ye."

The fact made him flinch.

"You were born with a veil over your face, Alasdair."

"A what?" He lowered his arm from the mantel.

"Some call it a caul. Few babies have it."

Alasdair grimaced. "What—"

"The woman who helped me with yer birth was a Gypsy. She said that those born with a veil could see between the worlds." Her voice lowered. "But only you can answer that."

He stumbled back like he'd been hit. "You would listen to Gypsies. I've heard enough." He turned toward the door.

"I want ye to have this, son." In Morna's hand lay a gold locket with deep, elaborate engraving.

Alasdair Cairncross
Born the 31ˢᵗ of October
At 12 of the clock at night
1857

Shock coursed through his body. Of all things he expected, this wasn't one of them. "What is it?"

"It's a locket."

"I can see that." He was afraid to ask what it contained.

"It's yer dried veil. The membrane that was over yer face that day."

He cursed. "Why would you keep it?"

"Because the Gypsy midwife said it would keep its owner from drownin'."

He looked away, disgust washing over him. Standing in Morna's room *was* like standing in a circus sideshow.

She could have sold the locket and come to London. She could have found him had she wanted to. "You should have sold the locket long ago. I imagine the melted-down gold would have sustained you for a while." Alasdair tilted his head as if he was observing a marching practice. He would see what she did with the comment.

Hurt reflected in the depths of her eyes. He had to give it to her, she was strong. The emotion was only visible for a moment. She pushed it away, the same way he'd seen soldiers push away their pain. The nuances were there—the way she tightened her grip on the chain of the locket, the slow way she straightened her back.

Morna was an expert at hiding. And it didn't matter what flashes he remembered of who she used to be—the hymns that she'd sung or the stories she'd told. This was who she was. Just as Father said.

Her hand moved toward him. "I've saved this fer ye in the hopes that one day I could—"

"I don't want it."

Morna's eyes closed as if he had hit her. "Please."

"Why?"

"Because it was always meant fer ye. And I never had the chance—"

"What?" He stepped forward. "To give it to me?"

"Yes." The word fell like a sigh.

"Should I feel sorry for you at this point?" Alasdair lowered his head so he could look into her eyes. "Is that what you want?"

"No." Morna placed her hand upon his arm.

He flinched but didn't pull back. Her touch was like a burn, but yet familiar. The weight of that hand made him feel small and vulnerable, worse than when he'd been stripped naked in the desert and paraded before Bedouin Arabs.

He hated this feeling—the feeling that he was out of control, that nothing he could do or say would make things go the way he wanted.

Tears pooled in her eyes. "I want to know that ye are well. I want ye to be well."

He regained some of his capacities and pulled his arm away. "No thanks to you, I am very well. As you can see, I have done well." A sick kind of heat spread into his chest. He wanted to be cruel, needed it.

He drew himself up to his full height. "The moment I left Torphichen was the best day of my life." His words were darkness. But he didn't care. He pressed in, like entering a hall of mirrors filled with smoke. This path would take him down, make him uglier than he wanted to be.

The curtains on the window lifted; a soft breeze ran over his face. He could choose to stop the words. He could soften them, because she was a woman, and she had borne him into the world.

The straight and narrow was less traveled for a reason.

"You ceased to be my mother twenty years ago. Your choices, not mine, have brought you to this moment."

Tears fell onto her freckled cheek, and with each one that fell, thorns bit into his soul.

"What did he tell ye about me?"

"What makes you think I'd reveal Father's secrets to you?"

"I know he lied about that night. It's not what ye think."

"We're done here." Alasdair strode toward the door.

"Ye've every right to be angry. I didn't protect ye that night, as I should."

"And you never came to find me, so that's that." He placed his hand on the doorframe. "Good-bye, Morna. Do better for poor Rowan than you did for me."

"Do ye know that he drugged me, that valiant father of yers?"

"I don't believe you."

"It's the truth. Ye can ask Angus downstairs, or anyone here. He wanted ye only because his mouse of a wife couldn't bear children. And it looks good in government to have a son."

His grip tightened. He glanced back at the carved *A*.

"Ask him, Alasdair. Pay attention to the look in his eyes. And I expect there's more he's lied about to ye, son." Morna walked to him and slipped the locket into his shirt pocket. "Take it. It's the only thing I ask of ye. If for no other reason than the fact that yer birth almost took me to the grave."

The locket was heavy in his pocket. His head swam with words he wished he hadn't heard. Air. He needed air. And the feel of Haven's mane beneath his fingers.

Alasdair stepped out onto the landing and had to hold onto the rail.

"She's not what ye think."

"Who?" He barely heard his voice over the noise from below. Morna moved into his line of vision on the balcony.

"Feya."

"Feya." He repeated the name with all the disgust that he felt.

"Ye'll be surprised in the end."

Alasdair felt nauseous—like he might spill every bit of the stew on the fools below him. Of course she'd choose something ridiculous like that for her last words. The woman sang hymns, painted prayers, and talked of superstitious rot as easily as one talked of the weather. And now she wanted him to believe that the thief was a heroine in disguise. A greater mix of contradictions he'd never before encountered.

But he'd make sure he'd never find himself in this position again.

Past was past. And a door, firmly closed and sealed, wasn't likely to open again.

Chapter Fifteen

The blacksmith had come back before the sun rose and fixed Haven's shoe. Now Alasdair rode hard. Sweat plastered his shirt to his skin and the wind chilled it, like a blade passing over his back. But the pain was good. Pain told him he was alive.

Orange colored the sky, lifting the thick, black sheet of heaven filled with stars. Alasdair knew that sky view well. At Holyrood, it meant he only had two more hours to go on his watch. Now the timing had more significance. In two hours he'd have the thief to Stirling. And be done with the madness that was Feya Broon.

Alasdair pushed Haven harder, shifting his weight to give him the command. The horse dug into the ground with his hooves, his body trembling with the need to burst through the trees and out into the field before them. Alasdair could hear nothing save the wind and the pounding of Haven's hooves. The sounds drowned out the misery and dulled it to an ache. Made him forget. And forgetting was good.

The opening in the forest widened. Leaves and dirt clods flew into the air. Branches whipped across Alasdair's calves, but then they were free, into the clear, open field.

The horse didn't wait for the request. The landscape blurred— grey, black, orange, and the soft tan of wheat. Alasdair's white shirt snapped against his chest and arms. There was only speed and the need to rise into the ether—become the sky or stars, something timeless. Somewhere where doubt didn't remain.

He leaned into Haven's body, becoming one. Closing his eyes, Alasdair erased the colors, real and imagined. Only the whip of Haven's mane against his cold cheek told him he hadn't died.

The noise of hooves.

The wind.

Dew in his hair and dampening his clothes.

It was easy, this place. Without expectation. Fears were weightless. He was weightless. Just one moment from falling.

It felt like trust.

Alasdair let the feeling linger. One second. Two. But that was all he could do.

He reined Haven in, hard, and immediately regretted it. The horse whinnied—high pitched—then danced in a circle.

Alasdair patted the side of Haven's sweat-soaked neck. "I'm sorry, old boy. I don't know what's gotten into me."

Haven rolled his eyes in answer and pinned his ears to his head. He was angry. And he wanted to run again.

"Perhaps later." Alasdair breathed in the crisp dawn air. "We have work to do." He turned his horse back to the village, cutting a row in the long grass.

The dampness of the morning had brought out the insufferable curls in Alasdair's hair. They fell over his forehead like a poet reborn, but there was nothing he could do. He should have cut it before now.

He moved Haven back into a trot and then regretted it. The locket in his shirt pocket thumped against his chest like the beating of a heart. He considered throwing it into the field, but then the sun rose, lifting over the trees like a solid curtain of light. The wind rose with the sun, whipping the grass around Alasdair's ankles and shoving his hair to the side.

Whispers in the breeze sounded almost like words—just like last night.

The back of Alasdair's neck pricked, as if he stood on a battlefield. He gave Haven the command to stop and scanned the field. Last night it had been dark and cold and given the illusion of waves. The cairn was far away now, out of view. Gripping the leather reins hard, he waited.

Something was coming.

To his right, sunlight filtered through the limbs and set the pine needles on fire. Green turned to soft, purest gold. But then the glow shifted into beams of light; they shot through the branches and reached for the grass.

He didn't know why, but as the light inched closer, he moved Haven back. Light exploded on the edge of the swaying grass—thousands of moving flames.

The whispering came. Alasdair strained to hear it, his flesh prickling. Warning went off in his mind, the same high alert before battle. He clenched the reins and slowly breathed, steeling himself.

Seconds fled in his mind. Moments stretched tight. The wind bent low in the trees, bringing a sound like voices.

Only the wind. The whispering was only the wind.

The corner of his lips turned up. Ridiculous. Alasdair relaxed his shoulders and settled into the slow, rhythmic shift of the saddle.

The sun took a breath and expanded—stretching its arms over the tips of the trees and the dismal grey buildings of Torphichen. Yellow ran into the cracks of the shingles, as if molten gold were being poured down.

"Beautiful." The word fell from his mouth, unbidden. Shock followed. How could anything in Torphichen be beautiful?

But it was. It truly was.

The sunlight touched Alasdair's forehead, then his cheeks,

warming them. The tips of his ears grew hot, and then his neck. The sun slid on, down his chest. Just before spreading into the sky, the light blazed its brightest on Alasdair's shirt pocket, directly over the region of his heart.

Feya squeezed the pillow in the kirk tower. Her heart raced and turned over, fluttering like a bird. Stabs came to her chest, as real as if someone plunged a dirk in her lungs, over and over again. She moved her shaking hands to wipe sweat from her forehead. It was a strange feeling, having your body rebel against you. This was worse than some odd sickness. Something was horribly wrong. She stared at the old stone walls of the small room and felt a chill rake over her. Once again she was lost in the dark and alone. Abandoned. Captured.

A voice, gravelly and slurred, wafted up the stairs.

"'Ae fond kiss and then we sever; Ae fareweel, and then for ever! Deep in heart-wrung tears I'll pledge thee . . . Warring sighs and groans I'll wage thee.'"

Feya sat up on the little bed, her body tense.

"'Who shall say that Fortune grieves him . . . While the star of hope she leaves him?'" The man hiccupped. The heavy bar scraped against the wood of the door.

Feya grabbed the candlestick on the side table. She moved to stand behind the door.

The heavy wood creaked on the old hinges. A shadow moved in the hall, fingers stretching toward the door.

One moment. Two.

His voice fell to a whisper. "'Me, nae cheerful twinkle lights me—'" The shadow stumbled and turned its head. "'Dark despair around benights me.'"

Feya squeezed the brass of the candlestick.

A hand wrapped around the edge of the entry. The sleeve of a robe came into view.

Feya stepped out.

The man was thin, like a stick wearing a bed sheet. He screamed, high pitched, and threw himself against the shelf. Books fell onto the floor. A glass tankard shattered. "A banshee! I knew my time was come!" He threw up his arms and sank to the floor.

"Just let me pass." Feya lifted the candelabra for effect.

He shielded his face. "I'm not ready to pass on!" His eyes rolled back into his head. He slumped the rest of the way to the floor.

Feya leaned over and narrowed her eyes. He was breathing. Good. She threw down the candlestick and stumbled toward the stairs.

Alasdair cursed when he saw her. Plain as day, there she was, running across the lawn right in the middle of Torphichen.

Apparently, Feya Broon was the lock that wouldn't stay bolted.

He spurred Haven on to a full run. He was going to enjoy this. Exceedingly.

She turned at the noise of the horse, almost tripping over her plaid skirt. The wench might have had the sense to stop. Instead, she hiked up her skirt and ran faster. As if she could outrun his horse.

Apparently Gypsies were eternally optimistic.

She was wearing his jacket, buttoned up. The tip of his mouth curved. How convenient. She'd made it easy for him, giving him something to hold onto.

He could feel the excitement of Haven beneath him. They were back on the charge. The horse snorted, and he spurred him on. The wind roared in his ears. He shifted in the saddle, anchored his left hand, and prepared to lean.

She spat curses at him, indiscernible in the wind.

Alasdair leaned to the right and reached for the back of his jacket. She screamed and flailed her arms when he made contact. Lifting her was no problem. The skirt that must have had twenty yards of fabric was. It wrapped around his leg and caught in the stirrup.

"I'll kill ye!" She swung her fist at his face.

Alasdair dodged and smiled. "Already tried that." He threw her across his lap like the primitive that she was.

"I'll do the job right this time." She kicked, but the angle was wrong. She met only air.

"Thank you, Gypsy, I haven't had this much entertainment in years." He adjusted his hold on her so her hands were pinned under her body. "Comfortable?"

She said something in Gaelic that sounded familiar. It was a word drunk men said at taverns before pounding each other's faces in. Fitting. He laughed.

"I'm glad ye find me situation funny." Her brown eyes were wide with rage.

"The fact that you keep thinking you can escape me is comical. Please, woman, save yourself the exertion. You'll need your strength when you're in prison." He commanded Haven to trot, just so it would be uncomfortable for her. "As I have said, I've had a lot of practice dealing with people like you. What makes you think you'll find a crack in my methods?"

She mumbled something and shoved, he assumed with all her might. Tendrils of her red hair came loose from her braid.

Alasdair spurred Haven into a canter. They circled wide on the village lawn. "There's a reason the British army controls the majority of the world. You might have considered that before you decided to go for a morning stroll."

"Yer right," she mumbled against the saddle. Her body went lax. "Don't know what I was thinking."

Alasdair relaxed his hold and inclined his head so he could look at her.

She turned her head and laid her cheek on his leg. Her brown eyes were as docile as a lamb. Alasdair raised an eyebrow. By Burns and Keats, had he finally tamed the fairy?

A smile spread on her pale face. She turned her head, quick, and bit his leg like a viper.

Alasdair jerked back, a mistake. The leather rein caught around his wrist, pulling Haven's head back.

The horse reared. Alasdair felt his weight shift dangerously. The Gypsy noticed. She leaned into him, pushing him the rest of the way.

The body of the horse slid away. The ground pounded into his stomach, and the wind flew out of his lungs in a rush. One moment later, the Gypsy tumbled onto his back, a double blow. The ground bowed and swayed, light flickering. Mud squished against his cheek.

He would not pass out. He'd fallen from a horse before. He would be . . . This would be . . . Alasdair's head dropped. He pulled up grass and dirt with his hand.

Cannot breathe.

The Gypsy sat up and scrambled to get away.

Air flooded his lungs, burning like fire as it entered. Alasdair lifted his head and looked for her.

She knelt not far away. Her breathing was quick and her face flushed.

Blood pounded in his ears. "Gypsy, you'd better run."

She had the audacity to flash her brown eyes at him and smile. "English, do your worst." Bunching the sides of her skirt in her hands, she stood and ran.

Like the devil, in fact.

Alasdair dug his boots into the ground and pursued. His muscles burned, his lungs seized from the exertion. He shouldn't have taunted her. He was severely disadvantaged from the fall.

They passed the church. The stable. Her skirts flared behind her as she veered onto the road that led out of Torphichen.

Alasdair pushed hard. He was gaining.

The Gypsy glanced back, saw him, then plunged into the woods, a blur of red hair amidst thick, green leaves. She dropped over a ridge and disappeared.

A crack sounded—multiple branches breaking. She screamed something in Gaelic. And then the sounds stifled, as if the words came from beneath a cloth.

Alasdair knew that sound. He skidded and threw himself behind a tree, shoving his back into the trunk.

No more words. No birds sang.

He made a fist and the leather of his glove creaked. In the unearthly stillness of the forest, the noise was too loud. He grimaced, his heart thumping in his chest, and listened again.

Nothing.

Slowly, he turned his head to the side to look past the tree.

The wind swooped, plowing through the underbrush, tearing off leaves and throwing them down. Branches shuddered and then stilled.

Alasdair scanned the ridges and the fallen trees. He took a step forward and stopped.

A flash of movement to his left.

He pivoted. "Show yourself!"

The blaggards had the audacity to laugh.

Alasdair reached for his sword. The sheath was empty. Black panic gripped his chest. He'd left it in the stable. How could he leave his sword in the stable?

Black floated by the bushes—vapors. Was it his brain ailment or was it the men? A flash of brown plummeted to the left. Yellow swirled in the air by his cheeks. "Show yourself," he said again. Control. He must gain control.

He adopted the stance for attack and slowed his breathing. Sweat broke out on his forehead. A flush of heat dove into his body. What soldier ever left his weapons in a stable?

Father's old words swirled around the trees. Incompetent. That's what he was. And, oh, how he felt that now. Shame coursed through his body, causing his hands to shake. Instead of guarding his charge, he'd been riding in the field with reckless abandon. Last night he'd stood in that copse of trees and played with colors like a child.

A mumble came from the right—words whispered too close.

Alasdair turned his head.

Down from the branches, they came—scores of them. And at the forefront a monster of a man, audaciously wearing a ripped top hat and a dirty red scarf. His large hands, wrapped in strange, fingerless gloves, held a club.

Alasdair lunged and ran at him, hoping to offset his balance.

The man was a Goliath. But Alasdair was no David. He'd abandoned that way long ago.

Something like regret flashed into his mind before the monster brought down the club.

Chapter Sixteen

An unlit lantern attached to the ceiling swayed. Feya squinted at the blurry apparition, glass and crudely shaped metal. A lantern. On the ceiling.

But the forest . . .

Her stomach clenched and her body felt strange, constricted. Everything ached, and the light was wrong somehow. Hadn't the sun just risen?

Feya tried to sit, but couldn't. Ropes held her wrists tighter than a blueblood's hatband.

"Bleedin' banshee." Panic scraped against her skin like claws.

A vardo . . . She was in a caravan. Feya's eyelids fell and the darkness pulled her down. Forcing her eyes open, she took a deep breath and focused. A man lay on the floor beside her.

Tall—stretched out from wall to wall. Black hair . . . White shirt open at the collar . . . Dried blood matted his hair to his forehead. His cheeks were pale, dark circles under his eyes. His eyes . . . She focused on the long coal lashes resting like raven's wings. "Cairncross?"

She remembered running through the woods. He'd been chasing her. But then she'd fallen. And now she was in a caravan. Why were they both in a caravan? Stranger still, his hands and feet were also tied, just like hers.

"Cairncross." Feya kept her voice low and glanced at the door. Her head ached. She had to try to think clearly. "Are ye dead?"

No answer.

The caravan hit a rut, throwing the lantern against the wall. Glass shattered. Shards ran down.

Feya turned her face into Cairncross's arm. She shook her head and glass tumbled from her hair.

A woman's sharp voice carried from outside. A man's answer followed.

Feya rolled onto her stomach and then scooted to her knees. The rocking of the caravan threatened to topple her over. She reached for the wood trim on a small, diamond-shaped window and pulled. Drowsiness weighted her body like water. It would be so easy to sink back into the darkness.

Her hand slid against the cold window latch. She took another breath and opened her eyes. "Concentrate on the latch . . ." She didn't know if she said the words. She brought her body closer and stared at the black iron.

Outside the window, there was nothing but blackness—a great rolling blackness. The noise of the wheels grated her thoughts, jumbling them into indiscernible rot.

She felt Cairncross behind her, helpless. "I can't save him. Shouldn't care." She thought of Morna's blue eyes. "Think of the bairns." Anger surged through her body. The cold of the window latch seeped into the bones of her palm. "And where could they be takin' us anyway?" She slid her gaze back to Cairncross's face. He was strong. He would get away.

Feya squeezed the handle. It turned by degrees, like a rusty clock. She cringed when it creaked, but surely the noise of the caravan wheels was louder. She pushed on the window. It opened a crack.

Pressure wrapped around her ankle.

Cairncross stared at her, his pupils dilated, his chest rising and falling. His hands were clamped onto her, barely spread apart, straining against the rope at his wrist.

"Let go." Feya tried to shake her foot loose, but his grip was too tight. She fell against the window, exhausted. A breeze pushed through, a vapor of pine needles and upturned earth. She pushed the window harder. It wouldn't move. It was nailed, just past the crack— a great iron nail like the spike of God.

Feya sank onto her knees and wanted to cry. Cairncross's hand was still wrapped around her ankle, as if she were a lifeline. "Ye can let go. I'm not goin' anywhere."

Cairncross relaxed his grip and brought his arms back against his chest. "Where are we?" His voice was hoarse, the Scottish and English accents muddled like dirty water falling into the sea.

"I don't know. Locked in a caravan."

"Help me up."

"What good will it do?"

"Woman, just help me up."

Feya brought her face down, close to his. "Why should I? I wouldn't be here if it wasn't fer ye. Yer the one who's been keepin' me from the bairns."

"Has it escaped your notice that our situation has changed?" He spoke slowly, like trying to make a child understand. "We are both captive now."

The caravan hit another dip in the road, jerking Feya's shoulders down. She steadied herself against the wall. "I should knock ye in the head and be done with ye."

"You could." His gaze never faltered. "But then, you don't know what you're up against, do you? Who do you think is outside those doors?"

Feya frowned and watched the way he tried to keep his eyes open. She knew very well who was outside those doors. Her people. Perhaps—if they were of the same tribe—she could convince them to let her go.

"We can help one another."

She closed her eyes and the blackness slid along her cheek, soothing, comforting, begging her to give in. The noise of the wheels roused her. "Help? As if yer capable of such a thing."

"You could attempt trusting me."

"Trust isn't somethin' I do."

"Me either." He took a long breath. The shakiness of it echoed in the small space. "Perhaps we could both make an exception."

Feya turned away and focused on the chipped paint of the wall. She knew he stared at her. Time stretched like a tight string, vibrating, pulsing with need of an answer.

"Not looking at someone doesn't make them go away."

"Pity." She hated that she needed his strength. She didn't want to need anything from him. "Say we're equal."

"I beg your pardon."

Feya turned and brought her face low, until she could see the smoothness of his cheek. "I'll help ye, but only if ye say we're equal."

"Given our situation, are you really going to insist?"

"Oh, I insist."

"In that case, it would seem I am inclined to be agreeable." He struggled with the notion, his deep-blue eyes told her as much. After a moment, calm bled into the lines of his face and softened his features. Finally, he gave her an unnerving smile—slow, with just the slightest raising of his eyebrow. "We are equal."

Still arrogant as the devil, despite his circumstances. "How many women have ye wielded that smile upon?"

"Enough to notice."

Heat flashed over her body. "I can tell when yer not being sincere."

"Can you?" He locked eyes with her.

"I'm not daft."

He looked like he considered. "Perhaps not."

"Shall I untie ye?" She raised her eyebrow to mimic him.

"That's the most reasonable course of action."

Feya nodded but didn't budge.

Cairncross raised his chin. It was a ridiculous gesture with him being laid out upon the floor.

"I'm waiting, Englishman. I might be able to loosen me own ropes somehow, but ye . . ." She frowned. "Not a chance."

"We are equal."

"What was that?"

Red shone in his face. "We are equal."

Feya nodded. For Cairncross, that was quite an accomplishment. "That's an excellent place to start." She leaned over him and curled her fingers around the rope at his wrist.

Whoever had tied him wanted to be sure he didn't escape.

"Please, help me sit."

The word hit her like the wind in the Highlands. It was a shock, that "please." The strangeness of it stilled her body.

"Yes, I said 'please.'"

Feya nodded, unable to respond. She grabbed his wrists and pulled. His shoulder lifted from the floor, and then his chest, the muscles in his neck straining. Finally, he sat, shoved up against her in the tiny space. "Hurry, try again."

His body against her in the dark was warm, and so large. Even bound as he was, he enveloped her with his presence—the scent of leather that hung about him, the smell of the forest on his clothes, even the faint way his breath moved the loose tendrils of her hair against her skin.

Trembling started, like a broad, wide chain shaking about her shoulders.

"Look at me."

Feya anchored her gaze on the floor instead.

"Please, look at me."

She looked up—his side, chest, and deep-blue eyes.

"I promise I will not hurt you. Would you try to untie me again?"

Feya moved her hands back over his. His pulse was strong beneath her fingers. Her own rope cut against her wrists, but she stretched her fingers.

"Good girl. That's the way."

Her eyes widened at the praise.

Their fingers slow danced—a shifting here, stretching there—wrist against wrist and rope against rope. After a few moments, his bonds fell away.

Cairncross stretched his fingers and started to work on the rope around her hands. "What do you remember? Details are important."

Feya fought the urge to pull away. His fingers brushed the back of her hand, the underside of her wrist. The caravan rocked again, and their bodies swayed in unison. "I remember runnin'. From ye. We were in the woods outside of Torphichen. I fell and then there was a man standin' over me. He was . . ."

"Yes?"

She closed her mouth. She didn't want to say the next part, even though it was obvious, them being in a caravan. "He spoke like a Gypsy. Had a white cloth in his hand. I think he put it over me mouth." The memory broke free and solidified. Her rope fell away.

"Come closer."

Feya snapped her gaze back to him. "Why?"

He closed his eyes as if gathering patience. "Now is not the time for questions. Put your face next to mine."

"Yer daft."

"Woman, just do it. If a chemical was used to knock us unconscious, I'll be able to smell it on your cheeks."

It made sense, she supposed. And, as he was a man of the law, he should know about these things. She wadded Morna's plaid skirt in her hands—something to hold on to—and she leaned in. His nearness was like embers burning.

"Closer."

It was the same word he'd used the day before to humiliate her, just before she'd dropped the belladonna into his water. Feya pulled back instinctively and took in a sharp breath.

"Do you remember what I said?" The gentleness in his tone lapped over her like waves. "I'm not going to hurt you."

Surely she was dreaming. He couldn't possibly be the same man.

Cairncross moved his body closer and the air shifted; heat came from between their bodies, rolling like a fire. There was only him. And her. Another wave of trembling ravaged her body and she felt ashamed, although she'd done nothing.

"My leg is jammed next to this table." His whispers came like feathers falling. "If you can move just a little more, I can reach you."

The lantern above creaked as the caravan swayed—back and forth, back and forth.

Feya stretched her body, like an animal giving itself to slaughter. He was so close now. Closer than the night she'd been wild with fever. Attacking someone with a blade of glass was one thing. Having the man pin you to the ground was another. But this—her face burned with his nearness. His breath fell softly against her cheek; chills plucked her neck like a Celtic harp.

The caravan hit a rut.

The stubble of his beard brushed her face. Feya jerked back, almost hitting the wall.

"There is something." His voice was quick. "It'll help if I can identify it. It could give us a clue as to who they are and what they have planned."

"Right." Feya flicked her gaze at him. He was right. Of course he was. And she was just being stubborn. She leaned back in.

"Be still. I do believe I know—"

The caravan dipped again. Feya's body tilted and fell. She slammed up against him.

Cairncross wrapped his arms around her and stiffened. He said something under his breath.

"I'm—"

The caravan bounced again, cradling her deeper into his arms. Just as quick, the caravan veered left. Cairncross lost his balance.

Feya reached for his shirt but only found air. Her cheek pressed against his.

He fell against the wall.

They both pulled away. Their cheeks slid together, and then their lips.

Another rut, and the false kissed deepened.

Cairncross slid the rest of the way onto the floor, a look of utter shock on his face. Feya fell on top of him, the length of her body sprawled against his. She shoved against his chest and rolled to the floor.

Only two times in her life had she wished to die. The first had been when Frank Rogers had kissed her. The second was now. "I'm sorry."

"Chloroform."

"I dinnae mean to fall against ye like that." Feya swallowed. Death could come now, and it would be all right. Death would be better than living with the memory that she'd put her lips against the Englishman's.

"We are not dealing with an average criminal." His gaze was on the ceiling, his body as still as a stone.

The whoosh of blood in Feya's ears drowned out his voice. "What are ye sayin'?" How had that happened? In all the possibilities in the world, how had that one come together? She hid her face in her hands, exhaled, and then moved to rub her temples.

"They used chloroform on you. I smelled it once at a medical university in London. Not easy to procure in the wilds of Scotland." His gaze shifted to her, but just as quickly he looked away.

Chloroform. Romani of her tribe would not resort to such things. Her people were few now, and scattered. But definitely not kidnappers. "What kind of devils are they, do ye think?"

"I can't say for certain."

There was a look in his eyes that made her think he knew exactly what all the possibilities were.

"Tell me."

"There might be a resurgence of body snatching in Scotland."

She thought of the men from Deacon Brodie's. And then the doctor at Edinburgh prison.

"Just like Burke and Hare, they don't like to dig up the bodies." Moonlight slid over his face, giving him the appearance of marble. "Being only *just* dead is more lucrative."

"I'm not goin' to be some medical man's experiment. I can tell ye that fer sure."

"I agree wholeheartedly."

"What's yer plan? I couldn't get the window open, but maybe ye can. Yer stronger."

"Nailed shut?"

"Aye. The sick buggers."

He looked at the door. "It's most likely locked."

"Do ye want me to try it?"

"No. Same scenario." He narrowed his eyes. "We wait."

"Have ye lost yer mind?" Feya looked at the window again. Perhaps she could force it open herself . . . But he was right. They would hear. And then they'd be upon them.

Panic clenched her body—squeezing her ribs and robbing her lungs of air. Sweat broke out on her forehead.

"Although we both agree that we don't trust well, I need you to trust me."

Her heartbeat was in her ears. She was going to die. And never see the bairns again. This was the end—butchered by body snatchers.

"Feya." The word sounded strange on his lips, especially with that Scots-English accent he had when he was rushed. "Feya." He said her name again, light as the wind stroking against a curtain. "I need you to trust me. I am accustomed to battle and difficult situations. This is not the first time I've been captured. Do you understand?"

Feya gazed into the blue eyes that she'd despised for days. The arrogance was gone. There was only truth. "Aye."

"Then say my name."

"What?" Feya closed her eyes like he'd shone a light. She knew what he wanted her to do, but to say it . . .

"Please say my name so I know you'll trust me."

Feya squeezed her lips shut. If she said his name everything would be different. It was a crash against the rocks, this difference.

The rumble of the wheels outside was painfully obvious. Feya opened her mouth and tried, but her breath fled over her lips and fainted in the dark.

"My name is Alasdair."

Feya nodded. The last time she'd trusted a man it had been Da. When he used to sing her good songs, before the drink had stolen that all away.

A whip cracked outside, followed by muffled voices.

Cairncross covered her hand with his, a simple gesture. The gentle pressure in his fingers said things words never could.

"Alasdair." She shivered when the last syllable flew away.

"All right." He squeezed her hand. "I'm going to get us out of here."

"What . . ." Feya pulled her hand out of his grasp. ". . . happens after that?"

"Survival is achieved one step at a time." Alasdair paused. "As soon as the caravan comes to a stop, I need you to pretend to still be unconscious. Can you do that?"

"Aye."

"Good. We might as well get into position. Lie down."

Feya brought her back against the cold floor and Alasdair loosely tied her ropes again.

He brought his body down, rubbing his shoulder against hers as he worked in the cramped space.

Feya's heartbeat increased with every turn of the caravan wheels. She studied the curved old boards on the ceiling. Tried to shift so she wasn't touching him.

She wasn't going to think about what had happened just a few minutes ago. It had been an accident . . . She fixed her eyes on a shape on the wall—a bookshelf, with a rope pulled across so the books wouldn't fall. So, the devils that'd kidnapped them liked to read. *More's the pity. It would be easier to outwit someone who never cracked a cover.*

Alasdair cleared his throat. His eyes were open. He, too, stared at the ceiling.

"How long . . ." She tested her voice in the dark, not trusting the tones. "How long do ye think it will be?"

"There's no way to tell."

"What direction are they going?"

"The roof outside that window makes it impossible to see the stars. Without that, I've no way to gauge it."

"I think it was six o'clock when I ran out of the church."

"How do you know that?"

She looked back at the ceiling. "I saw the kirk clock as I ran out through the chapel."

"Ah." His voice was soft, as if their conversation was perfectly reasonable. "That's good to know. We've been some hours traveling, I think."

She was proud of this fact, something she had done right. It was something to hold onto, some bit of something that made sense. The fact that she was lying next to an Englishman whose lips had just touched hers—that was not a fact to linger on. Neither was the fact that she had mint upon her lips from the experience. Feya stuck out the tip of her tongue and touched her lip.

Definitely mint.

Fire bled into her cheeks. She widened her eyes and turned her head.

He'd been watching. "When they come to get us, I'll be ready." His words were too fast. "Just be prepared to run."

The way he looked at her—a mixture of curiosity and something she couldn't name. "I wish I would have left the window cracked."

"Yes, it's hot. Hard to breathe."

"I wish I knew where they were takin' us." With each turn of the wheels outside, she could feel the distance between her and the bairns. She had the urge to claw at her skin.

"Breathe, Feya."

She opened her mouth and sucked in air. She hadn't realized that she'd stopped. Shivers shot over her body. Her lungs felt weak, as if she couldn't blow out a candle.

"The hardest thing to do in these situations is to keep yourself in a comfortable place inside your head."

Her shoulders rose and fell as she concentrated on breathing. "I can see that." She turned to him again. A lock of his black hair curled around his ear. His collar was rumpled. Somehow it made him look a little more Scottish than English—the lack of perfection. She lowered her gaze to the different colors in his beard and tried to focus on that instead of the sharp pain.

"Has it come to your attention that this appears to be a Gypsy caravan?" He didn't turn to speak to her. The tips of his ears were red.

It was a ridiculous question, given the fact that she'd told him the man in the forest had spoken like a Gypsy. "Of course."

"I assume you've been in a caravan before."

"Before me family moved to Edinburgh."

"Does anything look familiar? Would you be able to identify some kind of ornamentation? To distinguish a tribe, perhaps."

The bookshelf was scalloped. Papers stuck out at odd angles between the books. A table stood near her feet; wide bowls on top held candles. Thick tree branches formed the ribs of the caravan, like a fairy had built them. Dried flowers and herbs hung from the ceiling. "It was a long time ago. I'm sorry . . . Surely ye know that Romani ways have changed. Most travelers have moved to the city just to try to find work." Heavy sadness fell upon her as she said the words. "The old ways are gone." She didn't know why she said it, especially since they were in a caravan. Maybe part of her wanted them to be gone. Maybe she just wanted that part of herself she'd always despised to disappear. A clean wash, the heating of life—taking all the stain away.

But such things weren't possible. She could no more change the blood in her veins than she could hang ropes upon the moon. She'd tried to change her fate, but it'd come right back around and shoved her in a Gypsy caravan.

"I thought that was true before this morning—our society is modern, on the cutting edge. But then we went to Torphichen, and now we're here." He made a sound that was like a laugh. "This isn't exactly the latest model of a London phaeton."

"No." Feya hoped she sounded convincing. She had no idea what a phaeton looked like, or even what its purpose was. Leave it to the English to give carriages fancy names.

"I can't imagine why someone would want to live in one of these things and travel forever. Having no place to be secure, situated."

"It's better than the tenements." She couldn't trust her voice; the tones told her dark thoughts. "At least the air is good in the country." She squeezed her eyes shut to try to stop the burning in her lungs. It didn't work. "I ate better then . . . when we lived in a caravan."

Silence. The seconds passed.

"Was it very bad? Is it as bad as they say on the east side?"

Feya shoved down the bitter laugh. "What's the last thing you ate in Edinburgh?"

"Ham, codfish, and potatoes."

She exhaled at the mention of such things. "The last time I ate, before I broke into the palace, was three days previous. I ate one piece of bread that was filled mostly with air. I haven't had butter in nine months. Salt in six."

"Meat?"

"Before that stew ye sent to me when I was in the guard shack, it had been a year."

An unnatural quiet settled about his body. "My father says he has a new plan for Edinburgh. A plan to make things better."

"Does he?" She didn't want to tell him how many rich men had said things like that in the course of two years. They never made a difference.

"There's a bill in Parliament now. He's been able to influence the vote. It will pass." He shut his mouth like he didn't want to tell her that much.

"Ye talk of influencing the vote like that's a noble thing. I'm sure that's not easy to accomplish."

"Not at all. My upcoming marriage—" He stopped the words.

Feya widened her eyes in the dark "Yer going to marry to help yer father with his ambitions?"

"It is my honor to do so."

"The dutiful son." Feya didn't know why, but the information disturbed her. After all, what did she care for him? "As we don't seem to be stopping, what's her name?"

Alasdair rolled his head to the side and stared her directly in the eyes. "Miss Amberlyn Wanesley."

Feya snapped her head back to the middle and stared at the ceiling. Amberlyn. Of course she's have an elegant name like that. It no doubt meant something precious.

She didn't have to ask what the woman looked like. She'd be lovely, of course. And do everything right. Silver spoon in her mouth and all that. Everything Feya had never had or been or could hope to be. "I'm sure ye'll be very happy. When this is all over, ye can go straight back to her and start yer life."

"I intend to." He breathed a sigh. "I'm glad we had this talk. It's helped pass the time."

Wetness stung her eyes. It had to be the cramped quarters that caused it. Smoke, small rooms, crowded markets where she wandered all alone—it was always the same. Something was definitely wrong with her eyes.

"We'll get through this, Feya. I can see we'll work together well."

"Can ye now?" It was an ironic twist, those words.

"While we're here whittling the time away, I should tell you that no one has ever given me as much trouble as you."

"I suppose that counts fer something." She didn't want to talk anymore. If it were possible for the ground to open its gaping mouth and just be done with her, she'd welcome it.

"You've had to bear some very difficult circumstances. You've borne them as well as any soldier."

That was her. The strong one. Hadn't Da said the same words? And where had that strength gotten her?

"I've seen men in Egypt balk under lesser pressure."

Feya turned her face to the black wall, that place where the moonlight didn't touch. Alasdair said other words, but she didn't hear them. The only thing that was, was the night outside pressing in. The ruined lantern swaying. The books on the shelf knocking together. The turn of the wheels and the *clop* of the horses' hooves were like a clock, measuring off time.

Time. She'd always had that.

While the man beside her had been marching in parades and wearing fancy clothes, she'd had time. While he'd been living posh on the palace grounds, smiling at the fancy women, she'd been scraping away in the tenements. She'd watched time fade, as the light did over the ships in the Port of Leith she'd never sail on. She'd done nothing when time stole her mother away.

And when she'd risen up to fight—to change her destiny—she'd only failed.

Chapter Seventeen

"Whoa." A voice, thick with Romani accent, called from outside. The horses neighed, and then the caravan lurched to a stop. Feya squeezed her eyes shut and willed her heart to slow. She could feel Alasdair's anticipation beside her.

He was right. He had to be right.

And he was strong. His plan would work.

Someone flung open the caravan door. The sound of light rain was amplified. The caravan swayed as the person stepped inside.

The burning urge to look exploded in Feya's body; it pried at her eyes.

Trust me, Alasdair had said.

Their captor rummaged in a cabinet near her feet, then stopped beside Feya's knees. The scent of roses wafted down.

A cold hand touched Feya's throat. Feya sucked in her breath and snapped open her eyes.

"Ah, you're awake. I thought so." The woman pulled back her hand, and her bracelets rang together. Her voice was rich and her appearance richer. She was exotic and fine, the lines on her face somehow accentuating her beauty.

"Where am I?" Feya infused drowsiness into her tones.

The woman ignored her question and raised her eyebrows, revealing dark kohl lines around her pale eyes. She tilted her head. "You have Romani eyes, girl."

"And you don't." The words were out before she could think.

The woman's lips curved. "Aren't we all a mix, like oil and water in this country?" There was friendliness in the corners of her eyes, but also hardness, and some amount of cruelty.

"Aye." Feya's voice fell to a whisper. The woman was her contrast: the dark Gypsy hair of her ancestors, but eyes like the moon—light to Feya's dark.

The woman took Feya's chin and turned her head to the side. "Drabarni blood flows through your veins, I'm sure of it. Do you have the gift?"

Feya pulled her head away. "Do you mean can I influence others to do as I say?" Although he hadn't moved, Feya could feel Alasdair's disgust at the conversation.

"That's part of it." The woman dropped her hand. "Can you change the future?"

"Wouldn't that be a feat?"

The woman looked like she was thinking. "Indeed. And yet you wear Scottish clothes."

"You know how it is. I've survived."

The older woman nodded. "I do know that." Her gaze shifted to Alasdair. "You find yourself in very poor company."

Feya tried not to look at him. "I agree. Why don't ye take off these ropes so I can be done with him?" Rising heat flowed between her body and Alasdair's.

"I wish I could. Maybe soon. But right now, someone wants to meet you." The woman helped Feya sit, then drew a knife from the scarf around her waist. "You will decide if we are to be friends."

Her warning was clear.

A man larger than Alasdair stepped into the doorway. "I'm tired of the rain, and I could do with some supper. Are you finished chatting, or are you two settling in for tea?"

The woman smiled at Feya. "Don't be peevish, Emilian. It's so unlike you."

The man muttered something in Romani, then stepped away. The woman pointed to the doorway. "You've a long walk ahead of you."

"Where?"

She *tsk*ed. "So many questions."

"What about him?" Feya glanced at Alasdair.

"As he's been awake our entire conversation, he can join you."

Alasdair opened his eyes and smiled at the woman. It was a smile Feya had never seen—alluring, like the devil of seduction had come to call. "I'm sorry we didn't have the pleasure of an introduction earlier. As someone hit me over the head, I do hope you'll excuse my lack of manners."

The woman glanced down and tried to hide her smile. She was unsuccessful. When she lifted her eyes, she looked at Feya. "And that, my dear, is why you and I have mixed blood. The English are all too charming." She pointed at Alasdair with the knife. "On the surface."

"Come, come." Alasdair pouted and looked cavalier. "There's no need for that."

Feya looked him up and down. The man could do well walking the stage.

His smile never faltered and his voice remained light. "I suppose if I had to be captured, you are a most welcome candidate."

The woman brought the knife against his forearm, slid it to his elbow and then his shoulder. "You're going to take a walk with us, English."

"My pleasure."

The woman stood and rolled her eyes at Feya, as if they were sisters. She walked down the front caravan steps.

Feya whispered to Alasdair. "What do we do now?"

"We'll be free within the hour." He stood and walked to the front of the caravan.

Outside, the woman's thick black hair blew in the breeze. Moonlight shone, highlighting the water droplets on the strands. A makeshift awning snapped in the wind. Water dripped from the low side.

The man sliced carrots into a pot. "I don't like the look of him."

"Me?" Alasdair raised an eyebrow. "I was just wondering why you brought us all this way for dinner in the rain. Really, you could have just sent a card."

"You won't be eating." The woman turned and called three names. The men stepped out from behind the caravan. They eyed Alasdair like wolves set upon prey. Alasdair raised his chin and met their gaze.

The wind shifted and rain pelted Feya's face. A cold chill went through her, and she knew it wasn't just from the rain. "What do ye have planned?"

"Walk." The woman held out her hand. "Stay in front of me and don't turn around." The woman broke into Romani, perhaps thinking that Feya couldn't understand. "It won't be as difficult for her, as she has our blood. He'll take pity."

One of the men laughed. "Or maybe she'll be a nice addition to his other interests."

"Shut up. He only does what he must for the betterment of our people and Scotland."

"I think you're in love with him, that's what. Ever since the tragedy you can't keep your eyes away from his bum. Or maybe it's his pocketbook you're after."

The woman cursed. "Like you know anything. How many wives have you had now?"

"Not my fault."

"Oh, I'm sure."

"My stomach's about to burst. How much longer do we have with this English rotter?"

Feya lowered her gaze and pretended not to listen. There was a path between the trees.

"We're only supposed to take them to him. Then we're done. And we can celebrate all night if you want. We've captured the queen's favorite guard." The woman laughed. "Everyone said he couldn't be caught."

"Wasn't very hard when that vixen was always giving him pains."

Feya opened her mouth to speak, but then shut it. They all laughed behind her.

"How long do you think he'll last?"

The Gypsy woman took a deep breath, as if peace had settled around her. "That depends upon the master and what he has planned."

The men grunted, like that was the only explanation needed.

The way twisted to the left onto a dark hill. Feya climbed.

"Not that way," the woman said in English. "To the right."

The men brought Alasdair to the front of the line. The wind blew his hair, but other than that, he looked as still as funeral stone. The moonlight sliced across his face, illuminating his blue eyes. He flicked his gaze to Feya, and then back again.

The man behind Alasdair ground his fist into his back and pushed.

The wind blew like a soft silk veil. It rubbed its fingers over Feya's face and made the hair raise on the back of her neck.

The Gypsy woman stared at her. "What's the matter, girl?"

"Nothin'." Feya pushed her gaze to the rugged bottoms of the larch trees. "Beside the fact that ye've kidnapped us and I've no idea what ye mean to do."

The Gypsy woman's eyes shone like cold quartz and the touch of dead hands. "Move."

The hill they climbed was full of lush, green grass and ferns, like a carpet made for a king. The trees covered the knoll in slashes of shadows—stripes like the banner from an old, ragged flag. Further on, the grass changed into the dark purple of heather. Stone stairs appeared in the side of the hill. Walls rose on either side, obviously placed by the ancients.

A rush of wind came around the corner and pulled at Feya's skirt. She hesitated. The Gypsies had stories about places like this.

"Go on." The Gypsy woman pushed her.

Above her were two stone slabs as big as tables.

Sacrificing stones. Feya stepped back. The woman pushed her forward. Muffled voices came from further in.

"This is Tappoch Broch." The woman spread her hands in the air like a circus performer. Her bracelets rang together. She gave a shrill cry.

Out of a stone pit, hundreds of Gypsy faces met Feya's. They joined the piercing call, rejoicing like savages of old.

Feya sucked in her breath. This was much different than Da's family. There had only been ten caravans at most before they'd moved to the city. This—this was a real tribe, a gathering. Through the trees, the moonlight shone on countless caravans and horses.

"Welcome to Gypsy court."

Chapter Eighteen

Alasdair stumbled over the old ruins as he descended into the pit. Hundreds of Gypsies stared. Hundreds, not a few.

Above the fire, bursts of green flooded the sky like artillery explosions. A log fell and hissed, sending a stream of yellow into the air like a snake dancing. That was his normal; the bright white flash that followed was not.

Alasdair's heart surged in his chest. His breath accelerated. He tried to measure it so he didn't faint like a woman.

The landscape reappeared, like an eraser had swiped away the colors. But then the flash came again. *Flick, flick, flick.* The Gypsies were only shadows. The colors pulsated and spun—bright, a thousand times brighter than they ever had, mad like a lunatic's dream.

Pain sliced through his chest and his arms. "Stop." Sweat formed on his forehead. "Make it . . ." He doubled over.

The man prodded him in the back and threatened with words he could no longer hear. Alasdair wanted to cock him in the face and make him bleed. Blue covered his vision, like looking through rippling water.

Not now. He did not need this now. If he gave in, he'd lose their chances to survive.

The wind kicked up, throwing dirt against his legs. Slashes of orange followed the stones as they fell away. More flashes came—so strong he could feel them in the tips of his fingers and the roots of his hair.

Memories flooded him. The sting of sand . . . It had been the same in Egypt. When death was certain and hope was lost, the colors refused to be ignored.

Alasdair righted himself and focused on breathing. He'd have to let himself fade into the patterns.

White. Blue. Green. *Flash. Flash. Flash.* Swirling lines and dots like splattered paint.

Breathe. Just breathe.

The world came back like an expanding frame, pushing the symphony of color away.

"There's something wrong with him." The Gypsy's voice was gruff and strained. Wisps of grey floated over Alasdair's shoulder—the effect of the man's voice.

"Bring him here."

Another shove and his head split, both ice cold and boiling hot. His hands shook. He clasped them tight so the Gypsies wouldn't see.

The colors around the Gypsies changed; they spoke their angst without words—harsh blues and sharp greens, pushing and flaring.

Movement to the left caught his gaze.

Feya walked next to the fire and held her head high. Gold surrounded her like a halo—beautiful, brilliant gold, as bright as a candle behind stained glass. Through the haze, the focus helped. Watching her eased the pain in his head.

When she was especially angry with him, the colors around her radiated like a rainbow. To his shame he could now admit that he'd taunted her on the road just to see the shades flare.

Lies to oneself were a troublesome business.

In the palace storeroom, the colors around Feya had taken him aback—arched so wide around her body. Even when he looked into her brown eyes the colors pressed in around the corners of his vision, begging him to look. When he'd looked that first time, it hadn't felt wrong.

But then she'd cut him with the glass for his momentary lapse.

His only other indulgence had been looking at the tombstones in the ruined abbey.

A laugh escaped him at the ridiculousness of it. He thought of all the time he'd spent adding the numbers on the headstones. Not just to get the equation, but to see what color the answer would be. "Twenty-three is a soft blue like the sea's waves in Cornwall."

"What?" The Gypsy behind him dug his fist into his back again.

Alasdair only laughed harder. "You haven't lived until you experience the orange of seven and nine combined. I could fade into that orange. Feels like warm rain."

Two more Gypsies walked over. "What's he saying?"

"He's gone mad."

The biggest man punched him in the face. Alasdair reeled and spit out blood. "Fight me without the aid of ropes, coward."

The man answered with another punch. Four men jumped on him and pounded. Rage surging like a tide, Alasdair slammed his shoulder into the nearest Gypsy. Kicked the man with the red scarf. Before he could think, five more men piled on. They dragged him across the rocks, banged his knees on the ground. His shirt ripped. His trousers tore. They threw him into a shallow cave, dug out with iron bars conveniently placed.

Laughter followed the slam of the bars. Their spit hit the ground and splattered.

Alasdair fell back against the cold, stone wall. Adrenaline surged like wine in his blood. He'd been here before—captor and captive.

He knew this. It would just take watching, strategy, and withdrawing within himself like before.

One thing was different. He searched for Feya in the crowd. There was her beautiful gold, waving like a beacon above all the other angry blues and greens. Her skin was smooth for one who'd lived such a hard life, as pale as one of the queen's ladies. Her eyes had bothered him at first, so obviously Gypsy. But then there were moments when he couldn't help but notice the different shades—amber, cinnamon, chestnut—according to the light or her mood.

Alasdair focused on her lips as she spoke with the Gypsy woman. He'd be a fool not to notice that the gentle curve as she said each word was akin to art. A flash of heat went through him.

Behind bars, with a future uncertain, the feeling of freedom had never been so strong. The fresh Scottish air flooded the grotto—aged tree bark, wet moss, the lightness of bluebells. The colors swayed just beyond the bars, beautiful now. Like that *aurora borealis* in the north he'd read about. But only he could see this, he knew.

So lovely he just might weep. Let the Gypsy fools who'd taken them think him a weak man because of it. Let them think they'd broken him when he'd never felt so strong.

The time for restraining what he saw was over.

Alasdair settled back against the rough wall. Death sentence or not, the colors were his for a reason. They'd helped him survive in Egypt and they'd help him now.

Feya saw it all happen—the fight, the wild look in Cairncross's eyes, the way the Gypsies dragged him across the ground and locked him away. "What are ye doin' with him?"

The Gypsy woman stood. "Don't concern yourself. After all,

hasn't he been keeping you captive all these days?"

"Aye."

A man stepped forward and reached for Feya.

"No." The Gypsy woman threw out her hand. "She sits with me. There are more things I wish to know from this one."

Sounds of Romani conversation filtered all around. Men played cards, huddled together in groups. Laughter was as prevalent as the smell of herbed oil on their skin and the scent of rabbit on the fire. Feya closed her eyes and let herself fall into the sounds. A woman washed pans in the stream across the way. She sang the old songs. Someone in the woods to her right played the pipes. The sounds rolled over her like a lament, reaching deep down, tugging on something tightly bound, and frayed it.

The Gypsy woman spoke. "Had you not run into the woods, we probably wouldn't have caught you so early. We'd been tracking Cairncross since he left Edinburgh.

"Ye know his name." Feya brought her knees up to her chest. "Do ye know mine?"

"Of course, Feya." The woman's pale eyes burned silver in the firelight. "Do you imagine I don't know all about you?"

"That would be impossible." As Feya said the words, she shivered. She could feel the Gypsy men watching her, their gaze burning into her back like animal brands.

"Maybe." The corners of the woman's thin lips turned up. "Do you want to know my name?" The wind whipped through the camp, pulling at the fingers of the fire until they trembled.

Did the woman think she was that daft? "If I remember correctly, such things always come with a price."

"You did spend some time in the camps."

"Ye said yerself I had the look of a Gypsy."

"I'm Kizzy."

Feya nodded, wishing she wouldn't have said it.

Kizzy nodded toward Alasdair. "There are some who aren't fond of the Cairncross name."

"I expect so." Feya lifted her eyes to the treetops, which were starting to turn pink in the rising sun. "When were ye planning to capture him?" She winced. "Before I made it more convenient fer ye."

"After he dropped you at Stirling."

"Then I don't matter."

The Gypsy woman gave her a secret smile. "You do now."

"Ye could let me go. I'll walk away and not give ye any trouble."

"Is that so?"

"Yes." Feya swallowed when she said the word. Her heart picked up its pace. She wouldn't look at where Alasdair was.

"You'd leave the Englishman, then?"

"Yes."

"He means nothing to you?"

"Of course not." Feya looked away, heat burning her cheeks. She pushed dirt around with her shoe. Every time she thought of him, she thought of Morna and the love she'd seen there. Then she thought of little Rowan.

"I'd advise you against what you're thinking."

"And how do ye know what I'm thinkin'?"

"I'm a woman, Feya. Some things can't be covered. You have feelings for him."

Feya sat straighter. She decided to answer the woman in Romani, to let her know she knew their plans. "I do not."

The woman smiled, falling into the cant. "Don't care for the thickness of his black hair?"

"No."

"Those blue eyes that resemble deep water?"

"Especially not his eyes." The lie clawed on her. The realization was worse.

"Hmmm . . . And you haven't found yourself musing on the way the tones of his voice change? Or the velvet quality when he says your name?"

Feya's breath quickened. Sweat broke on her brow. She scooted back from the fire. "I think all this conspiracy and kidnapping has fogged yer mind. There is one thing I want, and that is to get back to the bairns. I want to get out of the city. I want to live free again, as ye do. As our people truly do." With the words "our" Feya felt like a betrayer. She felt no more Gypsy than Scots, only a mix—nothing pure.

She knew very well what it meant to be on the outside, to be always hated and looked down upon. She remembered the early years when the people in the villages they passed would spit upon the ground when they saw the caravans. And how she'd been hit by a local in Pitlochry just because she'd asked for a bucket of water.

"I saw you take the belladonna from the forest."

The shadows from the fire danced on the old stone walls surrounding them. Feya slid her gaze to the place where they held Alasdair. She could see only his outline behind the bars, like a specter lurking in the ancient grooves of time. "Aye. I did that."

"If you didn't care for him, you wouldn't have knocked his water flask away."

Feya reached for her braid and wove her fingers through the end. "Have ye watched me every move?"

"You above all people should know that our kind is good at watching. If what you wanted most was to get back to the bairns, you would have let him drink the water."

Feya put her hands on either side of her head. "I don't know why I did it. I suppose I took pity on him. How could I let him die when his mother—"

"That one choice may have killed your brothers and sister."

Feya tried to breathe, but her chest felt like someone squeezed it. "That can't be true."

The Gypsy woman picked up a stick and threw it into the fire. "Kingdoms have risen and fallen with lesser decisions. Every decision counts, Feya. Every decision alters time and the world forever."

Wetness sprang to Feya's eyes, but the heat of the fire stole it away. "Let me go. Please. I've already been away fer so long."

The woman hesitated. "I like you. You've got a lot of the same fire I had many years ago."

Feya thought of Morna and how she'd told her the same thing. She held her hands out, bound with rope. "Please."

Kizzy reached for the knife at her side. "Stand up." The rising sun cast the edges of Kizzy's dark hair into blue. "I know what it is to lose someone you love. You have convinced me." The knife slid through the rope.

Feya stretched her fingers.

The man behind her stepped forward. "What are you doing?"

"Something I wish would have been done for me once upon a time. Now go back to your hole, Chal."

Feya took a step. "Thank ye."

Kizzy nodded, her strange eyes tired. "You're welcome."

"I'm free to go?"

"There is a condition."

Feya's heart fell. There were always conditions with the Gypsies. They knew every angle, every possibility three days ahead. "Tell me, then."

"You only go back to Edinburgh when we're done with him." Kizzy inclined her head to the cave. "I have my reasons. You'd do best not to ask what they are."

"What am I supposed to think of that?"

"I'd be thankful if I were you. I've just given you freedom

throughout the camp. You'll do your part to help us, do you understand?"

"Help with what?"

"Whatever I say." The words were final, like the dropping of a great, ancient stone.

"When this business is done, ye'll allow me to leave?" She forced herself not to look at the cave and tried to quench the rising dread. "Ye promise?"

"When we're finished with Cairncross, we have business near Loch Leven. After that we can deliver you safely home."

With every word the woman said, Feya felt her hope slipping away. "Will these plans fer Cairncross be painful?" She thought of Rowan again, and the way the boy had sat on his older brother's knee.

"You'll know all in the end." Kizzy laid her heavily ornamented hand upon Feya's shoulder. "I have eyes all around. Don't think of wandering off on your own. That would not please me."

"I know mercy when I see it. Ye'll have no problems from me."

"Good. Some of the women could use your help down by the river. We leave within the next few hours."

The sun crept higher in the sky and took with it the last of her hope. "Can I ask where we're going?"

Kizzy smiled and the gesture forced a chill through Feya. "We're going to the end of the world."

"Feya."

She put her head down and ignored him, at least until the thug who followed her decided to take a detour around the broch. Then she tucked the pans under her arm and walked to the cave entrance. "Are ye hungry?"

Alasdair wrapped his fingers around the bars and ignored her question. "How did you manage it?"

"What?"

"Woman, how is it that you are free?"

"Free is an interestin' choice of words. I think the Gypsy queen's just made me an extra pair of hands fer now."

He drew his eyebrows together. "What are they planning? You have to know."

Feya reached into her pocket and withdrew some bread. "Ye'd better eat." She shoved it through the bars. "Take it. I don't know when that man will be back. There's no tellin' who can see us now."

He took the bread without his gaze leaving her eyes. "Thank you."

Feya wanted to laugh. "There's a first time fer everythin', I suppose."

"What do you mea—"

"Never mind." She came closer to the bars. "They're takin' ye somewhere. Whoever's behind this doesn't like the Cairncross name."

"What?" He brought his face close to the bars.

"I don't know how much I can help." Feya looked down to the Gypsies milling around the fire.

Alasdair reached through the bars and grasped her hand. "You can help."

Feya jerked and almost dropped the pans. "Look how many people there are."

He tightened his grip. "You're smart. And you're quick." He lowered his head so he was looking directly in her eyes. "Who cut me with a piece of glass?"

"Me." She could feel the scab on his hand.

Alasdair nodded. "Not even the Russian who snuck through Holyrood's gates managed that much."

Feya pulled away. "That doesn't mean anythin'. The way I see it, I've failed at every turn." She nodded, as if to convince herself. "If I'd done like ye said—always what was right—we wouldn't be here now. I should have thought of somethin' else, a decent job. Another job. Maybe—"

"I haven't always done what's right." Alasdair's voice was like the waves of the sea at low tide. "Forget what I said before. Things are different now. You get me out of this and I will get you home to the bairns."

Feya stilled, feeling the weight of his words. "This is the second time ye've asked me to trust you."

"Yes, Feya, it is."

"The Gypsies made me the same offer, ye know."

The information didn't seem to affect him. "And who do you think will carry through?"

"Every man in me life has hurt me. Betrayed me."

"I won't." Alasdair held his body still, as if he sensed her indecision.

Feya put her hand on her heart and fought the desire to shout. "I am here because of Da's choices."

"Maybe you're here so you can learn how valiant you are. As I know you to be."

The sun rose full force, pushing through the broch and stretching to the remnants of the fire. The rays hit Feya's shoes and slid along the bottom of her skirt.

"Yer lyin' to me." She gripped the bars. "As soon as we escape, ye'll take me to Stirlin'."

Alasdair sighed and searched her face. "We're already in Stirling. Turn around."

Feya turned and gazed across the valley. A castle gleamed in the sun. Birds took flight above it, black spots against a crystal-blue sky.

Alasdair's voice came from just behind her ear—velvet tones, English mixed with Scots. "That's Stirling Castle. The prison is just below."

"How long have ye known?"

"A while. Some of the men slipped into English and I heard them talk about Torr Wood. But I was only sure just now when the sun rose."

She turned back to him. His eyes were focused on something above her head. His pupils were dilated in a most peculiar way. "Are ye all right?"

"I'm fine." Alasdair brought his gaze back down. "Even if the Gypsies went away right now and you and I were left alone on this hill, I still wouldn't take you to Stirling."

"They drugged ye, didn't they?" She looked around for the evidence—a bottle, something.

"No." He smiled like he thought it was funny. "I believe you deserve to get back to your siblings. Seeing Rowan made me realize that. And I know you were telling the truth."

"I need to think." Feya rubbed the metal pot she held as if that would make the answers come.

Alasdair grabbed her wrist. "I promise I will never take you to prison. I have never gone back on my word."

Feya loosened herself from his grip. "And yer father will just pat ye on the head when ye come home without doin' the job ye were supposed to?"

Alasdair's face darkened. "No. There will be consequences. But those I am willing to face."

Her Gypsy guard appeared at the bottom of the stairs. "What are you doing there, girl?"

Feya stood straight. "Giving this English devil a piece of my mind." She kicked dirt at Alasdair for effect.

"You're supposed to help pack up."

"Right." Feya walked away, but turned back just before the path dipped over the ridge. Alasdair followed her every move with his gaze. The dark-blue depths of his eyes radiated something so honest, so naked in its sincerity.

Now she was truly terrified.

Chapter Nineteen

Curiosity was definitely Alasdair's downfall.

Here he was, locked in another caravan with no recollection of how he'd gotten there, except for the aching second knot on his skull. As if he didn't have enough worries where his brain was concerned.

If he'd fought off the Gypsy woman's three lackeys, he wouldn't be here. As he'd stepped down, a *fouetté* kick would have taken the first one out. Followed by a *chasse* and *revers*, the entire business would have been over. But no, he'd had to see what they planned and take that walk into the forest. It all sounded too familiar—for hadn't he followed Feya through the palace and started a chain reaction?

Where she was now, Alasdair couldn't say. From time to time, the caravan would stop, and he'd see the women gather around a fire and cook. He always looked for her, but she never appeared. Which was annoying for two reasons: he needed her help to escape, but more than that, he found that he wanted her company.

Alasdair settled back onto the wooden stool by the window and continued to carve the surface of the rough table. He used a small metal embellishment he'd taken off the empty water pot on the first day. After a thorough search, it was the only thing that could be deemed serviceable as a weapon. But, day after day, he'd had no chance.

The caravan jostled over a rut in the road and Alasdair's hand slipped. The sliver scored his palm. He laughed. He felt like a child with a wooden sword. Humiliating.

The caravan turned, and the sunlight slanted across the table like a clock hand ticking. The tip of the beam touched the edge of his deep carving—an *F*, of all things. An *F* like an elaborate chapter heading in an old manuscript. It had started out as a frustrated gash, but then the line changed—flourishes, intricacies, things he normally didn't allow.

By the fourth day, vines made a border around the letter. Then the vines turned into Scottish eternity knots. Because it just looked good. No other reason. And he supposed his childhood had tipped its hat in that stupid decision. There were more blasted eternity knots in Torphichen than people. As he had hours to do nothing else, it only seemed logical that influence would appear. He also found that carving helped him think. So that made it useful. A completely logical endeavor.

Today he pushed the sharp metal scrap deep into the wood, scattering twisted shavings over the table surface and onto the floor. A wisteria cluster took shape, very English. But only at precise angles, mind, and an equal number of petals on each side. Nothing was out of balance. In fact, he'd made his own ruler with a paper scrap just to be sure.

Alasdair brushed the last of the wood shavings onto the floor, then touched the carving. He dipped his finger in the grooves and followed the perfectly centered lines. As this *F* was also the first letter of Feya's name, it was the perfect opportunity for him to focus on the woman herself. The subconscious really was an amazing thing. Alasdair supposed that's why the *F* had appeared on the wood. He needed to analyze things more. It was probably the lack of food causing it. And the deprivation of proper amounts of water . . . once again. He could suffer much—endure much—but why must he be thirsty? Why that particular torture? Why that echo from the cursed African sands?

He threw the metal piece down and raked his fingers through his messed hair. A Cornish pastie would taste good right about now. Flaky crust with perfectly spiced lamb and peas, and potatoes that soaked up the gravy.

Alasdair slammed his fist down on the table. His stomach hurt like a knife shoved deep. The empty tea tin in the corner was a special kind of torture. As was the empty box of shortbread that had a mouse hole.

Feya had talked of hunger. Hunger that drove her to break into Holyrood Palace. It didn't excuse it—of course not. However, in his present circumstance he could see how someone might be driven to such madness.

Alasdair turned his face away from the window and the craggy Highland hills. Kilometer after kilometer taking him away from his destiny—Amberlyn, Father, all the plans. With their wedding date only a few days away, what would Amberlyn be thinking?

The sun stroked the back of Alasdair's neck like soft fingers of fire, asking him to turn. He shifted in the chair and gazed outside. Sodden green fields tumbled low and long to stacked-up clouds. Gold lined the horizon, breaking through the grey. Trees swayed, bowing their heads as they'd done for centuries, keeping beat with the groans of the wind.

Alasdair's eyelids drooped. Here, of all places, he'd experienced more sleep than was wise. But it felt good—this ability to rest. It had been so long.

The caravan lurched to a stop, forcing his eyes open. He braced himself, grabbed the metal piece, and hoped they would come.

The horses neighed. Footsteps sounded.

No one opened the door.

Alasdair made a fist and had to restrain from punching through the small window.

As each ray of the sun dipped lower in the sky, his body relaxed into nothingness. Another night with no change. Captivity once again laughed her cruel, familiar tones.

Gypsy men milled about, making campfires and watering horses. Some pitched tents, their colors as varied as the places of the world. Conversations, low and confiding, filtered in on either side of his caravan. Alasdair couldn't understand the words, but the sentiments were always the same: Friendship. Camaraderie. Love. The whispered tones made him long for the barracks. And, worse than that, it made him miss taunting a certain half Gypsy who might even be dead.

A Gypsy woman came into his view. She laid chicken onto the fire spit. After a few moments, the savory smells of fowl reached him. Alasdair gritted his teeth and looked at the floor of the caravan. Breathe. He just needed to think of something else and breathe.

Violin music wafted in. A man wearing a long waistcoat stood by the fire. He pulled a bow against a very old instrument, the dents and wear obvious. The melody was slow at first, but then he quickened it and played like the entire world was dying and it was his last song.

And the colors—oh, the colors as the man played. Red in the air, mixed with purple. The perfect meld, like the bleeding of ink coming from the strings. Yellows flowed behind that, and then white. White so pure not even sun-lined clouds could compare.

The man changed the tone. The notes quivered. Circles of gold fell in the air like bubbles being blown by a child.

Alasdair leaned closer to the window. The Gypsy closed his eyes at the high point in the song and his bow hand stilled. He swallowed, and then the notes came again—deep and trembling and then high and faltering like a bird. Tears flowed from the man's eyes. Such expressions were never seen on the musicians' faces at court.

Alasdair sucked in his breath and waited. He gripped the edge of the table.

The man lowered the violin and walked out of view. And the lack of him—the lack of the music—was like a cavernous ache. Something hulling him out and making him raw inside. He raked his hand over the stubble on his jaw and sighed.

Gypsies filtered around the fire and sat. An old man stood and started telling a story, Alasdair presumed. Surely this man's stories weren't new to them. They gasped just the same. Their laughter filled the night, full and free. Crescendos of color burst from the Gypsies' mouths—ripples of orange and blue and grey.

Alasdair found himself smiling, the sound of their laughter infectious. But then his smile fell. Being captured was desperately lonely.

Two men fought in the corner of the field. That, he was used to. He took his anger out on the rugby fields. But he employed strategy and skill, something the Gypsies seemed to know nothing about. They lived on dreams, it seemed, and floated like dandelion seeds. True travelers.

A child passed by the window. She smiled at him and waved.

Alasdair held up his hand and felt his lips tilt again.

She toddled out of view, dragging a doll behind her.

He rested his face in his hands. Perceptions were cracking. And he didn't like it.

For one thing, Gypsies were not as dirty as everyone said. Even now, the women were washing pans and clothing in the river. And they had very strict rules, which he never would have guessed or believed, had someone told him. They always washed things in running water, never in ponds or lakes. Forks and spoons were washed separately from dishes. Clothes were washed upstream, but only clothes that went on the upper body. Alasdair reckoned that clothing such as trousers must be deemed unclean by them, because they were washed downriver, as were all the unmentionables. The people must have washed upriver because they always disappeared in that direction and then came back with their hair wet and their clothes changed.

He would give fifty pounds for a bath right about now. But there was little use in thinking about that.

He had to admit the Gypsies took right and proper care of their horses. The thought depressed him. Every time he saw them with their beautiful black-and-white horses, Haven came to mind. And that spiraled him into a depression the likes of which he hadn't experienced since Egypt.

Across the field, a door opened on a blue caravan. Women stepped down whom he hadn't seen before. They were dressed differently from the rest, their skirts and scarves more elaborate.

"And there's their Jezebel queen." Alasdair scowled at the sight of her. She looked just as pompous as he remembered, holding her chin higher than Queen Victoria herself. Her earrings fell past her shoulders and the same bracelets decorated her arms.

One of the younger girls brought a chair for the queen and set it under the yellow canopy. Another girl hung lanterns all across the front and sides.

The woman was nothing if not dramatic, apparently holding court in the middle of the Highlands.

Five women came from behind the caravan and sat at the Gypsy woman's feet. They spread their skirts upon the grass in perfect circles and swayed with tambourines in their hands.

Alasdair made a fist and leaned his cheek into it. At least he would be entertained while he starved.

The door of the Gypsy queen's caravan opened again. A delicate hand appeared. And then the tips of red hair blew in the wind.

Feya stepped down.

"She's alive." Hope surged within him. "Clever woman." He scooted his chair closer to the window.

She wore Gypsy attire, from the dark-blue embroidered bodice to the ruffled gold skirt. Coins hung about her waist and decorated her arms. Some sort of veil was draped around her hips—shimmering aquamarine blue and hints of green. The setting sun glinted off her earrings, necklace, and rings, giving her the illusion of moving light.

Alasdair sat back, stunned. Fairy stories had long since faded in his mind, but blast it all if he didn't feel like he'd just stepped into one.

Feya reached into a wicker basket and withdrew a hairbrush. She lifted the queen's dark hair and began to brush.

"She's turned her into some kind of bloody handmaid." He didn't know why it made him so angry. There were worse things that could have happened. They really could have killed her. Or let the men use her for sport. Alasdair's eyes widened. Maybe that had happened. From the downtrodden look on her face . . . Alasdair stood and kicked the chair. He paced, all of five feet, crossed his arms, and sat back down.

The wind blew Feya's hair to the side, and in the firelight it looked as though she wore a copper veil. Her braided hair had been a transformation. But this—this was something all-together different. Once she had washed the dirt away from that first night, her metamorphosis only continued.

Alasdair frowned. Another thought occurred to him, like water on a sleeping soldier. "Where's my jacket? My medals were on that jacket. Medals that took a lot of bloody time to earn. What did she do? Trade it for the privilege of riding in that sham of a queen's caravan? Divide it in pieces for the men to cast lots over?"

The queen stood. A girl took the chair away and the women formed a circle, including Feya. Now even she held a tambourine in her hand.

"What the devil?"

The women began to sway, just a bit. They lifted their hands in the air and tapped the tight skin of the tambourine with their palms.

Alasdair watched one hand in particular—Feya's. His gaze went to her wrist. She had a small wrist, very fine. And the way she moved her fingers . . . She wore rings, which were bells. And curse it all if that wasn't slightly interesting. But just slightly, mind. Most men in London would think it downright peculiar.

Feya closed her eyes. That wasn't good. For some reason Alasdair found that small act more intriguing than a week of performances at the London Opera House.

Feya had such peace on her face, but also pain. It was the thing she always carried—the abuse she'd suffered because of her father's addiction to drink, the death of her mother. And then there were her siblings to consider. She must be wild with grief and worry by this time.

Feya moved to the left and then the right, swaying her hips in a most unnerving manner. The wind blew through the veil of her hair again—the red tips of it reaching out into the watching darkness. Alasdair put his chin in his hand and then bit his finger. It was blasted hot in the caravan. Couldn't the fools have the compassion to allow him an open window?

The women wove in and out, dancing in an elaborate pattern. Seeing Feya now, it seemed odd to think of her as living in Leith. He couldn't even imagine her slaving away at the rubber mill. Or making potato soup in the hellhole that was the tenements. And collecting rags to make tuppence? Such a thing seemed impossible.

The woman dancing in the open field could not be that woman.

Even the trees bent down in the wind to see.

Alasdair dropped his hand onto the table and found that he couldn't move. Nor did he want to. He only wanted to watch her, every nuance, every gesture—the tilt of her hands in the Scottish air, the movement of her skirt.

Feya bent low and reached, as if she scooped up some otherworldly offering. Her dark brown eyes followed her hands as she raised them to the sky. Firelight painted shadows upon her face, casting her into a relief of marble and silk. The corner of her lips tipped up, as if she could see beyond the sky into the eternal.

The movement jolted him. Alasdair shook his head as if drunkenness had taken hold.

Feya drew her hand back, close to her ear, as though she held a bow. Alasdair almost expected one to appear. He wiped his forehead, and his hand came back wet.

The women dropped the tambourines and the dance changed. Feya brought her hands to her mouth and closed her eyes again. Finally, she pushed her hands out in front of her like the wind carried a kiss.

Alasdair's heart pounded like a schoolboy who'd noticed a pretty woman for the first time. He closed his hands and then opened them. His fingers had no circulation.

There was a look on Feya's face that held such longing—pain about the corners of her eyes. And then it faded; her features softened and gave way to release.

Knowledge came like the mist flooding over the riverbank behind her, soaking into his bones. Alasdair drew his eyebrows together. He swallowed. His mouth fell open—in surprise or horror, he didn't know which. He'd never felt this way about any other woman.

Especially not Amberlyn.

Amberlyn was beautiful, yes, but in an entirely different way. Amberlyn said all the right things. Wore her hair and clothing exactly as she was supposed to—like the perfect ornament in a frame. And he desired her, as any man would. But it was a different feeling than this. This was an ache beyond the pangs of mourning. This was a wound plunged deep—and the salve to heal it.

Feya radiated an inner beauty that was like the timeless Highlands of Scotland. Rough in so many ways, but obviously formed in a rare mood of the Creator. Something one couldn't help but be in awe of.

Alasdair exhaled slowly. The coming cold made the window fog and Feya's image fade. He wiped the mist away.

Truth wrapped around him and pulled tight. Ever since Edinburgh the wildness of Scotland had compelled him. He'd seen sunlight that mimicked the portals of heaven on a clear day and heather spilled like paint upon the mountains. He'd never been able to admire Scotland before. But now . . . The wild beauty of Feya and Scotland were the same.

Alasdair closed his eyes against the flare of Feya's skirt as she turned. Looking upon her more might drive him to the edge of sanity, and he was already dangerously close.

This either had to be killed or embraced. There was no middle ground.

He opened his eyes.

The music stopped. Feya leaned against a tree with her face turned toward the river. Suddenly, she looked back—across the field and to the caravan he was in.

Fire crept across his skin, but he didn't look away.

Chapter Twenty

There was always the fear.

Fear stayed with her through the hours, like a shawl. She thought about giving in to the emotion—believing that the bairns were dead after a week of being away—but she had to hope, didn't she? Because if they were gone, she would know, wouldn't she? Wouldn't it come upon her like a cold, rushing wind and push her finally into the grave?

But none such feeling had come. Not when Alasdair held her captive the first two days, and not when her captor had changed to a Gypsy queen. And now, as she pretended to be the perfect Gypsy, she had only a feeling of urgency, like a great clock ticking. The bairns still breathed, but maybe not for long.

Ma had called this faith, but to Feya it had always looked like walking in the dark with hands outspread, feeling for something solid to grasp.

Feya stood by the Gypsy queen's caravan and pretended she didn't see Alasdair. She turned her face away but still felt the heat of his gaze burning like a hot coal.

She busied herself with pouring water for the queen and then took her own drink, tipping the glass high until the cool liquid was gone.

It didn't help.

He still looked at her. Feya knew that. He waited. And he was full of need. She was the only person in the world who could change whatever fate the Gypsies had planned.

Trust him, he'd said. Two words that carried the weight of the world. If her fate was already written in stone—cursed blood of the Gypsies—shouldn't she be true to that part of herself and trust the Gypsies instead? She'd seen the way Alasdair tried to charm the Gypsy queen. He was probably doing the same with her.

Feya crossed the field and went to the tents set up by the river. "He's not of my world." She nodded to convince herself. Just because their lips had touched in the caravan, it meant nothing. It was only an accident. The fact that the moment had replayed in her mind more times than she'd breathed was foolishness. It was only her heart searching for comfort. And the way one glance of his blue eyes shook her deeply . . . He was handsome, that was all.

Thoughts like these brought women down low. Gave them more children than they could feed. Soon men's pretty promises wore out, and women were left wondering what happened to the sweet words. By the time it was all over, they were just like Ma—dying in the tenements, their life's blood spilling onto the floor.

Alasdair Cairncross could take her to that place of wanting. And it wouldn't be very hard. She'd be worse than when she started the journey in chains.

Feya passed a copse of wood; the trees huddled together and shivered in the wind. She stepped inside, longing for a place of hiding. She put her hand upon her side. Tightness . . . always the tightness. She took a breath, and still her lungs didn't feel right. Of all the times to catch a sickness. Why did she have to fall ill that fateful night at Holyrood? From the feeling of her lungs, perhaps she would never be well.

The bushes rustled. A fluttering of scarves. The Gypsy men who always watched her weren't far away.

She turned and walked out of the woods.

She'd heard the girls in the tenements talk about being fancy on a man. The symptoms were ridiculous: lack of appetite, nervousness, feeling like the world was on fire. Before long, they were heavy with the man's child . . . and no marriage vows were ever said. It was always the same.

It would not happen to her. The bairns came first, and that was that.

It didn't matter that Alasdair had more money than Da and a good position. He was still a man. And she had no illusions that he'd actually want her for more than a tumble in the hay. If he even wanted that.

Feya touched her cheeks, which still burned. "I must be goin' crazy. All this trouble's meltin' me brain." She put her arm around the tree and leaned in. The cool bark felt solid, stable. "I'll put these illusions out of my mind."

A limb snapped behind her. Her constant Gypsy shadows closed in.

"What are you doing there?"

"Takin' a rest." She turned to the big one and scowled. "Don't ye have anythin' better to do than watch me like a babe?"

"No." His voice scraped like a shovel on muck. "Whatever it is you should be doing, do it. Or do you want me to tell Kizzy you're acting suspicious?"

"I'll talk to her meself. And tell her what I please." Feya raised her chin and strode past the brute. She acknowledged the other man by bowing her head. He wasn't as hard, and the extra sugar she put in his tea on the first night had softened his opinion of her.

He smiled as she passed and looked at her a little too long.

Feya had seen that look on other men's faces at the tenements.

That look scared her more than cruelty. She held onto the sides of her skirt and quickened her pace to Kizzy's tent.

It hadn't taken a lot of work to make herself a Gypsy again. Her childhood and teenage years in the camp were an old cloak, and one that fit comfortably. It was easy to lose herself in the music and dance in the light of the lanterns.

Feya walked around the queen's tent. Fine, colored sheets were draped over ropes, as well as animal hides. She had learned earlier that this place was their permanent dwelling, wherever here was. It was a place totally hidden from the world. A place she never would have dreamed existed. These people had done it—what her father hadn't been able to manage. They'd kept the old ways and not let the regular people drive them out.

The door of the tent snapped impatiently in the wind.

"You may enter, Feya." It was the queen's voice.

Feya lifted the tent flap. "How did ye know I was there?"

"I know a lot of things." The queen sat on the floor, applying makeup around her eyes. The incense Feya had smelled outside was thicker—like woods and earth and something else she couldn't name. Pillows were scattered upon the rugs, thrown about like an angry child had tossed them.

"How are you feeling today, my dear?" Kizzy followed the curve of her eyelid with the pencil and then fanned it out onto her temple in an elaborate scroll.

"Better." It was a lie, but at least the walk had cleared her mind somewhat. "I've come to ask ye fer a favor."

"Is that so? You must think I'm in a good mood." Kizzy turned her face and added sparkle to her cheek. "In fact, I feel quite peevish."

"How can I ease yer discomfort?"

Kizzy placed the beauty powders upon the floor. "Do I look old to you?"

"I beg yer pardon?"

"You can tell me the truth." She narrowed her eyes, the green powder a stark, beautiful contrast to her strange silvery eyes.

Feya stepped closer. "Ye are very beautiful, Kizzy. Much prettier than me."

The queen sighed. "If that were so, I wouldn't have the problems that I do."

Feya wanted to ask her to elaborate, but it was hardly her place. She was at the mercy of this woman. One word from her and she'd be dead. Over the past few days, Feya had seen her rule with a rod of iron.

Kizzy stared at the tent wall billowing with the wind. Shadows of people fell on the makeshift walls as they passed between the tent and the fire outside. Someone put their hand against the cloth of the wall as they walked. "I have loved a man for years, and he has never returned my affection. What do you think about that?"

"I hardly know." Feya swallowed. The queen's entire mood had dropped, and Feya felt it. "Love is not my specialty. I'm better at peeling potatoes and washing pans."

Kizzy stood. "Give me your palm."

Feya took a step back. "I don't think that's a good idea."

"Why not? Too much Gypsy for you? If there's one thing I know about you, it's that you're not afraid." She raised and eyebrow. "Or am I wrong?"

Feya extended her hand.

Kizzy slid her index finger down Feya's palm. "Even more interesting than I thought." She narrowed her eyes.

Feya tried to pull her hand away but Kizzy held it still. "What do ye see?" She rolled her eyes to the ceiling, frustration clawing on her like fingers. "A romance to rival the ages? Ten children with rosy cheeks and silk ribbons in their hair?"

Kizzy's expression changed to stone. She dropped Feya's hand, stepped away, and widened her eyes. "Sometimes it's better not to know."

Feya's stomach dropped despite the fact that she didn't put stock in such things. "Bad news, is it?"

"Worse than that." Kizzy sat down and looked as if she considered her words. "You don't have a love line."

The information brought a flash of heat into her body. "Well." Hadn't that been what she wanted anyway? Men were trouble, plain and simple. "That's better than having me heart broken."

"There's nothing better than love."

"I suppose I'll never know." The wind kicked up again, and it must have brought dust into the tent, because her eyes stung and watered. "I thought ye said yer love wasn't returned. Why would ye say there's nothing better than love?"

"The pain that I feel is better than not loving."

Feya laughed and used her sleeves to wipe her eyes. "Seems I don't have a choice." Some things were set in stone. Hadn't Robert Louis Stevenson said the same thing at Deacon Brodie's?

Kizzy took Feya's hands in her own. "We always have a choice."

"Is that why I was captured? Is that why my brothers and sister are starving?"

Kizzy stepped away. The hard look was back on her face. "Some people believe that only the people you were born to are destined. That the rest is our choice, and every choice matters." She paused. "But what do I know?" She stared down at the pillows. "What can I do for you? I'm sure you didn't come here to discuss fate."

Feya looked at her palm and then squeezed it shut. "I want to talk to the Englishman."

Kizzy's hand stilled over a container of rouge. "You should know that we've reached our destination."

"Have we?" Feya crossed her arms and held herself. "And where is that?"

"Loch Ness, darling."

"Loch Ness?" Feya dropped her hands. "That's ages away from Edinburgh."

"I told you we were going to the end of the world. You didn't believe me?"

"But . . ." Feya put her hand on her forehead. Strange things happened in Loch Ness. Everyone knew that. "What business does Cairncross have here?"

"If you were a full Gypsy, I'd have no problem answering that question."

"Haven't I pleased you in all these days?"

"Yes. But something lingers in your eyes."

"I have to go back to the bairns."

"A noble cause, but probably a fruitless one."

Anger made Feya sway. She measured her voice to be calm. "I know yer not that cold hearted. I've watched ye."

Kizzy studied her for a moment and then waved toward the door. "Go if you must. But don't dally." She went back to adding more green powder to her eyes. "I'm taking him soon with a group of men. Someone is very anxious to meet him."

"Thank ye." Feya turned to the tent flap.

"Why do you want to talk to the Englishman?"

Feya stopped. Her heartbeat quickened. "I want to let him know that he didn't win and that I'm leaving. It would bring me a great deal of satisfaction."

"Very well. As I told you earlier, we can take you back to Pitlochry. But we'll be here another week at least."

"I can't wait that long."

"You'll go alone across the wilderness to try to get back to the bairns?"

"I have to." Feya wanted to ask for a horse and supplies. She kept her mouth shut instead.

Kizzy called the names of her watchers. The two men entered the tent.

"She's free to go now. You can go back to your business."

"Very good." The big man bowed.

"What?" Surprise flicked across the other man's face. "She's leaving?"

"She says she is. Does that bother you, Emil?"

Emil drew his eyebrows together but said nothing. Kizzy returned her focus to Feya.

"I'm not in the habit of giving things away with no return. You'll leave the jewelry, of course. And change back into that Scottish dress we found you in."

Feya slid the bracelets from her arms and removed the earrings. She placed them all on the side table. Wherever they had come from, they would have brought a hefty price to aid her back to Edinburgh. But she'd not risk such a thing. Not even a coin from this woman.

"You would have made an excellent Gypsy, Feya." Kizzy reached for a few scarves and arced them into the air. "You can have these to remind you what you turned your back on. And when you're tired of slaving in the city . . . don't come back to me."

Feya caught the scarves and squeezed them in her hand. A thought formed in her mind, like the edge of a knife. "Might I ask ye fer one more personal favor?"

"You *do* think I'm feeling generous."

"I'd like to have his jacket back. As a souvenir. The girls in Leith would laugh for a year if I brought it back to them."

"Take it. It's in the trunk. I doubt he'll need it where he's going." Kizzy fanned her hand in the air as if it were beneath her to even discuss it. "Now leave me. I must prepare."

Feya acted quickly, her heart near bursting. "Since the Englishman thought it good to inflict such terror in me, I'd like to do a little of the same. What's in store fer him?"

A slow smile formed on Kizzy's face. "Mr. Cairncross has a personal invitation to Aldourie Castle on the shores of Loch Ness."

"Sounds lovely," Feya said flippantly.

"Oh, it won't be. I can assure you of that."

Feya ran through the woods, clutching Alasdair's jacket. She'd made a wide arc around the camp and stopped just before the clearing.

"I'm an idiot. A complete numptie." Her breath pushed from her lungs and wheezed on the way back in. What had she been thinking, running like that when she felt so poor?

Moonlight stretched over the roof of the caravan, falling like a blanket over the eaves. No one appeared to be on guard.

Feya crept to the window where she'd seen his face. She knocked on the cold glass pane.

Nothing. Crickets answered in a bush not far away.

She cupped her hands around her face to peer inside.

Only shadows and darkness. An old wooden stool.

The trees creaked in the wind, groans from the centuries.

Surely the door would be locked. But the doorknob turned with ease. The door squeaked as it opened.

"Hello?"

No answer came.

"Alasdair?" Feya whispered his name and rubbed her arms from the cold. It was colder inside than out.

He was gone.

Books lay on the floor as if they'd been knocked from the shelf.

The blanket was half on the bed and half off. The pillow was indented, as if he had just lain there. She touched the woodstove. It was dead cold. He should have had a fire hours ago. Long before she'd seen his face in the window.

Moonlight slanted on the table. Shadows fell into what looked like a carved *F*. She traced it with her finger. Wood shavings scattered under her touch.

It was a recent carving.

Feya jerked her hand back. "Why?" The pain in her lungs returned. Her feet felt heavy and stiff. She forced herself to move to the door.

To the right, three sets of footprints pressed into the dirt and gave evidence of a struggle. The trail led into the woods. She followed. The moonlight bent low through the trees and shone on fading bluebells, turning them white like fairy lights. The trail grew thick with ferns and flowers. Tree roots heaved up like great mossy fingers.

Men's voices wafted through the trees. And the trees kept groaning. The thick limbs kept reaching into the inky sky.

The sound of a fist making contact echoed through the woods.

Feya dropped down in the ferns.

Footsteps approached, snapping twigs.

"The English dog almost took my nose off!" A Gypsy man walked past her, his eye black, blood running from his nose.

Another man laughed behind him. "That's what you get for taking your eyes off him."

Feya crouched lower, next to the scent of pine and rich earth. The men walked away, back toward the camp.

Alasdair's voice reached her—English mixed with Scots, although she couldn't understand the words. Heart beating wildly, Feya clutched his jacket and rose, sneaking along the line of ferns and wood moss. The forest floor took a dip. Slowly she crept along a ridge.

Below, Alasdair stood tied to a tree. His hair was wet, whether from sweat or water, she couldn't tell. He looked so strange—more wild Highlander than London gentlemen. A bloody gash sat just above his right eye. His head was down. He had a beard.

Another Gypsy stepped out from the trees and punched him. Alasdair doubled over and strained against the ropes. "Is that as hard as you can hit?" He brought his head back up and spit blood on the ground.

The man drew back again.

Feya stepped forward. "Wait!"

Alasdair turned. Surprise bled onto his face.

"What are you doing here?" The Gypsy narrowed his eyes. "Where's Ian and Emil?"

Feya scrambled down the ridge, knocking leaves and sticks to the side. "It doesn't matter. I'm free to go. I've met the queen's agreement."

"So go, then."

"I've unfinished business." Feya inclined her head toward Alasdair. "With him." She put a look of anger on her face. "Thought ye could get away with treating me like an animal?"

Alasdair's eyes widened.

"I'll show ye what it means to cross a Gypsy." Feya drew her hand back and slapped him across the face. Hard.

The Gypsy behind her laughed. "Oh, she's a spitfire. I should let her get you ready to meet the master."

Her hand stung. Red appeared on Alasdair's cheek in the moonlight. He raised his eyebrow, but said nothing.

Leaves and loose dirt scattered the ridge. Another man made his way down. "Get over here and help us with the transport."

"And here I was having so much fun." The Gypsy walked past her. "You can have your way with him for a little while."

Torches appeared above. When the Gypsy met them, the lights faded and then disappeared over the ridge.

"I deserved that, I suppose."

The rich English tones of his voice washed over her like a deep calling. She stepped back to him and grabbed his shirt. "They're taking ye to Castle Aldourie. This is Loch Ness."

His eyes flicked to her hand upon him. "Why do you tell me this?"

"Because I don't want ye to die, ye stupid half Englishman."

He smiled. "You have my jacket, I see."

"Is that all ye can say at a moment such as this?" She searched the ground. If only she could find a sharp rock.

"Feya, I can take care of myself."

"Ye were doin' a fine job of that just now." She crouched and threw some leaves aside.

Noise sounded from above.

"They're coming." Alasdair's breathing came hard. "Just go."

Torchlight reached for the trees.

"I can't just go." The words surprised her. But they were the truest thing she'd said in days.

The clouds shifted. Moonlight washed onto Alasdair's face, revealing worry lines she hadn't known existed. "Rip the piping from my jacket."

"What?" She threw more leaves aside.

"There's a wire that keeps the shape. See if you can get to it." His gaze went to the trees and the growing light.

The yellow piping was loose. Feya tore it and found the wire.

"That's right."

Feya rushed to him and threaded the wire under the ropes. "Hurry."

"What do ye think I'm doin'?" She pushed her sleeves down over her hands for makeshift gloves and moved the wire back and forth.

Voices filtered through the trees.

"You'd better hurry, half Gypsy."

She sawed and sawed until her fingers hurt. Until she was sure they were both done for. Fear pulled on her skin. It rode upon the wind in the valley like a harpy of old.

Alasdair's sharp intake of breath made her stop. She'd nicked him with the wire.

"Go on." He lifted his eyes to the ridge. Where the glow of the campfires flickered, crested the shadows of the men—cast them closer than what they were. Or were they?

Any moment they would descend.

The queen would kill her for sure.

Her fingers trembled, so she gripped the wire tighter. It stung against her thumbs and her fingers, but she had to go faster. Back and forth. Back and forth.

Rope fraying.

Heart fraying.

Her own dark blood smeared on her nails.

Alasdair's breath quickened. "Just a little—"

The rope snapped. He flung off the remnants and held out his hand. "Feya, run with me."

Chapter Twenty-One

Gypsy voices grasped in the dark. Behind the trees, over the ridge, the wind carried the guttural Romani tones and changed them, casting them into the forest. Howls skittered across the leaves above them. Sharp cries rose up from the ground.

Find them.

You won't escape.

Kill the woman.

The Gypsy who'd hit Alasdair stood on top of the ridge. Torchlight flickered behind him. The red scarves around his neck flowed through the air like blood. The men's shadows were demons in the darkness—stretching, running, flooding down the hill.

Feya slipped on wet leaves. Her knees buckled. She dropped Alasdair's jacket. A rock, bathed in moonlight, sliced through her palm.

"Hurry." Alasdair pulled her up. His eyes widened at the sight of them all.

Feya's heart beat frantically, straining in her chest. She reached for the jacket, but Alasdair pulled her away. Morna's skirt wrapped around her ankles, catching on her boots.

Trees blurred beside her as they ran—hazy moonlight and black. Cold pushed into her lungs, shoving in great spikes of ice and flame.

Her head roared, and her heart—it would burst into a thousand pieces and shatter against the sky. And the thick dome of black pushed down lower, floating ever more close. Her body—if it even was hers anymore—swayed numbly.

Running. Was she running? She was always running. But what from or what to she could not tell. Because thoughts didn't exist in the pain exploding in her chest. And breath—that precious commodity—was reserved for those who were well. Great ropes must be threaded around her throat. And lead poured into her lungs, burning away everything.

Alasdair looked back. His mouth moved. She couldn't hear any sounds.

The forest floor arced toward her. Moonlight magnified and glowed, burning the black tree trunks white, turning them all into tall ghosts of men, walking.

Sinking . . .

A force like an anvil hit her in the chest. She opened her mouth to breathe. Her lungs were tight stone.

The edges of the world dimmed—the forest, the shivering leaves, and Alasdair beside her. Blackness pressed in, warm and safe.

Somewhere distant, she felt a hand, and then fingertips.

"Feya!" Alasdair's faint voice turned into the wind and became nothing.

Falling . . . into the dark. She didn't care. There was no pain in the darkness. There was nothing. She was nothing.

Only a misbegotten thought on an ill wind.

Blue spears of light shot onto the forest floor. The light shifted as they ran, illuminating the path and sometimes swiping it away into nothing. Thick ferns, black in the darkness, caught like fingers on Alasdair's boots and pulled at his legs.

Even the land was against them.

The Gypsy torches were great orange eyes in the woods, darting in and out of the trees and getting closer.

Feya's grip slipped.

Moonlight spilled over her face. Her eyes were wide and full of pain.

Her head tilted back. She was falling.

Alasdair threw himself to his knees, dirt and leaves scattering in the wind.

Feya's body slammed against his chest. He wrapped his arms around her before they fell. Her head fell against his shoulder, as limp as a babe's. Blue seeped into her lips.

"Over here!" One of them spoke in English.

Alasdair flinched, his heart pounding, his breath coming too fast. The lack of food had made him weak. He tightened his grip on Feya.

"I saw them!"

Tall ferns swayed in the wind, rustling like curtains. There was only one way of escape, and that was over the hill and into the denser part of the forest.

A cloud passed and the moonlight shifted. The ferns swayed again, black again from lack of light. Perhaps it was possible to hide. If the cloud stood still.

Feya's blouse was white, a sure signal to the Gypsies.

"I saw something!" Shadows stretched closer.

Alasdair lowered his ear to Feya's mouth. Faint breath shifted his hair. Her next breath didn't reach him.

He had to act. Now.

He went to his knees, grasped her under the arms, and slid her across the ground. His muscles strained with the weight of her unconsciousness. Wet ferns slapped across his face, splattering water down his neck and into his shirt.

The ground turned to a pit of mud and debris. Cold water seeped into his trousers, the mud sucking at his boots. Feya's skirt caught.

Beneath his hands, the gold waves of color around her body faded to dull brass.

Alasdair tightened his grip and pulled. The mud pulled back, but finally, they were free. He tugged her into the thick covering of ferns.

Her colors drained into darkness. Only a faint glow remained.

She wasn't breathing.

Two men crashed through the trees.

Alasdair dropped, gathered her into his arms, and covered her.

God, help us. Keep the cloud still.

It was the first time he'd prayed in years. He slowed his breathing, the way he'd been taught in training. He put his cheek against Feya's and covered her head with his arm. He looked through the waving ferns and into the starry sky.

The Gypsies were close. He could hear their footsteps.

Alasdair slid his thumb into Feya's mouth. Her lips were as cold as death. No breath brushed his skin.

He wanted to tell her to breathe, shake her to make her do so.

The wind shifted the ferns above him.

"Where'd they go?"

"They have to be close. I can't believe you left her alone with him."

"How was I supposed to know she had a fancy for him?"

"Idiot. All you had to do was look at the way she watched him."

Alasdair drew his eyebrows together, hardly believing the words.

"Look. Footsteps." The man crouched down, so close his shadow fell just beyond the ferns.

Alasdair dug the toe of his boot into the ground, ready to pivot and attack.

"Something happened here. Look how the mud's disturbed."

Alasdair inched his arm away from Feya's head and placed his palm upon the ground.

The man slipped in the mud and fell, only a few meters away. He cursed and the other one laughed.

"Are you blind?"

"Shut up."

The wind blew again, cutting through the forest like a scythe. The ferns bent low over Alasdair's back. The tips trembled against his neck.

God, please stop the wind.

"Must have been a deer." The Gypsy stood. "Let's go over there with the others. They look like they've found something."

Alasdair waited until their footsteps faded. He raised his head. The torches were out of view.

"Feya." He turned her face toward him. In Egypt, a soldier had stopped breathing after the charge. The doctor had used something called the Silvester Method. It hadn't worked.

The clouds shifted again, flooding moonlight onto Feya's countenance. Alasdair lowered his face, put his lips on her mouth, and blew.

Her cheeks expanded with his breath. He pulled away and looked down. She didn't move.

"I'm doing it wrong." Alasdair swallowed, feeling the moments slip away. "What did the doctor do?" Sweat dripped into his eyes. He wiped it away. His hand stopped on his nose. "That's it." He pinched her nose and tried again. This time her chest rose with his breath.

"Come on, Feya." He blew again, then put his ear over her mouth and listened.

Nothing.

He should have told her to go on and not bother with him. He could have done it on his own. Even if the Gypsies beat him to death, it would have been better than this. She looked so fragile. And the gold about her was almost gone.

"Please breathe." He lowered his lips to hers and exhaled.

Pink tinged her cheeks. Her arm twitched beneath him.

"That's it. Good girl." He bent his ear, so close that her lips touched it.

A wheeze started low in her throat.

He tilted her face more, lowered his lips to hers, and blew hard. He could feel his breath going out of his body and into hers. Her chest rose and her throat expanded under his touch.

Feya's eyes flew open. Her gaze was frantic, her brown eyes focused on nothing. She coughed viciously and then choked. Her arms flew out, clawed the dirt, and thrashed the ferns.

"Breathe." Alasdair turned her onto her side. "Try to breathe." He stroked her back and looked over his shoulder. Still no sign of the Gypsies. He scooped her into his arms. "If you can, hold onto me." Her head dropped against his chest. She shook violently in his arms.

"I'm afraid." Her voice was faint.

"I've got you." Alasdair rolled her into his body and stood. He glanced at the sky. The clouds moved again, revealing the Big Dipper. He followed the constellation's outside lip to the North Star.

He swallowed with relief and then turned. Feya's skirt flared out and twisted around his back. The Southern Cross was just where it should be. An old friend. He followed the imaginary line downward to the ground. There. Just between those trees. South. To Edinburgh.

"Where are we going?" Her teeth chattered, he reckoned from shock.

Alasdair adjusted her weight and then walked. "Don't worry. I'm going to get us home."

Alasdair stumbled and almost dropped Feya. A muscle wrenched in his back. Rainwater dripped into his eyes, blurring everything.

He'd been walking so long he couldn't feel his legs anymore. And how long that time had been, he had no idea. The past hours blended like the slashes of rain. He'd carried her until he no longer could, then he'd draped her arm around his neck and helped her to walk. Now he was back to carrying her again. She shivered in his arms and turned her face into his chest. Her cheek against his soaked shirt was cold—too cold. And still her breath came in quick, whining gasps.

"Just a little farther." He wished he believed that. Numbness caught the muscles of his throat, casting his voice to the indifferent wind. A wave of exhaustion swept through his body, setting stone into his fingers and his feet.

There was nothing but a black, assaulting forest. The rain ripped the leaves and thin branches, throwing them to the ground. Oh, how he could fade into that tumultuous strain. And the burden in his arms—she didn't feel so heavy anymore.

Another pelt of rainwater slammed against his face, jarring him awake. Alasdair looked behind, sure the Gypsies were upon him. How long had he faltered? How many moments had been lost just now?

He'd cut across the land, left to right—night-laden streams and gullies too many to count. He'd followed the moonlight paths until there'd been no more paths to see. Backtracked and then gone forward. All the tactics he'd painstakingly learned in training. It had been twice the effort, but perhaps now they had some sliver of a chance. Although *perhaps* was an awfully vast word, full of unspoken things and possibilities. Especially since the Gypsies knew they were headed back to Edinburgh.

Alasdair trudged on, through ruts and thickets. For Feya's sake. For those siblings of hers. That was the only thing that drove him now.

The barrage of storm was both blessing and curse. Their tracks melted away. But if their bodies survived the beating, wet, and cold, it would be a miracle.

Puddles sloshed in his boots, very dangerous indeed. Shelter was imperative.

An outcropping of rocks cut through the inky horizon. Mist rose up, like God shook a blanket. Whites and greys melded, shielding whatever lay beyond.

Jagged rocks sliced his jackboots, tearing the highly waxed leather. Alasdair misstepped again, sending his right foot down hard. The chain on his boot caught on a low-lying branch. He ripped his foot away and the spur dropped to the ground.

Ruined. His boot was ruined. And only his arrogance was to blame. Of course he'd worn his dress boots instead of practical ones. And now, with his jacket cast away, he looked like a sopping wet vagabond. Alasdair closed his eyes for a moment and swayed. The palace was a world away, and that man—the one bearing the honor and representation of the queen—seemed like another.

"A two-day journey to Stirling. That was all it was supposed to be." He opened his eyes and considered just lying down in the field. The exhaustion—the pure, raw exhaustion of fleeing . . . Warmth was beginning to spread into his body.

Alasdair lowered his head and looked at the woman in his arms. The rain gathered on her eyelashes and her hair plastered against her pale cheeks. Thoughts swam like the wind and the rain, barraging his senses. Somewhere in the back of his mind he knew he was going into shock. He knew not to give in to the illusion of warmness. He cleared his throat and widened his eyes, forcing himself to focus.

The plunk of rain from his hair onto Feya's collarbone brought magenta, splattering and twisting above her. He took a long breath and just watched it spin in the air above her and then dissipate like smoke. A drop from his nose landed on her cheek. White—a rivulet of white followed the water. Another drop brought blue, swelling in the air between them. Cobalt like the deep, ever-moving sea. Calm flooded his body. Another breath brought more.

Alasdair took a step and then another. Once again, the colors made him not feel alone. Like God somehow cared for his plight and was ever present. Even if they meant his death, they could come. Because beauty was his—his own, private beauty, this madness.

Crags rose up beyond the field of muck. There—a space of black in the rocks. A cave. It had to be a cave.

Relief shook his body. "Look, Feya. A cave." He slid his arm from underneath her knees and placed her feet upon the ground. "Wake up." He shook her a little, holding her about her waist.

"Where?" Her eyelids flickered. She gripped the collar of his shirt, but then her head sagged against his shoulder.

Her cheek was in flames. "All right. Just try to move your legs." He half dragged her and forced her to climb. Step by step. Rock outcropping by jagged precipice. Higher and higher, so long he had no idea if she was alive or dead. Still he supported her.

Finally, they reached the cave. He stumbled inside, instantly assaulted by the lack of pounding rain. Chills like he had never known raked his body. Gently, he laid her down beside the wall, far enough in not to be touched by the white curtain of rain.

He wiped water from his face and caught himself before he fell. Exhaustion called to him again—a sweet song, low and deep. He jerked awake. He had to start a fire. Dry clothes would mean the difference between life and death. If they weren't dead already, which was a possibility.

He moved slowly, his arms stiff and his back screaming. "A little dry wood." He said the words aloud to remind himself of what he should be doing. "Start a fire." He took a step and kicked something.

Green sparks flew into the dark, flashing for a moment and then disappearing like they'd never been. Something was on the cave floor.

Alasdair knelt and slid his hands over the cold rock. A thin stick came into his grasp. "Thank you, God." He felt like a traitor saying the words. How long since he'd muttered them?

Feya wheezed in the dark. The sound was a relief. At least she still lived.

Far-off lightning illuminated the cave. Sheets of it came, accompanied by thunder.

Moment by moment, he found more sticks, leaves, and debris. He put them into a pile and then fished in his pocket for the piece of metal from the caravan.

There, behind a rock, were larger sticks. He collected them, shaved a point on the one, and made a long groove in the other. Now was the part he might not have any more strength for—the rubbing. The furious rubbing until the groove filled with shavings and then an ember.

Finally, after what seemed like an eternity, smoke curled from the stick. He added the kindling and blew, near delirious when the first flame appeared.

His shirt was the first to go, and then his trousers. Down to his undergarment, he rubbed his hands over the flame, knowing he hardly had time.

He went to Feya and kneeled. "Feya, you're soaked. You need to take some of your clothes off and get warm."

No answer.

Alasdair clenched his teeth until he felt pain radiate in his jaw.

Not this. Hadn't she endured enough? He stifled a curse, placed his hands underneath her, and lifted. She needed to be closer to the fire.

She sighed when he lay her down, but she didn't wake.

Alasdair shook her. "Feya, please. I need you—" The words died upon his lips. She obviously couldn't help herself.

Alasdair pulled her boots off, one by one. He peeled her drenched socks away. Her feet were ice.

"Sweetheart, you'd make this a lot easier on me if you woke up." He cringed at the use of the endearment, but it fit. Much more perfectly than he cared to admit.

He placed his hand on her cheek and shook her, but still she didn't wake. She muttered something unintelligible. That wasn't good. Not good at all. Dreams had taken her down. Most likely, she was delirious after what she'd just endured.

Layered scarves adorned her waist. He looped his fingers in the knots and pulled the first one away. Her hips rose with the movement. A flash of heat rushed over him. He sucked in his breath.

"Move quickly and think of England." Her blouse slid off her shoulder, revealing skin as soft as butter cream. The fire moved over the curve and turned her skin the color of honey. Alasdair bit his lip. "Get hold of yourself, man. Think of the queen, fat and eating meat pie."

Sweat broke out on his forehead. He moved his hand to the laces of her bodice and tugged. And curse it all if his hands didn't shake like he was drunk. The laces slid through his fingers like water.

Alasdair put his hands on his hips, turned away, and focused on breathing. "All right." He thought of curry, which always made him vomit. And the pungent rank of offal on Morrison Street. He glanced back. Off. Her clothes had to come off.

He clutched the laces again and pulled. The ribbon snapped and the last metal grommet on her bodice gave way. He tossed the ribbon into the air as if it had burned him. Which wasn't far off.

His heartbeat was in his ears. Suddenly, he wished he hadn't made a fire, as foolish as that notion was. His entire body was aflame, his thoughts even more heated. Which made no sense given the situation. She was in dire need of his help, and he couldn't get his mind off bedding her.

"Top-notch, Cairncross." He stood and walked to the other side of the cave. Never had he been more disgusted with himself. Never before had he experienced such lack of control with his mind.

After a moment to compose himself, he walked back and leaned down, putting his arms around her back, and lifting her. "Forgive me." He slipped her bodice off one arm and then the other. Her blouse was next. He inched it up and pulled it over her head, careful not to catch any of her hair on the buttons. The only thing left was her corset and chemise, but those would stay.

He lay Feya back down, and even in her feverish sleep she embraced him. The feel of her naked arms around him sent a bolt through him, like the rolling of summer thunder high on the Scottish hills. He turned his face into her neck and closed his eyes. This close, she smelled like everything he had forgotten: sunlight on the hidden wild grapes near Torphichen where he used to walk and where the fruit had dropped heavy in his hand. The tasting of it was as sweet as the low wind.

Feya moaned in his ear.

Alasdair pulled himself away and cursed. He grabbed the sides of her skirt and pulled it past her hips, her knees, and her feet. He tossed the sopping heap of fabric to the side, then took her foot in his hand and rubbed. "You'll be warm soon." He ran his hand to her knee and then down her shin.

Feya opened her eyes and looked down. Her eyes widened.

Alasdair gripped her calf. "You were—"

Her gaze lost focus. Her eyelids closed.

Alasdair relaxed his shoulders. "Thanks be to God for His unspeakable gifts."

Chapter Twenty-Two

Feya woke with a start. Her ribs ached, and when she took a breath, her lungs burned like a coal was set against them. Cold rock was at her back. A rock arch loomed above. She moved to sit.

"Stay there." Alasdair walked across the cave and knelt beside her. His hair was wet and curled around his ears. His shirt was ripped at the collar and gaped open, revealing his chest. "How do you feel?"

Feya lay back down and widened her eyes at the sight of him. Nothing about him spoke of the English palace guard. If anything, he resembled a Highlander—all wildness and hair askew. Water drops from his hair slid down his neck and pooled at his collarbone. Feya stared at the liquid, the way the firelight made it shimmer on his exposed skin. "I—Were we runnin'?"

"That's right." He hesitated. "What else do you remember?"

"The Gypsies." The room shrank, and the fire seemed too hot. Her lungs ached with a vengeance. She coughed, but that only made it worse.

Alasdair laid his hand on hers. "We escaped them."

"We did?"

He nodded and raised his dark eyebrows, concern lacing his expression. His hand was still cold from the rain, but something more rested in the weight of his touch. Comfort. Safety. The feelings moved along her arm like fine cloth. A shiver dove between her shoulder blades and trailed down her back.

"Are you cold?"

"I don't think so." Feya avoided his eyes and glanced over his shoulder to the fire. They were in a cave and it looked like they were hidden deep within. She could see no opening or entrance, only the rough arched ceiling and the orange shadows stretching over the walls.

"My chest hurts." She placed her hand on her breastbone as if the outward pressure would relieve it. It didn't. "Did I have an attack of the vapors? I've heard some women talk about that."

Alasdair smiled but then covered it by drawing his lips into a thin line. Seriousness passed over his face. "A spell of the nerves would have been preferable to what you experienced. You stopped breathing."

"Stopped . . . ?"

"I'm afraid so." He placed his other hand upon her shoulder.

Feya knew his gaze was set upon her, searching her face. She only had to lift her eyes and she'd be looking into the most astonishing blue. She thought of the night at Holyrood Palace when she'd first locked eyes with him and how that had tilted everything within her. That was nothing compared to this.

Her cheeks flared with heat. "Did I die?"

The weight in his touch increased. He paused for a moment too long. "Not that I could tell."

"Well." Feya shifted her eyes to the dirt smeared across his shirt and the ripped piece of his collar. She swallowed, her mouth dry. She should say something—something to break his touch. "I thought it was impossible to live after one stopped breathin'. Did ye do something to me?"

Alasdair cleared his throat and pulled back, brushing his fingers along her arm like an afterthought. "It wasn't your time to go." He turned, picked up two long sticks, and moved to the fire. The orange glow washed over him like a blanket spread over his shoulders. He picked up a stone from deep within the fire, using the sticks like prongs.

"What's that fer?"

The corner of his lip tipped up. "You'll see." He carried the rock a few meters across the cave and lowered it into a small pool of water. Steam rolled up and the water bubbled. He reached for a pile of pine needles and tree bark and threw them in. After a few minutes, he dipped a curved piece of tree bark into the pool. "I regret it's not strong and black, but it's the best I can do at present."

"Ye made tea?" Never in all her wildest days would she have imagined that he would be able to do such a thing, especially in the wild.

"The pine needles have some sustenance. And I reckon the hot liquid will do you some good."

"Thank ye." Feya took the makeshift cup and sipped. It was strong and bitter, but the heat and the steam were like instant medicine. As the liquid went down it felt as if her chest loosened a bit. "It's a wonder the Gypsies didn't catch us." She took another sip. "How did ye manage it? Where was I?" She laughed, nerves running through her. "Passed out on the ground?"

"Quite." He watched her over the lip of his own improvised cup.

"Fer how long?"

He looked into the fire and his expression turned deathly serious. "Long enough to scare me."

Feya gripped her cup tighter. To be scared, he would have to care about her. And that seemed impossible. "I don't think anythin' scares ye."

"Really?" He sat casually, leaning one elbow on his raised knee. "Who do you think I am? Some kind of Prometheus?"

"I don't know who that is." She laughed out of shame. Their differences in education were apparent.

Alasdair sipped his tea and winked. "Never mind."

Feya reached for a lock of her hair and fidgeted with it. Suddenly all she could think about was how horrible she must look—like a wild red sheepdog, she was sure. "Yer dauntin', ye know." A flash of embarrassment flooded her cheeks. She raised her eyes to his, worried she would see anger there.

"Am I?" Alasdair's smile grew. "Good."

"How's that good?"

"Comes with the job. I worked very hard to get a scowl like Prime Minister Gladstone and the intimidation skills of the queen's dogs."

Feya almost spit out her tea. "I'd say ye've been successful."

"Hmmm." The look he gave her said he was teasing. "Now I'm curious. What did you think of me that night at Holyrood?" He looked down into the tea and lowered his voice. "Chose your words carefully, half Gypsy."

"I thought ye one of Satan's minions."

Alasdair made a *tsk*ing sound. "Harsh." He glanced above her, and his pupils looked larger. "Has your opinion changed at all?"

"Yer . . ." What did she think of him? What could she say? Her lips closed as she was at a loss for words. In this light the color of his eyes reminded her of the royal blue in the queen's parades. Why did they have to be so compelling? Why couldn't they have been dull, ugly brown like hers? "Yer more than I expected."

"As are you, Feya." He sucked in his lower lip. "More than I expected."

Feya closed her eyes again. Every time she looked at him the oddest sensations coursed through her body. It must be the lingering sickness from Holyrood. Perhaps it was the effects of lack of breathing. And precisely this minute her breath was coming too fast.

Alasdair's hand was on her cheek. "Can you breathe? Perhaps you should lie down again." He placed his hand upon her back as if she were too weak to recline. Feya lay back and rested her weight against his arm. Above her, sitting so near, Alasdair filled her sight and blocked out all the darkness and shadows of the cave.

He moved his hand to the back of her neck, cradling her. "How do you feel now?"

"Better." The thoughts she'd had at the Gypsy camp—they moved on her like a reckoning. Him. Her. Together. But the possibility of Alasdair Cairncross wanting her . . . She knew it was a wispy hope, floating on a sea of dreams.

Such were his eyes, she realized. There were things unreachable in those dark-blue depths. She saw them now. It was in the powerful way that he looked at her—studied her every move. There were things in his eyes, fresh and unsullied by the filth that was her constant companion. He was full of life and unquenchable warmth.

He slid his hand from her neck and laid it at his side, casually. "Feya, if you're worried that you're dying . . . Well, I don't think so."

Yes, she was dying. But perhaps not in the way he spoke. "No?" The word came out raspy. He still hadn't looked away. The orange light of the fire arched over his head, pulsing and reaching, reflecting her desire to touch him—to feel the skin of his cheek under her hand.

"You're much too strong to give up now and die. Look how you've handled yourself." Color spread into his cheeks. He looked at the ceiling and swallowed. "I already told you no one else got as far as you did against me with your glass shard. And no one else has ever tried to poison me with belladonna, I can assure you."

Shame coursed through her at his words. She'd repent of that forever, she supposed. Without thinking, she laid her hand upon his wrist. Immediately she regretted it. His pulse quickened beneath her thumb, but she couldn't pull away.

Alasdair lowered his gaze to her hand. This close, she realized how long his eyelashes were. The firelight cast the shadows of them over his cheeks, like raven's wings.

"I'm sorry," she whispered, but she didn't know if she said it because of the belladonna or because she had touched him . . . or because she had yet to draw away.

"You were in a difficult situation. I would have done the same."

His voice lulled her, like the moments before slipping into a dream. "I don't believe ye."

"When I was in Egypt, there was this devil who—" He paused. "—was rather sadistic. I can assure you, I would have poisoned him, given the chance."

A stick fell in the fire, casting shadows over the smooth planes of his face. Feya tightened her grip, wanting somehow to let him know she could see the pain in his eyes and comfort him, as he had her. "Sadistic?"

"Creative in his methods of torture. Stuffed rags in prisoners' mouths and then poured water down their throats." His voice trailed off and left no doubt that he had experienced such a thing. "That was only one of the things he did." His lips closed, as if he regretted the words.

"It was as bad as that?"

The sound of the fire echoed off the cave walls.

"Worse." The last bit of palace guard fell from his eyes, leaving an expression so naked and honest that it twisted Feya's heart. A moment passed as she saw deep within him—the corners of his soul that he tried to hide.

She moved her thumb to caress the bottom of his wrist. *I'm here*, she wanted to say. *I'm sorry that ye've suffered.* She couldn't speak the words.

Alasdair flinched, as if he heard the phrases anyway. His lips parted, and then, suddenly, he drew his hand back and ran his palm over his face. He took a deep, shuddered breath.

Feya looked away to the rough, opposite wall. She was a fool. He must be disgusted with her now. She the gutter rat, daring to reach for someone like him. She could feel the emotions flowing from him, washing over her body like waves.

"Have you had problems with your lungs before?"

"Aye. It's been gettin' worse now fer a while." Feya moved her fingers against the floor of the cave and shifted the pebbles, turning them over like the quick, bad decisions of her life. "When ye were chasing me in Torphichen, I felt an awful burnin' in me chest." She dropped the rocks and covered her eyes, wishing he would go away, just walk out of the cave and never come back.

"Perhaps it is only because you've been sick."

Exhaustion wove through her bones. She allowed her mind to go numb. This feeling she was used to. It was a cloak easily donned. She used it with Da when he was speaking daggers into her heart. And when the men leered at her as she walked to the mill. And when the Farcy brothers held her down in the alley and almost had their way.

"Feya, are you all right? Your chest hurts again?"

"Aye. It hurts." She could feel tears at the corners of her eyes, but she wasn't going to show him that. No one saw that. It was the last thing she still owned.

"I'm sorry, Feya. I wish—"

"I'm strong like ye said." Da's words came back to her and raked along her wasted body—the lungs that didn't work right anymore, the hair too red, the skin too dark, and the eyes so brown they might as well be black.

"It's my fault we were kidnapped. If I hadn't lied to you at Torphichen and locked you in the church . . ."

A tear rolled down her cheek. She hated herself for it.

Alasdair moved quickly, lowering himself down beside her. He reached for her, turned her into his arms, and said nothing.

A shudder went through her. She froze. Having him so close was like sudden, bright lightning over the water when floating in a boat. His scent was pure and fresh—earthy forest and high, tempestuous rain.

Alasdair moved to cradle her neck, pushing her head against his chest. His heartbeat was strong and pulsing. "Cry." His voice above her was like the whisper of wings.

"What?" Her shoulders shook. The force of holding back tears was breaking her apart.

"You can cry now." Alasdair tightened his arms around her and brought his mouth close to her ear. "You don't have to be strong all of the time."

Feya closed her eyes and shivered, his breath upon her cheek. She brought her arm around him and let her fingers hover above his back.

"Feya, surrender your grief to me. I can bear it."

She brought her hand down upon his back and embraced him. As soon as she touched him, great soul-wrenching tears flowed from her eyes. Sobs ripped through her body, wracking her frame. The more she cried, the tighter he held her, an anchor in a nameless sea. She splayed her fingers out over his back and gathered his shirt in her hands.

"That's right." His voice was gentle, like the sun's first rays upon snow. "Cry until your heart's content. That is the only thing that is required."

Her tears seeped into his shirt, but he didn't seem to care. That alone made her cry harder. He'd endured torture and hardship and come out on the other side. He was the true measure of strength, not her. If ever there were a man she'd marry, she supposed it would be him. That thought brought another wave of grief.

Alasdair stroked her hair. "I'll get you home. I promise you'll see the bairns again."

Feya pulled away so she could see his face. There was nothing written there but sincerity and a promise she was sure he meant to keep.

"I promise," he said again.

She took in a shaky breath. "I believe ye."

He lay his head down on the ground beside her and stared into her eyes.

She was lying with a man. And not just any man. Alasdair Cairncross. Painters across the ages had painted faces like his. She followed his dark hairline down to his jaw and the stubble there.

"You have the most beautiful eyes." His voice was thick, and his accent had fallen into half-English, half-Scottish tones.

Feya's hand stilled upon his back. Fire licked the air between them.

Alasdair threaded his fingers into her hair. "There are so many variations of color in your eyes. I've studied them for days."

So this was how it happened. This was how Ma got herself pregnant with her. This was the weakness a man worked on a woman. And, oh, how she felt it. It would be so easy to lift her mouth to his and kiss him. It would be so easy to do anything that he asked. Every small movement that he made—the way he traced a pattern on the back of her head, the rise and fall of his chest against her, the warmth that his body brought to her coldness—it was an ancient melody, like the passionate Gypsy dance. Her body seemed to know the tune. She moved her hand over his shoulder blade, because it felt right.

Alasdair sucked in his breath. "After you fell, I laid you under the ferns." His words were strangled and drawn tight.

The muscles of his back quivered under her hand. "Where did ye hide?"

"I hid with you."

"Under the ferns?" It was a foolish question, she knew. But words were fading, and all thoughts but one: she longed for him. As she longed for a good life for the bairns.

"Yes. Nestled against your body." He took a shaky breath and pulled her closer. "Much like this."

His closeness made her head swim and her legs turn to jelly. "How long were we there?"

"You weren't breathing. I was more focused on that." Red spread along his neck and into the tips of his ears.

"Me face was pale?"

"Like death. Your lips were blue." The firelight on his chest turned him to bronze, like some great statue of old. He lowered his voice to a whisper. "I wish—" He closed his eyes and took a breath. His hand stilled in her hair. "Sweet Feya." Her name dropped like honey from his mouth.

"What do ye wish?"

"You make me wish my life was different." A thousand words were said within his eyes. His gaze fell to her lips. "How is it that I feel I know you so well? And yet . . ." He closed his eyes and breathed, as if trying to gather strength. "It's only been a matter of days." A little of the palace guard was back—the steel in his gaze, the way he clenched his jaw. He moved to pull himself away.

The gesture jolted her. Feya gripped his shirt to keep him close but the fabric slipped through her hand.

Alasdair stood and walked into the shadows.

The lack of him instantly made her cold. "Ye know I have a worthless father, and the bairns in me keepin'." The words came too fast. She wished he would turn so she could see his face. "If ye were listenin' to my conversation with yer mother, ye know me ma left this world almost two years ago."

He turned. Tenderness bled onto his features. "I was listening." His blue eyes darkened. The firelight turned them to sapphires. "I was also listening that night at Holyrood when the fever gripped you and you were talking out of your head."

"Is that so?" She wanted so badly for him to take her back into his arms, to feel the safety that his body brought to her.

He nodded. "You dream of living in a cottage by the sea."

He couldn't have stripped her more naked had he actually done it. "What did ye say?"

"You also want to teach Brenna to read. And have time to play with Gillis."

Her hand went to her heart. The ache was back, like a bandage ripped away too soon.

"And Hamish . . . You just want to hold him close to your face. And smell milk on his breath and know that he's eaten well."

"Aye." Tears welled up in her eyes and spilled over again. "That's what I want."

"You're a good woman. Despite what you think."

"If I was good, I wouldn't have left them, ye ken?"

"You have been nobler to me than some of my comrades in arms." His gaze was upon her again, burning and soothing at the same time. "Something runs through you more fierce than this Scottish rain." He looked out to the mouth of the cave and the moonlit white curtain of water pouring down. "You have only done what you thought was right. I am in awe of you."

Her eyelids fell at his words. If only she could believe that she was right and noble, as he was. If only she could wash the filth of her experiences away. And now, with him knowing what she really desired, he would know the other thing too—the thing she could hardly admit to herself.

She wanted him. In the way the sick pine for the morning. In the way the well pray for those who are ill. He was her candle in all the years of her darkness. The part of her that was still worth something. He called to that. With every glance, and even the way he tried not to look at her now—everything that he was, she only wanted to be something to him. To make him smile. To make his life somehow easier to bear. To take his father's mistreatment and his time in Egypt away.

But, most of all, she wanted to give him secret things. The short time in his arms confirmed it. Feya's heart thudded. How would he treat her if she did?

As if noticing the change in her thoughts, he scrutinized her with one raking gaze. He seemed to be choosing his words carefully. "Feya, you saved me twice. Even when I treated you as less than human. I need to know why."

Heat flashed over her body like a blanket on fire. "I can't answer that."

"You don't want to answer." He stared somewhere above her. "It's not that you can't."

"What are ye lookin' at?" She glanced above and behind, but saw nothing of consequence. Only the hard ceiling of the cave and a trickle of water dripping down the wall.

Alasdair flushed deep crimson. "I see things."

"What sort of things?"

He drew his lips together, as if he were shutting down the words. Finally, he spoke. "I need to know why you risked your life for me."

Feya stood and spat out the words. "Because ye were worth savin'." Dizziness pushed against her. Other words flooded in on her and pressed. *And because of what ye make me feel when ye look at me.*

His breathing increased. Conflict waged on his face.

Anger flooded her. Because he wouldn't touch her. Because of the passion she saw in his eyes. "What's the matter, Alasdair?"

"Honor. And duty."

"The kind of men who use words like that are usually the ones who are as far from them as Ben Nevis to the sea." Anger flashed in his eyes and it made her glad. "I imagine yer father said such things when he left yer ma heavy with child and alone."

"Feya." He said her name as a warning.

"Yer mother told me she loves ye. She longs to be with ye again."

"Don't call her that."

"Why not? She bore ye into this world."

He stepped toward her. "That's all she did."

"Ye don't believe that. I can hear it in yer voice."

"Woman, how is it that you think you know the intricacies of my heart?"

Why shouldn't she? He seemed to know hers. She stepped closer and mocked his tone. "I know ye. Yer a handsome man who's used to getting what he wants. Especially from women."

He flinched.

"That's why yer engaged to Amberlyn." Saying the woman's name brought another wave of dizziness.

"How dare—"

"What do you really want, Alasdair? Is it her? Or are ye marryin' her because yer father told ye to? I think it's time fer ye to be honest with yerself."

He walked past the fire but then returned and pointed at her. "You wouldn't even have an opinion to give if I hadn't given you my breath."

"What?"

"You should keep your opinions to yourself." His eyes flashed. "Especially about my choice of wife."

"What do ye mean ye gave me yer breath?"

Alasdair held his hand up as if he was trying to gather patience.

"Lie back down and go to sleep."

"What did ye do to me?" Feya swayed.

Alasdair moved quickly and put his hand on her elbow. "Woman, lie back down."

Feya lifted her chin and looked him square in the face. "Not until ye tell me what ye did."

"I lay on top of you. I prayed the Gypsies wouldn't see you, then I covered your head with my arm."

"Go on." Her heartbeats came too fast and the longing only deepened with every tone of Scots-English.

"I tried something very unconventional. Something I saw in Egypt. I put my mouth over yours and blew my breath into your body." His blue eyes stared deep into hers. "Again and again. Until finally, you breathed."

Feya drew her eyebrows together. She hadn't expected that.

Alasdair gave her a hard look. "Rest. We have a long way to go."

She wanted to cry again. And that disgusted her all over. He truly had saved her life, just as she'd saved his. "I'm sorry fer being contrary."

"Come now. I'd hardly know how to act if you lost your contrary spirit. Your vehemence has been my companion for some days now." His words were light but she knew he was angry. He led her back over to her place by the fire. "Get some sleep."

Feya took the hand he offered and lowered herself down. "What about ye?"

"I'm used to not sleeping."

"That's unnatural."

He rolled his eyes and threw more sticks into the fire. "Maybe for some."

"I hope ye know what yer doing."

"I was trained for situations like these, remember?" He tried to mask the weariness in his voice but was unsuccessful.

"That had better be true." She put a bite in her tone just to spite him. Because she wanted nothing more than to be back in his arms again. "If ye forget yer trainin', those Gypsies will be upon us again. If they catch us, I can tell ye fer sure our blood will be seepin' into the ground." She knew he didn't deserve the words, and she felt sullied just saying them.

A shadow crossed his face. "I told you I will get you back to Edinburgh, and I will." His hand stilled on the firewood. "Those words don't seem to be the ones you really want to say, Feya. What do you really want from me?"

Her heart pounded in her ears. Her voice fell to a whisper. "I don't want anything."

Alasdair laid the wood upon the fire, like strategically placing a chess piece. "Is that so?"

Feya pulled at a loose thread on her skirt. "Ye know I just want to go home."

"Your eyes say something different."

Her hand froze over the fabric.

"And the way you touch me says even more."

When Feya had the courage to look up, he was gone.

Chapter Twenty-Three

Alasdair stepped outside the cave and breathed hard. He counted in multiples of three. Grabbing a nearby tree branch, he shook it until cold rainwater poured down. It soaked him once again, but he didn't care. Maybe the chill would do something against the fire in his blood and the onslaught in his mind.

He shook the tree again and turned his face to the cold glare of the moon. The liquid drenching his hair, face, and shirt didn't help. Trickles ran over his shoulder—an acute reminder of where her fingers had stroked him and nearly driven him mad. "I didn't expect—" Alasdair squeezed the tree branch and forbid himself to look back to the entrance of the cave. All doubts about her feelings were gone.

He'd been a heartbeat away from kissing her, and kissing her madly—dragging her into the frustration he felt, giving her the release she sought. And, most likely, reaching heights of pleasure they both had never known.

Alasdair pushed away from the useless tree and walked a few paces away. He bent and gripped his knees, forcing himself to focus.

Down below, a lush valley stretched out in the moonlight. Green and white mingled together, contrasting but complementing at the same time. An owl hooted somewhere, and then he saw it, expanding its wings and bursting through the forest canopy and into the night. Wisps of red trailed the bird—the effects of his condition.

Another breath, and he was near himself again. He stood and crossed his arms.

The ledge was a perfect vantage point to watch for the Gypsies. But oh, what a climb. The hours wore upon his body. He had no idea of the time, but it was late—near morning.

Anger was an easy substitute for desire, and one he could easily employ.

Feya was the most ungrateful person he'd ever laid eyes upon. How dare she accuse him of not taking the proper precautions with their escape? What did she think he'd been doing for the past six hours? Playing whist and stuffing his face with cake?

The retorts he could take. The bites and jabs were easy. He knew as sure as the queen reigned that Feya said such things because she didn't know what to do with her pain. She was like an animal in a vice most times. Being away from the bairns had made it so.

He walked to a puddle and splashed his face.

The worst part of all of this wasn't that they were fugitives. It wasn't even that there was some unknown plan for his detriment in the Scottish hills. The worst was that even in his anger, his arms still tingled from holding her. She'd fit perfectly, like a puzzle piece. Like that was just the place she was created for. One look from her and he felt adrift—a man ablaze with no thoughts but one. And that scared him more than he liked to admit.

If the experience he'd had while watching her dance could be compared to a war, what he experienced now was bloody Waterloo and he was Napoleon. He'd been lying to himself. The attraction hadn't started with her Gypsy dance in the camp. It had started the first time he'd seen her. It was the fire in her eyes when she'd defied him. It was the way she'd longingly looked at Rowan and obviously wanted to reunite them. It was the way she'd stood in the moonlight after she'd knocked the water flask away.

He owed her his life, two times now. He supposed he'd returned that payment tonight, but what about when they made it back to Edinburgh? Could he really just let her go back to the tenements?

"Anything but that." Alasdair cast his gaze to the sky and the crystalline stars. "One True Living God, what do I do?" The old name for his Creator pulled at his heart. He'd not uttered those words since before the Guard. It was how Morna addressed God, the way she'd taught him as a child. They were the words of the prophet Elijah as he called down fire on the Baalite priests on Mount Carmel.

Memories came back as the cold wind gusted. His blood mingled with Egyptian sand. The horror. The pain. But then the feeling of not being alone. God's presence real and tangible.

He headed back to the cave and then made his way in the dark until he saw the glow of the fire. He'd purposely chosen a deep place where the smoke and glow wouldn't be noticed. Feya couldn't see those details, and he supposed she never would. Nor would she know that as every kilometer had passed, the thought of Hamish, Brenna, and Gillis had torn him apart. He wouldn't be responsible for the death of three children.

He went back to the fire and sat some distance away from Feya. The gentle rise and fall of her chest told him she was asleep.

The beautiful gold was back exactly where it should be.

It was folly to look at her. He knew that. Just as he knew the elaborate drills of the Guard. Her strength made him think that he could be a better man. And her passion . . . He ran his hand over his face.

He was dangerously close to falling in love with Feya Broon.

He began thinking the strangest things. Like that if he had a woman like Feya beside him, he would finally be able to rest. Perhaps even laugh again. Not think about every angle, every decision. Finally, he could just be.

Amberlyn wouldn't have had the courage to set him free back in the woods.

He thought again of Feya's siblings. Just one month of his wages would solve most of their problems. And that cottage that Feya dreamed of? How coincidental was that? The sea sang in his blood no matter how much he tried to lie.

This was a very dangerous endeavor. More dangerous than being captured by the Gypsies for only God knew what purpose.

He threw another stick into the fire. To get back to Edinburgh, it was at least four days walking with no rests, and that was impossible. It would be grueling and hard. And with no horse, even more dangerous. Cold was coming from the north, probably early snow. Just like Scotland to lavish more cheer.

The best thing would be to find the first town and get some work. But that would take more time that Feya didn't have. She was ill, despite what he'd told her. Something was definitely wrong with her lungs, and she needed a doctor.

Alasdair leaned back against the wall. He wished he could sleep like Feya. But the innocent were always like that. As soon as their heads lay down, they were gone to the world. Free of regrets.

As he would never be.

Despite the rain of the previous day, the bright yellow rays of the sun stretched into the cave like fingers—over the rocks and Alasdair's boots by the fire.

Feya had been staring at him for quite some time, ever since the first bird had dared to make a song. Her sleep had been good and deep. Surprising, given the circumstances. The fire had long since died, and she hadn't moved to stoke it. The coals still warmed her feet, though, like the putting on of an extra blanket by a mother.

"Aren't ye such a man to be reckoned with, then?" Feya leaned her hand on her cheek and watched him breathe. The moments built upon one another—the rise and fall of his chest, how much she wanted to brush his hair away from his forehead. It made her feel unstable, like she'd just downed one of Da's whiskey bottles.

She stood and headed for the cave entrance.

"Where are you going?"

She might have known that Alasdair's senses were that sharp. "Just outside."

"Not before I check the perimeter." He sat up. "How do you feel this morning?"

"Better. What's yer plan?"

"To get as far away as possible."

"Good plan."

He walked past her and outside. After a few minutes, he came back in and scattered the burnt wood coals. "I'm sorry for being harsh with you last night. I was angry."

Feya scowled, more from shame. "I'm the one who should be apologizing. The last thing I said to ye was unkind. I was just angry because . . ." Feya forced herself to look at him. The thoughts she'd had last night—they were even stronger in the daylight. She loved him. And he could break her into a thousand pieces if he chose. "I'm a simple woman, Alasdair. My temper sometimes gets the best of me."

He hid a smile. "You are anything but simple. And we should save our tempers for the journey. We're both going to need our strength." He flicked his gaze to her. "And resolve. Plenty of that."

"Whatever ye say." Feya nodded. "I'll do whatever ye want."

The corner of his lips turned up and a bit of his devil-may-care look returned. "*Whatever* is an awfully vast word."

"They what?" Ranald brought his fist down against his library desk. Fury burned the back of his neck and seeped deep inside.

Kizzy flinched. "Escaped. I'm sor—"

"How do two people manage to escape in the company of two hundred? Tell me that." He moved around the desk, his hand still pointed at the half-written paper he'd been ready to send to Edinburgh. "How?"

Kizzy frowned, and it made her age show through her face paint. "It was the woman—Feya. We trusted her."

"Trust no one. Isn't that what I told you a month ago when you stood in this exact place?"

Kizzy looked down. "She was different. One of us."

Ranald ran his hand over his eyes. "She's obviously in love with him."

"I . . . I didn't think—"

"That's right. You didn't think." He closed his eyes and felt the pressure wrap around him like a vice. This could not happen now. It was the critical moment.

"We've been combing the woods for hours. It's like they disappeared."

Numbness seeped into his body. "Only God can do that. Only He can disappear." He went to the chessboard and moved the black rook a space forward. He purposely softened his features and let his fingers brush the top of his queen. When he turned, he had the look upon his face that he knew Kizzy loved. "I'm being too hard on you.

Of course you've done your best." He stared into her eyes and held his revulsion at bay. "Have you eaten?"

"Not since last night."

"Come." He placed his hand upon her back and rubbed it for effect. "We will talk. I want to know everything about this Alasdair. I'm sure you have much to say."

"He's not like his father."

That made him pause. "No?"

"He has a weakness for Feya. So much so that he carved her initial into my best table in the caravan."

"Sentimentality." The old version of himself might have commiserated. "How unfortunate for him." He tapped the edge of the table. "But very good for us." He led her to the doorway and looked back over his shoulder at the men. "They're on foot. And they're not far."

"We'll find them today," Kizzy said. "Make no mistake."

"Of course you will." He lifted her hand and kissed it, letting his lips linger just until he saw complete adoration in her eyes.

"How far do ye think Pitlochry is?" Feya squinted at the glare of the sun against a rock face.

"Far enough. Don't focus on the distance. Just take one step at a time."

It was good advice, but it annoyed her. What annoyed her more was that for the past half hour she'd been trying to engage him in conversation just to hear the honeyed tones of his voice.

"What's bothering you?" He climbed the rocks and stood beside her. "You've been peevish all morning."

"Ye must be imaginin' things, Alasdair. I feel fine. We've escaped. I'm very happy."

"Mmm." He narrowed his eyes and studied her. "Is that right?"

"The sooner we're back in Edinburgh, the better."

He flicked his glance to her and then back, as if he was afraid to look in her eyes. "On that we agree."

She crossed her arms. "Where are ye goin' to live after you're married?"

"And why, pray tell, would you want to know that?" He turned and crossed his arms. "Planning on sneaking in some fateful night and disrupting my life?"

"No. I wouldn't dream of it. I doubt we'll ever see each other again after this. Not even in passin'."

He worked the muscle at his jaw. "You're right."

"I know."

"Look. If you are in some bizarre way worried about me—"

"I'm not." She was worried about herself after he was gone. "Yer a very capable man."

"Usually."

"What does that mean? Why are ye doubtin' yerself?"

"It's not important. And neither is this conversation. Shall we move on?" He gestured to the path beyond.

Feya raised an eyebrow. "Every time a man tells a woman that something's not important, he's not tellin' the truth."

He walked a few paces and then stopped. "I'm dying, Feya."

His words were like buckets of water pouring down from the tall, shivering trees. "What did ye say?"

"I'm afflicted with some sort of ailment of the mind. I don't know . . ." He swallowed and looked away.

She crossed the boulders to stand before him. "What in the name of Bonnie Prince Charlie are ye sayin'?"

He lowered his voice. "There's something wrong with my brain. There always has been. I reckon I don't have long because the symptoms . . ." He looked above her, in the same strange way he had the night before. "The symptoms are increasing."

Feya opened her mouth to speak but could find no words.

"I told you in the cave that I saw things. For example . . ." He widened his eyes like he didn't believe he was about to speak the words. "Right now there is a very melancholy silver around your body. It's quite depressing. And your name tastes like . . ." Red bled into his cheeks. "Cherry cordial. But only the kind you can get from Prince's Street during Christmas." He stood straighter, as if he expected some rebuke to come.

Feya put her hand on her hip. "Cordial?"

"And letters have colors too. *R*s are blue, like the sea at twilight. *H*s are brown, similar to that tree over there, but not quite. And *G*s . . ." He winced. "Very hard to describe. Like a mix between Irish butter and clotted cream. But there's an undertone of something dark and sharp."

Feya squinted, trying to understand. "What else?"

"I . . ." He gave her an odd look. "You actually believe me?"

"Why wouldn't I? Yer not lyin' to me."

"No. I am not."

Stories came to mind from the Gypsies of long ago—people who saw things that others did not. "Alasdair, I don't think yer dyin'."

"Truly?" He shifted his weight. "You don't think I'm making this up?"

She laid her hand on his arm. "There are strange things in the world. Just because somethin' can't be explained . . ." She pursed her lips together. "Maybe it just doesn't have a name yet—this thing that allows ye to see. I'd say it's a great and terrible gift, ye ken?"

"A gift?" He spoke the words slowly.

"Just because ye see differently than me, who am I to judge?"

He noticeably relaxed.

"These things ye see . . . the colors . . . Do they put ye in a bad way?"

"Crowded places are particularly difficult." He studied her, waiting, she assumed, for laughter or some rebuke. "Certain sounds are unbearable. And certain things cause me to hear sounds. If I believed in curses . . ." His eyelids fell, as if he'd had the thought too many times.

And, oh, didn't she know about feeling that way.

He hardened the muscles at his jaw. "I haven't told anyone except for Father."

"I'd wager that went well."

Alasdair laughed. "Perhaps your Scottish ideals about the upper-class English are not so off after all."

Feya smiled, but it brought her no pleasure to be right. "What did he do? Laugh ye out of the room?"

He opened his eyes and looked sad. "Never mind."

"He beat you!" She paced. "The devil."

"He has good intentions."

She fell into Gaelic, and none of the words were nice. About how his father had stolen him from Scotland, from his mother and everything that he was. And then forced him to deny the gifts within him. To be someone he wasn't.

"It was a long time ago, Feya."

"And how does that make a difference? Ye've got scars that are not in yer flesh, but in yer soul. Things ye can't see just by looking."

"And you can?" Some of his English arrogance was back.

"Oh, aye. I see things. I have a way of readin' a person too."

He flung out his hands in a noble gesture and bowed. "Look your full." When he stood, he raised his chin and gave her a look that would have melted most women. It was his court look again.

"Oh, no." She gave him a wicked smile and inclined her finger. "You come here."

"As the Gypsy princess requests. Of course." He strode across the ferns. "Better?"

"Not quite close enough." She smiled again. "I have to look past all yer pretenses, and that's hard."

Alasdair rolled his eyes. He lowered his head slowly, toward her. "How about this? Can you see my pain yet?"

Everything within her quieted. She brought her hands up to rest on either side of his stubbled face. This was different than looking in his eyes at the cave. The light there had been dark, making his blue eyes all silk and suggestion. Now there were no shadows to hide anything. She pulled him toward her before she knew what she was doing.

Alasdair's smile dropped. Haughtiness fell away and another emotion replaced it.

But it had to be her imagination. It couldn't be that he wanted her. It couldn't be that he thought she was a possibility.

Alasdair placed his hands on her hips.

Feya sucked in her breath at his touch.

The wind clenched the fallen leaves and tossed them, sending them into a spiral above the ground. The tall alder trees above them groaned in the wind.

Alasdair pulled her closer.

When she'd seen his eyes in Holyrood Palace, Feya had known that this man would be her undoing. But she never could have guessed in what way. Love. He was both the sickness and the cure. The needing and the balm.

The wind blew gently through his hair. She knew then that there was indeed a God. For He'd chosen this man to be hers. Everything pointed that way. Alasdair's blue eyes. His birth in Torphichen. Him being a soldier.

The knowledge made her shiver. If God was that knowing, then none of her life had been an accident.

The longer Feya held him, the more he had to fight not to kiss her. And he didn't just want to kiss her. He wanted to keep her. He wanted to marry the woman. To save her from the hellish tenements, make the bairns his own. Care for them all as his family.

That's what he wanted. But those things weren't his to give. He'd made that promise to Amberlyn. He'd made that promise to Father.

Father held affection—if that is what it could be called—for him because he was the dutiful son. Because he'd conformed to the mold. Amberlyn wanted to marry him because of what he could give her—stability, security, and closeness to the queen.

He saw in Feya's eyes that she loved him. She didn't have to say the words. The thought was terrifying. She didn't love him for ability to serve. She just loved him.

Feya felt such uncontrollable longing. She wanted to tell Alasdair so many things. She wanted to kiss him—that's what she wanted. Her hands shook with the need of it. All she'd have to do was raise her chin and make her lips meet his.

And what would it hurt? Just one kiss?

Conflict bled into his eyes. His grip tightened on her waist.

She loved him and he should know. "I—"

He pulled her against his chest and out of the range of his lips. "I know."

Two little words—they knocked upon her heart and promised, without saying anything more.

Chapter Twenty-Four

Countless things would change if she told him. Giving someone your love was final, like the deep crevices in the windswept rocks of Bynack More. The way she felt for Alasdair Cairncross was like that. If she didn't tell him, she might break.

As if he knew what she wanted to say, Alasdair held her there, crushed against his body like the strength of his embrace would hinder her words.

Feya leaned into his warmth, hating that he stood so still. "Alas—"

"Please, don't tire yourself." His voice was flat, laced with the weight of the ages. "We have so far yet to go."

Feya breathed in his scent—wood smoke from the fire last night and the lingering freshness of rain. His words pressed in like the low obscuring clouds.

There was only one reason why he'd stop her from saying it. Her love to him was only a bother—something he'd been shackled with along the way. She felt it in the iron grip of his arms. And the way his breath fell ragged against her throat.

Feya wrenched herself out of his arms. There was always pain—deep, scoring, jagged rips in her soul. The pain of hunger. Want. Grief for a mother lost. The pain of wanting Da to be the man she knew he was.

And then there was the weight of wanting to give the bairns more than they had. Feya lowered her hands and looked at her wrists, her fingers too pale from cold. She'd spill her own blood if that would do it. If the drops of her own life could somehow make all their terrors go away—keep the evil at bay from claiming them . . . Aye, she'd do that. Without looking back or shedding a tear, she'd watch her life's blood seep into the ground if that would make the cold Creator smile.

Feya clenched her hair at her scalp and pulled. What did He want from her, this silent, unchanging God? This God who seemed to favor only nobles and kings. And men like Alasdair Cairncross, handsome devil with his life all planned. And beautiful Amberlyn waiting at the end of the journey to open her arms and comfort him.

The wind slammed against her back and reminded her of all the kilometers to go. And the bairns . . . What was she doing mooning for a man—a man who didn't want or need her at all—in the middle of the Highlands when they needed her?

Alasdair crossed the old sheep path and came to her. He gently laid his hand upon her shoulder. "Are you all right?"

"No." She took a step and then walked on, not caring that she was off the path and the weeds ripped at her boots.

Alasdair halted her and placed two fingers under her chin, lifting it. His blue eyes held kisses and whispers in the dark—but not for her. "We need to talk."

"Is that so?" She jerked her chin away. "I cannae think of anythin' I have to say."

"You're a horrible liar." A smile flickered across his face. "And you're wasting your strength by traipsing around in these—" His gaze froze and his words stopped. He pulled her to the side, throwing them both behind a tree.

"What is it?"

"Quiet." He looked over her shoulder and into the valley below. "There's a dwelling below."

Feya stole a look. Far below, a lone white cottage stood in the open field. Smoke billowed from the chimney. "Do ye think they have any food?"

"Of course they do." Alasdair frowned, scanning the vast expanse of green and snaking crystalline stream. "I don't like it. We move on."

Feya pushed against his chest, her voice raising. "But they have food."

"I've learned over the years to trust my feelings about survival. It doesn't feel right." He grabbed her hand and pulled her away from the tree.

The cottage door opened, a sliver in the blotch of faraway white. It looked like a woman came out and threw slop to the pigs. "There's a woman."

"Doesn't matter. We go on."

"She's harmless." Feya pointed down the mountainside, although he wouldn't look. "What do ye think she is? Some kind of Gypsy spy?"

Alasdair pushed tree branches aside and pulled her deeper into the forest. "I don't care to speculate on who she is. I can only tell you that I've never been wrong. This feeling has been my aid in many battles." He looked back at Feya, wariness in his eyes. "You do trust me, don't you?"

"*Trust only yerself.*" That's what Da always said. It was the Gypsy way. And the way of the tenements. "Maybe I could go down and talk to her."

Alasdair pulled her harder, deeper into the woods. "And what would you tell her? The truth? That we were kidnapped by Gypsies?" He shook his head no. "We'll stay tonight in the woods. Perhaps we'll reach a town by morning."

It was too much. And the thought of lying beside him underneath the stars wasn't comforting. It would get cold, and she knew that he'd offer to hold her and share his warmth. "How long since ye ate?"

"That is inconsequential."

"No, it isn't." Feya tore her hand from his grasp and waited for him to turn around. "How long? I know the Gypsies didn't feed ye well."

"They didn't feed me at all."

Feya drew a deep breath and nodded. "What am I goin' to do if ye get weak? I cannae carry ye through the Highlands."

Her logic played into his mind. She saw it in the way he averted his gaze. "Going down there is risky."

"Like life, hmmm?" She tilted her head to scrutinize his face. "We'd be disruptin' the order of the centuries, is that it? Ye with yer perfect duty and obligation. Is it deviatin' from yer plan that's botherin' ye?"

"No." He took a slow breath, looking like he was trying to gather his patience. Her double meaning was not lost to him. "I told you. It just doesn't *feel* right."

"What are the odds that the Gypsies know about her?" Feya threw up her hands. "She's one woman livin' in the middle of nowhere. If I don't get somethin' to eat, ye'll be carryin' me again." She stepped toward him. "And we both know what a burden ye think that is."

Alasdair narrowed his eyes, said something under his breath, and paced around a tree. After a moment, he stopped and pointed, like one would point at a disobedient child. "All right, I'll go. I'll make sure the house is safe and that the people within are trustworthy."

"We go together." She raised her chin. "Isn't that how we've been since Torphichen? With yer pretty face and me wits, I'd say we make a very good team."

He pinched the bridge of his nose and closed his eyes. When he looked back up, the anger was gone. "Backward, Feya, but accurate."

"What are ye sayin'?"

"Never mind." He placed his hands on his hips. "Just come here."

"What for?"

"Questions, always questions. I need you to make me look Scottish."

"Excuse me?"

He looked heavenward as if he was asking her to dump him face first into a cattle lot. "You know the current Scottish backwoods dress better than I." His words were clipped. "Is there anything to be done with my appearance?"

"Alasdair, I can't make ye look Scottish. Ye are Scottish."

"A very minute detail. And I'm only half Scottish, or did you forget?"

"Oh, I beg yer lord's pardon. Yes, yer right. Half is a vast difference. Like the journey from Lerwick to Port Ellen." She circled him and mimicked his stance, hands on hips. "Well, it's the English we'll have to weed out first. Ach, it seeps from ye."

"Does it?" He raised his eyebrow, arrogant as the devil, and smiled.

"First of all, don't stand so proud."

"There's nothing the matter with standing straight. In fact, it's a very good indication of a proper gentleman's character."

She snorted. "When ye stand like that ye look like yer fit to escort the queen. It shows. Got yer nose so high in the air—"

"I do not have my nose high in the air." He narrowed his eyes at her.

"Be careful. If a heavy rain comes, ye just might drown."

He slouched and adopted a pose something akin to a street clown. "Is this any better?"

Feya scowled to hide a laugh. "Don't ye remember yer time in Torphichen? Ye were born and raised a Scot fer yer early years."

"It was a long time ago. And lower your voice." He looked over his shoulder. "Voices carry on the wind in the Highlands."

"How would ye know?"

"Read it in a Robert Louis Stevenson book."

She decided to leave out the part where she'd almost tried to sell herself to the author. That information wouldn't benefit any living soul. "Um-hum." She stopped in front of him. "Well, yer beard does help, at least. Mess yer hair."

He obliged. The wind caught it and splayed it out, messing it more.

"Good." She searched the ground for a sharp rock. Finding one, she went toward him. "Ye might not like this part."

He eyed her with suspicion but stayed still.

Feya reached for the stripe on the side of his trousers. "This has to go obviously."

"Of course." He blew out his breath, as if he were resigned to being hanged. Feya grabbed the loose edge of the stripe on his right leg and cut the threads. It ripped loose and curled in the wind like a kite string.

He turned, his arms over his chest. "Proceed."

"Thank ye fer the consent, yer majesty."

"Witch." He held back another smile. "Just tear off the stripe."

Feya bit her lip to keep from smiling. It was devilish hard to stay mad at him. "Untuck yer shirt. Good. Now roll up yer sleeves. And that chain on yer boot . . . Throw it in the weeds. Excellent."

"Well?" He held out his hands. "Do I pass muster?"

He more than passed muster. If anything, his disheveled hair and shirttail flying in the wind only made her think of the country life that she longed for. He resembled a simple farmer, but that angel face of his was anything but. Her mind wandered, like the breeze blowing up from the valley. She would love him better than any woman had ever loved a man—doting on him and easing his woes. She imagined that life. The bairns would be asleep, safe and full of supper, and Alasdair would blow out the candle and carry her to bed.

Alasdair raised his eyebrows, still waiting for an answer.

"All right." Feya cleared her throat. "Ye look all right. I pray the woman has some decent food, a kind heart, and the means to share it." As she said the words, she realized it was the first time since Ma had died that she'd wanted to pray. She supposed she actually just had. And that was strange.

"Let me do all the talking, just in case."

"Are ye sure? Yer voice . . . Ye can sometimes sound so English."

He lowered his eyes, and a dimple appeared in his cheek. "I can manage it. If occasion does arise when you are asked a question, use that clever head of yours and find a way to say as little as possible. A hard task, I know, for a woman such as yourself."

"Anything else I should know?"

"As a matter of fact, yes." He reached for her hand and headed toward the rocky ledge. "Our current relationship won't serve our purposes for this endeavor."

"What do ye suggest?" The wind tore at her skirt, whipping her words away and scattering them.

"A marriage." His unbuttoned sleeves trembled in the gale.

Feya swallowed and suddenly felt the air too thin. Another few meters and the entire valley spread out below them, full of sunlight and promise. "A marriage?"

The sunlight broke between the clouds, casting yellow rays upon him. It highlighted the red in his beard and brought depth to his eyes—gold flecks in a fathomless sea. "Ach, Feya. Isn't that just the thing that's needed in our circumstance?" His English accent was completely gone. He sounded Scottish through and through. "Could ye pretend to be me wife?"

"Aye, Alasdair." She untied her Gypsy scarves and tucked them into her pocket. "I'm good at pretendin'."

They cut through the long, green grass and headed toward the little cottage. His nearness whispered love to her. It was in the way his arm draped across her shoulders and how he held her close to her side—as if she might disappear on the low Scottish wind. And when she didn't think he knew she watched him, he'd squeeze her shoulder. Or weave his fingers through the ends of her hair.

How natural it would be to feel Alasdair beside her every day. And his touch—it was the worst longing. Unending longing. With every bit of kindness he showed her, the more she craved.

Alasdair indeed looked like he was born for the country, with his easy way of walking and his modified clothes. It did nothing to stifle the ache within her. "Ye were foolin' me back there on the mountain. Ye have no problem actin' the country man."

He winked at her and pulled her closer. "Do ye ken, yer not so daft as ye pretend."

She smacked his back with her hand and laughed. And laughing with Alasdair was easy. Also, the fact that she fit perfectly beneath his arm and at his side didn't escape her notice. He'd turned her head to oatmeal and her heart to warm syrup.

Alasdair bent low and matched her pace. "Have I coaxed a smile from ye at last?"

Feya closed her eyes and leaned into him, allowing him to guide her steps. The sun was bright behind her eyelids. She sank into his warmth and the light. She wanted to say so many things.

"Why, Feya, ye look shy. Whatever's the matter?"

She reached for his hand on her shoulder and threaded her fingers through his. "Nothin's the matter. Don't all good wives find themselves at a loss in the arms of their husbands?"

"I suppose as much as a husband finds himself lost in the arms of his wife." His stare was as bold as the wind rifling through the trees.

Feya had to look away. The man was the sweetness of summer nights and the heaviness of rain. The gentle drifting of thoughts unbridled and the sharp sting and tightening of a noose.

Her steps slowed. When this charade was over, he'd be gone. She knew that just as she knew the songs in the Scottish wind. Like the Gypsy fires and the filth of the tenement, some things just were. Alasdair Cairncross, beautiful man that he was, was not of her world. And that was why he wouldn't say the words that would easily pass his lips if he had another station in life.

They came into a low place, hidden and secret. The stream sang beside them, an ancient song for the rocks and the hills and the trees.

The clouds moved low in the valley, as if God Himself had pushed them off the shelf of heaven.

Feya reached for the long grass and pulled. After this dance they were moving through was over, they'd be torn apart, and things would be worse for the knowing.

"Wait." Feya stopped. Her heart beat frantic. She let go of Alasdair's hand.

"What is it?" His English accent was back. Sunlight shadows filtered through the trees and made dark patterns upon his shirt.

She could choose not to do it. She could pretend that what she felt was just passing fancy for a handsome man. But she'd lied to him—she wasn't good at pretending. Feya closed the distance between them, placed her hands upon his broad shoulders, and looked him straight in the eyes. "I want to give ye somethin' so ye'll remember."

"Remember what?"

Feya wrapped her hand around the back of his neck, stood on her toes, and pressed her lips against his.

The softness was the first shock. She'd expected his lips to be hard, much like the stoic palace guard she'd met all those days ago. But no. A tremor went through her like a flash of light. Alasdair's lips were velvet warmth—the deepest, truest thing she'd ever known.

Feya pulled back and breathed lightly between parted lips. Wonder soared through her body. Lightness pulled at her heart and whispered that she was free.

Alasdair's breath was like the sun against her face. The wind rose and shook the grass into a frenzy. She couldn't look into his eyes. Warring emotions seeped from him, trembling in the air.

Feya threaded her fingers into his hair. She pressed her lips to his again and hoped she was doing it right. With everything within her, she wanted to kiss him right and proper and give him a memory he'd carry to his grave. Even if he wouldn't let her say the words, she'd tell him with the brushes of her lips.

Alasdair moaned and swayed. He brought his arms up and splayed his hands out over her back. His lips moved against hers like the warm caress of waves against the shore.

Feya pulled him closer, daring him to admit what he felt.

His lips turned demanding, drawing her into a fire she'd never known. Wave after wave washed over her until she was dizzy. Nothing existed on the vast Highland plain but him and her.

Yes, his lips said with every movement. *Yes, I love you.* He grabbed the back of her hair and echoed the words with the touch of his hand.

Feya melted into him as the currents of the water melt into the sea. With his left hand he drew long patterns on her back. The movements coaxed her to part her lips further.

Lightning plunged deep into her soul and set her aflame. She took his bottom lip between hers and sucked.

Alasdair pulled away, his face flushed. Red spread across his neck and dipped below his collar. "You are in quite a lot of danger."

"Danger?" A tingling washed over her, so strong that if he let go she would fall.

He nodded, seemingly at a loss for words. "Unless you want me to make love to you in this field, we should walk." He moved his hand to her shoulder, turning her away from him, but keeping her close to his side.

Feya put one foot in front of the other, although her legs felt like warm strawberry jam. At least he'd put his arm back around her. Had she just kissed Alasdair Cairncross? Brazenly? Openly? She couldn't think worth a tinker's curse. "I'll be pickin' up these pieces till the trumpet sounds."

"Pardon me?" His words were breathless and strained.

"Nothin'."

He nodded like she'd said something worth sense.

They crested the hill and the little white cottage drew closer. Laundry snapped on the line.

"Can you do this?"

By "this" she assumed he meant the charade. There was no way she could tell, given that her insides were mush. "Aye."

"Good girl." He slurred the Scottish tones and then knocked on the door.

She'd been right: the woman who opened the door had weathered the ages. Her hair was pure white and the skin on her face looked paper thin. "Well, now. Look what the wind's blown in."

Alasdair took it as his cue. "Good afternoon to ye, me dear lady. Me wife and I are travelin' south and we find we've miscalculated a bit. Ran out of food, we did." He drew his eyebrows together for effect. "We were wonderin' if there was any work ye might be needin' done?"

"Well, I don't know . . ." She looked around them as if she meant to dismiss them as soon as she could think of the words.

"I see yer fence there could use a man's hand. We'd be much obliged even fer a piece a bread."

"There are a few things 'round here that could use patchin'." She narrowed her eyes at Feya, taking in her clothes. "Are ye travelers?"

"Anything but," Alasdair said quickly. "Newlyweds. You can see how lucky I am to have this one beside me." He squeezed her shoulder. "Isn't she a prize?"

"She looks solid enough. She'll bear ye lots of children, that's fer sure."

"Ah, and a happy man I'd be too."

Heat burned Feya's cheeks and spread through her body. Just the thought of it, especially after what she'd felt just kissing him . . . She dropped her eyes to the woman's shoes.

"Well, the Good Book says not to be forgetful to entertain strangers. Truth is I'm in want of more company than work." The woman pushed the door wide. "I just made stovies if that interests ye. I have oatcakes as well."

"How about that, me love?" He put on a smile that would make the hardest of women weep. "Would that perk ye up a bit?"

"Aye." Feya choked out the word, overcome at his endearment.

The woman clapped her hands together. "Good. Yer timing is perfect." She shuffled off, leaving them to follow behind her. "It's not often I get company. The Good Lord sure has smiled today. And perhaps this will be a honeymoon ye'll not soon forget."

Feya searched his eyes, but he wouldn't look at her. How she wished the woman's words were true.

"Come further in, then," the woman called from beside the stove. Savory beef and spice filled the room. "Come warm yerself by the fire. Ye both look a tad weary. Have ye traveled far?"

"We come from the north." Alasdair sat down at the table and gestured that Feya should join him. "We're travelin' to Edinburgh. Lookin' fer work. Somethin' a man can do to better the situation fer his woman."

Alasdair *was* good at pretending. The thought forced nervousness into Feya's bones.

"There be pros and cons to that venture, I can assure ye." The woman passed food to them both and then sat. "Many have gone before ye hoping fer a better life. I can't tell ye how many young people I've seen pass by here on their way to the big city. I often wonder how it worked out fer them."

Feya wanted to laugh bitterly. Moving south hadn't worked out for Da. It was the beginning of all their problems. She scooped as much as she could into her spoon and lifted it.

"Time will tell, I suppose." Alasdair put a bite into his mouth and closed his eyes. He chewed, slowly, reverently.

"It's good, then?"

"Aye." A shade of the Englishman was back in his eyes. He'd been starving, but still, he took bites slowly and measured. "It's delicious. Thank ye."

Feya's heart broke for him. He'd been so hungry, and he'd never even said a word.

"Ach, 'tis nothing." The woman smiled like spring. She watched them for a while, glancing back and forth. "I can see that ye love her. It does my heart well."

Alasdair stopped his spoon mid-air.

Perhaps he'd deny it. But how could he after their kiss?

The corner of his lips tipped up in a private smile, but he said nothing.

"And ye . . ." The woman turned to Feya. "When did ye first know that he was the man fer ye?"

Feya moved a potato around in her bowl. "It took me by surprise," she finally said. And once the words were out, more wanted to follow. "It was when he was kind although he didn't have to be. It was what I saw in his eyes a hundred times although he'd said no words." Shaking started deep down within her, and she wanted to run—or just be still again in Alasdair's arms. "It was when I felt his presence in the room before I saw him. And the way I'd hang on his words and still do."

Alasdair lowered his spoon. He, like the woman, stared.

Feya reached for her water glass and drained it. She was an idiot. The stupidest numptie in the world. It was a simple question and she could have answered it a hundred ways. Any way but that way would have been better. Why did she tell the truth?

The woman's gaze seemed to reach back through the years. "It was the same way with me dear departed Collum. Lord, I had it fierce fer that man." She wiped her mouth, her hands shaking. "Girl, I saw it on yer face before ye'd even spoken a word. It's why I let ye in, in truth." She turned to Alasdair and reached for his hand. "Yer a blessed man, fer sure. Love like she's givin' doesn't come often in this world. Hold onto it tight, me boy."

"Aye." His voice was thick. He was struggling with the Scottish tones.

Clouds shifted in the valley, darkening the windows. Moments passed in silence, and then the food was gone.

"Let me clean up." Feya rose and reached for the dishes.

"I won't argue with that." The woman put her hand on Alasdair's shoulder. "Come and sit with me by the fire. Ye look like a man who's seen a lot fer yer age. Would ye oblige an old woman and tell me some of yer travels?"

"I'd be honored." His gaze shifted to the door. "But first, the fence, as promised."

"All right. And then ye'll be stayin' here tonight."

Alasdair leaned forward in his chair. "I don't wish to impose."

"Yer not." The woman laid her hand upon Alasdair's arm. "Look upon it as a weddin' gift from an old woman who remembers what it's like to be young and desperately in love."

When the dishes were clean, Feya took the soap and headed for the stream. The rain had gone and the night was beautiful. She plunged into the water and nearly screamed from the cold. In a deep pool she floated on her back and studied the full, sultry moon.

From the cottage window, Alasdair's laughter mixed with the old woman's. She washed quickly and then crept back inside.

The old woman's laughter rose and fell, over and over again. She quieted when she saw Feya. "I've kept ye too long, Alasdair. It's late."

To her surprise, his beard was gone and his hair was wet. Somehow he'd managed to wash. If he'd managed warm water, she just might kill him. But then again, the sight of him without his beard made her throat catch. He was himself again.

"Thank ye again, Millie. I haven't spent such a pleasant evening in so long."

"Until tomorrow, then." Millie rose from the chair and reached for a lantern. "Ye can sleep in the same room where ye washed. It's a spare room that I keep fer me son when he comes." She handed Alasdair the lantern. "I'll go make the fire."

"Please." Alasdair placed his hand upon her shoulder. "Let me do it."

"As ye wish, then. Sleep well."

When the woman disappeared down the hall, Alasdair held out his hand to Feya. "Did ye have a nice moonlit swim in the freezin' water?"

Feya took his hand. "I really might hurt ye now."

"It might be fun to see ye try." He stifled a smile. "At least we're both clean." He led her into the bedroom and softly closed the door. Then he put his finger to his lips, indicating that they should be as quiet as possible.

That was fine with her. She was sure she couldn't manage words. She scanned the whitewashed walls and the long, cedar rafters. Finally, she dared to look at the large iron bed. All teasing died, and she was suddenly terrified.

Alasdair placed the lantern on the old, cracked mantel and set to work on the fire. He stacked the wood on the metal grate at precise angles and perfect distances apart. Every movement was purposeful; he'd lay the wood down and then narrow his eyes at it as if it had to pass inspection.

Through her nervousness, Feya bit back a smile. She'd hated him for being so precise that first time in Holyrood Palace stable. Now his careful movements made her swoon with want. No man in her life had ever been careful. No one from the wrong side of Edinburgh was ever careful. Everything was done in haste and anger, just what was necessary to get through the day. But this man—Alasdair Cairncross—everything was an art to him.

Especially the way that he kissed.

Feya fiddled with the fringe on her sleeve. She could smell the fresh soap on his skin, and it made her feel like an awkward child. He'd combed his hair neatly back, like he'd worn it in Holyrood. "Do ye need any help?"

"Not in particular." He struck the tinderbox and it sparked. He glanced at her and seemed to be weighing his words. "It was a very good meal."

His English accent sent shivers through her. Why hadn't she thought of braiding her hair after washing? And her tattered clothes—they must repulse him. "That it was. A very good meal."

"I admit you were right. There is no danger here. Only a sweet widow woman with a heart of gold."

Feya nodded, too quick. "What a shame we couldn't know her under different circumstances."

"Yes." He reached for the iron stick and poked the fire. The carefully laid wood caught fire with a whoosh. The flames stretched and reached to lick the inner wall. "We covered a lot of ground today. You must be tired."

Feya laughed, completely out of place.

"Would you like to sit by the fire? I know that stream water really was cold. I don't want you to get sick." He patted the floor beside him.

Feya walked and stretched her hands to the flames. Even that movement felt wrong. But after a moment, the heat seeped into her bones and eased her a bit. "That was very nice of ye to fix her fence."

Alasdair gave her a lazy smile, the fire also lulling him. "I used to fix things as a boy in Torphichen. In London, I'd take things apart just to see how they worked." A whimsical smile tipped his lips. "Much to my stepmother's dismay."

Feya chose her next words carefully. "How did she react when ye came to live with them?"

"She didn't have a choice. They were childless. Father retrieved me and made me his heir."

Retrieved. Not stole. "Was she kind to ye?"

"She was like oil and I was the water. She died five years ago."

Feya fisted her hands and pulled them into her lap. "I'm sorry."

"*C'est la vie.* Such is life." He leaned back against the foot of the bed and crossed his feet.

Feya followed his lead and did the same, but took off her boots and stretched her toes close to the fire.

Thoughts passed upon his face, none of which she could discern. She turned to the fire and became lost in the patterns of the flames. Only inches separated her body from his. She would only have to move a little to the right and perhaps he would hold her again. "I made a discovery today."

"Oh?"

"There's a God. I've decided." She swallowed, hardly believing she'd said the words. The room rushed hot, as if the flames reached out and touched her skin.

"Good to know He has your approval. What brought you to that conclusion?"

Feya snuck a look at him. "Meetin' ye."

"Is that so?" He raised an eyebrow. "I don't know whether to be pleased or terrified. Was it because of my cruelty early on? Did that drive you to Him?" He looked genuinely concerned.

"No. It was something else." She bit back the words that would naturally follow. If she could believe that God had orchestrated their meeting so perfectly, maybe she could accept some of the other things in her life.

Conflict warred on his features. He stared into the fire. "I used to think about God quite a lot." He drew his eyebrows together. "When I think about the person I used to be—" He swallowed. "I . . . felt God in Egypt."

His words jerked her from her thoughts of destiny. "When ye were being tortured?"

"Not specifically. Afterward. There was a comfort in that sand hole that I can't explain."

She nodded like she understood, but she didn't. "He takes care of ye, then, does He?"

The seconds drew out as Alasdair considered his words. Finally, he spoke. "He used to feel closer than my skin. But now . . ." He took a deep, troubled breath. "Mostly I block Him out. But I'm pretty sure He's done with me, anyway."

She wanted to ask him what he meant, but the moment felt too sacred.

"He has questions for all of us, I suppose." He dropped his head and looked disgusted with himself. "The problem is our free will. He never forces His way; we get to decide."

"Yer talkin' in riddles."

"I know." Apology was in his eyes. "The first thing is deciding if you want your way or His—His plan or yours. And then, after that— then He wants to know how much you want to know Him." Deeper things lay in his words than what he was saying. He sighed, his spirit disturbed with some memory.

"Know Him?" Feya leaned back again, feeling strange. Like being able to see behind a curtain that was never meant for her.

"Yes. Intimately. As few do. It is possible. I have experienced it before. But then I . . . I went another way. Too consumed with my own plans." His words seemed like a revelation to himself. He put his hand over his heart. "I felt Him here." He moved his finger to his forehead. "And I knew things here." He slid his finger to his temple. "And I suppose while I'm telling you all this, I might as well add that I also recognize Him in the things that I see. I've been denying that too."

Feya flinched and sucked in her breath. This God, she didn't know. She only knew of Ma's God—the one who had to be appeased by rituals and prayers. Visits to church and wearing the proper clothes. This was different than an almighty God orchestrating a few things to come together. This was personal. And raw. And terrifying. Much like the way Alasdair looked at her now. And the kiss they'd shared in the meadow.

He held back his words, she knew. He waited for her to say

something, but what, she didn't know.

Feya hugged herself and stood. She was tired now. She only wanted Alasdair to hold her and make her feel safe. To lay down on the bed with her and make her forget. She didn't want to think about questions from God or allowing Him into her heart. That place was only for the bairns—and Alasdair, if he wanted it.

She went to the bed, pulled down the blanket, and laid her hand upon the snow-white sheet. If he asked . . . If Alasdair wanted to . . . She wouldn't say no. This was what she wanted. She'd wanted so long just to be loved. "Are you . . . Would you like to . . ." She closed her eyes and took a breath. It should be easier than walking down that hallway at Deacon Brodie's, so why couldn't she say the words? She loved Alasdair. And he would be gentle, wouldn't he? She swiped her hair out of her face and realized her hand shook.

Alasdair turned and looked over his shoulder. The firelight raked over him, turning his white shirt orange. "Pardon me, Feya. Did you say something? I was lost in—" He stopped the words. Realization must have dawned.

"Ye have only to ask." The words came out in a whisper. "Fer ye, the answer will always be yes."

"I—" He sat up, seriousness in his expression. "As much as I want to . . ." His eyes were a sea of desire and regret. "I think you'd better give me that extra blanket." He tore his gaze away. "I'll sleep here by the fire."

Disappointment and shame raked over her like claws. She grabbed the knit multicolor blanket and tossed it at him, then collapsed upon the bed, hot tears once again threatening. What did she expect? She'd kissed him, after all. Not the other way around.

Alasdair stood and blew out the lantern, casting the room into shadows and long orange patterns of flame.

This was worse than trying to sell herself all those days ago. Now, even when she'd tried to *give* herself to a man, he'd refused. Curses did sing in her blood. And no closeness of any God could change that. She was a cast-off, by Alasdair and by Him.

Alasdair crossed the room and sat upon the bed. The frame creaked with the weight of him. He reached for her and pulled her against his chest. "Woman, you do try me."

"What are ye doin'?" Feya pushed against him, but he held her still.

He brought his hand up and smoothed the back of her hair like a lover, the same way he had in the field. "Shhh. I want you to listen to me."

Feya laid her head upon his chest because it was easy. Being numb was easy. And, after all the kilometers and all the struggles, her fight was finally gone.

"It's not because I don't want you."

His words hardly reached her. Somewhere they made sense. She remembered the girl she'd been once—the one with all the dreams and a future that looked bright. And now she felt like that little waif again, staring in a fancy window at things she could never own.

Alasdair lowered his mouth close to her ear. "How much you undo me—your eyes, your smile, every time our hands touch, that kiss . . . Everything about you seduces me, calls to me. It scares me. And that's probably the truest thing I've said in years."

Feya pulled back and looked into his eyes once again awash in fire. "Then why not? Ye are a man and I am a woman. I feel the same fer ye."

He cupped her chin with his hand. "I don't know what the future holds yet, Feya. I'm only trying to protect you."

"I don't want ye to protect me." She reached for his wrist. "I want ye to love me, Alasdair, as I love ye." She threw the words at him. They reached in the half light and caressed. She saw it in the faltering of his eyes.

He ran his thumb against her cheek. "Yes, I am a man, and you are not just any woman." The fire crackled. The light of the room surged and grasped.

Feya ran her fingers down the hard planes of his stomach and tugged at the hem of his shirt. The moment suspended like a note trembling on the air.

His eyes turned the color of the sea at midnight. And the reflection of the fire danced in them. Long orange flames melded with blue. And desire—so much of that. And *yes*. Sweet, sweet *yes*. He reached for the back of her neck and brought his lips down upon hers.

Tears spilled from her eyes as she closed them. She wrapped her arms around him as he lowered her upon the bed.

His kiss became urgent, like the need of the cold winter ground for the rays of the sun. Like the stretching of the spring flowers to be warmed. Memorizing her with his lips. He whispered against her neck—words she could no longer hear because all she could do was feel. Feel his heartbeat against her. Feel his strong back beneath her hands. Feel his lips at the base of her jaw, below her ear, at the curve of her collarbone.

Her breath came, in and out, although how she was breathing, she didn't know. She threaded her fingers into his thick black hair with one hand and clenched the soft blanket beneath her with the other. Death must be a little like this, she thought. Because she couldn't distinguish where her body ended and his began. She was lost and she was found. He had unraveled her and wound her back together again. Nothing remained but his touch, his scent, this moment and then the next.

Alasdair pulled away, his face like a handsome dark angel above her. His breath came out ragged. His chest rose and fell. "I need to know if you're sure. Just tell me—" He swallowed, trying to gain some kind of control, it seemed. "Do you want to be heavy with my child and no wedding to go with it?" He swept his gaze over her face. "I will not lie to you: that's a possibility if we indulge in this."

Her feelings had nothing to do with reason or consequences. Another tear slid down her cheek. Her words came out as a whisper. "I was yers forever ago. I don't care."

A hard look bled into Alasdair's eyes. The firelight highlighted the tips of his black hair and made them glow red-orange. He traced the path of her tear with the tip of his thumb and then took a deep, labored breath. He removed his hand, placed it on the bed beside her, and turned his face away. His hand made a fist on the mattress. His arm shook.

"What is it?" Feya reached for his cheek, soft and smooth.

He flinched as if her fingers burned him. "I will not use you as my mistress, Feya." He ground out her name and tore himself from her arms. "You deserve more."

Chapter Twenty-Five

Feya woke to the blank, white ceiling and the empty room.

If Alasdair had slept, she didn't know. He'd left the room when he'd left her arms. And great was the lack of him—a sucking void, cold like death.

Birds sang somewhere outside, but their melodies were shattered—too fragile to be beautiful. And beauty—what good was that anyway? There was always a lecher in the alley or a Gypsy in the dark waiting to steal all goodness away.

Feya slid her hand over the empty sheet beside her. Its coldness mocked her. The blanket spilled over the side where he'd wrenched himself away. The pillow still held his scent and, like being drunk on the sweetest wine, it made her skin come alive in remembrance. Maybe what Da did she could now understand—in drink there was no remembrance. In drink you could fly away from memory and dreams.

Such dreams had haunted her in the wee hours of the night. The bairns' cries had been soft and mournful like doves.

She should get up. But maybe it didn't matter if she did. Perhaps she could die in the bed where Alasdair had almost loved her. That would be fitting. An accurate end for all the ways she'd tried.

A crack and thump wafted in from outside. Her eyelids were heavy so she closed them. What did it matter? Maybe Alasdair would bury her in the Highlands, for surely she'd never see Edinburgh again.

The sunlight reached through the thin curtain and fell upon her face like a hand. Warmth flooded her cheek. She imagined the wind blowing in the field where she'd first kissed him. Maybe he would bury her there, for that was where she'd given the last of herself and died.

A light knock sounded at the door.

Feya gave no answer. Answers were for those who knew things for certain, those who didn't live in a world of grey.

"Are ye awake?" Millie's sweet voice intruded like the sound of breaking glass.

Feya slung her arm over her eyes. She couldn't let Millie see her like this—spread out upon the bed like a wasted woman. Millie had enough troubles in this barren land without adding Feya's angst to the mix.

"I'm comin'." Feya stood, tugged on her bodice and then righted her skirt. There was no hope for her hair, she supposed. Alasdair had made sure of that last night—raking his fingers through it and grabbing it like a lifeline.

She jerked open the door with all the pain that she felt.

"There ye are." Bathed in morning light, Millie poured tea by the window.

"I'm sorry. I dinnae mean to sleep so late."

"Everyone needs a long sleep now and then." The older woman set down the kettle. "I'm glad ye were able to rest."

There was something Millie wasn't saying. She'd probably heard them last night, maybe even some of the conversation. It was a very old cottage and the mortar most likely thin.

Feya brought her hand up and touched her blazing cheek. As soon as a bed had been available, she'd tried to make use of it with a man. Once again, the filth that she was tightened around her. "Where's Alas—my husband?"

"Likes to work in the moonlight, that one. I get up before the sun and he was chopping wood before then." Millie handed Feya a cup. "I'm not goin' to say I don't appreciate it. I think I'll be set up fer the entire winter after yer gone." Millie eased herself down upon a weathered rocking chair that had probably been used to comfort her children.

Thwack. Pause. *Thwack.* Pause. Although she couldn't see him, she felt his frustration with the noise. It cracked through the valley, reverberating off the cottage windows, sounding like the Day of Judgment had come to call.

"Sit beside me, love." Millie patted the other chair's cushion. "Take a sip of tea. It'll do ye good."

"Thank ye." Feya's throat caught. To her shame, tears welled in her eyes.

In the kind way of the aged, Millie looked away. "It's been a while since you've had tea, I'd wager."

She gulped the liquid. "It's been years since I've had any this strong."

"This is what's left of the tea my son brought down last time he come from Inverness."

The warmth from the teacup seeped into Feya's hand. "That was decent of him."

"Aye." Millie drew her mouth into a thin line. "He was a good boy once." Sorrow pulled at the corners of her eyes. "Took up with the wrong friends a while ago." She shook her head as if the weight of it was too heavy to bear. "I pray fer him. Not much else I can do."

Feya leaned back. The ache and groan of the decades came from the old wood. The chair had probably been Millie's husband's. And how they must have spent the hours, loving each other, forcing out the biting cold of the Highlands and listening to the mournful high notes of the wind.

Thwack. Alasdair brought the axe down hard. The sound split the world in two. Feya jerked, and tea sloshed over the side of the cup. The wind breathed, and the lace curtain lifted up and into the room. Alasdair's shadow outside stretched across the grass. The axe lifted.

Feya clenched the cup. He was straining his muscles and tiring his body trying to rid her from his mind.

"I've seen that look before in a young woman's eyes."

"Hmmm?"

"Yer afraid of losing him."

Feya looked down into the dark, swirling tea.

"It's how ye cling to him with yer eyes when he's in the room. And, I suspect, how ye feel adrift when he's not."

Feya smiled, bitterly.

"Yer afraid he'll leave ye fer another woman, perhaps?"

The woman's name was Amberlyn. "Maybe."

"Well, with the looks that one's got I can understand why."

The information did nothing to comfort her. Feya opened her hand. She didn't know which line the Gypsy queen had been talking about, but she'd obviously been telling the truth.

"Ye need not fear."

"Why?" Feya closed her hand.

"Alasdair only has eyes fer ye. He'll not be leaving."

Feya closed her eyes against another *thwack* of his axe. "Ye seem awfully sure."

"There's a look a man has when a woman holds his soul. He's got it when he looks at ye."

"Truly?"

"Do ye feel it when he holds ye?"

Feya drew in a shuddered breath. "It's like dyin' and bein' reborn."

"The good Lord orchestrated your match, and there's no mistake. Ye needn't fear." Millie nodded as if confirming the words. "That one will be with ye till you're as old as me. Faithful until the end."

It was what her heart said—that they were meant to be. "Thank ye fer yer beautiful words."

"Here now, child." The old woman stood and rubbed Feya's back, the same way her ma used to do. "'Twern't nothin'. I only say the truth as I see it."

"I wish I could pay ye fer your kindness." Most of all, Feya wished she could just tell Millie the truth. She reached for Millie's hand instead.

"Ach, there's to be none of that." She patted her as if the matter was final. "Have faith, child. Wait and see what the Great Author will do."

"The Great Author?"

"God, of course. Who do ye think invented love in the first place?"

"I . . ." Feya widened her eyes.

"Oh, the religious and the lies they spread. Such ideas about the Creator." Her hands stilled, as if she was thinking. "Ye know, one of the best parts of being married—the part that takes yer breath away and makes ye lose yerself. That was His idea. What does that tell ye about Him?"

Had everyone gone mad? Millie's ideas about God were just as strange as Alasdair's. She searched for something to say. Her tea lent the inspiration. "You said this tea was from the north. The north's seen its fair share of hard times. All of Scotland, I think."

Millie went to heat more water. "Yer right there, and no mistake.

Worse since Minister Aldourie gave those Gypsies sanctuary."

The cup slipped in Feya's hand. "Gypsies, ye say?"

"Aye. Hundreds of 'em. They camp on Aldourie's land. Ever since his wife died, strange things been happenin' up there."

"What things?" Feya whispered.

"I don't know fer sure, although there's plenty of talk. His wife died at the hands of an Englishman. Oh, what was his name?" She searched the ceiling as if looking for the answer. "Cairn somethin'."

Feya sucked in her breath. "Cairncross?"

"That's it. Do ye know that story?"

"No." Feya swallowed. "But I've heard the name."

Thwack. Pause.

Thwack. Pause.

Feya stood. She should go outside and get Alasdair. They should be on their way.

"A tragic accident, some say. Others say the Englishman killed Aldourie's woman on purpose."

Feya paced and the old boards in the cottage groaned. The chopping sound stopped. She looked at the window but couldn't see his shadow.

"Cairncross was up there to run the Gypsies out. A cleansin' of sorts. Somethin' went wrong. I don't know the det—" Millie's expression froze. Her eyes were fixed on the window. "Ye have to go."

Outside, a Gypsy caravan crept across the field. The wind blew the horse's mane out like white flames.

Alasdair burst open the door, his hair wild and his blue eyes wilder. "We have to go." The English tones were back, all hints of Scotland gone.

Millie stood and drew her eyebrows together, as if looking at him for the first time. "Hurry. Go with God."

Feya reached for her. "What about ye? The Gypsies—"

"I know how to handle the Gypsies." She inclined her head to the rear of the cottage. "Go out the back just fer good measure."

Alasdair stopped in front of her. "Thank you."

Millie gave him a small smile. "Give us a kiss then, Englishman, and be gone."

He bent and kissed her cheek.

The sound of the caravan wafted through the open window.

Feya clenched Alasdair's hand. They stepped toward the back door . . .

It opened. A man walked in. His clothes were Gypsy, through and through. "Hello, Mother."

Three more men stepped into the room.

Millie's son shifted his weight. "I should have known it would be ye that was harborin' 'em."

Millie rushed to the stove and picked up the pan. "Ye must be hungry, and yer friends there. How about some breakfast?"

"Shut up." The man stroked his beard as if trying to decide what to do first. "We don't want yer food."

Four more caravans pulled into the yard.

"Watch your tone, Tommy." Millie cracked an egg. Her hands shook. "My guests will think ye've gone bad."

"If I have, 'twas ye and yer prayers that forced me into the dark."

The lines around Millie's mouth deepened. "Step aside, Tommy. Me friends were just leavin'. Honeymooners, they are. Ye wouldn't want to dampen their joyous mood, would ye?"

"Honeymooners? Is that what they told ye?" Tommy's voice was like silt from the river—smooth and dirty with things that didn't belong.

The old woman's hand froze in the air. The second egg missed the bowl and oozed onto the table.

Alasdair's expression was calm. "The women are not to be harmed. You have orders to take me. Here I am."

Feya reached for him. "No—"

"I'll go quietly." Alasdair laid his hand upon her shoulder and the weight in his touch said things his words couldn't. "She stays with your mother."

"And who are ye to be makin' bargains? As if anythin' ye could do or say would sway me?"

The men filtered their laughter through the hard look in Alasdair's eyes and the challenge in Tommy's.

Alasdair's gaze shifted to Millie. "Forgive me."

"Fer what?"

Alasdair's fist slammed into Tommy's nose.

Blood sprayed onto Feya's blouse.

"Tommy!" Millie lunged for him. The bowl of eggs crashed to the floor.

Feya grabbed the frying pan from the stove and hit the long-haired wastrel in the face. The man's surprise turned dull. He crumpled to the floor.

A body flew to the right. Alasdair crouched down and plowed into another.

The old woman backed up, her entire body shaking. "Dear God in heaven, preserve us!" She dropped to her knees by the stove and lifted her hands to the ceiling. Her prayers fell into mutters.

The front door opened. More Gypsies poured in—swarms of them—a flurry of scarves and pushing bodies.

Alasdair locked eyes with Feya as the men took him down. At the same moment a hand came over her mouth, a cloth with chemicals rank and sharp. Tears blurred her eyes as the Gypsies held her—too many of them to fight, although she tried as her body failed her.

Alasdair's name passed over her lips, but it wasn't good for anything. There was only darkness and things which couldn't be avoided—the thrum of other men's wishes against her own.

The last thing she saw was the look in Alasdair's eyes that said he was letting her go.

Chapter Twenty-Six

The letter fell from Edan Cairncross's hand. It fluttered and then wilted upon the floor. Words. They were just words.

"What does it say?" Miss Wanesley took a step, her yards of silk fabric rustling.

"Don't." He made a fist but couldn't reach for the letter. The gold clock on the mantel ticked off the seconds.

"Mr. Cairncross? Are you well?"

"I am not." The paralysis broke and he bent. He crumpled the letter. Words disappeared into the folds. *I have your son . . . An eye for an eye . . . You know what you must do regarding the vote . . .*

"Is it news about Alasdair?" There were tears in her eyes. But there'd been so many of those these past days. "It's just a letter of state. Some nonsense about the duke of Sussex arriving soon."

Sir Walter burst through the door. "Look here, Cairncross, I've spoken to the consulate and they think something's gone wrong."

There was a bit of intelligence gone to waste. And an understatement. Alasdair had been kidnapped. And if he didn't make his way to Loch Ness by Thursday next, his son would be killed. "What else did the consulate tell you?"

"The soldiers you sent have just returned." He gazed at his

daughter and took off his hat. "Alasdair never made it to Stirling."

Miss Wanesley rushed to the window, her sobs evident.

Edan squeezed the crumpled letter. He wanted it to go away. He thought it had. All these years . . .

"His horse was found at Torphichen."

The name wrapped around him like a vice. He crossed the room and stood before Sir Walter. "Did you say Torphichen?"

"Do you know it?"

Edan took a long breath to collect his thoughts. It was impossible. Morna was dead, wasn't she? "It's a small village with even smaller people. Very unrefined."

Miss Wanesley pressed her hand against the window pane. Outside, a soldier brought Alasdair's horse into view.

"You're right." Edan was careful to put an indifferent look on his face. "The time for waiting is past. I leave within the hour."

"Where are you going?"

"Torphichen first. I assume the soldiers asked questions, but they often lack the resolve to get the answers."

"I'll go with you." Sir Walter put his hat back on.

"I'd rather do this alone. Questioning can be an unsavory business. I will find out exactly where my son is."

Miss Wanesley wiped her tears. "You don't think he's dead?"

He put his hand against her cheek and felt the large teardrop diamond earring against his palm. "Do you not know my son to be one of the most resourceful men you have ever met?"

She nodded, and the softness of her cheek reminded him of another's from long ago.

"Did he not escape from the deserts of Egypt? Does he not possess the Victoria Cross for his bravery?"

"Yes." Her expression relaxed with the word. "That's true."

"He is the best of men." Edan looked into her clear, doleful eyes.

"I will find him."

She took his hand. "When you do, tell him of my love."

"Miss Wanesley, there is no woman in the world as devoted to my son as you. No one more deserving. When we return, you'll be married immediately."

"Thank you." Her eyes shimmered and her lips eased into a smile.

"I'll send you updates as I can." Edan tossed the crumpled letter into the fire. "Have no fear. I always get what I'm after."

When the door clicked, her father nodded. "Do it."

Amberlyn rushed to the fireplace, picked up the poker and fished out the letter. She beat out the flame. "If he lied to me, I'm going to kill him." Her hands trembled as she unfolded the page and gasped.

Father's heavy hand was upon her shoulder.

Amberlyn ran her finger over Alasdair's name. Just seeing it written made her heart clench. "Why would Mr. Cairncross lie?"

"Many reasons. I've told you before about him."

"But he's always been so wonderful to me."

"He knows what he will gain by your marriage to his son. That is all."

Amberlyn set her mouth into a thin line. She strode across the room.

"Where do you think you're going?"

"I'm going to tell Mr. Cairncross exactly what I think!"

"No, you're not." He tossed the letter back into the fire. "He will do what he thinks he must, and perhaps that will help your fiancé."

Amberlyn put her hands over her face and took a deep breath. Tears welled again in her eyes until she couldn't see. "I want him back, Father. The world is grey and useless without him." She brought her lips to Alasdair's engagement ring and kissed it.

"I, above all people, know how you feel about Alasdair Cairncross." He pinched the bridge of his nose and then lowered his hand.

Her gaze fell to the clock. "We would have been married an hour ago." Her laugh turned into another sob. "I just realized that."

Her father took her into his arms and patted her back. "Money is good for a lot of things, you know."

She clenched his waistcoat. "What are you thinking?"

"We're taking matters into our own hands. I recognize this handwriting. It's unmistakable, in fact. Pack your things. Looks like we're taking a bit of a diversion."

"Where exactly?"

"Loch Ness, of course. But more specific, Castle Aldourie."

Either Feya was dead, or she was dreaming.

The sound of a harp washed over her. High and deep, light and dark, rounds and rounds of thoughts suspended on plucked strings.

Sounds pressed in on her—the tick of a clock, the shuffling of feet. Feya opened her eyes and took in red-velvet wallpaper that stretched up to an elaborate white ceiling.

"Where am I?" A thick counterpane slid into her lap as she sat. She wore a fine nightgown—lace cuff sleeves and pale blue ribbons the color of moonlight.

The music came again—strange tones full of beauty and regret.

Feya held her head. Why would she be in a bedroom that looked like it belonged in a palace?

She slipped out of bed, stumbled, and fell. The thick carpet burned her knees. Again the music rang in her mind. Dizziness blended with the tones.

The door was unlocked. She put her hand against the wall and followed the corridor. Curtains blew in the wind. Like ghosts in a dream, they danced.

At the end, shrouded by the dark, she heard it. The harp was in the corner. A hand moved against the strings.

Feya squinted. "Who's there?"

"That depends on whom you ask." The man's voice was deep and daring, seductive as the low plucked string.

Feya swayed. She'd obviously been drugged, and the thought did nothing to comfort her. "I'm asking. And, as I assume I'm standin' in yer house, not wearing me own clothes, I suggest ye start talking'."

He smiled in the dark. She could feel it. "Good answer." The notes of the harp plummeted, like a deep plunge into the heart of the earth. "They said you had spirit. I am happy to see that to be true."

"Ye seem to have the upper hand, as ye are hidin' in the dark."

A match was struck; the small light floated and then grew. The flame touched a candle and spread, illuminating his face. The lines there told of pain and too much sorrow. He must have been handsome long ago.

"Dearest Feya, I am Ranald Aldourie. At your service."

"How do ye know my name?"

"I know a lot of things." He plucked the harp again, as if to accent his words. "These are strange times, are they not? A strange, strange world."

"Aye." The word came out in a whisper. She lifted her gaze to the fancy molding on the ceiling. The walls were the color of blood.

He stood and walked to her. He wore a fine black shirt and a gold waistcoat that shone in the dim light of the candle.

Feya stepped back.

"There is no reason to fear me." He held out his hand.

"I'm held here against me will." Her gaze flicked to the nightgown. "And as I have already said, these clothes are not me own."

"You are not my prisoner." He drew his dark eyes over her, a slow smile spreading upon his face. "You are free to go at any time. I wouldn't recommend it now, however. As you can see, it's quite dark."

Feya met his stare and narrowed her eyes.

"The gown was procured for you by a maid—Glenna, should you need her. Shall I ring for her to come to you?"

She didn't answer.

"You were sleeping like the dead when you arrived. Sorry for that, by the way. But the young man made things difficult."

"Yer behind the Gypsies?" She walked closer, wanting to see him.

"I give them sanctuary here on my land." He gestured to the windows and whatever lay beyond the floating curtains. The breeze shifted. The smell of water wafted into the room.

"I suppose ye might know me next question."

"I can guess." He stepped closer and towered over her. "You remind me of someone from long ago. There's something about your eyes that is kindred to her." He paused, taking his time to look over her face. "I'm sorry for the hardships you have undergone."

Feya narrowed her eyes. "Who are ye, really?"

"I told you. As far as what I mean to do with you, well, I'm not a barbarian. Come and go as you like. You are my guest. I only hope you stay so I can get to know you better."

Feya opened her mouth to speak, but no words came. None of it made any sense.

"I'm sorry about Cairncross." Something flickered in his eyes. "You must have held some affection for him."

"What do ye mean? Where is he?"

"I never meant to hurt him. It's a nasty business, politics. Sometimes certain strings must be pulled."

The room closed in. Air escaped, leaving nothing but a tight void.

"Feya, sit down." He reached for her hand.

She pulled it back. "I'll stand."

"Very well." He went to the window and pushed the billowing white curtain aside. "He died quickly. On the road to Inverness."

The words didn't make any sense. Feya shook her head. "What?"

"The fool who caught up with you, the old woman's son . . ." A look of pain crossed his face. He slid the edge of the silk curtain between his fingertips. "I told them only to bring him here. The fool put too much chloroform on the rag."

His words hit her like a fist. She dropped to the chair. She tried to search her memory. The last thing she remembered was the old woman praying on the floor. "Yer lyin'."

Mr. Aldourie let go of the curtain. "No, Feya, I am not."

Deep pain ripped through her. She would wake up now, surely.

"I only meant to talk to him. But he refused all my invitations. I have friends in Edinburgh who knew Alasdair was supposed to take you to Stirling. It seemed the opportune time for persuasion."

Feya pushed her hands into her hair. She thought of Morna and Rowan. "He has a family."

"So do you."

Her hands stilled in her hair.

"You told Kizzy about them. Had you not been so foolish as to rescue Alasdair, you would have saved yourself a lot of turmoil. I never meant you any ill. I will send for them, if you like."

"Ye'll what?" The sound of lapping water reached her. The dark, and whatever water lay outside the windows, was pressing in.

"Brenna, Gillis, and Hamish could be here in a few weeks. You can all stay here on my land. Safe from everything. Protected."

Hearing their names was like a deep, resonating bell. Tears fell down her cheeks. "Ye would do that?"

"The Romani have suffered too long. You have that blood, and so do your siblings. My wife was a Gypsy, and she was taken from me. It is my life's goal to use my status and wealth in Parliament to protect others from what happened to her."

His words pushed in like light that was too bright. She couldn't think. Somewhere far away she thought that she must be cold because she shivered.

"Sit for a while. Allow yourself the chance to grieve. I'll play you something from the ages." Mr. Aldourie laid his hand upon her shoulder.

She was trapped in her own body, wearing clothes owned by another man. She wanted to run through the great house, calling Alasdair's name. But he wouldn't be there. And she knew this not because of Mr. Aldourie's words, but because she could no longer feel Alasdair's bright burning soul.

She thought of the cave where she'd felt safe in his arms, and the feel of his lips against hers. To think that he wouldn't walk the earth anymore . . . She was the cause of it. If she hadn't cut his ropes in the Gypsy camp he'd still be alive.

"I understand why you tried to save him." His voice mixed with the harp, low and mournful. "I don't blame you for delaying my plans. And I'm not angry. I understand the power of a Romani woman's love."

In the dim light, Feya's tears fell, and no one remarked upon their falling except for the harp. The mournful notes played, all strung together and desperate. Plunging. Digging. Each one prying away any hope of brightness from her soul.

Chapter Twenty-Seven

Ranald couldn't look away as Feya slept. Her eyes, even closed as they were now, resembled Elspeth's.

Need stirred within him at the curve of her lips. And memories . . . such memories pulled tight on his heart until he thought it might break, as stated by poets of old. A ragged breath escaped, and he lowered himself onto the couch, gently. Only a few inches and he could touch her, see if her skin was as soft as Elspeth's. See if his fingers would remember touching a woman in adoration.

Feya stirred, as if she could feel his scrutiny. She turned into the cushions of the settee. The young man's name escaped her lips, the syllables a sigh full of wanting.

He reached for the long, red hair falling over her shoulder. Between his forefinger and thumb, its softness whispered kindness—things that could ease the pain. The loneliness . . . She would be the cure.

The lace parlor curtain lifted, billowing over them like a white portal in the early morning light. Shadows danced upon the smooth lines of her face.

The smell of the loch wafted on the wind, and with it the memories that caused him to ride the dark tide. The scream of the women as the soldiers barreled down upon them. The breaking of glass and the burning of the caravans. The children wandering the woods. Elspeth . . . His beloved Elspeth, lost forever . . .

Feya stirred, her pain evident even in her sleep.

The only thing that remained now was a bit of distastefulness—not much. Just like the careful facts of a parliamentary debate, one must not present evidence too late or too soon.

"I will sway you," he whispered to the woman who would be his salvation. "It won't be long."

Chains rattled when he moved his arms. And with the sound Alasdair came fully awake. He took a deep breath, trying to bring himself into check. The atmosphere was stale and musty, like the air underground. Behind him, bone-sapping cold reached out of the stone.

Something slid against the wall.

Alasdair widened his eyes, but couldn't see. Not a bloody thing.

He grasped the chains and pulled, as if that would make a difference. Instantly, pain lanced his side. His rib was broken. "Who's there? Show yourself."

The *drip* and *plunk* of water answered. He sucked in short breaths and swayed. The chains jerked him back to consciousness.

"Feya." Her name slipped from his mouth. Images accosted him, one after the other. The cabin. The Gypsies. He'd fallen, and then . . . "Feya."

She didn't answer.

The knowledge fell upon him like death—like the Egyptian sun and the madman's blade. What had they done with her? They wouldn't be kind after she'd blatantly defied them all and helped him escape.

He saw her pale face gripped by another man's hand. She'd cry out, but he wouldn't be there to help her. They'd drag her to the woods and use her. One after another. Take her down into the weeds and steal her innocence.

Alasdair's stomach churned. Had it happened already?

In his mind's eye he saw the bairns—they always resembled Feya when he thought of them—brown eyes like the depth of the forest and faces that broke down the walls of the heart.

"I promised her."

The walls bore down on him in the darkness, as if they had lips to snarl and breath to rake across his skin. The room was suddenly hot. And was that the call of the Muslims? The voice of the devil with the knife . . .

He took a breath and then another. "Just imagining."

He squeezed his eyes shut in the dark and saw the colors, like he always did. They came in waves, like ripples across a lake—blue, purple, green. He followed the pattern and counted them off.

Sweat pooled at his waistline. He tried to focus back on the colors, but they merged and blended, becoming nothing but deeper black behind his eyes.

Alasdair opened his eyes. The room had changed.

Even in the dark, a soul could be felt.

Someone was there. Waiting. Watching.

"You seem to have yourself in quite a predicament." The voice was definitely Scottish, but refined. "I do apologize for these less than desirable accommodations. However, it's not as if I can just put you in one of the guestrooms." A match was struck. A faint light burned and the glow expanded. His scarred hands were the first thing that Alasdair saw. And then the elegant cut of a finely tailored suit. "I heard you speak a name earlier. Feya, I believe."

"What do you want?" Alasdair made a fist against the chains.

"Ah. Hit a nerve, did I? I can assure you that she is well. Very well, in fact. Happily installed above, basking in the finery I am more than happy to give her."

Alasdair closed his eyes. He knew that tone, that particular intention. "Might I presume that I am at Castle Aldourie?"

"You are clever. How ever did you deduce that?"

"I've learned to listen."

"Well." The man moved, bringing the lantern closer. "Perhaps you'd like to listen some more." He pulled something by the wall and it tightened Alasdair's chains. "Once upon a time there was a man who loved a woman—the only bright star of his existence. But then your father decided to come to the north and make a show of cleansing the Gypsies. She was at the camp that day, visiting her mother. Your father came barreling down upon them, scattering those who could run. But my wife . . ." He brought his hand to Alasdair's throat. "Your father set the caravans ablaze and she was trapped."

Alasdair widened his eyes. "No."

That brought a sound like laughter from him. "Lied to you all these years, has he? You would have done well to investigate that father of yours before you decided to be the dutiful son."

Morna's words came back to him with a vengeance, rushing through the cavern. *"Ask him, son. Pay attention to the look in his eyes. I expect there's more he's lied to ye about."*

"By the time I saw the smoke . . . And then, when I finally was able to reach her . . ." The man squeezed, hard, focusing on the scars on his hands. "Do you know what it's like to hold your dying wife in your arms?" Tears formed in his eyes. "Of course you don't. I've often wondered if your father would have hesitated if he knew that she was with child."

Blackness pressed in, hard. Alasdair's heart beat quicker, resisting.

"How sad that you're caught up in this. How awful for you." The man pressed harder, until Alasdair was sure his neck would break. "I've never been a violent man. I'm a . . . lawyer. An esteemed member of Parliament." Tears streamed down his cheeks. "Revenge does hold a certain sweetness." He focused on his hands. "In fact, the more I squeeze your throat, the better I feel."

Feya woke facing a window. A rolling lawn met the edge of a loch. Gold from the sun touched the dark-green trees. Higher up, into the disappearing sky—smudges of pink, white, and grey, like a painter had drawn his hand across the colors in frustration.

Crushing weight bore in on her as she remembered. It hadn't been a dream. She turned onto her back and stared at the elaborate molding on the ceiling. "Alasdair." Her tears cut off his name, as he had been so cruelly cut off from the earth.

"That devil, Aldourie." She waded the velvet coverlet in her hands. "He'll show me Alasdair's body or I won't believe."

"Begging your pardon, miss."

Feya leapt for a water pitcher on the side table and stood. A platter crashed to the floor and shattered.

"Oh, Lord!" A woman dressed in maid's clothing flung herself against the wall.

"Who are ye?" Feya lifted the pitcher higher.

"Glenna, miss." She curtsied, awkwardly. One brown curl fell out of her cap.

"What do ye do here? Have ye come to spy on me?"

"Oh no, miss." Her eyes widened. "The master only wants me to help you if you desire it."

"Help me with what? What makes ye think I'll trust ye—or him, fer that matter?" She jabbed toward the door with her finger as if Mr. Aldourie stood there.

The maid cowered and held up a curling iron like a shield. "He said you were rough 'round the edges. Don't hurt me."

Feya raked her gaze over the girl. She was probably not a day over sixteen. "What are ye supposed to do, then? Dress me like a babe?"

Glenna relaxed a little. "You're not accustomed to being dressed?

Feya lowered the pitcher. "What do ye think?"

"You're more like me, I think."

"Where are ye from then?"

"Just up the loch. Inverness."

Feya sighed and felt the weight of all the distance she had come. The Gypsy queen's words came back to her. "The end of the world."

"What makes you say that?"

Grief pressed her down upon the bed. The pitcher rolled from her fingers onto the blanket. "It's a long way from Edinburgh, that's all."

"Is that where you're from?"

"I suppose." Feya stared back out the window. "Yer master . . . What sort of a man is he?"

"Oh, miss, only the best sort. Even though the mistress was gone, he let me stay. He knew I needed help because me mum had taken ill and the winter was coming."

"The mistress?"

"Elspeth." Glenna whispered the word like it was sacred. "Her death was a true shame."

"What happened?"

"I'll tell you if you let me dress you and do your hair. It's been a long while since I've gotten to make up a fine lady."

"I'm not a fine lady. But I suppose I can't wear this nightgown."

"It wouldn't be wise. Not in such a castle as this. The clothes you wore here are being washed. While you're here, the master thought we should treat you like the honored guest that you are." Glenna went to a wardrobe and flung open the doors. The light gleamed off satins and velvets.

"He thinks a lot, yer master." Feya narrowed her eyes. Most likely, they were the dead woman's clothes.

"He says you've been through a lot and you might be staying with us for a while."

"Is that so?" Feya walked to the wardrobe and touched the velvet sleeve on a deep-green dress.

"Oh, that's one of my favorites." Glenna's face lit up. "With your hair, you'll look like a dream."

A profound sadness washed over Feya. She didn't want to dress up in fancy dresses. She just wanted Alasdair. She wanted to see his handsome blue eyes and his long eyelashes. She nodded to keep from crying.

Glenna took the dress from the wardrobe. White lilies were embroidered in the silk. The leaves were trimmed with gold thread.

Feya turned away, gripped the poster of the bed, and shut her eyes. She wished the woman would leave. She had the urge to scream and then break things. The mouse of a maid wouldn't take it well.

The girl tugged on the nightgown. "They had a great romance."

Feya glanced at her and squeezed the bedpost. "Did they?" The last thing she wanted to hear about was a romance.

"They weren't about the house much, if you get my meaning."

"They traveled?"

"No." Glenna leaned forward and whispered. "Kept to their bedroom most days."

Feya exhaled and leaned her forehead against the post. Perfection. She'd been stuck with a maid who loved gossip about romance.

"And when they were about the house you couldn't stand to look at 'em."

Feya rolled her eyes. "Why?"

"They undressed one another with their eyes. Didn't matter what time of day."

Love always came to torment her. Dangled like a carrot and then taken away. That pain in her lungs stretched everything taut, including her mind. She slid her hands down the post and felt her body sway.

"Here, now. You look a little pale." Glenna took her by the shoulders and led her to a cushioned chair. "The master said you had a long journey. I'll ring for some tea." She pulled a thick tasseled cord that came out of the ceiling.

A cord to ring for more servants. Such a waste.

Glenna picked up a black brush inlaid with pearl. "May I brush your hair now?"

"Why not." Feya stared at her own hollow eyes in the mirror, and the dark circles that rimmed the ugly brown. Each tug of the brush took her back—to Deacon Brodie's and the stroke of Maggie's wasted hands. It was the same, that and this. She was being prepared for another man, and not the one that she longed for. "Why not," she repeated again. She closed her eyes against the vision of the only thing she was ever meant to become.

Chapter Twenty-Eight

Mr. Aldourie lowered his newspaper and stood. "Good morning. Did you sleep well?"

"I slept." Feya stared at the breakfast table and all the food heaping there. She couldn't take the steps that were needed to enter the room.

"Please, come in." When she hesitated he added, "I've had the nursery readied for your siblings. If that is what you desire."

"Ye told the truth?"

"Of course." The lines at his eyes deepened. "Why would I lie?"

Feya walked to stand beside him. "Tell me again." The fragile early light revealed his eyes to be the color of amber. Last night they had looked as dark as hers.

"My dear, you should sit down. You've had a shock, and I am sorry for it." He took her arm and nodded at a servant. "A tonic, if you please."

Quick footsteps followed, taps against the wooden floor.

He led her to a parlor chair. "Breathe, Feya." Anger flashed upon his face, deepening the many lines. "I never meant for you to be tied and drugged like animals. I will deal with those Gypsies who brought you here."

Feya wrapped her fingers around the crushed red velvet of the chair. Its softness felt out of place with the ache that raged within her.

Mr. Aldourie knelt before her. "There were a few unruly men in the camp. Travelers from the west. I'd never met them before." He shut his eyes as if in pain. "I cannot abide a loss of life. Not since my wife . . . It's all such a waste."

Feya took short breaths, the room spinning.

"They say he was cruel to you at first, but then he started to change after Torphichen."

"Alasdair was only doin' his job in the beginnin'."

Mr. Aldourie reached into his waistcoat pocket and retrieved a white handkerchief. "Here."

She buried her face in it, not caring what he thought.

"I wrote his father. It was my duty to do so."

"Ye what?"

"I informed him of his son's death."

His accent was suited to someone who lived in a castle. Feya hated him for it. She hated the kind way he looked at her now. She hated the concern in his eyes.

"What did ye say? That ye had him kidnapped?"

"I am a man of government, Feya. Of course I left that delicate matter out." He looked at her like they were conspirators.

"Right as rain, I bet ye did. Ye've made a fine mess of things." She pulled her hand back when he tried to touch it. She wished that she was like the mist on the loch and that she could just float away. Be nothing. Not hurt anymore.

"Feya, your accent . . . and your eyes. What tribe are you from? What part of Scotland?"

His voice called her back from the loneliness. "Some of me childhood is just shadows—Gypsy fires, police knockin' on the caravan at night, songs and sellin' flowers and baskets just to stay alive. Don't ask me where I'm from." Her voice caught. "I'm not from anywhere. I'm not anybody."

"You're a strong woman who managed to outwit two hundred of my men."

Her voice rose. "And what did strength ever do fer me?" She could never get away from it—people insisting she was strong. Her strength had killed Alasdair. And he was the only one who had told her it was all right to be weak sometimes. To be carried by others at times.

A tear rolled down her cheek. Mr. Aldourie wiped it away with his thumb. She was too weary to protest his touch.

"'Clouds symbolize the veils that shroud God.' The French writer Balzac said that. It's a favorite phrase of mine. It reminds me that there are many mysteries in the world. One of them being your strength and how you came to be here." His smile was hidden, like a magician just before pulling off a cloth. "Everything will be revealed in time—the reasons for your pain and the joy that will follow."

"Yer a strange man, Mr. Aldourie. I don't know what to make of ye."

"You may call me Ranald. And why label me like a science experiment? Sometimes the best surprises are the ones that can't be classified at all."

Feya sat in the same place where he'd left her. He'd opened his pocket watch and then apologized like they were friends. "Dash it all, but I find I have to go into town to conduct a wee dram of business. You will forgive me, won't you?"

It was such a posh thing to say. Flowering the phrases just for the sake of exploring the words. It made her miss Alasdair even more.

The tick of the clock on the mantel echoed throughout the room.

She sat on the couch, her shoulders stiff and her back straight as an embalmer's board. With each tick, her body jerked. She didn't know what she was guarding against, but she felt the need anyway. The servants were far away in the other corners of the house, probably talking about her.

Feya walked over to the harp. Places on the top were worn away, like Mr. Aldourie had stroked the carved wood many a time.

Ma used to do that with her harp when she was worried.

Feya ran her finger down a long, gold cord and plucked it. The deep, pure sound rang throughout the room. The vibrations shivered against her. "Who are ye, then? The devil or my savior?"

Nothing was right.

Alasdair had said he felt God closer than his skin. Apparently not. Because Alasdair was dead. Gone. Without so much as an inkling of divine intervention.

Feya walked like a ghost, feeling like she was floating—stuck between two worlds, never fitting in. Everywhere she wandered, the windows were open, curtains expanding in and out like the castle breathed.

She turned into a hallway lined with windows. The light flooded her vision, forcing her eyes shut. The warmth should have been welcome. A full sun hadn't shone its face in so long, and yet it chose to now. Now, when she wanted only the darkness. Now, when she wanted only to hide.

She placed her arms around herself and pretended that she was with him: Alasdair the palace guard, because even hating him would be better than this. Alasdair of the road, smelling like the forest and all things forbidden. Alasdair who scowled and teased and kissed. Alasdair who saw strange things and had trusted her enough to tell. Alasdair Cairncross—all of him. Alasdair like a vine in her blood. Every smile and word that he'd said. All the times she'd spent longing for him before she even knew he was alive.

She opened an oak door at the end of the hall. A fountain stood in the middle of the room. Plants spilled from lacquered pots. Glass lined the walls like facets of a rich woman's ring. Feya collapsed on a bench. The light caught the water drops as they fell and made them look like tears.

The melancholy pressed in . . . but there was something else there too. A presence—someone in the room she couldn't see. She turned. No one was there.

"I'm losing me mind now." Feya reached for Ma's wooden cross. It rested in her hand, just like always. Just like the day Ma had died and pressed it there. Just like the night she'd clutched it in the tenement before heading out into the rain.

"Bloody waste of wood." If Mr. Aldourie really was the man he said he was . . . If the bairns really were coming. Well, then, she'd found her rainbow. The perfect solution.

It had only cost the life of Alasdair Cairncross.

The pool of the fountain circled and bubbled. How much did it cost to make this water disappear and come back again? Waste. Want. Plenty.

Feya dangled the cross above the drain. What did it matter if she opened her hand? No one would see.

Just like God could have stopped her from getting sick the night she went to Holyrood Palace, He could have stopped Alasdair from dying. He didn't.

He'd turned his back when she'd been scared out of her wits, just about to give her body. Turned His back on her and the bairns.

Feya opened her hand and felt the leather string fall.

God hadn't helped them at Millie's cabin. Thirty more minutes and they'd have gotten away. Alasdair would be alive.

The leather string slid through her fingers like the last bit of her prayers.

The cross floated on the surface. The water sucked it down.

Feya's heart caught at the sight of it. "There's no room fer the weakness." Alasdair was wrong. There was no God who wanted to be closer than her skin.

She had to do it—this thing called life. She had to do it for the bairns. And, cursed blood or not, she would give those babies more than had been given to her. Even if it meant lying with Mr. Aldourie. She'd seen the way he'd looked at her when she'd come into the room. And here she was wearing his dead wife's dress. Men were so predictable.

All except one.

But men were men, Maggie had said. What did it matter which one took it from her? A woman could use her body to manipulate and get what she wanted. It was the only thing she could ever offer. It was the only thing she had ever had. And this would be a good life for the bairns.

"Easy." The word came on its own from her mouth. She nodded and clenched her fists. "It will be easy."

A noise came from below the floor—a sucking sound and then a great crack. The water in the fountain changed, trembling, sending ripples to the sides. Trickles of water came from the fish's mouths like a drunk man's spit. "Idiot! I should've thrown it into the loch. What possessed me to do such a thing?" She knelt beside the fountain and plunged her hand into the drain.

The water rose to the edge and then lowered.

She felt the slick drain. Nothing.

The cross was gone, out of her reach forever. And her fragile hopes, like the trickling water, disappeared into the darkness.

Chapter Twenty-Nine

He was going to drown.

Alasdair widened his eyes at the water coming from the ceiling. At first, the shaft of light had made him think that he'd died. After that devil Aldourie had finished with him, Alasdair had wished for death and prayed for it. His mind was frayed. His body was broken. And Feya . . . The things the man had said about Feya were worse than the torture in Egypt.

Alasdair jerked back to consciousness. His weight against the iron shackles caused the metal to slice him once again. Blood ran down his arms like payment. Not much longer and it would be done.

Cold reached into Alasdair's veins—stroking death fingers that wouldn't take long. The water fell from the ceiling crack like rain.

Rain. Always the Scottish rain. Pouring down upon him since he'd been a child. Torphichen. Morna—Mother—calling him out of it so he wouldn't get cold. Watching it flow down the panes of the old windows in the inn as she told him stories . . .

If only he'd not been so hard when he'd seen her. How much he'd wanted to embrace her. He could admit that now. But the carefully constructed man that he had become—the Queen's Guard— couldn't allow it.

That man was nowhere to be seen now. He was only Alasdair. Alasdair of Torphichen, London, Egypt. Alasdair guarding an empty palace in Holyrood, standing alone in the rain. Until she had come— Feya. But now he was Alasdair forgotten, dying under a madman's castle. Once again dying in the rain.

He looked down at Morna's locket around his neck. His birth caul—the veil over his face—rumored to keep men from drowning. The irony of it would have been comical in another life. Now it just lay on his chest, an icy weight, reflecting the drops of water like all the tears he never cried.

He let his mind slip back to Millie's cabin—to kissing Feya and how hard it had been to pull away. She'd awoken in him what he'd long locked away. He could feel his heart again—all the desires he'd once had and all the desires he wished could be. The call was deep and resounding, like a ship through fathoms of blue. But now he felt too much. It came as the water, pouring down.

"One True Living God, I know You can hear me. I shouldn't have locked You away. You aren't someone who can be controlled and measured. I remember what it was like when we spoke face to face." The water ran in his eyes and dripped from his chin. "I know what You asked of me in Egypt, but I chose my own road. You fulfilled Your end, but I didn't fulfill mine." He closed his eyes and listened to the endless water, a clock measuring his life away. "If I must die, save Feya. Hide her in the shadow of Your cross."

A crack echoed in the cavern. The earth above heaved, and dirt rained down. The stream of water swelled like a gaping mouth.

Alasdair pushed against the wall, fighting for the small ledge. The water reached, lapping closer and closer. Up to his waist now.

Rays of light plunged in the fall like spears, as if the sun rose above somewhere. A small black blur fell in the quickening stream. Alasdair squinted. The black smudge spun on the surface. A leather string trailed behind it, curling around.

It floated closer, carried on the rhythms of the water. It came into the light.

A cross. It was Feya's cross, nudging him on the leg. But how? He stared at it in bemusement, his eyes tracing its edges—then realized what it meant.

If he could just reach it . . . he might be able to pick the locks.

Chills came over his body. The cold racked in spasms. Tears came, falling like the water, tumbling down.

Elspeth's dress flared out behind her as she paced. The material was too heavy, the bodice too big. Feya pulled it up again on her shoulder. Slipping—it kept slipping. And time . . . Time unraveled like the light—brighter and brighter until she couldn't stand it. How she longed for the rain. And a cave. And the scent of Alasdair beside her.

His absence was an ache like the death of the Highlands in winter.

Sleep. Death. Either was favorable. It was all the same without him and the bairns.

The early morning light slanted from the window, reaching across the harp, making shadow bars fall across her borrowed shoes.

Waiting was a kind of death. Waiting was like the tenements.

A door slammed deep in the castle. A woman's voice wafted through the hall. Feya knew that voice. She ran behind the piano and crouched.

"What do you mean, you're letting her stay?" The Gypsy queen strode into the room and turned, her finger in Ranald's face as he followed.

"It is my affair, Kizzy. Not your concern."

"That little rat caused me a great deal of problems. She lied to me."

"And you've never lied when you've been in a fix?"

"That's different." Kizzy narrowed her eyes.

Mr. Aldourie stepped closer. "What are you really upset about?"

Kizzy raised her face. "You know." She looked as if she would cry. "I should be here and not her. How many years have I doted—"

"I cannot give what I don't feel. I have told you this before."

Feya's mouth opened wide. Kizzy was in love with Aldourie. When she'd talked in the tent about being in love with a man . . . it had been Ranald.

"At least let me take Feya back to the camp where she belongs. We'll make her comfortable. I won't punish her for going against me."

Ranald plucked a low string of the harp. "I'm not so sure about that. And until I am, she stays here if she desires it."

"Listen to you, talking about her like she was a princess."

His hand stilled over another string. "Please, Kizzy, I have a headache that would wake the dead. Be a good girl and go back to the camp."

Kizzy's eyelids fell. She played with the bracelets lining her arm and fought back tears as she left. Strange to see on a woman such as her. But women were women, Feya supposed. And nothing could break a woman faster than lack of love.

"Well, that was tiring." Ranald collapsed in a chair. "You can come out now, Feya."

Feya stood. "I'm sorry. I heard every word."

"I thought so." A smile pulled the corner of his mouth.

"How'd ye know I was there?"

He pulled a book from the side table and opened it. "Let's just say you're hard to overlook. "How was your morning?"

"I broke somethin'." She crossed her arms and braced herself for his anger.

His turned a page. "What was it?"

"Yer fountain."

"Which one?"

"Ye have more than one?"

"Yes."

"Down the hall. Lots of windows."

"Ah, that one. I brought it over from . . ." He looked up. Instantly, as he met her eyes, his expression softened. "Never mind. How did you manage that?"

"I dropped somethin' in the water."

"Making a wish, were you?"

"Somethin' like that."

"Put it out of your mind." He brushed his hand in the air as if moving the thought away. "It's only a material possession."

"Yer not angry?"

"Of course not." He stood. "There are far more serious things in life." Gentleness shone in the depths of his eyes, but there was something else there too. "Would you trust me for a little while? I'd like to show you something."

Clouds passed over the windows of the parlor, casting the light into sliding shadows.

"I suppose."

He held out his hand and she took it. The feel of his palm was rough, not the palm of a nobleman. Scars wove in and out of his fingers, a tangled white web.

"What happened to ye?"

"It's hardly worth mentioning." His smile was a little too perfect. He led her up the stairs. Paintings crammed the upper stairwell. The scenes were ghastly and dark—abandoned shacks along a lonely road, phantoms and specters, a lone tree in a field, and the biggest painting of them all—a man before a table full of bottles, his gaze turned heavenward.

"Are you frightened, Feya?"

She looked at the scars on his hands again. "Should I be?"

"Fear doesn't exist as a thing. It is planted there by ourselves or others."

Feya loosened the grip on his hand. "Only wicked hearts desire to plant fear in others."

"Not always." They reached the end of the long hall. "These are desperate times. Sometimes fear must be used to achieve a greater good."

Feya studied the weathered lines in his face. Only a man who spent hours in the wilderness had a face such as that. Blown by the wind, chapped by its bite. But yet, here he stood, dressed as a London duke, his silk sleeve rubbing against her wrist.

"You have nothing to fear from me." Ranald ran his thumb over the back of her hand. "I want you to believe that you are safe here."

"Thank ye." It was the proper response, but she didn't feel it.

"I wouldn't take you in here, but I feel . . ." He drew his eyebrows together.

"What?"

"Some things can only be understood through the eyes." He turned the doorknob and swung the door wide.

Dark blue colored the walls of the bedroom. Elaborate white molding reached down the wall in scrolls. Faded red roses wept in a vase, their shriveled heads hanging low.

"This was Elspeth's room."

On the bed, blue velvet cascaded in perfect folds. Blue would make her think of Alasdair until the day she died.

"Go to the window. Tell me what you see."

Feya pulled back the heavy curtain. Far below and across the dense forest, smoke curled from Gypsy fires. Hundreds of caravans dotted the woods like splattered paint—maroon, aqua, gold. People moved like ants—washing, cooking, dancing just because.

"We set up the settlement soon after we married." He ran his hand along the bedpost. "You're the first one to be in here besides the servants."

"Is that so?" Feya dropped the curtain. It shushed against the floor.

"I have a question, my dear, and I'd like you to think carefully upon it."

"Yes?"

"If Alasdair was here, would you leave with him? Or would you stay and start a life here among your people?"

The question plunged into her heart. The room disappeared, along with Ranald's presence beside her. She was on the bed again in the cabin. And Alasdair . . . strong, beautiful Alasdair held her in his arms. *"Do you want to be heavy with my child even if there's no wedding to go with it?"* Her heart shattered as she realized the full intent of his words. Even though he'd loved her, there'd never be a future for them together. In his mind, she was only the momentary comfort—the available woman. The fact that he'd refused to lie with her had been a kindness—a gift that she hadn't realized at the time.

Ranald's voice filtered through her thoughts. "Consider carefully, please. For the sake of my philosophical mind. You will excuse a gentleman's curiosity, won't you?"

If the bairns truly were coming, why would she go back to Edinburgh? Feya looked back out at the Gypsies and the perfectly serene picture of the camp. Never had she experienced such freedom and solitude—such safety as they had under his protection. "Do they have to steal?"

"Excuse me?"

"The children." A great unwinding started within her. It was every doubt she'd ever had. It was all the times villagers had spat at her family as they'd passed. "Do they steal to live?"

"There's no need for that here. If I have anything to do with it, there won't ever be the need for that again. There's a bill in Parliament . . ." He searched her face, as if looking for the depths of her soul. "It's called the Moveable Dwellings Act. If passed, all Gypsies will have to have their caravans registered. Searches of those caravans can be made at any time. Beyond that, there are hidden things in that bill—things to punish and snuff out your people."

"Truly?" The word came out as soft as the curtain lifting, as soft as the velvet cover on the bed. The castle—this place—it was hidden from the world. And the words he said must be true. If the Gypsies were ever to be safe—if she and the bairns were ever to be safe—it would be here.

Ranald stepped toward her. "Families would be broken. Children would be taken away."

Feya closed her eyes and saw the harsh greys of the tenement. She rubbed her arms and felt the grime upon her skin that never seemed to come off.

His hand was light upon her shoulder. "I know what your people have suffered. I know what blood has been shed and what promises were broken."

A breeze came through the window and chilled her skin. She was alone now. And if she left, there'd be no one. No beautiful Alasdair with handsome blue eyes, his presence like an anchor beside her. She floated now. Who would she be if not a Gypsy? She'd tried so hard just to be Scottish. And that had only brought hunger and want. And too many tears from the bairns. "Da bricked up the window because of the tax." The words slipped out and she didn't know why. That's where it had begun.

"What did you say?" His voice was gentle.

"It all started with the whiskey. And then he had the mortar and

I couldn't stop him." She swallowed against the void that she felt—the man Da had been and never would be again. "The bairns were so hungry. What was I supposed to do? He left—"

"The window tax? Is that what you said?"

"Aye. The wastrel landlord—"

"Feya, the window tax was repealed in fifty-one."

His words didn't make sense.

"The window tax hasn't been in effect for thirty-four years."

She exhaled hard and grabbed his arm to keep from falling.

"I'm . . . sorry Feya. Whiskey, you said?"

Everything that had happened—Deacon Broodie's, the palace, Alasdair, and now being here—it was all because of Da and the drink. Worse than that, it meant meeting Alasdair wasn't meant to be.

Final. No intervention by God. No plan other than her own.

Mr. Aldourie took her in his arms. "It's all right. You're safe. I am here."

"I would stay." The words slurred against his chest.

"Are you sure?"

Elspeth's dress slipped on her shoulder. "I am now."

His body noticeably relaxed. Time became the sound of the loch waves lapping. "Feya, let me love you."

The Torphichen Inn door opened with a force like the final judgment. Leaves blew inside, skittering upon the floor.

Morna inhaled sharply and dropped the cleaning rag.

Edan Cairncross stood in her doorway, a haunted look on his face, just the same as the last time she'd seen him.

The years slipped back, as they were wont to do—hateful things, tempering memories until they were too bright or too dull. "Rowan, go into the back."

The raindrops on Edan's cheek fell into his collar—seeping away like the rivers of tears she'd spent on him. His eyes, just as handsome as the day he'd first walked through the door, searched her face. It made her feel like a girl again, and she hated him for it.

Rowan stopped by the fireplace. "Who's that, Ma?"

"I said go." She gripped the chair. Rowan's dog made her way across the room and nudged Edan's hand like a traitor. "Nessie, out!"

"The beast isn't doing any harm." He patted the dog's head as if he were a gentle man. "It's been a long time, Morna."

"Thankfully, it has." She hated how her heart caught at the sight of him—the hair still as black as a raven's and not a touch of grey.

Rowan and Nessie disappeared in the back. The kitchen door beat against the frame.

"I have thought of you often." He swallowed and clenched his hand, as if the words were difficult. "When I was with my wife—"

"Don't."

"You know the truth, even without the words." He stepped toward her, and the wind outside pressed against the window—sliding, forcing, whispering things from long ago. "I have missed you. Don't say you haven't thought of me."

He stood so close she could feel his warmth. She lowered her gaze to keep from seeing the scar at the corner of his right eye—made from the blackberry thicket where he'd chased her just to make her laugh. "I only think of ye on special occasions. Like when I have the grippe, or I'm in a great deal of pain. Apart from Alasdair, ye were the biggest mistake I ever made."

"Don't say that." His wish to touch her was between them—as real in the air as if he had done so. "The years have been kind to you."

Morna laughed bitterly. "Ye think that if it pleases ye."

"The boy . . ." His gaze went to the door where Rowan had gone.

"Aye. He's mine. A better man filled the place ye ripped from me heart." Even though the words didn't ring true, she raised her chin just to taunt him. Let him feel what she had felt. Let him take in the sickness of being thrown over for another.

The arrow lodged deep; it showed in the way the muscle twitched at his jaw. "Did you marry him?"

"Aye." Morna clenched her fist. "He had more honor than you."

"Is that so?"

"Aye."

"And how does he make you feel in the summer?"

Rage flashed in her veins. She clenched her hand. Her fist met his flawless face.

Blood spilled from his nose. He tilted and tripped over the table. His back slammed against the floor.

Morna jumped on his chest and pinned his arms with her knees. She slapped him hard. "How could ye leave me after what ye said?" She lifted her hand to slap him again.

Edan caught her hand and twisted. She fell to the floor. "There's the woman I know. Glad you haven't lost your spunk."

His face loomed above her as she'd seen it so many times in her dreams. She lifted her free hand and slapped him again.

Edan closed his eyes, gritted his teeth, and released her. When he stood, the sound of his greatcoat was like the rush of the wind. "Is your husband good to you?"

Morna gripped the table and stood. "Better than ye ever were." She wouldn't tell him that Brochan was dead. Wouldn't give him the satisfaction that apart from Rowan she was alone.

"That's good." He leaned on the fireplace mantel and stared into the fire. "I often wondered." He said the words softly, like the last falling leaf just before snow.

Morna raked her hands through her disheveled hair, suddenly weary to the core. "What do ye want? Or did ye just come here to torment me?" All the years between them bore down hard. All the things spoken and unspoken. Every look that never was. All the things never destined to be.

"I want to ask for your forgiveness."

She sucked her breath in at his words and turned to the window. Anything but that.

The trees outside bent under the weight of the wind. The dark clouds pressed lower, reaching for the ravished ground.

Some days, hating him was the only thing that had kept her alive.

"Did you hear me?"

His words pressed in like the night she'd found Alasdair gone. "Sorry fer what? Sayin' ye loved me and then leavin' me without a word? Not answering when I wrote ye that I was with child? Or coming here and stealing Alasdair away?"

"Everything."

Morna clamped her lips shut. The words required were few, but oh, how hard to let them pass her lips. The rage of the fire and the howl of the storm used the seconds like an overbearing master.

Soft whispers came on the wind. Branches tapped on the window. She'd borne the anger for so long. What would it be like to open her hand and set it free?

"I understand." He dropped his gaze to the ashes scattering the floor.

The moment was gone. Scattered forever as the leaves outside used by the wind.

"Alasdair . . . He came here."

"Aye."

"Is he not handsome, Morna?" Edan closed his eyes. "And strong. A man above men."

"Aye. That he is." She wrapped her arms around herself to try to keep out the cold that wasn't from the weather. "If only I'd seen him grow."

"I gave him a life. He wouldn't have had one if I'd left him with you." The words were tired, as if he'd said them to himself too many times.

"Well, I'm glad ye have the mind of God." She walked to the kitchen and poured water over her shaking hands. Edan's blood swirled in the bowl.

"You know what his life would have been in Torphichen."

"At least he would have had his mother. Yer care has made him hard." Tears formed in her eyes at the thought of it. How she'd longed just to hold him, or talk with him for days. A lifetime. But Alasdair would have none of it.

"There was a woman with him."

Morna stilled, the towel in her hands.

"How did they seem together?"

She would not tell him there'd been an obvious spark between the two. That seeing them together had reminded her of herself and Edan. "I don't know what ye mean. He was taking her to Stirling. She was handcuffed like an animal."

"Could she have manipulated him?"

Morna almost laughed. Out her bedroom window, she'd seen them standing in the stable like lovers—him holding her arms in the moonlight after she'd knocked his water flask away. Feya had almost poisoned him. "Manipulated him how? Enlighten me, as ye seem to be the expert in that area."

Edan placed his hands on the counter. "How did he seem around her?"

Angry. Trying too hard not to look at her . . . "He was her captor. Ye obviously trained him well."

Edan lowered his gaze so he could look her in the eyes. "You're a smart woman. You always had a way of seeing what was below the surface."

"Aye," she whispered. "I can see." She saw the way he struggled now—holding himself away but longing to step forward.

"Would he bed her given the chance?"

"How would I know? That's yer area of expertise."

He cursed and wiped his hand over his face. "Something's happened."

"Aye." She braced herself for the words she dreaded most. "It would have to fer ye to come back here."

"Alasdair's been kidnapped."

Morna flinched. The rain outside pelted the windowpane like stones. "He's not dead, then?"

"He—How did you know he was in trouble?"

Morna closed her eyes. "A mother knows. I felt it some days ago. I've been prayin'."

"He was intercepted on his way to Stirling. I wouldn't put it past the woman to have set it up."

"Why would ye think that?"

"I have been told that she wore a Gypsy scarf."

"And that incriminates her, does it?"

"Surely you know what kind of people they are. I have worked very hard to rid this country of their disease and insolence."

"They are people, Edan. Ye have to look on the inside before ye can tell what sort."

"Do you know how they treat their children? Their lack of education—"

"What do ye care about children except fer stealin' them?" She came around the counter and pointed in his face. "I wouldn't be surprised if ye were the reason he was kidnapped."

"What—"

Something fell behind the kitchen door.

"Rowan. I know yer listenin'."

The door creaked open. Rowan's innocent face stared back at her, as well as Nessie's massive snout. "That fancy man who was here . . . The one with all the buttons."

"Yes, love. He's yer half brother. And this is his father."

"Well, then." Rowan hooked his thumbs in his waistcoat pockets. "What are we standin' around talkin' fer? Me brother's in trouble. Family helps family. We certainly don't abandon them." He leaned toward Edan and scowled. "Or steal them in the night."

Morna walked to stand by her youngest son and wrapped her arm around him. "Ye heard the little man. What is yer plan? Ye have quite a lot of explainin' to do, Edan Cairncross. And I fully intend to hear all the details."

Chapter Thirty

Through the open window, Feya could hear the lap of water and the rush of trees dancing in the wind. She had stood with Alasdair in that wind. She'd fled with him to a cave where he'd let her cry.

But it didn't mean anything. Just a man with a woman. It was just the way. The way as old as time.

She was cold. Ranald's touch helped a little. Maybe she could pretend it was Alasdair. Maybe that would make it easier. Maybe then she could feel.

Ranald pulled her close, but it didn't mean anything.

Feya. Feya on the wind. Feya who might have been.

Somewhere children laughed and had no worries. Somewhere every tomorrow was a promise destined to be filled.

Somewhere. But not here.

She smiled when he pressed his lips to hers. Because that was how women survived, wasn't it? That was how you kept in a man's favor.

He would protect her and the bairns. They would have a life. The price she paid now was such a small thing.

The smell of him was musk and wealth, choices he could make, things he could accomplish. His hand on her back was quiet power, a longing undercurrent.

"It will be all right." His voice was low and hazy like the fog over the loch. "I promise to take care of you." His lips on her neck were warm. "Trust in me." He brought his lips to her ear. "Lean into me. Now is the end of all your suffering." Ranald walked toward the bed. The back of her knees hit the mattress. He lowered her down.

His weight was the weight of sorrows.

Feya turned her face toward the wall.

Words. He said them. But she didn't care.

She clutched the velvet blanket and stared at the crushed blue. *Alasdair, I'm slipping . . . Catch me.* Breath came too shallow.

Ranald reached for the hem of her dress. "Shhh." He smoothed his hand over her hair. "Don't cry."

Help. The word echoed but she couldn't say it. Panic was a sliding, raking beast upon her skin. Poisoned breath and the weight of a thousand tons.

"No." She ground out the word, and that dragged another. "Stop."

"It's all right," he said in that fine, sick way of the proud.

Feya sucked in her breath, sharply, and forced her hands against his arms.

Crushing, grasping, devil of a man.

She thought of Alasdair, holding her hand in the woods, telling her to run. *"Hurry, Feya. Run with me. Just a little farther."*

Feya clawed at the bed but only came back with the soft velvet cover.

His hand slid up her thigh.

Help me, God. The cry came from deep within her soul. *You're the only one who can.*

Panic was a freezing weight, numbness in her arms, stone throughout her body that forbid her to move. *Help,* her mind cried out. But her lips couldn't form the word.

Footsteps sounded somewhere. A great noise and then a crash.

Feya opened her eyes. She must have died, because Alasdair stood in the room. It was odd, though. He looked as if he'd been drowned. His shirt hung in tatters. Even stranger, her cross necklace hung from his neck.

Deep-blue eyes met hers. Water dripped from his hair and trailed down his face. The moment stretched like fine silver, hot from the refiner's fire.

Blackness played at the edges of her vision, pressing in.

So this was death. Ranald Aldourie had killed her.

How kind of Alasdair's ghost to come.

More crushing weight. The last of her breath flew from her lungs. Feya snapped her eyes open, pain like a burning rope around her ribs.

Elspeth's room. Why was she still in the room?

The white bed canopy ripped from the posts. Ranald slid off her body. Alasdair threw him to the floor.

Alasdair.

She wasn't dead.

Alasdair wasn't dead.

Feya reached for the bedpost. She gasped for air.

"Look at me!" Alasdair grabbed Ranald by the shirt collar and picked him up. He hit him hard, causing him to stumble into the wardrobe. Glass rained down, sparkling shards into his hair and over his shoulders.

Feya came to herself, the shatter of glass like a bucket of cold water. Alasdair was alive. He needed help. They needed to escape. She stumbled to the fireplace and reached for the iron poker.

Alasdair slipped. Glass crunched beneath him.

Ranald came down hard, grinding his knee into Alasdair's stomach.

Voices yelled from the hall.

Feya raised the poker and aimed at Ranald's head. Her hands shook, as well as her body. She should hit him, soundly and sure. Send him to the abyss he'd almost placed her in.

Alasdair grabbed Ranald's leg and pitched him to the floor. "That's for Feya." His fist slammed into Ranald's stomach. "That's for me." He drew back and kicked, his foot meeting Ranald's ribs. "And that's for the bairns."

"Do you expect me to give in?" Ranald gasped and spit blood. "They are all counting on me! I will exhaust . . . every . . . resource."

"Ye can't very well do that if yer dead." Feya's breath came too fast. "What did ye do to Alasdair? He was here all along." She stepped forward and lifted the poker over Aldourie's head.

"No." Alasdair wrenched it out of her hands. "Feya, no. My father . . ."

She saw in his eyes things that had happened—terrible things. But he was different too. Some kind of knowledge stayed his hand.

"Yer father what?"

Ranald's eyes rolled back in his head. His moan turned into a sigh. The master of the castle lay upon the floor, covered in glass and blood like a common criminal in the alleyways.

"Tie him up." Alasdair turned to her. "Let's just go." His voice was a whisper. He swayed and caught himself on the bed. The poker clattered on the floor.

Feya hurried to him and cast her arms about him. The feel of his body was the sweetest relief. "Yer alive."

"Of course I am." He tried to smile but failed miserably. His entire body trembled.

Tears spilled down her cheeks. "He said . . ." She grabbed him tighter, moving her hands up his back and then flinching when she felt his blood.

"It doesn't matter. Put your arms around me. I want to feel you."

Their bodies swayed together, his from tumbling out of death, hers from nearly tumbling into it. Shaking came upon her like a reckoning. She couldn't stop it—her hands, her arms, her legs.

"I'm here." Alasdair brought his cheek against hers. It was freezing.

More voices came from the hallway.

Alasdair's grip tightened. "Let's go home."

"The bairns. He said—"

"He never sent for them. He was waiting to see . . . what you would do." He stumbled toward the door, taking her with him.

She didn't ask him how he knew this. Aldourie certainly had demons no man should have to bear. But that wasn't her concern anymore.

They headed for the stairs.

Glenna stopped in the hall. "Miss?"

The housemaids gaped. One dropped her bucket.

Alasdair stumbled.

"Hold onto the rail." Feya led him down and threw open the front door. The fierce Scottish wind hit them full in the face.

"Which way?" The wind made her shiver, worse than the shock.

"Stable." Alasdair swayed again. "I'm sure Aldourie could spare some . . . horses." His head lolled. He twisted in her arms and collapsed upon the ground.

"Help!" Feya fell to her knees. She looked back at the castle door. "Glenna. Someone!"

The door cracked open but then shut again.

Her voice rose. "Don't ye have a mind of yer own? Or has Aldourie purchased that too? He kept this man prisoner."

The door cracked open again.

"His name is Alasdair Cairncross. He earned the Victoria Cross fer servin' his country. So that the lot of ye could be free from Turks and Arabs and all manner of bloody men. And now here he lies in the company of fellow Scotsmen who won't even give him a blanket."

Glenna pushed open the door and ran to them. "I'm sorry, miss. Perhaps you should come back inside."

"We can't, Glenna. How far to the town? He needs a doctor." Feya kissed Alasdair on his cheek and smoothed his coal-black hair. "Fight. It's what yer good at. Fight, ye noble man."

"Miss, what happened to the master?"

"Nothing he didn't bring upon himself. Glenna, your master kidnapped us both. He held this man captive. We need yer—" Feya's voice broke.

"Someone go to Inverness and get a doctor." Glenna's small voice took on the tone of a warrior. She flicked her gaze back at the servants standing in the doorway. "That's not a request."

"We'll lose our jobs," a woman said.

Glenna stood. "What would you rather have on your conscious? A lost job or a murder?"

"I'll go." A servant stepped through the doorway and headed down the lawn. Some went back into the house without a word. Doors shut.

"Bring me tea!" Glenna pointed at a housemaid. "Now. And a blanket."

The girl skittered across the marble and disappeared.

"The master is hurt." The butler strode out, scowled at Alasdair and headed for the stable. "I'm going for the constable."

"I think you'd better." Feya scowled at him. "And then yer master can explain what he's done."

The housemaid came back with a tea cup. The hot liquid dripped and sloshed as she ran.

Feya pulled Alasdair up to sit. Glenna held the cup to his lips. "Can you drink?"

Alasdair coughed and jerked. His eyes flew open.

"Good." Feya smoothed his hair away from his forehead. "That's a start."

Alasdair sucked in a breath and pushed against the ground. "Help me up." Red seeped into his cheeks. Rage was the fuel that he needed to go on, and he was using it. His eyes were locked upon the castle door. "How long was I on the ground?"

Feya wrapped her arm around him again. "A little while."

His gaze shifted to an upper window. "Head for the woods."

"But I thought—Someone's goin' fer the constable."

"There isn't time." He worked the muscle at his jaw and then looked at Glenna.

"But, sir, we sent for a doctor too. You certainly need one."

"Yes. No . . ." His eyes were fire against the paleness of his face, his lips smudges of blue.

"Yer too cold." Feya's voice shook. Holding him against her had caused the freezing water from his shirt to seep through Elspeth's dress. "I don't know if ye can make it to Inverness."

"Just walk, Feya. One step at a time." He threw his gaze to the swaying pine trees and the mist rolling in. "I picked the locks with your cross. How did it get down there, I wonder?" The tones of his voice were too dark, too fleeting. When she didn't answer, he continued, "You saved me once again." He reached for her face and caressed her cheek. Focus left his eyes but then came back again. "I have an aunt in Edinburgh. I want you to go to her. Tell her everything—"

"No." The word choked in her throat. "Don't talk like that. Yer going to be fine."

"I'm not cold anymore." Alasdair rested his head against her.

"That's good." She rubbed his back frantically.

"No. It's quite . . . bad." His weight sunk into her. "Just hold me,

Feya. I won't last much longer." The Scottish slurred into his voice. "I'm sorry. . ."

"No." Feya shook him. "Stay awake." She grabbed his face and kissed him full on the mouth. His lips were ice. "Ye promised ye'd get me back to Edinburgh."

"I'm sorry, love." His eyelids closed.

"Don't do this." She shook him again. "Fight."

The noise of carriage wheels wafted through the trees.

"Take him, Glenna."

Feya ran past the proud walls of the castle. Past the line of the trees and the far stone gate. Tears streamed down her face as she reached the road. The carriage was a black blur, coming too fast. "Stop!" She doubled over. "Please!"

The rumble of the coach ceased.

Feya looked up, her lungs heaving.

A man dressed in fine clothes stepped down. "What is it, my girl? What's happened?"

Feya fought for breath and pointed behind her. "At the castle . . . He needs help."

A woman stepped down, her fine skirt billowing behind her. "Who needs help?"

"Alasdair Cairncross."

Recognition shone in the woman's beautiful eyes.

The heat from the roaring fire made her sweat, but Alasdair still needed it, frozen as he was. He was alive. And resting comfortably in the bed just across the room.

The moments in the coach with Amberlyn and her father were a blur. They'd made it to the hospital and then the Royal Highlands

Hotel. It didn't mater that the woman he was engaged to hovered over him; she kept telling herself that. It didn't matter that Amberlyn's love for him was thick, like the blanket the woman now laid upon him.

Alasdair was alive. He had saved her. She should think of that. Not the way Amberlyn looked so perfect beside him. Not the way her blonde hair complimented his black. Not the way her blue eyes and pale skin would ensure that their children looked very English.

"Well." Sir Walter stood and headed for the door. "I think I'll go talk to the police inspector again."

"Good idea." Feya stood for no reason. "Perhaps . . ."

"Yes." Sir Walter gave her a smile. "Perhaps they've found that miscreant Aldourie."

"They said they searched everywhere?"

"Yes."

"The entire castle? All the grounds?"

"They will find him. What he's done to Alasdair will not go unpunished." He reached for the doorknob. "The guards are still posted outside the door and throughout the hotel. However, you two are not to go out of the room, do you understand? We don't yet know who else was working for him. And we don't know if he has anything else planned."

"Aye."

Amberlyn reached for Alasdair's hand. "Yes, Father. I wouldn't dare leave him."

Alasdair turned his head upon the pillow, sleep thankfully still with him.

Sir Walter spoke with the guards but kept his voice low. He glanced one last time at Alasdair and then shut the door.

Feya crossed her arms and then uncrossed them. If only she wasn't wearing Elspeth's dress. She could feel the questions Amberlyn wanted to ask.

"You didn't tell me how you know him."

Feya took a breath. There was no use delaying it any longer. "I was his prisoner. He was takin' me to Stirling when we were captured."

"Is that so?" Amberlyn looked like she'd just read a good part in a novel. "Whatever did you do?"

Feya looked at Amberlyn's expensive shoes. "I tried to steal somethin' because me brothers and sister were hungry. I was hungry too."

Moments passed. Finally, Amberlyn spoke. "You poor dear."

Feya tore her gaze away and stared at the fire. Above all else, she did not need Amberlyn's pity. It made it worse—that place she had fallen to, and the slow gentle steps of Alasdair leading her out.

"But you ran to us. You rescued him."

"We did a lot of saving each other." Feya dared the other woman with her eyes. Let her think of everything those words meant, and the unspoken ones between.

"Well." Amberlyn folded her hands in her lap. "I am grateful to you."

Alasdair drew his eyebrows together as if in pain.

Feya went to the other chair beside him.

He sucked in breath and opened his eyes. He searched the molding on the ceiling. "Where . . ."

"It's all right." Feya wanted so badly to touch him, to reassure him in some way.

"Feya." Alasdair reached for her hand and wove his fingers in hers. "Are you all right?"

She should pull away. She knew that. It would be the decent thing to do. But decent things . . . What did she know about them? She held his hand tighter even though she could feel Amberlyn staring. "I'm fine. Everything is going to be fine."

"Alasdair."

His grip faltered. He turned his head slowly on the pillow. "Amberlyn." He whispered her name, as if he dredged it up from somewhere lost and far away.

She gave him a practiced smile. "Darling, you gave us all quite a scare."

Color returned to his face, full force. "You've met Feya." He nodded, almost as if trying to understand.

"Yes, we've met."

"Excuse me." He swallowed. "Where are we?"

"Inverness. As Feya said, you are safe. All will be well." Amberlyn lifted his hand and kissed it.

Alasdair pulled his fingers away from his fiancée and pushed himself up to sit. "How is it that you're here, Amberlyn? Forgive me. You have me at a disadvantage, as the last thing I remember is the castle."

Amberlyn paused for a moment. "Feya, would you be a dear and go and get Father? He'll want to know that Alasdair's awake."

"He said not to leave the room."

"But this is important."

"She stays." Alasdair voice was firm.

"If you like." Amberlyn's voice was practiced honey.

"I need to know everything." He moved to take the blanket off and then muttered something under his breath. "Do I have any clothes?"

"You're to stay in bed," Amberlyn said. "The doctor said you need to rest."

"The doctor doesn't know what I know. Feya, where are my clothes?"

"Over—"

"I'll get them." Amberlyn stood and retrieved the new grey suit.

"Father purchased you some suitable attire a few hours ago."

"Ladies . . . please, would you go behind the screen? If Sir Walter has said that you must not leave the room, there's a good reason, and I intend to find out what it is."

Feya stood and dutifully went behind the screen. Amberlyn followed.

Alasdair ripped off the blanket with a whoosh. The fire cast his shadow on the wall.

Amberlyn leaned in close. "I don't know what happened between you, but know this: I am his fiancé. That isn't going to change."

Feya lifted her chin. "I know exactly who ye are."

"Good. Then we can be friends."

"That I doubt."

She pouted, falsely. "What a shame. I'd hate to upset Alasdair, and a rift between us most likely will. What I said earlier—I meant it. I am grateful to you. But don't think I'm stupid. I'm a woman. I can see what you feel as you look at him."

Feya clasped her hands behind her, for Alasdair's sake. He might not want Amberlyn's perfect face marred, or her perfectly arranged hair ripped from her head.

"You were both in a difficult situation, and I understand that. People do strange things when they are about to die." Amberlyn nodded as if trying to convince herself.

"I agree. There's no reason in the world why ye need to know what happened all the other days."

Amberlyn folded her hands. Her knuckles were white with restraint.

"Please come out." Alasdair stood by the window, looking like a prince in his charcoal suit. He searched the street below, and all the faces. He'd combed his hair.

Feya's heart caught. He looked like the old Alasdair—the one who had paraded her in chains on the Edinburgh streets, the one who'd thrown her the dried meat just outside Torphichen.

"Well, my love." Amberlyn's smile was brilliant. "You look much better."

"I feel more like myself than I have in days. Now, tell me everything."

Amberlyn closed the distance between and stood in the light of the window. Their voices lowered like lovers of old.

Feya turned away, searching for a place to stand. Everything was too perfect—too good. She still had dirt on her fingers from the woods. Her hair was in tangles. And the dress—the stupid, stupid dress—it gaped in the front and told of everything she had been.

Chapter Thirty-One

"I need to see about our departure." Alasdair bowed to Amberlyn. "If you'll excuse me." He moved toward the door, keeping his eyes upon the carpet.

Look at me, Feya wanted to say. *Don't walk past and pretend like I'm not here.* She wanted to grab him and shake him because of the way he held himself—too proper, too tall.

He drew his eyebrows together as if he'd heard her thoughts. He stopped, locked eyes with her, and everything they'd been through was in his gaze. "Are you well?"

"Aye." It was the furthest thing from the truth, but the only word she could manage.

He gave her a ghost of a smile and looked over his shoulder. "Amberlyn, would you happen to have anything in your trunk that would fit Feya?"

Feya crossed her arms. Wearing Amberlyn's clothes might be more than she could bear. "I'm fine, Alasdair."

"No, you're not." The look he gave her wasn't pity; he was merely stating the truth. "I'd take you shopping, but our circumstances prevent it now. We've lost too much time all ready."

"Of course. I should have something." Amberlyn crossed the

room. "I'm sorry I didn't think of it earlier."

Red flared upon Alasdair's neck, just above his starched white collar. "I'm surprised as well you didn't think of it. You thought to have clothes purchased for me but not for her. If you knew what she's been through, and what she risked to save me . . . She deserves more than she's been handed in this life. Frankly, I'd have expected the grace and kindness you've so often shown me to be shown to her." He cringed, as if knowing his words were harsh. He pushed on anyway. "And yet here you stand, draped in diamonds while the woman who saved my life twice wears the same dress she was accosted in."

Amberlyn paled, if that was possible. "I didn't mean—"

"You didn't think." Alasdair reached for Feya's hand and lifted it. He inspected the bruises on her arm and the grass stain from the forest. "When I get back, I expect this dress to be gone." The muscles at his jaw hardened. "Throw it in the fire."

Amberlyn blinked back tears. "Of course."

The doorknob clicked back into the frame as he shut it.

Amberlyn wiped her eyes with a fine lace handkerchief. "He's right. I'm ashamed of myself."

"I shouldn't have provoked ye earlier. It wasn't right." Feya looked away from the tear streaks on Amberlyn's face. "I have a sharp tongue. It hardly ever serves me well."

"Can we start again, please?" Amberlyn held out her hand.

Feya knew what taking her hand would mean. She'd have to stop seeing Amberlyn as the enemy. She'd have to put aside her fear that Alasdair would chose this woman over her. In other words, she'd have to be the kind of person she'd always prided herself on being—not judging Amberlyn just because.

Feya reached for her hand.

Feya sat as straight as she could, not a hard feat in Amberlyn's whale-boned corset.

Amberlyn poured tea from a teapot that was made for women like her—fragile, beautiful, every accent perfectly placed. "Tell me, what do you do for pleasure?"

Feya stirred the tea as Amberlyn did—careful not to hit the metal against the porcelain. "That's not the easiest question to answer."

"Whyever not?"

Feya closed her eyes as she sipped the tea. The warmth felt good. She let it rest upon her tongue before swallowing. "Because people like me don't often have time fer pleasure."

"I'm sorry." The firelight reflected in her light-blue eyes. "I wasn't thinking—"

"Flowers." The word came out suddenly. She couldn't bear Amberlyn's distress any longer. It separated their statuses even more—the fact that she now felt she needed to apologize. "I like flowers. I like to arrange them. Make garlands and things like that." Feya smiled at herself. It wasn't that far off. She had enjoyed making garlands for the Gypsy caravans and making crowns for her friends' hair.

Friends who were long gone. Girls she hadn't thought of in years.

Amberlyn's soft voice cut through the memories. "You would enjoy the Marché aux Fleurs in Paris. They sell the most beautiful flowers—thousands. Father and I spent a very pleasant morning walking through that flower market." She poured more tea. "Afterwards, we toured the cathedral Notre Dame."

"I'm sure it's lovely." Feya looked down at the yellow sleeve of Amberlyn's borrowed dress. It looked odd against her skin, turning her the color of old oatmeal. It certainly didn't go with her flaming red hair.

The door opened. Sir Walter and Alasdair came in.

"Everything is set for our departure."

"Excellent." Alasdair closed the door behind him. He looked at Amberlyn first, no doubt knowing that was expected.

Feya sat straighter. The time when he'd been out of the room had been like a long, dry desert. She wanted to hold him again. She wanted to breathe him in again and smell the scent of forest and rain. Maybe then it would seem real—that they really were alive and had passed through Aldourie's fire. Maybe then it wouldn't seem like a dream where they were both wearing fancy cloth that were too good to get dirty from laying in a cave or walking through fields of heather.

Pick me, her heart cried. *Please, pick me.*

Alasdair walked to the fireplace and stoked the fire.

Sir Walter sat down at the table and Amberlyn poured him tea. They fell into easy conversation—a father and a daughter—kind words filled with love. Sir Walter patted his daughter's hand.

Amberlyn had that too—everything.

Still, Alasdair stood with his back to her, plunging the poker into the flames—over and over again. Sparks flew up, rolling and hissing against the bricks.

Feya felt Amberlyn looking at her, judging her every move.

Surely Alasdair would turn and nod in her direction. She deserved that, at least, didn't she? After all they had been to one another. And everything Feya hoped yet to be.

I would love ye to the ends of the earth. Let me.

The noise of carriages sounded on the cobblestones outside. Alasdair went to the window. His knuckles turned white on the sill.

Sir Walter stood. "By George, it's your father."

"So it is." Alasdair drew a deep breath.

Amberlyn went to them and laid her hand on Alasdair's arm. "But who's that woman with him?"

Feya crossed the room and looked down to the street.

Morna. Beautiful, kind Morna. She stepped down from a coach, her red hair blowing in the wind—a jewel amongst a backdrop of grey. Soldiers surrounded her, flanking every corner of the street.

"That's my mother." Alasdair stepped back from the window and ran his hand over his jaw.

Feya wanted to throw her arms around him. If he could say Morna was his mother, he truly had changed.

"Excuse me?" Sir Walter lifted and eyebrow. "Your mother passed away some time ago."

"Happily, she did not." A smile crossed his face. "Sir Wanesley, Amberlyn, I need the two of you to do something for me."

"Anything, my boy."

"You have but to ask."

"Feya was never here." Alasdair looked them both in the eyes. "Do you understand? If asked, you never saw her."

"Whatever you need, my dear boy, but I don't—"

"I'll explain everything later. I promise." Alasdair reached for Feya's arm and led her to the side door. He lowered his voice. "You have to trust me now."

There were a million things he could have said. A million things she wanted him to say. He led her down the hall and into another room. "No one will look in here." His went to the middle of the room and glanced out the window. "I had hoped to be able to talk with you, but there isn't time."

"Why not?" Feya went to him, standing so close she could smell his scent—the same way he'd smelled on the road out of Edinburgh. Wealth. Privilege.

"Morna will help you. I don't know why she's here . . . And with

Father, of all people. But I'll persuade her."

She felt the meaning of his words. It was in the way he held his body away from her and wouldn't look her in the eyes. "Why does she need to help me when yer here?"

He closed his eyes as if her question were too much. "You'll have to wait a day." His voice was want and regret. "Then go back to Edinburgh. As soon as you get into the city, go to my aunt. She is kind and good."

"So this is yer way of gettin' rid of me. This is yer easy solution so ye can be with *her*." Feya turned away.

Alasdair turned her back. "This is my way of saving your life. If Father sees you, there won't be anything I can do."

His touch was like fire, creeping up her arm until she couldn't think. "If ye told him what happened, surely he'd understand."

"Feya, do you really think him to be a reasonable man?"

"I don't care what he is." She closed the step between them and held onto his arms. "I only care what I am to ye."

Alasdair cupped her cheek in his hand. He searched her face and looked deep into her eyes. "I used to think, before you, that I was strong."

"I love ye." The words came tumbling out. "With all me heart. And I might just die if ye leave without me."

Alasdair wrapped his arms around her and crushed her to his chest. His voice was low and warm, like a caress and a sigh tumbled together. "Woman, how you try me."

They were the same words he'd said to her when they been in Millie's cabin, right before he'd kissed her and laid her down. "Now is not the time to think of what was or is, or what shall be. I am once again trying to protect you, whether you believe it or not. The restraint I had to employ to not make love to you was . . ." Whatever he'd meant to say died up his lips. He pulled away from her and glanced at the door. "This is no easier."

"I want to tell ye so much." Alasdair blurred before her eyes—the grey cashmere suit, the beautiful black hair, the conflict in his eyes. "When I thought ye were dead, a part of me died too. I can't see ye go away again."

He moved toward the door. "I'll get the bairns. I promise you." Footsteps sounded in the hall. "Whatever happens, you will never want again."

Her breath quickened. The seconds were stealing him away. Clouds passed over the window, casting him into shadows. "I want to be yer wife." The words were freedom and a prison all the same. She could feel Amberlyn in the next room, and the weight that placed upon him.

Alasdair flinched. He reached for the door handle. "Princes Street." His voice was choked. "Number twenty-one."

Feya looked into the eyes of the man who would hold her heart forever. Still, there were no promises there. The deep blue was like the gathering rain stretching itself across the city—dark, brooding, trying to decide how much of itself to let go.

The door creaked as he cracked it open. "Say it, Feya. Do it for me."

"Princes Street. Number twenty-one."

"Good." Alasdair stepped back. "I wouldn't leave you if there was another way. Remember that." His palm slid against her arm. His fingertips brushed hers.

And then he was gone.

An hour later, Feya stood at the same window where he'd left her. Down below on the street, Alasdair walked to the waiting coach,

Amberlyn beside him. His gaze was straight ahead. He held his head high, like the trained soldier that he was.

If only he would look up to the window. Then she might be able to endure it.

Alasdair held out his hand to Amberlyn, the perfect picture of a couple well matched. Her dress billowed in the wind as she stepped inside. Alasdair joined her.

The slap of reins made Feya jerk.

And now they had all the kilometers back to Edinburgh to talk.

Sudden rain splattered against the window, blurring the view.

Morna wrapped her arms around Feya as if she knew her thoughts. "Ach, lassie. I cannot tell ye how happy I am to see yer face."

The coach pulled into the street. Feya watched it maneuver in the flow of traffic until it became a black spot amongst the grey buildings of Inverness. "He's gone."

Morna put her hand on Feya's cheek. "Fer now."

Feya returned Morna's embrace. "I'm glad yer here."

"And where else would I be?" Morna smoothed her hair, much the same way she had in Torphichen. "I'm glad to be able to help ye and him. Ach, the sight of ye both does me a world of good."

"But he's gone now." Saying the words brought the fire back to her skin. Tears spilled down her cheeks and onto Morna's shoulder.

Morna held her like a mother, rocking her in her arms as they stood. "Why do ye think he tried so hard not to look back at the window?"

"I don't know." But she did. She had felt his restraint as he walked, seen it in the stiff way he held his shoulders.

"He cares fer ye, Feya. More than he can show right now. Don't blame him fer that."

"How do ye know such things?"

"Ach, a mother feels deep, past rhyme or reason. I saw it when he asked me to stay with ye. There's a look a man has when his heart's been claimed."

Feya squeezed her eyes shut. Alasdair had opened the floodgate of her tears in the cave and now there seemed to be no end of them. If Morna could see such a thing in her own son, surely it was true. And now he was on his way to rescue the bairns.

God, don't let him fail. Let them be alive. Please, I beg ye.

It was easier to pray with Morna to hold onto. She seemed so sure of so many things.

The rain came harder, dropping a grey curtain on the world. It danced on the street below and washed away the rubbish on the ground. Morna stroked Feya's back. "Everything changes. The old passes away to make room for the new."

Feya listened to the sound of Rowan playing in the next room. The child was carefree and happy. "I can't say that yer words bring me comfort." Deep longing washed over her like the rain had that first night walking up to the palace.

And now, the grey Scottish rain flowed between her and Alasdair Cairncross. He was there somewhere past Inverness—slipping away as the rain beat. And here she stood, next to a window once again— wishing she had something just out of reach. This was a window of Alasdair's choosing—his way of protecting her, he'd said. He hadn't taken her to Stirling and placed her behind the bars. Instead, he'd caged her with glass.

Feya laid her hand on the cold window. The shop window on the Mile had been much the same—the wedding dress there had seemed too good, too bright for the likes of her. And then there was their window at the tenement that Da had bricked up in his drunken madness. And the window that had been behind her and Mr. Stevenson as they'd talked.

Windows. Always windows and never doors.

"Ye fear the worst." Morna spoke the words softly, as if she understood. "But now is the time to trust. Lean hard into the One who made ye and has better plan fer ye than ye have fer yerself."

Feya pulled her finger down against the glass, making a crooked streak in the condensation. "Ye know he's engaged to Amberlyn? They're supposed to get married when they get back to the city."

"Aye, I met her. That is what she says."

Feya turned to face her. "Ye don't sound worried."

"Alasdair's blood is as wild as the Highlands. No matter what mask he tries to put on, his heart has a long memory."

She hoped so. She desperately hoped so. She'd seen so many sides of him on their journey: fierce guard, unsure son, protector, kind as the heat of the sun in winter, and passionate . . . Ach, he was that. He'd rescued her from the Gypsies, Aldourie, and even death when her breath gave out. And still, he'd been gentle enough to tease her in the field, pretending to have no idea how to be a country man.

The shadows of the rain made patterns across Morna's pale cheek. "He roamed the hills until he was eight years old with naught but God fer company."

If Feya could see into Morna's thoughts, she knew she'd see a young Alasdair there—hair blown by the wind, the sun most likely shining upon his shoulders. Maybe he'd have a stick for a sword, shaking it at all the dragons to come.

"He was meant fer more, and he knows it."

Feya crossed her arms. "What's better than a privileged life?"

"A life full of purpose. To feel the One True Living God beside ye every day." Morna paused for a moment and then smiled. "Alasdair has ye in his mind even now."

Feya glanced back out the window. He'd be far from Inverness now. Southward bound with all that had passed between them just a memory. "I sincerely hope yer right."

Morna looked out over the streets and further on, as if she, too, was looking for him. "Amberlyn has a problem she doesn't know about yet."

"What's that?"

Morna smiled and winked. "She's not you."

Another pothole in the road forced Alasdair to brace himself against the coach seat. Amberlyn held his arm tighter and exclaimed something feminine, something expected. As if the worst thing in the world was a bump in the road.

What he really needed was to be alone. To feel the wind on his face and just to walk nowhere in particular. It was a strange sentiment, given what he'd just come through. But the comfort of the carriage, the warmth—it all seemed more than he deserved. He was a thief of the worst sort, and what he'd stolen could never be replaced. Love. He had Feya's love. It bore down and wrapped around him like the finest silk. Breathless. Ageless. Ancient like the hills they passed now, feral and free.

Alasdair closed his eyes and feigned a headache, rubbing his forehead. If only Amberlyn would let loose of his arm. Every subtle movement of her fingers was like a public announcement: *My hope rests upon you, Alasdair. Don't let me down. I'll be shunned and ruined if you don't marry me.*

Sir Wanesley's top hat tumbled to his lap. He snorted, a very aristocratic sound, then promptly went back to snoring. Eating, sleeping, spending, shooting the occasional grouse. What else did the man do?

Alasdair leaned back against the plush seat and stared at the velvet ceiling. The fading light shifted over the crumpled fabric as the carriage turned and twisted farther away from Feya. And the colors . . . They were quite dim now, floating about in the carriage like a wispy afterthought—the dullest sort of green, a simplistic yellow that brought him pain in his side when he looked upon it. He turned his head. Amberlyn's colors were like ripples of water, pulsing toward him—shades of rose and silver. An overwhelming flush, that.

Alasdair cast his gaze out the window to the cold Scottish rain; it still came, pouring down like all the decisions he had yet to make.

Feya wrapped her fingers around the bottom of the coach seat. The wheels rumbled, pavestone after pavestone, carrying her closer to the bairns.

They turned into New Town, the best part of the city, and the sun broke over the fancy townhouses like God stretched wide his arms and set it free. Pale pink and misty orange—soft, delicate colors, but so bright. Colors for children. The beauty of it was fragile, much like the hope that she felt. Only a few more moments and it would be answered or gone.

The light hit the tan sandstone of the houses, filtering through the carefully manicured trees. Shadows from the leaves hit the entrance to the houses, trembling at the doors like beggars. Still, the coach rumbled on. Feya's hands shook and her stomach dropped low. People spoke of dying from heartbreak. If the bairns weren't at the house . . . if Alasdair had failed . . . if they had died . . .

Princes Street. The sign was welcoming and terrifying just the same. Through the window, the warmth of the sun caressed Feya on the cheek. She turned her face into it and prayed. *Please.* Just one word.

The house numbers gleamed in the sunlight. *24 . . . 23 . . . 22 . . .*

Feya stepped down from the coach before it stopped. She ran and pounded against the shiny blue door. She hardly saw the man who opened it. "Are there children here? That is—" She swallowed. "My brothers and sister?"

"Madam—"

"Alasdair Cairncross . . ." How could she put into words who she was and how she knew him? How could she possibly explain? Feya widened her eyes at the man in the black silk clothes. "I . . . he . . ."

The man's expression softened into pity. "Madam, do come in."

The house was fine, just like Feya knew it would be. She followed the man into the hallway, clasping and unclasping her hands.

A woman walked into the hall. She looked at Feya and took what looked to be a breath of relief. "I'm Alice, Alasdair's aunt. And you must be Feya."

"My brothers. And sister."

"Of course, my dear." The woman crossed the thick rug and laid her hand upon Feya's shoulder. "What an ordeal you've had. He said . . . Never mind. Did you go to the tenement?"

"No. I came here straight away. Just like he said." There was no question as to who he was. There was something about Alice that reminded her of Alasdair. Maybe it was the calm she had about her— the gentle way she looked in Feya's eyes, as he had done at times.

"Perhaps you'd like to come into the parlor for a moment." Alice's voice faltered. "I have some bad news, I'm afraid."

Feya grasped Alice's hand. "Are they alive?"

"Yes, dear. They are well and just upstairs. It's your father."

Pain flooded Feya's heart. The words she feared the most came: "He's dead."

Alice reached for her. "I—" She drew her lips into a thin line. "I'm so terribly sorry."

Feya looked away. The tears that so easily came now flowed from her eyes.

"Would you like to sit down?"

"No." The word came out breathless. "I need to see them."

Alice handed Feya a handkerchief and rubbed her back. "And they want to see you very much. Just this way." She led her up the stairs. "I shall be sorry to see them go." She pushed open a door at the end of the hall.

The sunlight poured through the window. Feya squinted. Slowly, her eyes adjusted.

Brenna sat in the window seat, brushing a doll's hair. She was clean. Her dress was new. Her shoes weren't scuffed.

Gillis pushed a new wooden horse upon the floor. Baby Hamish sat beside him, not a speck of black on his face from the coal.

"Bairns." The word shook.

Brenna ran to meet her. The doll fell to the floor, cast aside. The feel of her was like the sweetness of the deepest summer.

Gillis fell into Feya's arms and cried.

Alice helped baby Hamish walk to her. Feya breathed the scent of him in deep—fresh soap and sweet, sweet baby. On his breath there was the scent of milk.

Some time later, Brenna and Gillis were tucked into their borrowed beds. Hamish slept in Feya's arms. She held his face close to hers and sang. Songs from the old time. The time of threshing barley and campfires.

Alice watched Feya when she didn't think she noticed. The clock on the mantle struck nine. She put her sewing down. "Would you sit with me?"

Feya eased down into the overstuffed chair opposite her. "I can't thank ye enough fer taking care of them."

"I was more than glad to do it. Ever since Charlie died . . ." Memories flooded into the woman's eyes. "The nursery has been too quiet. John and I have longed for other children, but I suppose it's not meant to be." She looked down like she'd revealed too much of herself. When she looked back up, she smiled. "You're just like Alasdair described you."

The mention of his name brought a flash of heat not from the fire.

"I wish I was as brave as you are."

Feya laughed, not knowing what to say. Suddenly she wished she could go and hide somewhere, not to hear words of how she was brave or good. "Stupid, more like. If it hadn't been fer you and Alasdair . . . How you told me he found them, huddled in the corner of the workhouse . . ."

Alice's forehead crimped. She stared into the fire. "'A proverb haunts my mind as a spell is cast. The mill cannot grind with the water that is past.'"

Feya furrowed her brow. "That's a beautiful saying."

"It's true. You're going to have to forgive yourself, Feya. What's done is done. The bairns are safe."

Feya nodded for Alice's sake, but remorse over what she'd put the bairns through would probably never go away. She stroked Hamish's cheek, as if to say she was sorry, for the thousandth time.

"He's fond of you, my nephew."

Feya's hand stilled on Hamish's baby-soft hair.

"Would you go to the secretary drawer, Feya? There's something there for you. I'll take Hamish for a moment."

Feya stood and gently passed him to Alice. She crossed the room and opened the drawer. A beautiful blue purse nestled in the corner. Elaborate glass-bead fringe trailed from the sides. Instantly, she knew it was from him. The blue was the color of his eyes, although she was sure he'd not been thinking that when he'd bought it.

"Open it." Alice smile held secrets, but there was also something else: sadness.

Feya reached for the gold clasp and twisted. "It's full of money!"

"Yes. And something else." Alice walked to her. "Shall I take Hamish up to his bed? Would you allow me?"

"Of course." Hamish yawned in his sleep.

Feya waited until the door shut and then went to the fire. She pulled out the money and placed it upon the couch. Rolls and rolls of bank notes covered the cushions. "Bleedin' banshee!" She widened her eyes at it all.

A sealed envelope was at the bottom of the purse. Feya lifted it. The orange of the fire lapped over the ivory parchment like waves. She carefully broke the seal, her hands shaking.

Dearest Feya,

I hope the journey was not too laborious and that my mother was good company and able to afford you the comfort you so rightly deserve. I smile as I think of what your reunion with the bairns must have been. I found them in the Edinburgh Charity Workhouse. I am glad I arrived when I did. That is all I shall say on that matter. It was my privilege to have rescued them.

Please accept my deepest condolences for your father. When I arrived at the tenement and asked after him, I was told that I would find him by the docks. They said he often walked there at night. After I brought the bairns to Alice, I searched for him. I found him barely alive. He died at Royal Edinburgh Hospital. I was at his side. His last words were of you, Feya. "Tell her I'm sorry," he said.

Feya's tears fell upon the page, smudging the words.

I'm sure you saw the bank notes. There's enough for your cottage by the sea. Take it and make a new life for yourself and the bairns.

I only ask one thing: when you look out upon the sea, think of me. I will be thinking of you. Your memory will be with me all of my days.

With gratitude,

Alasdair Cairncross

Feya held the letter to her chest. There it was—his decision. The wail that erupted from her came on its own. Waves of anguish wrapped around her and tightened. Seeing in it words made Da's death settle in like the worst grippe. Spasms rocked her body until she collapsed to the floor.

"Alasdair . . ." Her voice gave way.

It was over.

Amberlyn would be his wife.

If she wasn't already.

Chapter Thirty-Two

The coals of Alice's fireplace spent themselves into dead, white ashes. Hours split and shattered like shards—fragments of the life she'd imagined. A little memory here, a sharp jagged thought there. And, at the center of it, Alasdair Cairncross beat upon her mind like a flogging. Tears were deep and raw, the only thing that made sense.

Feya clutched the blue purse to her chest once again. Just feeling its softness was an acute torture. She rubbed her hands over the velvet as if the action would somehow conjure to Alasdair's mind what they had been and change it.

If only.

If time could be bent. If more words could be said. If she'd been good enough. Better than Amberlyn, who shone like a silver star to her red, common earth.

In the end, she didn't fit. And Alasdair knew that well.

She had the money. It would give her and the bairns a good life. Safety. Food. Something she never thought possible.

Light hovered at the edge of the window. The sun was rising. The day would go on regardless of what she wanted.

Feya dropped her chin and indulged in a good, strong cry one last time. Time to hold her head up like a thistle, as she'd told Brenna in the tenements. Time to be strong for the bairns. That was what a common woman did in times like these.

The window glowed orange. The light shifted and spread, catching the beveled glass and splaying out like long fingers. On the wall, a light beam fell into a corner. A rectangular painting hung there. Lilies surrounded words: *I am the door: by me if any man enter in, he shall be saved, and shall go in and out, and find pasture.*

It was a Bible verse; it had to be. Looking at it made her heart beat fast and hard.

God—the Great I Am, Ma had called him often. And there were those two words again—I AM. Could she never escape Him?

In the tavern when fear had taken hold and made her shake like a child, His presence had been there, no matter how she's tried to taunt Him and doubt His existence. When Da sang his ranting songs. And when Aldourie had almost claimed her. God had seen it all.

The hot yellow sun rose further, unashamed; it spread into the room, across the carpet, reaching for her, wavering over her shoes.

The parlor door opened. Alice stopped when she saw her. "You didn't sleep?"

"I'm sorry. I was . . ." She searched for words that weren't there. How could one describe such thoughts? The torment of the hours that had passed. "Are the bairns awake?"

"Still sleeping. Would you like some break—"

"Is Alasdair married?" The question pushed from her lips, like the way the light grew.

Alice took a deep breath, like she was trying to decide something. She looked into the hall and then shut the door. "I have something to tell you." She pulled a book from the bookcase, opened it, and took an envelope from between its pages. "I've agonized over showing you this." Her eyes, a light shade of blue, flashed in the sunlight pouring through the window. "I think you should see it."

Feya stood and took it, knowing before she looked down she wouldn't like what she saw. She ran her thumb over Alice's name and opened it.

Sir Walter Wanesley and Lady Wanesley request the honor of your presence at the marriage of their daughter, Miss Amberlyn Wanesley, to Sir Alasdair Cairncross.
St. Giles Cathedral. The 10th day of August, 1885.

Feya sucked in her breath. The wedding was tomorrow.

"Feya." Alice's voice was soft. "When Alasdair was here and he said your name, there was more than friendship in his voice."

Feya handed her back the invitation. "He's made his choice." She wanted to run away and never been seen again. She wanted Alice to stop looking at her with pity. She just wanted.

"Who's to say he hasn't made the wrong choice?"

Feya cringed and looked back at the painting. Alice spoke the words her own heart said. But what did it matter? "Long before I came along Alasdair made a promise to Amberlyn. His world— Those things can't be easily broken."

"Maybe."

"I've met her. She's perfect." Feya rubbed the side of her face, wishing she could change so many things: the wild redness of her hair, the dark of her eyes, the hue of her skin that whispered of lands far away. "She's what he wants."

Alice looked away as if memories flooded her mind. "She's a good choice for Alasdair, I do admit."

"There, ye see."

"But perhaps not the best choice for what he really needs. As far as what he *wants*, I'm fairly certain it's you."

Feya ran her hands over her face. This was a different kind of tired—like throwing yourself against a wall that would never break. "We saved each others' lives. That bonds people." She went to the window. The light washed over her body like warm water. "Whatever he feels fer me . . . It's only because of that."

"And you? What do you want?"

Feya clutched the windowsill. The sun had warmed the wood. "Something that's not meant to be."

"There are many paths in life. There is one path where you and Alasdair are married. It is a possibility."

Feya placed her forehead against the glass. It was still cool from the long night. Why wouldn't Alice let it be? She felt the woman step closer, hovering just behind like a tormentor. Or maybe an angel.

"Amberlyn came here for tea a while ago. She loves the idea of Alasdair, not who he really is. She loves the life he has and the fact that he's close to the queen."

"Did she say those things?"

"She didn't have to." Alice opened the book she held. It was a photograph album. "I showed this to her."

Feya's heart caught at the sight of him. Had Alice held the rarest treasure in the world, still the photograph before her would have drawn from her more awe. She placed her hand over her mouth for fear of sobbing again.

In the photograph, a younger Alasdair stood barefoot at the sea, his toes dug into the sand. His clothes hung limp upon him, dampened by the waves. In his hand he held seashells. His smile was like the freedom of spring—unapologetic and wild.

"Alasdair adores the sea." Alice's voice was wispy and light. "He's happiest when he feels the warmth of the sun upon him. He can't stand the cold." Alice took a deep breath, as if pulling the memories to the present was hard. Tears welled in the woman's eyes. "His father's plans interrupted so much. My brother . . . My stupid, stupid brother."

Feya searched her eyes, wanting to say something that might comfort them both. "Alasdair has a good life."

"Maybe. But how good is it if one ignores the heart and the desires God has placed within?" Alice closed the photo album like something final—an ending. Or maybe it was just her anger at how things had gone.

"What do ye mean? What desires?"

"When Alasdair was young, he spent a great deal of time with us. He didn't care for his stepmother, I'm afraid, and the feeling was mutual with her. Every holiday was spent with us, every weekend." She reached for two leather-bound books next to the photo album. "These were Alasdair's."

Feya touched the first embossed title. *China: Its Spiritual Needs and Claims* by James Hudson Taylor. The pages were worn, some falling out.

The next book was much the same. *Rivers of Water in a Dry Place* by Robert Moffat.

"And this was his favorite." Alice pulled down a third book and handed it Feya. "*Missionary Travels and Researches in South Africa* by Dr. David Livingston." She smiled. "Alasdair volunteered with me at the London Missionary Society."

What Alasdair had said in Millie's cabin came back to her. When he'd spoken of God, he'd seemed to be holding back details—holding back a part of himself. The curtain had almost parted, but then he'd dropped it.

"Long ago, Alasdair felt called to be a missionary. He wanted to go to the South Seas. He had a very strong burden for the people there."

Feya dropped her gaze to her shoes. Had Alice told her the moon was made of haggis, she might have believed that more. "Could I see his photograph again?"

Alice handed her the book.

With this new information, she could see it—the passion in his eyes for something other than the water. His heart was settled. And what was stranger, she could see the man he'd been in the cave when he'd told her to cry. And when he'd laughed with her in the field. When he'd told her of the things he saw . . . And the look in his eyes when he said he would not make her his mistress. All that—Feya didn't know how it was possible to see so much from a photograph, but she did.

"I showed this picture to Amberlyn when she was here. I told her everything I just told you."

"What did she say?"

"It's what she didn't say that's important. Her displeasure was apparent, I can assure you." Alice pointed to the photograph. "That part of Alasdair she'll never accept. It doesn't suit her plans at all."

"If that is what makes him truly happy . . . If he truly has a callin' . . . Why wouldn't she want that fer him? I would."

"Thank God." Alice exhaled and her shoulders relaxed. "That's exactly what I hoped you'd say."

"He'll be miserable with her, won't he?"

Fire burned behind Alice's eyes. "'To fall in love with God is the greatest romance; to seek him the greatest adventure; to find him, the greatest human achievement.' Augustine of Hippo said that, more than a thousand years ago. It's still true." She placed her hand on Feya's shoulder. "When Jesus died, the veil of the temple was rent. Intercessors were needed to get to God before, but after . . ." She smiled. "Now we can go within the veil. True intimacy."

Feya closed the album and held it close. Outside, the sunlight hit the roofs of the townhomes and turned them into blazing lines against a cotton sky.

She had sought God all those days ago—in the darkness of the tenements, holding Ma's cross. As her feet headed toward Deacon Broodie's. That had been the dare in her heart: *Show me if You're real.*

God had shown her. He'd done it through Alasdair and all the trials they'd come through.

More than any love of any man, God's love was deeper. He had seen her. And He wanted her, truly wanted her. Desired her company, even. Just like Alasdair had said, He was closer than her skin. And, unlike Alasdair, God would never choose another against His own heart.

Alice came up behind her. "Feya, until we're in heaven, nothing in this world will be perfect. It's broken down here, you know?"

"Aye." The word came out in a whisper. "That I do know."

"We're all under a curse when we enter the world—the curse of sin. But Jesus took the curse when He died on the cross. The payment was made so that our souls could be made clean. His salvation makes us free from the power of the evil one."

All Da's words about curses came back to her. If what Alice said was true, all mankind was cursed, not just the Gypsies. All blood was tainted. And Jesus was the only way to be set free.

Alice studied her, as if she saw the realization in Feya's eyes. "God gave us something very important: our free will. We have to chose to accept this free gift or deny it."

"I want it." Feya nodded. No hesitation. No doubt. This was what she'd been searching for when she'd set out upon the Royal Mile. And as she longed to be in Alasdair's arms, it had been this longing all along: to be loved. To walk through a door and never be turned away.

"Then ask Him." Alice's eyes were full of years of loving and knowing God. "He won't turn you away."

Feya drew her eyebrows together. She wanted that. She wanted to have confidence, as Alice had it. Her heart beat so furiously now she could feel it in her whole body. "Should I go to a church and pray?"

"There's no need. He's right here." Alice smiled and knelt by the window.

Feya lowered herself down. There was an electricity in the air she couldn't explain. Everything looked brighter, sharper, as if seeing something for the first time. "I don't know what to say."

Alice took her hands. "Just say what you feel. He already knows."

Feya took a deep breath. Morna's name for him would be best. "One True Living God . . . hello?" She cringed.

Alice closed her eyes and nodded. "Go on. It's all right."

"Thank Ye fer bringing me here and protectin' the bairns. Fer Alasdair . . . And fer Alice's kindness. I believe what she says is true, God. I know it's true. I believe in Yer son Jesus and what He did fer me—takin' the curse and payin' fer me sins with His own blood." The feeling that she was being watched came upon her like the wild Highland wind. Like the moment when she'd thrown her cross into the fountain. Like all the times she'd tried to be strong. There'd always been a hesitation, a shift in the air. A brightness in the light. It was with her now—He was with her now.

"There is no greater power than Yer power. I know this because Ye raised from the dead and Ye live. Forgive me, please. Fer all the sins that I've committed. Fer trying to go me own way. Wash me. Save me. I believe."

Lightness came into her body like a great weight was lifted. And joy, deep joy, rushed to the corners of her heart and flew like a bird. Chains around her heart broke and fled away as if they never had been. Warmth spread over her like a fine silk blanket. And it wasn't the warmth that she'd tried to substitute—the warmth of a man. This was better, pure, cleansing. The light flooded her in pure, white abandon.

Great rolling tears trailed down Alice's face. "Yes, Feya." She threw her arms around her. "So many times yes."

It was finally settled. She was truly loved. She wasn't Feya of the tenements or Feya the Gypsy. She wasn't even Feya begging a man to love her. She was Feya, forever in the light, daughter of God.

Alice pulled away and looked deep into her eyes. "There's an Officer's Ball tonight at Holyrood Palace. If you like, you can take my place. Alasdair will be there."

This path, Feya knew by heart. Only now she wouldn't ever be walking another path alone.

In Holyrood Abbey the setting sun blazed, drowning Alasdair in a shower of golden warmth. The heat of it seeped through his black evening tailcoat. He'd dressed early for the ball and come here on a whim. Better to pass the time in the place he knew better than his own soul.

He laid his hand against the cold, ancient stone of the wall. Not even this rare sun could warm the old masonry. Too much wind had battered against it for centuries. Too much rain . . . But rain in Scotland did have a certain practicality. The land needed the water; of course it did. Therefore there was order. It made the day predictable.

The sun waned, flickering over the mountain of Arthur's Seat. A little red, a little orange . . . Almost gone. Almost done.

Now he'd kill the last part of himself that begged and pleaded like a fool. That part that ached and wanted. That part that cried out for Feya Broon.

The light hit the crest of the hill and shone through the ruined window, casting a beam to the ground. He didn't know why the light seemed so important, as if he should pay attention to it, or perhaps remember something. He was tired, that was all.

One last indulgence. Only one.

Alasdair breathed deep and let his shoulders relax for the first time in days. "Feya." Although the wind stole the sound, speaking her name was the sweetest release. How he'd longed to say her name out loud.

"Feya," he said again and gripped the corner of the wall. "Feya." The most uncommon woman in the world. The woman who simultaneously accosted his mind and eased it. The woman he had to forget.

Had to.

Must.

Would.

The shaft of light wavered on the gravel, moving up and down like shaking shoulders. Laughter. It reminded him of laughter.

Alasdair turned and strode back toward the palace. The night before one's wedding obviously strained a man's mind.

Chapter Thirty-Three

Feya picked the dress because it was the color of Alasdair's eyes. She chose it—that was a fact more beautiful than all the hidden coves in Scotland. It wasn't borrowed like the dress from Morna or the dress given to her by the Gypsy queen. And, most of all, it wasn't the dress forced upon her by Ranald Aldourie or the one begrudgingly given by Amberlyn. No, this one was hers. And in this dress her future would weave together or unravel. This night would decide it all.

She held onto John's arm and to be truthful, Alasdair's uncle was the only thing holding her up as they passed through the main entrance.

The palace on the night she'd broken in had been a sight to behold. Now, with hundreds of candles blazing all around, it was overwhelming—like standing beneath a waterfall of silk and falling diamonds. Far beyond, she could hear the click of heels and the echo of music. The crush of people made her breath catch. So many masks, their bearer's shadowed eyes accusing. They followed her with their stares.

She was here to steal a man from a woman.

Feya touched her cheek, sure there must be sweat there. The

fringe of her gold mask only swayed against her fingers.

She wanted tomorrow. Every tomorrow with Alasdair Cairncross. And that was worth fighting for. She had to trust that the path she walked might be God's. And that felt more vulnerable than just wanting. Because now that she'd given herself to the Creator—now He held her heart and all of her tomorrows—He could break that fragile hope she held in her heart if He wanted. Or He could do more than she imagined, like Alice said.

John leaned close, his black cape falling against Feya's shoulder. "Do you know how to dance, Feya?"

They stepped into the ballroom. Couples swirled and mingled, so many colors, elegant steps and intricate movement. "Not really. Not like that."

Behind his mask, concern bled into John's eyes. "Let's start slow. Some punch, perhaps?"

"Aye." Feya nodded, sending the feathers in her hair bobbing. They stood in the line for refreshments. Feya searched the crowd, looking for hair as black as coal. And his height—she knew that well. No matter how he was dressed, she would know him. She only hoped she saw him first.

As they approached the table, Feya widened her eyes at the sight of it. Flowers cascaded like a fountain—roses, hyacinths, as many colors as there were costumes in the room. And at the bottom punch trickled into a deep crystal bowl. On either side glasses made a tower, eight feet tall at least. It stretched up to the ceiling like a drink offering of old. The candles reflected there, small flames burning in each cup.

"Bleedin' banshee, there's no end."

John chuckled beside her. "Not for the wealthy, no." He handed her a glass.

Feya gulped it, the cold liquid soothing.

A servant approached her holding a silver tray. A black mask covered his face. A feathered hat shrouded his eyes in shadow. Ach, but the man was unnerving, staring at her like that. Could he tell that she didn't belong?

The glass clinked a little too loud when she set it upon the tray.

The man continued to stare. He took a step toward her.

Feya stepped back. Perhaps it wasn't the right place for glasses. She turned back to John, trying to ignore the odd feeling the servant gave her. "What should we do first?"

"We dance. That's what one does at a ball." John cut through the crowd. "Do what everyone else does."

Feya took a deep breath and stepped onto the polished wood. The couples formed a line.

"Smile," John said. "It's more fun if you do."

Feya tipped up the corner of her mouth and held tightly to his hand.

They turned a corner, and John pulled away. The women separated and turned again. Thankfully, it was only another line. The music beat in time to their steps, and after a moment, she relaxed.

The ladies formed a circle and held hands. They all walked to the right, much like the game children played, "Ring Around the Rosie." The chain broke, the men joined them again, and then they all formed a large circle. They stepped in and out, and Feya had to admit that this type of dancing was contagious, light, very different from the passionate Gypsy steps she was used to. But light and jolly was just what she needed.

John broke from the others and came for her. "You're a natural. I thought you said you didn't dance."

"You should see her dance around a fire, with coins about her waist and scarves in her hair. It's quite something to behold."

Feya sucked in her breath. Alasdair's voice washed over her the way his kisses had. She would know that voice if the sky turned to ash and the earth fled away. She turned. He stood there, his shoulders stiff, his jaw hard. He was pale, as if the days had taken their toll. He wore medieval clothes, all black velvets and gold. His blue eyes watched her from beneath the mask—stoic, hard despite his words.

"Hello." She wanted to throw herself against him. She wanted to take him from the room—all the prying eyes—disappear somewhere so they could talk.

"I suppose I have you to thank for bringing her here." Although he spoke to John, his gaze was locked with hers.

"The garden . . ." John stammered. "I hear it's beautiful at night. Excuse me." He left them standing upon the dance floor.

Alasdair placed his hands behind his back, as if he was the palace guard and they were once again upon the road. "Did you receive my package?"

"I did," she whispered. "I thank ye. And the bairns . . ." The words choked in her throat. "Alasdair . . ."

His gaze scanned the crowd. "Not here. Please."

The music began again, this time a soft strain. One lonely note trembled in the air, like the wanting that she felt.

He bowed slowly and held out his hand. "Will you dance with me, Miss Broon?"

Feya curtseyed and took his hand, glove against glove. "Always."

A woman stood behind him, checking her dance card. She scowled and stomped off in the crowd.

But what did Feya care that she'd stolen the dance? It was hers to claim. It had been since that moment she knocked his water bottle away. Since her lips fell against his in the Gypsy caravan. Since he saved her from death and gave her his breath. There were so many reasons, and her heart beat fiercely with them all.

Alasdair drew her close, as the other couples did. And time . . .

Time was a slow sheet of silk. His eyes lingered on her face and then traveled down to her gown. His other hand came around to her back. When he touched her, he flinched.

So did she.

His voice was husky, full of the thoughts yet unspoken. "You shouldn't have come."

"Is that so?" Feya raised her chin and curled her fingers around his hand.

"My father is here."

"I figured as much."

He lowered his voice. "Amberlyn is here."

"I would imagine she is."

"And that doesn't concern you?"

The music swelled. "Concern is one thing. What needs to be done is another."

Red flashed in his cheeks. "Feya Broon, can you waltz?"

"Alasdair Cairncross, what do ye think?"

"I think you barged in here like the headstrong woman you are, without any thought as to how you would get through the evening." He cleared his throat and stood straighter. "This is the waltz." He pushed her away and twirled her in front of him. In one fluid movement, he brought her back. "You'll have to follow me."

Feya smiled, full and free. "I can do that."

"Really? And you follow directions well, do you?" The music picked up. Alasdair scowled and stepped to the side. "Step right. Back. To the left . . . Again."

"All right?"

He used his weight to guide her—the pivot of his arm, pressure against her back. "Not bad." He gave her a small smile. "Although what you shall do on the turns I have no idea. We'll most likely end up in a heap in front of all and sundry."

Feya laughed then, but had to concentrate. The dance moved faster.

"Left . . . Turn . . . Chin up, if you please."

Feya adopted a regal pose befitting any English lady—nose in the air, shoulders back. "Is that better?"

Alasdair laughed. "Not quite."

Feya's gown fell around her legs and flared out as he turned her again. "Well, regardless, yer an excellent teacher." She pouted. "Surprisin', given yer temper."

"My temper?" He looked like he bit his cheeks to keep from laughing. "You always were a horrible flirt."

"If I was flirtin' with ye, Alasdair, ye can be sure ye'd know it."

His expression grew serious. "I thought I made myself clear in the letter."

"I don't accept yer letter."

Alasdair spun her again at the corner and then brought her back. "That's a pity."

"Why?" Feya tightened her grip. The feel of him so close was a deep ache in her heart. How she longed to stop dancing and just throw her arms around him. Beg him not to say what she knew he wanted to.

"I'm getting married tomorrow."

Feya took a breath and weighed her words. "Are ye now?"

He looked away. "She's already had to change the date because of the kidnapping. Five hundred people, Feya."

It didn't pass Feya's notice that he wouldn't say Amberlyn's name. "Invitations can be burned. It's ye who has to live yer life, not them."

The pressure of his hand increased. "You act like this is easy for me. As if I don't want—" He cut off the words and slowed his steps.

"Ach, ye silly man." She anchored her hand to his shoulder, as if that could convey the love she felt. "How ye do try me." They were the same words he'd said to her at Millie's cabin. She saw from the look in his eyes that he knew it too. "How could I not come? How could I not see ye again? And all the days after?" She was close to tears.

"Hush, Feya. People are staring."

What did it matter if they all stared? She kept looking into his eyes. "We're good at rescuin' each other. Let me rescue ye now."

Alasdair's jaw hardened. He turned and pulled her from the dance floor, leading her by the hand like a child. He wove in and out of the crowd, saying nothing.

Heads turned. Masks lowered. Eyebrows raised. Whispers floated all around.

Who is she?

Did you see the color of her skin?

Alasdair pulled her behind a heavy curtain and into an empty corridor. The music in the other room strained and beat like wings fluttering against a brass sky. "I cannot accept what you're offering."

Feya pulled off her mask. "Tell me that now. Look into me eyes and say it. Ye don't have to pretend with me. Ye don't have to live out some duty or obligation. Ye don't have to be strong all of the time. Ye taught me that." She took a step toward him. "I'm the one who was runnin' through the forest with ye. I'm the one who kissed ye in the field, terrified to do it. Don't ye remember everythin' we went through?"

"I do remember, woman." He stepped forward and wrapped his fingers around her shoulders. "Every moment I spent in your company replays in my mind." He closed his eyes as if in pain. "The sweetest, most acute torture of my life is you."

Hearing him say it was a kind of balm—something healing, something deep. They weren't the words she longed for, but they were a start. Feya reached for his face and placed her fingers on his mask.

He sucked in his breath but didn't move to brush her hands away.

Feya ran her fingers along his jaw, lifted off the mask, then cast it to the floor. "There ye are. Here's the man I know. Not the pretender I danced with, worryin' about other people's opinions."

"Feya, you think you know me." He placed his hand upon her cheek.

"I know ye've been runnin' from God fer a long time. Alice showed me yer books. She told me everythin'."

He flinched. "And what do you think of that history of mine?"

"I think it's beautiful. And I believe, too, Alasdair. It happened just this morning. I'm a true Christian now. Alice explained it all—what ye couldn't say in Millie's cabin but knew. Ye lit the lamp that showed me the way." Feya stepped forward and kissed him on the cheek. His warmth was like sweetness in the dark. "God has plans fer ye. If ye want, I'll be part of them."

Alasdair looked into her eyes, his breathing hard.

"Dear man, do ye want me to stay?"

No answer. Just a hardening of his jaw.

"Alasdair, I need to know. Are ye gettin' married tomorrow?"

His eyes still locked with hers, he gave the slightest nod.

The small movement sent a sharp blade through her heart. Feya took a step back and stumbled. He reached for her, but his face was still as emotionless as a statue. She stumbled past the heavy curtain and into the ballroom. The music was loud and horrible, none of it making sense. The candles were too bright. The bodies too many. She pushed past them—groups of never-ending feathers, silks, and masks. People who didn't care. People who never would.

She heard Alasdair's voice, but she couldn't make out the words. But it didn't matter anymore. He didn't want her.

Across the room, a man who resembled Alasdair was heading straight for her, rage upon his face.

His father.

She had to get out. For the bairns. For herself. Only prison waited if she was caught.

Breathing was too hard. Her chest ached like Alasdair had plunged a knife into her heart and twisted. Feya pushed past the people, sobbing like a child. The tall balcony doors loomed ahead, swallowed by billowing gold curtains.

People whispered and laughed and pointed. The noise of their scoffing was like the drum of demon's wings. Alasdair called again, his beautiful voice mixed into the fray. She couldn't make out the words. He was lost to her. Lost by his own choosing.

She pushed open the glass doors. The cold air hit and she stumbled again.

"Feya?" John stood by the stairs.

She couldn't answer. He'd been so kind, tried so hard to help her. And for what? Nothing. She ran, past the Abbey where her life had first crossed with Alasdair Cairncross. Through the gates where she'd tied the scarf and tried to be a thief.

As the sky broke free and poured down rain like that first night, Feya stumbled down the Royal Mile, getting soaked like the fool she was.

She walked past the bread shop where she'd almost broken the window. Past Deacon Brodie's where laughter still wafted from the upper windows.

Most of all, she walked past the path where she and Alasdair were together. Forever. Once and for all.

"Wait!" Alasdair lunged for her, but the blue silk of her dress slipped from his hand. "Feya!" Panic clenched his chest. He couldn't see her.

The red of her hair mingled with the crowd, and the colors were too many—great brown slashes, blue hues, orange strips floating in the air from the music.

His head had been splitting from the colors all evening. When he'd seen her dancing, he'd been about to slip outside to take some air. Alasdair cursed his gifting, if that's what it was. For as she'd stood there, he'd only been able to stare at her—the gold he'd missed so much, the calmness he felt in her presence, the rightness of it all. It became clear, as if two years of fog lifted from his mind.

The memories flooded back to him—the missionary society and the burning deep within his soul, the people of the Pacific Islands, the peace he'd once felt when he was at rest with God. He'd nodded from the simplicity of it all and the reasoning. It all made sense—where he'd come from, what had happened, and God's leading all the way. He'd nodded and been just about to tell Feya that he loved her when she ran away.

The crowd was massive—a great, roaring, laughing, unfeeling thing. He reached above the cacophony, his white-gloved hand a smear against the opulence of the room.

"Don't go!" His voice bled into the music.

"I say, old chap." Charlie's hands were upon him, holding him back. "What has gotten into you? Richard said that's the thief you took—"

Alasdair's fist slammed into his face.

He went down, his tailcoat splayed out. Blood poured from his nose.

"She's not a thief. She never was."

"Explain yourself!" Amberlyn's voice was behind him.

Alasdair turned, and as soon as he did, black jagged lines shot through his vision. Pain split behind his eyes. The color faded and he saw what had caused it. Flutes. He hated flutes. They were of the devil's making.

"Can you not even speak?" Amberlyn crossed her arms. People had stopped dancing. They stared. "After that fiasco of a waltz, I figured I'd better follow my fiancée and see who the woman was who caused such a commotion. I saw her. I saw Feya run out of here."

"Amberlyn, I never meant to hurt you." He put his hands on either side of his head. The flutes reeled off a string of high notes, a particular torture. Blue spun violently, melding into the colors of all the conversations. And why, for the love of God, was yellow flaring up in the corner?

"Even though my intuition was screaming at me, I gave you the benefit of the doubt! Are you even listening to me?"

"I—" Alasdair massaged his temple. Purple obscured his vision now, crowding in like a shroud.

"Have you kissed her?"

"Yes," he said without hesitation. "More than once."

Her slap echoed. Flames engulfed his cheek. The force of it jolted his face to the side. "I deserved that."

Another slap came. It was like a gong went off in his head. And the colors . . . *Just dump them all and boil them, then shoot them into the sky with a cannon. That would compare.*

Lies glared at him in Amberlyn's eyes, true and raw—the life he had tried to construct out of fear, and all the ways he'd been running. "I'm sorry. I can't marry you. I never could."

Hurt, raw and pure, replaced the rage. "I only wanted you to love me."

Yes, she wanted many things from him, never to give as Feya wanted. She wanted be able to say that her husband won the Victoria Cross. She wanted to move in the right circles and for them to climb socially together.

Father pushed through the crowd, his eyes speaking louder than words. Disappointment. Anger. That, too, he felt, like lances to his heart. Great black sheets wobbled in his vision, pouring heat upon his head like a molten fire.

Father reached him and grabbed his arm. He rushed them to the corner of the room. "Am I to assume that my son has just broken off his engagement?" His voice ground into Alasdair's ear. "The night before the wedding."

Alasdair pulled his arm away. "You don't have to assume anything, Father. Please allow me to be absolutely clear. I will never marry that woman. And your sordid political ambitions will not be accomplished with my aid. I am only sorry that I did not have the strength to say this earlier."

Disbelief shown on Father's face. "Do you dare, sir?"

People gathered around, trying to appear as if they weren't listening.

"Indeed I do." Alasdair raised his chin a fraction higher. "While I am at it, I might as well say that you have quite a lot of repenting to do. I know what happened with the Gypsies. I will think better of you if you start by confessing your crimes and resign your post."

Father stepped closer, grabbing him again with an iron fist. "You had better think very carefully of where you are, my boy, and to whom you are speaking."

Alasdair stood a little straighter, this time not from duty or some childhood fear. "I know exactly who you are, Father, but I don't think *you* have any inkling."

The look in Father's eyes that had terrified him through the years grew. "You always were a little too much like your mother. I have tried to weed it out, but I see—"

A strong unease hit Alasdair full force. Something was off. He turned to the left. Three servants set down their trays and moved toward the front of the room. Once near the center, they split in three different directions, veering toward the strategically placed tables.

Alasdair turned back to Father. "Get out of here. Alert the—" His words stopped. There—a figure moving through the people—another servant with a dark mask, moving toward the table near the door.

A servant who wasn't a servant at all.

Ranald Aldourie turned, lifted his mask, and smiled directly at him. He reached for a candle, then lifted the tablecloth. The other servants did the same.

Barrels stood under the tables.

Gunpowder.

Alasdair ran, pushing people aside. "Get back! Get—"

Aldourie and the three servants lit the fuses.

"Stop them!" Alasdair held out his hand, powerless to move against the crush of bodies on the dance floor.

Smoke billowed in the air.

Across the room, women screeched and pushed, a merge of silk, feathers, and masks. The effect was like a wave—a living, roaring wave—spreading throughout the room.

"Run! Get away!" Alasdair moved forward, pushing people away, grabbing others and pitching them toward the balcony doors. If he could reach the punch bowl, he might use it . . .

The crowd split. Aldourie was there, also caught in the crush, attempting escape. Alasdair flicked his gaze to the gunpowder kegs and then lunged, knowing it could mean his death. He reached and snagged the back of the man's cloak.

Time. There was never enough time. In the heat of battles, in the African sands, and in the moments before one's life was forever changed.

Glass shattered. Screams split the air.

A force like a calvary charge hit Alasdair in the chest.

Then everything—everything—went black.

Her Majesty, Queen Victoria, was quite up to snuff on the sordid exploits of men. But this was the height of madness—an insult in the extreme. At the other end of the courtroom stood her favorite guard—Alasdair Cairncross—being questioned like a common thief. There he was, stripped of his honors and his lovely red uniform. But those eyes—those eyes were the same. And that smile . . . He smiled it at her now.

Every head in the room turned, gasping when they saw her. Typical.

She strode forward, very aware of the quivering she left in her wake. "It would seem, gentleman, that you have all been very busy in our absence." She paused for effect. "Imagine our astonishment to arrive and find our palace ballroom in ruin. And now . . ." She gestured toward Alasdair. "Am I to understand that one of my own guards has been accused of treason?"

"Y-yes . . ." The counselor stammered as he lowered his head. "Yes, Your Majesty."

She raised an eyebrow. "Do enlighten us."

"He was seen last night dancing with a woman known to be a Gypsy. Three Gypsies were posing as servants and lit the very kegs of gunpowder that molested Your Majesty's palace. Happily, these men have been apprehended, along with a former parliamentary member who was also posing as a—"

"I do beg your pardon! Are we to understand that one of our members of Parliament is implicated in this mad, wicked folly?"

"I am sorry to say that it is true, Your Highness."

"Well." She didn't have to ask which one. She had long suspected that Ranald Aldourie had been slipping into madness. She tapped her fan against her palm and slid her gaze throughout the room. Upon seeing Edan Cairncross in chains, she felt not the slightest tinge of surprise. "And here we see our bailie of Holyrood."

"Indeed, Your Majesty, Edan Cairncross has been found to be—"

She lifted her hand and silenced him. A great, angry sigh escaped her lips. "First, to the matter at hand . . . Sir Alasdair Cairncross, are these allegations correct? Have you plotted against your queen and your country?" There was hardly the need to ask, but for the simpletons of this court. Alasdair had been seen helping people to safety last night. And had been moving toward the explosives instead of away, no doubt trying to save lives. All facts that these ninnies took into no account. Dancing with a Gypsy, indeed!

A look of absolute sincerity came over his features. "No, Your Majesty. I would never contemplate harming you or endangering this country that I so love."

She nodded. Once. That's all the fools in the room deserved. "We are not amused by the charades that have been taking place of late. And I do hope you gentleman know what happens when we are not amused."

Fear spread through the entire room, as it should. All but one man—Alasdair Cairncross—quivered. And that was also as it should be. My, but that guard was a handsome fellow. Out of all of her guards, he had been the only one brash enough to smile daily at her. And that smile reminded her of her dear, departed husband's. He'd also brought her a handkerchief once when she'd been crying in Holyrood gardens, grieving Albert once again. He'd broken protocol, and she could have had him dismissed for it. But sometimes—just sometimes, mind—a woman liked to be treated like a woman and not a crown.

She'd always felt that this guard meant only to be kind to her, and that he had no further ambition. Such a rare thing in all the lands where she reigned. Even when she'd awarded him the Victoria Cross, he'd accepted it with humility and the attitude that it wasn't deserved. But it was deserved. She knew of his torments for her in Egypt. And now she would doubly repay what he had suffered.

She only hoped that he had a plan for his life, this astonishing young man. For even as much as she might wish it, he could not remain one of her guards after this hoopla. One could only abide so much gossip in one's household. And the public—they were never very forgiving.

Queen Victoria drew out the moment and scowled. She lit her gaze upon this one and that, just for amusement. Silence stretched in the room. She adored this part—making them tremble. It was certainty past time to clean the proverbial house. "Well, then, let us explain everything that shall be done."

Ranald Aldourie sat in the prison cell and reflected upon the hours. What else was there left to do? No one visited. Not one of the parliamentary members. But why would they now that his shame had been paraded in the papers for all to see? Of course they left out the part where children had laughed and a people had lived because of him. They left out all the bills he had been instrumental in passing for the betterment of Scotland. And now, what was left? An empty castle on Loch Ness that would soon fall into disrepair. No legacy. No support. Nothing. That's what he was.

And the Gypsies that he had so desperately loved—where were they now? He'd thought one of them would come to brighten his pathetic existence. That an escape plan might even be arranged.

Vanity. The stories he told himself just to be able to take another breath. Well, those stories were dead now. And the Gypsies? They most assuredly had moved on. Traveling. Always traveling. And while he rotted in jail they would still be roaming the world.

The guards opened the door at the end of the corridor. Keys jangled, followed by the shuffling of feet. Another unfortunate prisoner, no doubt. Another man guilty or not guilty. What did it matter in here? Every man who walked the earth was guilty of something. He had been guilty of too much love. The love of a Gypsy woman and her people and then the fantasy of love with Feya Broon.

The cell door beside him opened. An unfortunate soul was thrown inside. "Welcome to purgatory." He glanced over and then widened his eyes. Edan Cairncross was sprawled upon the floor. The man looked up and paled.

The door opened again at the end of the corridor. Footsteps sounded on the pavement. Alasdair Cairncross stood on the other side of the bars.

"Well. Hasn't this been the scandal of the century? At least the papers say so. A member of Parliament imprisoned over trying to keep a bill from being made into an act. And the bailee of Holyrood imprisoned over bribing men to pass it." He clasped his hands behind his back. "As of this morning all support has been withdrawn from the Moveable Dwellings Bill." He paused for effect. "I hope that you can both now behave as gentleman. Although you have struggled with that in that past."

Ranald stood and looked at both of his enemies. "How is this possible? You were also accused of treason."

Edan Cairncross dusted off his prison uniform as if it was an evening jacket. "Everyone forgot to take into account one thing."

"Queen's favorite guard." Alasdair shrugged. "It's all in the smile, you see." The man employed it now. "Good-bye, gentleman. I have already been delayed too long, and there is someone I'm very keen on seeing." He turned and walked away, his footsteps echoing once again on the cold pavement. "Have no fear, Father. I will write."

The door closed, metal against metal.

Ranald stared at the monster, the one who was responsible for it all.

Edan Cairncross stared back.

Metal against metal. That's how it would be from now on.

Chapter Thirty-Four

Sometimes Feya managed not to think of him. But even then, there was always the ache, especially when the sun dipped low over the ocean and turned the sea the same blue as his eyes. When she laughed, which she did often, there was always a part of herself that couldn't quite join in. On long walks down the beach with the bairns, she always had the same thought, no matter how she fought it. She always looked down expecting to see another set of footprints there beside her. It was foolish. But that didn't draw her eyes away from the place where the sea kissed the shore. He would walk there, she knew it somehow. That would have been his place. The "might have been."

He must be happy. He had to be. Because if he wasn't, how could she forgive herself for not fighting harder? At the time, it had seemed as if she'd begged and pleaded and done more than most women would have. But now, with the hours stretched long with the waning days of summer, she wondered. She speculated too much.

She'd purchased the cottage in a remote part of Cornwall, England. The doctors had said the climate would help her lungs. She'd had too much time in the tenements, they said. Too much coal smoke and cramped conditions. Perhaps she would recover. Perhaps.

Feya uncapped the medicine bottle. She hated the vile liquid. It made her mind turn to mush and the coughing was much the same. But the doctor had assured her it was helping and he wanted her to take a double dose this week. She sighed, tipped the bottle back, and swallowed. "Fer the bairns." She lifted the teacup she'd brought outside and drank deep. That would help the taste. As for the other, the fog in her brain would roll in soon. Better to take it just before bed, when the bairns were settled down and safe.

Feya hugged herself as the sun set in the sky, dipping its toe in the water like a bashful woman. It was her ritual, this. Taking the medicine and sitting outside the cottage, witnessing the remains of the day. It was the time she gave to Alasdair and their memories, as stupid as that was. But sometimes—sometimes—it eased the ache a little. And she prayed for him as the sun dipped low. That eased the ache a lot.

The long sunlight fell upon her shoulders, so warm it made her smile. It was God's comfort, the sun, and she felt Him in it sometimes, as she had all those months ago in Alice's parlor. As she felt Him in the Bible Alice had given her. As she talked with Him through the day.

The sea sang low now, crashing against the rocks, reaching and moving back. Down the cottage path, the blue strip of water lapped just beyond the waving sea oats. White crests and so many shades of blue. Over and over again. Longing was in the sea. And longing she did well, so it suited.

Since she'd come, some of the villagers had whispered she was some man's mistress. Why else would she have money to buy such a nice cottage? They laughed and whispered when she said the bairns were her kin. And then there was the word that always came when her back was turned—Gypsy. Gypsy woman with the brown eyes, going to steal their husbands and leave them all with a curse.

Tiresome people. Always the same.

Feya dug her bare feet into the sand and ran her hand over its softness. Brenna's voice carried out the window, a beautiful sound. She sang English songs now, only happy ones, and they suited her. What a young lady she was turning out to be.

The waves crashed on, as they always did, lulling like a mother's tune. The fog of the medicine pressed upon her, harder. The wind brushed over her, bringing the sting of sand and the smell of salt. Feya breathed deep, willing the medicine to work so her lungs would open. So she could be free of the tightness and the pain.

The same barrier came halfway through the breath, like a clog. She rolled her head to the side and tried not to cry. The bairns needed her. And they always would. If something happened . . .

"Stop it." She always spoke to herself when those thoughts came. Feya held her legs tighter and thought of Alasdair again. She supposed she would always feel his arms around her and his kisses against her lips. And his safety. That's what she missed most when she was afraid.

"'What time I am afraid, I will trust in thee.'" The verse brought calm, as it always did. She was able to concentrate on the roaring of the waves again—constant, always moving, like God.

But after the sailboat she'd been watching turned toward the cliffs, the medicine's seductive voice called once again. Her hands shook. Scenes from the ball washed in like the water. Thoughts came that served no use but to torture. *By this time, Amberlyn's probably carrying Alasdair's child. By this time, they've moved to London . . .* Feya closed her eyes against the thoughts. But it didn't help. It never did.

The touch of little hands was on her face. Baby Hamish fell into her arms. "I thought Gillis was readin' ye a story."

"All done." He laid his head against her shoulder.

"What is it, then, me wee little man?"

"'Member what ye said."

Feya smiled, knowing what was coming. "'God takes care of us,' is that it?"

"Yep. Don't worry Fey-Fey." He grabbed a strand of her hair and wove it through his fingers. "Got any scones?"

"Of course we do." Feya kissed him, rose, and took him into the cottage. It was the first time she'd not stayed and watched the entire sunset. She took a deep breath and nodded. Maybe it was time to let Alasdair go.

Gillis looked up from his book. "It's a particularly winsome evening."

Feya smiled. "That it is." Gillis was her word lover. He could wax on for hours about stories and books.

She went to the larder, brought out the scones, and then poured the fresh milk.

Brenna came into the room. "Are ye feelin' all right, sister?"

"It's the medicine. I'll be going to bed early tonight."

A knock sounded at the door.

Gillis pushed away from the table. "Maybe it's Henry come to play with me."

"It's a little late fer Henry." Feya went to the door. The wild sea wind hit her in the face—the smell of salt and lands beyond. But nothing else.

Brenna walked to stand beside her. "Who is it?"

"No one . . . Strange."

"Maybe it's the ghost of the fisherman come to haunt Gillis." Brenna turned back to her brother and wailed as if dead.

Feya scowled. "Don't tease yer brother."

"But it's so fun."

Gillis pushed up his glasses and looked back down at his book. "Simple minds resort to ghost stories."

Feya stepped out past the doorway. Something clinked against her foot.

A bottle lay on the doorstep, a rolled up message inside.

"Pick it up, Feya." Brenna nudged her like she was afraid to touch it.

Feya bent and lifted the cork.

Two words were scrawled across the page: *Forgive me.*

It couldn't be . . . Feya searched the bluffs. The handwriting . . . She ran back inside and headed for the dresser where she kept his letter.

"What are ye doing?" Gillis asked.

"Fey-Fey!"

Brenna stepped back inside. "Have ye finally gone mad, Feya? I knew it was comin'."

Gillis turned a page of his book. "Stop speculatin' on the state of her head. It's not funny anymore."

Feya jerked opened the drawer and reached for Alasdair's letter. She unrolled the message again and put the writing side by side. "Oh . . . it is! How? Oh, me . . ."

"I told ye," Brenna said. "We might as well find the constable. It's the orphanage fer us."

"Shut up, Brenna! I'll not take yer abuse!" Gillis reached for the remaining loaf of bread from supper and flung it at her.

"Ow!" Crumbs rained upon the floor.

"Gillis . . ." Feya stared at the handwriting, her breath coming fast. "Don't hit yer sister."

"Even when she's being a monster?"

"Especially then, love."

"Raspberry!" Hamish threw his scone against the wall and laughed.

Brenna picked crumbs out of her hair. "What's it you've got there, Feya? Who's it from?"

Feya shoved the letter back into the drawer and rolled the message into her hand. "I'll tell ye later. I need ye to watch yer brothers for a short spell."

"Ah, corkers." Brenna threw herself into a chair and rolled her eyes. "I was just about to braid me doll's hair."

"Watch them just like I taught ye. Especially Hamish."

"I've got it." She pouted, but then she stood again and smiled like a haughty queen at court. "Listen, y' lot, I'm in charge. Ye both are going to behave like gentleman or I'll have yer guts for garters, do ye understand?"

Hamish laughed and threw more scone.

Gillis shut his book and frowned. "Don't make me play dolls again, Brenna. It does things to a young man's mind."

"Fifteen minutes, at most." Feya pointed to each one of them. "I can feel when yer disobeyin' me, even when I'm not in the room."

"Eyes all over the place, I know." Brenna cleaned her throat, flung her hand out, and started singing and dancing for Hamish.

Feya rushed out the door and ran down the path. There were footprints in the sand. A man's footprints. She searched the horizon. Only the sun moved, blazing toward the sea.

The wind whipped her dress around her knees as she climbed the sand dune.

There . . .

Alasdair stood by the shore, his hands in his pockets, staring out to sea. He wore a white shirt and dark trousers—sailing clothes, from the looks of it. His shoes were cast aside, heaped in the sand. The water lapped his bare feet. He stilled, as if he sensed her, and turned. "Feya." He took a long breath. "You look well . . . You look very well."

Her heart broke at how well he looked, and how perfect he looked in the place she'd come to call home. She crossed her arms to keep from flinging herself at him like a fool. The medicine thrummed and beat in her blood. What a pretty dream this was, so different from the rest. "What . . . brings ye to this corner of the world?" Her words were thick on her tongue.

"Cornwall." He smiled and threw a shell into the sea. "Of all places, you chose Cornwall."

"I like it here." She nodded as if that was enough. "It suits me. It suits the bairns."

Again, he didn't speak. He was looking above her and all around her. His eyes were so blue. She was right in thinking they matched the water.

Feya furrowed her brow. "Do ye need the money back? Because . . ." Feya pointed behind her at the cottage. "I can sell this place if I have to."

She looked down, feeling like a complete ninny. He had that ability—to make her feel like a wobbly pudding with just one glance. And this time she felt wobblier than ever. She shouldn't have taken a double dose of the medicine. It was like being held under deep water. Surely she would wake now.

She opened her eyes and her gaze fell on his white shirt. His open collar flapped in the wind. He was standing so close, looking down at her with those eyes. And his scent . . . Ach, her mind really was fraying. Because breathing in this dream made her smell the earthiness of him, the way he'd been in the forest.

"I didn't come here to have you sell the cottage. I wouldn't want to do such a thing. I want to—" He stopped himself as if struggling with the words. "Are you married?"

She laughed. It started small and ended up shaking her shoulders and doubling her over to the ground. Bouts and bouts of it came, like a dam breaking. The wind whipped her hair around her face until she couldn't see.

"Are you?" His voice was urgent. "Just tell me, woman. Yes or no."

"Ye want . . ." She wiped a tear from her eye. ". . . to know if I am married?"

"Yes, that's it." He raised his chin. "Exactly."

"Are ye really that daft? Ach, sweet man, I'll always be pinin' fer ye. I couldn't do that—betray what we had. I never would." Dizziness swirled around like the water and the wind and the feelings she would always bear for him. "I'm tired. I'm so . . . tired." She turned toward the cottage. This was a long dream and it hurt too much.

"I'm not married either. And I love you."

Feya stopped near a clump of sea grass. She smiled at the words her mind so often had him say. How lovely a moment, replayed over and over in her mind. When she was awake. When she was asleep . . .

"Feya, I love you. I always have. And I always will. And that call I had before—the missionary life I denied . . . I was wrong to think that I could arrange my life better on my own. Whatever God asks, I want that now. I want it with you."

She wiped away another tear. "I'll wake soon and ye'll be gone." A sigh came from deep within her. "It's always the same."

He walked around and stared at her. He cupped her cheek in his hand. "Are you well? Have you taken something?"

"They say I could die soon because of me lungs." She looked at their feet together in the sand. "I haven't told the bairns."

He drew her into his arms and laid his cheek against hers. "I don't accept that. And I don't care how difficult, how costly the need, it will be done for you. I am here now. I am going to take care of you." He drew back and took her face in his hands. "We are good at rescuing one another, remember?"

Feya sucked in a breath and brought her hands up to cover his.

She'd told him that at the ball. "This—You're real."

"Very." His smile was the warmth, the thaw, against the medicine.

Feya curled her fingers around his. "Alasdair." More tears welled in her eyes. "I'm sorry. I took some medicine."

He turned his hand into hers and brought it to his lips. "Can you understand me right now?"

"Aye." Another tear streamed down her face. "A moment ago I thought—"

Alasdair removed a handkerchief from his pocket and wiped her eyes. "You thought what?"

"That ye weren't real. I've dreamed of ye so often."

"Would you like to sit down?"

"No." Feya took a deep breath and focused on the wind, forcing precious oxygen into her rebellious lungs. Her blood thrummed with his presence—all the things she'd longed to say to him, all the ways she'd imagined them together. "Better now." But it wasn't. The pain in her lungs was like a lead weight in the bottom, rolling around until she was afraid again—like spun glass stretched too thin, she could feel it waiting, the breaking that would claim her in the end.

"Doctors know nothing these days." Alasdair drew his eyebrows together in concern. "We shall have to see about that. In the mean time . . ." He lowered himself to the sand, kneeling. "I have a question for you."

Feya's heart caught. Surely Alasdair Cairncross couldn't be proposing to her. She was broken; she'd just told him as much.

"You are smart and brave, and so beautiful my heart hurts when I look upon you. That doesn't even begin to describe the beauty you have inside." Alasdair closed his eyes, as if all the moments they'd had together played before him. "I was a fool." When he opened his eyes, Feya saw it all—love and regret bound together. "But let me remedy that now. Please be my wife." Alasdair rubbed his thumb over her fingers. "I promise I will love you desperately, as you have always deserved."

Feya went to her knees. "Do ye mean it?"

"Every day. Every hour. Every moment." Alasdair placed her hand over his heart. "I pledge myself to you and the bairns. It would be my greatest honor to be your husband and their father."

"Yes." Feya fell against him with the word, her hands weighted like iron. She tried to hold on, but her palms slid against his back.

Alasdair's strong arms came around her and he lifted her like a child. He kissed her on the forehead and walked toward the cottage, his steps shifting in the sand. Behind him, the sun blazed bright, drowning him in a shower of gold.

As he'd rescued her from herself once, he'd come again.

Alasdair Cairncross carried her, as he had in the forest with the rain pouring down. As he had when he'd given her the permission to first cry. As he had, and always would—lover, husband. She was his completely, forever ago. When she had been a Gypsy. And even when she had been a Scotswoman, pining away for she knew not what.

With him she could weather the tempests. They already had. She would protect his heart and hold it close and he would do the same. And if the days came when they forgot what they had gone through, and who they were becoming, then they would whisper the truth to each other—be each other's remembrance. Wasn't that what a marriage was anyway? Helping each other be the best versions of themselves—the truest part.

Feya reached for his cheek and felt the warmth of him on her hand. Alasdair Cairncross stared into her eyes with complete love.

Now was just the beginning.

<h1 style="text-align:center">Epilogue</h1>

Samoa, Pacific Islands

The boat rose and fell in the gentle waves. Alasdair's smile was wide and warm, full of the nights and days they'd shared together. He tried to keep his eyes on the horizon, and the island that had just come into view. "Love, please, I really need to concentrate on the sailing."

Feya wrapped her arms around him from behind and kissed the place just below his ear. "Was I distractin' ye? Poor lamb." She rose on her tiptoes to whisper in his ear. "I'm so, so very sorry."

Alasdair cleared his throat and adjusted his grip on the helm. "You do realize I shall make you pay later."

Feya slid around, bent under his arms, and stood between him and the wheel. "That's what I'm countin' on, husband."

"Ach!" Brenna's voice came from across the deck. "Avert yer eyes, bairns. They're at it again."

"Yay!" Hamish clapped. "More kiss!"

Gillis' voice amplified over the music of the wind and the flap of the sail. "We're all goin' to meet watery graves. How can he see, kissin' her like that?"

Alasdair smiled against Feya's lips and pulled away. He cleared his throat. "It's quite simple, young man: a gentleman has many talents and can easily combine them at will." He raised his eyebrow and gave Feya a look of playful warning. "Women, however, are the most distracting of creatures and should be approached with caution." He smiled. "Lesson number one hundred twenty-eight, I believe."

"Thank ye." Gillis scribbled in his journal. It was their way of bonding, and bonded they were, thicker than blood. Gillis wrote down everything Alasdair said of note. He entitled the book *Rules For A Gentleman As Told By Alasdair Cairncross, Most Esteemed Father.* Sometimes Feya would read the book and let her own husband's wisdom wash over her. Other times she was amazed at his ability to calm Gillis' fears or simply make him smile.

Alasdair projected his voice so it would carry over the wind. "And how is my Brenna girl?" She'd grown quiet, and he'd noticed.

Brenna walked to him, her pretty new dress flaring out. "I just don't know about this, Alasdair. What if some Samoan boy carries me off and tries to marry me in some devilish tribal ceremony?"

Alasdair bit back a smile. "A weighty concern, indeed. Do you really think I'd let that happen?"

"Well, no." Brenna placed her hands upon her hips. "But what if it was the middle of the night?"

Alasdair removed Feya's hands from his waist and shooed her away with mock displeasure. "Brenna, darling, I don't exactly achieve the required hours of nightly rest. I would know if anything was amiss and come to your aid immediately."

Brenna took a breath, as if the answer didn't satisfy. "But why don't ye sleep enough, Alasdair? Yer in the bedroom often enough."

"Ask your sister," Alasdair said quickly. He turned the color of the fiery-red eastern sky. "Gillis, this would be the perfect time to read lesson number five. For Brenna's sake."

"Yes, sir." Gillis stood and flipped back in his journal. "'Women must be protected at all times.'"

Alasdair turned the helm toward the shore. "With passion, man! This isn't a soiree. We're on the high seas embarking upon grand adventure."

Gillis raised his chin and adjusted his posture. "'This rule is to be obeyed especially when ye think ye don't care fer a woman. Hypothetically speaking, if ye were a palace guard and she tried to break in, still be kind. If she is sick, make sure she gets stew and a warm blanket. Some of life's greatest moments happen in the unexpected.'"

"And?" Alasdair adjusted the rigging beside him.

"'Footnote.'" Gillis rolled his eye and sighed. "'This rule is especially to be obeyed with sisters. A true gentleman protects and loves his sister always.'"

"Exactly so." Alasdair winked at him. "Well done. You may sit down."

Feya smiled secretly and went to the rail. Their new home loomed just beyond—so alive, green, and beautiful. Palm trees swayed in the breeze, a tropical chorus waving their fringed hands in greeting. Feya breathed in—so easy now since Alasdair had taken her to London and found a doctor who knew what he was doing. And this climate— the longer she breathed in it, the more her lungs relaxed. The air was fragrant and sweet—gardenias, hibiscus, coconut oil. Alasdair had told her stories of this place. And now, smelling its beauty as well as seeing it, it made her love him more.

A man ran down the coast. "Hello, there!"

Alasdair called back to him and waved. The man looked oddly familiar—something about the way he held himself. He bent over, out of breath from running. "I heard an English accent. Am I mistaken?"

"Alasdair Cairncross, at your service." Alasdair dropped the anchor and prepared the small boat.

"Ah, the new minister. We've been anticipating your arrival. And this . . ." He shielded his eyes from the sun. "Madam, I do believe we've met before."

Feya looked closer. As she lived and breathed, it was Robert Louis Stevenson. "I can't believe it."

He adjusted his hat and smiled. "Didn't I tell you that you had the look of adventure?"

Feya nodded. Of all the people to meet, in all the places of the world.

"I beg your pardon." He looked to Alasdair again. "Allow me to introduce myself."

Feya watched him talk and her mind slid to that night when she'd almost betrayed herself in the worst way. And had Mr. Stevenson not made her angry, causing her to abandon the horrible notion, she'd not be here. She'd not be married to Alasdair. None of it would have ever happened.

Cause and effect. Choices. Moments when a person's life hung in the balance and she wasn't even aware.

Mr. Stevenson's voice filtered back in through her thoughts. ". . . and we shared a cup of tea on a rainy night. I was just tossing around the idea of Jekyll and Hyde, I believe." Mr. Stevenson continued to study her face and she could have sworn that he laughed softly. "Not much to tell, really."

"Aye." Feya nodded. "Just a short conversation a long time ago."

Mr. Stevenson nodded, as if he understood. "But your story!" He gestured to them all and the ship they sailed on. "Now that's a story I'd love to hear."

Feya took her husband's hand as he helped her descend the stairs. The warm water lapped at the little boat that would take them to their destiny.

Mr. Stevenson wanted to know their story. Where should she begin the telling? She would begin where everyone's story began, she supposed, in the heart of the Creator.

Once upon a time . . .

AUTHOR'S NOTE

Thank you so much for taking the time to fall into Feya and Alasdair's story. I'm so glad that you've been drawn to *Within the Veil.* When I finally typed the end of this book, I burst into tears. The crying didn't stop for three days. That's just how much these pages are engraved upon my heart. I'm going to miss traveling through the wilds of Scotland. But don't despair—if the longing gets too bad, I'm sure that unparalleled place will find its way into another book down the road. I'll forever have a little Gypsy in me now. Feya's already starting to show up in the jewelry I choose and the clothes I gravitate toward. Maybe that's just my way of remembering everything that she learned.

There really was a Moveable Dwellings Bill in Parliament. From 1885 to 1926 it made quite a few appearances. Although it never passed, there were many opinions on both sides. One of its avid supporters, George Smith of Coalville, wrote various pamphlets and books in support of the bill. I have to admit, I was shocked at many of his opinions of the Gypsies. His book *Gipsy Life being an account of our Gipsies and their children, with suggestions for their improvement* became an invaluable resource for gauging the political climate and opinions of the time. In my mind, Edan Cairncross would have been involved in many such ventures—called a philanthropist by some and, by today's standards, accused of prejudice by others. And yet, in many European countries around the world, Gypsies still live a heartbreaking life. It is sobering to read current events and opinions that are not much different than Feya's time.

Robert Louis Stevenson really did get some inspiration for *Dr. Jekyll and Mr. Hyde* in Deacon Brodie's Tavern. However, his real breakthrough with the story came after he had a nightmare in the fall of 1885. I had fun imagining Feya meeting him, and as he was known to have a fascination with Edinburgh's dark side, I don't think this imagining is so off base. When I visited Edinburgh in 2011, I had the pleasure of having lunch at Deacon Brodie's Tavern, and it's in that exact spot that I placed Feya and Stevenson, sharing their conversation over tea.

Robert Louis Stevenson did end up in Samoa and in fact died there. He arrived in 1889 and was affectionately known by the locals as Tusitala, which means "Teller of Tales." Since *Within the Veil* takes place in 1885, I did take a little artistic liberty with the epilogue. But you can very well imagine that Feya and Alasdair were married in London where Alasdair's comrades could wish him well and where Feya could receive the proper medical attention that she would have needed. Perhaps they then moved back to Cornwall for a couple of years for her health to continue improving and for them to prepare for their adventurous missionary endeavors.

Although I never mention it by name, Feya's struggle was with asthma. In 1885 it had no such designation.

There really was a Gypsy queen of Scotland. Esther Faa Blythe lived from 1803 to 1883. According to H. Murray, one of her contemporaries, she had a pleasing aspect and an olive completion. She was intelligent, shrewd, and had a fiery temper. She was often seen with her clay pipe. She lived in a whitewashed cottage, known as the Gypsy Palace, and you can still visit it today. I loved looking at her pictures and delving into her world for research. Although it didn't make it through editing, one of my earlier drafts of *Within the Veil* had Feya speaking of the death of Esther Faa Blythe. In real life, some of Esther's relatives tried to keep the traditions going, even crowning Charles Blythe as king of the Gypsies in 1898. Ten thousand people came to the coronation at Kirk Yetholm. Kizzy, the Gypsy queen in *Within the Veil,* was my reimagining of that interesting fragment from history.

Alasdair had synesthesia, a neuropsychological phenomenon where all of the senses are combined. Many gifted people throughout history have had synesthesia, including Nikola Tesla, Franz Liszt, and Vincent van Gogh. I gave Alasdair quite a few types of synesthesia including Grapheme-color (he saw letters and numbers as being colored), Chromesthesia (sounds trigger colors), Lexical-gustatory (he tasted words, especially Feya's name), and Auditory-tactile (he experienced sensations in his body when he heard specific sounds). I also gave Alasdair the ability to see auras. While many in the New Age community speak of this, researchers at the University of Granada, Spain, have found that this is a type of emotional synesthesia and published their results in the medical journal *Consciousness and Cognition.*[1]

Within the Veil has been a very personal journey for me for many reasons. When my son was in the sixth grade, we found out that he had synesthesia. He came home from school one day and asked me if I thought people could see colors when they heard music. The look on his face told me that it wasn't just an ordinary question. I responded that I thought it was possible, and then I did a frantic Internet search that forever changed our family. At first I was scared, not knowing what this meant for my child and wanting to protect him. But knowledge is power, like the old adage says, and I'm very thankful to live in the days of such easy access to information. I poured myself into learning everything that I could about synesthesia.

As I asked my son, Abishai, more questions about what his daily life was like, I was blown away. He was surprised that I didn't have the same kinds of experiences. Synesthetes often think that everyone experiences the world in the same ways that they do. I'm still learning about this beautiful gift and every time I meet someone with synesthesia, I am amazed.

In many ways, scientists think that we are just beginning to understand this tremendous gift. Some scientists believe that the study of synesthesia will unlock more secrets of how peoples' brains work. In many ways, we are on the frontier, especially in regards to how synesthesia affects learning. In classrooms, synesthesia is rarely taken into consideration. I think it's important that we see that change. Although the numbers are conflicted, as many as one in three hundred people are said to have synesthesia. Other sources say one in two thousand.

If you would like to know more about synesthesia, please contact the American Synesthesia Association. You can find them on the web at http://www.synesthesia.info. Our family went to the 11th Annual Synesthesia Conference in 2015, and it was one of the best decisions we ever made. Meeting all of the beautiful, creative synesthetes was a true gift. Hearing all of their stories was an eye-opening experience that I will never forget.

I can only guess what it would be like to have synesthesia in other time periods, but I explored the idea with Alasdair. I very well do imagine that you might think, as he did, you were dying—especially depending on what type of synesthesia you had.

If you have synesthesia, please know that you are not alone. I hope you are encouraged and that you can see your synesthesia as a blessing and a gift. If anything comes out of the writing of this book, I hope it is that. I do understand that it's not always easy. I know how certain environments make you struggle and sometimes even cause you physical pain. I know that you often feel different, and rightly so. As Feya told Alasdair, "It's a great and terrible gift, ye ken." I'd love to hear from you and discover how you experience the world. You can connect with me via Facebook or Twitter @BrandyVallance, or you can use the contact form on my website at www.brandyvallance.com.

1. E.G. Milán, O. Iborra, M. Hochel, M.A. Rodríguez Artacho, L.C. Delgado-Pastor, E. Salazar, A. González-Hernández. "Auras in mysticism and synaesthesia: A comparison." *Consciousness and Cognition* 21 (March 2012): 258–68.

ACKNOWLEDGMENTS

No book is ever possible without the support of others. For me, there are a few who wouldn't let the dream of *Within the Veil* die.

First, my husband: When doors closed on this book you opened one and made it possible. You encouraged me and fought for my calling. Without you, these pages would have stayed on my computer. Thank you for investing in my dreams.

Abishai: Thank you for cracking the door of your beautifully complex inner world. I count it a privilege to be your mom. I am very excited to see where synesthesia takes you but remember this: even if you didn't have synesthesia, you'd still be amazing. Together with God you are going to do wonderfully astounding things. Thanks for being patient during all the times I asked, "What do you see when . . ." and "Describe what happens when . . ." Here's to a million more cups of good, strong tea and deep conversation. You still owe me a cappuccino at Saint Mark's Square in Venice.

To my daughter, Eleason: Out of all of the people who like my writing, you are my biggest fan. You encourage me every day and your love keeps me going. Knowing that you are proud of me is a wonderful gift. I endeavor to keep making you proud. You are going to transform this world, my darling. Keep singing and dancing and talking to the Creator of your dreams.

To my editor, Leslie Peterson: We did it! Thank you for being patient with me and for falling in love with Alasdair. I hope you find yourself in Scotland again one of these days. And if you do, I hope you'll think of the mournful wind, all the beautiful windows, and Alasdair's lips, which definitely tasted of mint.

To Steve Gardner: Thank you so much for the beautiful cover. You captured Feya without reading a word. You are a true artist.

To Evangeline Denmark and Carla Laureano: How many conversations did we have during the writing of this book? Some of my fondest memories will always be those times. Not only did you help shape this story but you have helped me discover who I really am. Here's to all the truths we have yet to uncover. Let's continue to be transformed through our writing. Many lampposts await.

To Cindi Madsen: You always know how to make my writing better. Your help and support have kept me going. Shine on you beautiful supernova.

To Bob Spiller: Now there is a second book because you started our critique group all those years ago. Your wisdom—guitar strings, bulls, and water in a river—I won't forget. The times you have made me laugh cannot be counted. I'm so honored to be able to call you my friend.

To Jackie McKnight: Thank you for supporting this book through a really difficult time in my career. Knowing that you loved *Within the Veil* made a difference.

To everyone who prayed for me, and some special mentions: Julia Johnson, Eva Ficke, Bernice Wheeler, Rachel Lawry, Angel Oldaker, Priscilla Quevedo, Daniela Milam, Lorraine Phillips, and Diana Cessna. Please keep praying! I still have many more books to write.

To my grandmother, Minnie Cole: I'm pretty convinced that your love and prayers keep me alive.

And finally, to my father, Tim Cole: "Go on and rain on me now." Thanks for teaching me how to let go. And for telling the best stories. Talking to you is always the best medicine.

ABOUT THE AUTHOR

Brandy Vallance adores history and frequently has to be told in museums that it's closing time. She loves to travel, plays the cello, and thinks all teacups should be bottomless. In 2011 she fulfilled a lifelong dream and went to England, Scotland, and Wales. Being a complete Anglophile, it was difficult to bring her home. Bribes may have been involved.

Brandy fell in love with the Victorian time period at a young age, fascinated by the customs, manners, and especially the intricate rules of love. Since time travel is theoretically impossible, she lives in the nineteenth century vicariously through her novels. Unaccountable amounts of black tea have fueled this ambition. Brandy's love of tea can only be paralleled by her love of BBC period dramas, deep conversations, rain, and a good book.

Brandy lives in Florida with her adventurous husband, a debonair son who has adopted her love of all things British, and a beautiful daughter who reminds her to pay attention to moments and never lose the wonder. You can visit Brandy on the web at www.brandyvallance.com or connect with her via Facebook, Goodreads, Pinterest, or Twitter @BrandyVallance.

If you enjoyed this book would you consider sharing it with others? Here are some ways you can help spread the word about *Within the Veil*:

- Write an honest review on Amazon, Barnes & Noble, or Goodreads.com. The number of reviews a book receives really does influence sales.

- Recommend the book to your friends, family, and book club.

- Recommend the book to your local library. You can usually do this through your library's website.

- Post a picture of yourself with the book and tag Brandy Vallance on Facebook. You can also post a picture of the book in an interesting location. This can be as simple as the book (or your e-reader showing the cover) next to a cup of coffee. Don't forget Instagram and Pinterest.

- Mention the book on Twitter and include @BrandyVallance.

- Like Brandy's Facebook author page and post a comment about what you enjoyed the most.

- Post a book review or book spotlight on your blog.

- For interviews, guest posts, or appearances contact Brandy Vallance at www.brandyvallance.com

ALSO BY BRANDY VALLANCE

Bianca Marshal is holding out for the perfect husband. Finding a man that meets the requirements of her "must-have" list in the foothills of the Appalachian Mountains has proven impossible. Bianca's mama insists that there's no such thing as a perfect true love, and that Bianca's ideal man is pure fiction. On the eve of her twenty-fifth birthday, Bianca discovers a devastating statistic: her chance of marrying is now only eighteen 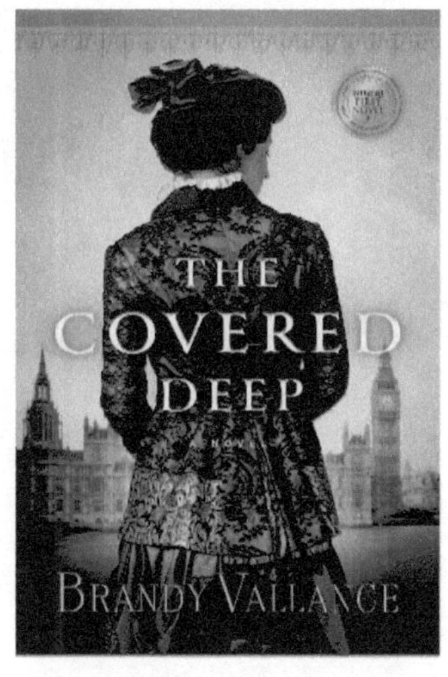 percent. Unwilling to accept spinsterhood, Bianca enters an essay contest that propels her into a whirlwind search for her soulmate. Via the opulence of London and the mysteries of the Holy Land, Bianca's true love will be revealed, but not without a heavy price.

"Lovely lyrical prose sets the scene for Victorian romance, while layered mysteries and a diabolical plot of emotionally—and psychologically—devastating proportions combine to bring the story and its characters to life in *The Covered Deep*. Beautifully written and showcases a breakout talent that isn't afraid to push the boundaries of what is 'expected' in an inspirational historical romance." *~ USA TODAY*